F

Gravy, Grits, and Graves

Gravy, Grits, and Graves

Vicki Blair

TATE PUBLISHING
AND ENTERPRISES, LLC

Published by Tate Publishing & Enterprises, LLC
127 E. Trade Center Terrace | Mustang, Oklahoma 73064 USA
1.888.361.9473 | www.tatepublishing.com

Tate Publishing is committed to excellence in the publishing industry. The company reflects the philosophy established by the founders, based on Psalm 68:11,
"The Lord gave the word and great was the company of those who published it."

Published in the United States of America
ISBN: 978-1-62295-237-3
1. Fiction / Crime
2. Fiction / Mystery & Detective / General
13.03.01

Dedication

I'm so honored to be from the "real" McWhorter, Kentucky. It's a very special place with some of the finest people in the state including three of the most wonderful ladies I know— my McWhorter sisters: Penny Greer, Paulette Vaughn, and Kathy Feltner.

Acknowledgments

I have to start by thanking my wonderful husband and children. Buddy, Nik, Alex, and Gabe, you are my greatest blessings. I know how each of you sacrificed over the last three years— I hope it was worth it! A special thanks to my husband whose law enforcement expertise proved invaluable to me. Thanks, Bud, for answering those million questions ranging from what a firing range looked like to helping me to understand police protocol. I love you all and appreciate all your help!

Although they will be watching from heaven, several family members and friends were helpful in the completion of this book. Roy Tincher, Allen Young, Danny Young, Alene Young, Hazel Tincher, Sue Jones, and Julia Collier all played a part in my life and my book.

To my parents-in-law, brothers, sisters, nieces, nephews, and cousins, your help and encouragement were invaluable. A special thank you to those who went above and beyond the call of family and friendship to help me: Paulette Vaughn, Penny Greer, Lanny Greer, Kathy Feltner, Courtney New, Linda Downer, Vickie Ann Dill, Kyle Rush, Lee Tincher, Patty Tincher, Jon Kristen McCowan, Misty Vaughn, Shelly Hyatt, Misty Jones, and Blair Vorbeck, thank you for each of your contributions to the book. For helping me name the book, a big shout out to Christy Jones and Tammy Blair. Linda Downer, your encouragement and cheerleading was what got me through at the end!

Senture, LLC has blessed me! Thank you, Mr. Deaton, Chris Deaton, Cheryl Hubbard, and Jim Gayhart, for helping to make my dream a reality. Reva Brown, Ruth Ann Caldwell, Kelly Sizemore, Nancy Workman, Carol Reed, Cindy Hutson, Deronda Medlin, Delores Deaton, Rebecca Gilbert, Stephanie and Joyce Fouts, Kimberly Shackleford, Lorraine Jones, Lisa

Smith, Andrew Depew, and Scott Noble, thank you for all your support, even if it meant cooking in order to help my cause. Also a shout out to Rebecca Gilbert Photography for my back cover photograph.

Thanks to each of you who I bribed, begged, or conned into reading the book during each of my rewrites. Your feedback was invaluable. A special thanks to Dave Caldwell for my lesson on firearms!

Also a special thanks to my prayer partners—Kim Whitson, Cheri Weaver, Pam Lamb, Minnie Reed, Beth Maggard, and the Senture Armor bearers. I'm convinced that your daily prayer coverage made all the difference. Also a special thanks to Trevor Weaver who God miraculously used after my last computer crash.

Last but not least, my largest debt of gratitude goes to my teacher, mentor, and friend—Mrs. Judith Brown. I could not have done this without you. I will never, ever forget you for all your support and help.

CHAPTER 1

Tuesday Club - The Beginning

Tuesday, October 4, 1938

In night blacker than pitch, six men crept into the heart of the Cumberland National Forest. The October night was eerily quiet as each of the six men, pillars of the community and respected leaders, could feel their heart beat in unison with each step. The *ka thud ka thud* of their drumming heartbeats was soon replaced by the thuds of shovels meeting the black Kentucky soil.

Several of the men were still dressed in their fancy work suits while others still had the farmer's stink hanging onto their overalls. Although the night air was cool, the men were sweating like pigs, but they paid no never-mind to their own odor because they could only smell the sickening sweet scent of warm blood. It was a smell these men would never soon forget. The stench would serve as a reminder of the night they witnessed Jon R. Ledford kill the Mayor of McWhorter in cold blood.

Nary word was exchanged as the six men finished digging the mayor's final resting place. This unmarked grave in the middle of a thick wilderness would be a safe place to hide their sin. The gravediggers' silence was not because they had nothing to say to one another; they didn't speak because they valued their own lives.

Jon R. Ledford hadn't planned on pulling the trigger and murdering one of his lifelong buddies, but it had happened, and he learned long ago not to look a gift horse in the mouth. Jon R. knew this was his opportunity to create a dynasty where he called all the shots as McWhorter, Kentucky's rightful leader.

Feigning fatigue, Jon R. took a break from digging, but actually, he never felt more alive in his life. His presence loomed even larger over the top of the grave as he rested his body weight on the shovel and examined his reluctant partners in crime. He smiled inwardly because he knew he had them in the palms of his hands. Although their intelligence was no match to his own, they were still smart men—smart enough to recognize their only options were to follow his lead or follow the dead mayor into another shallow grave.

In the three short hours since the shooting, Jon R. had formulated his plan. Every town loved a good scandal, and McWhorter was no exception. Every tongue would soon be wagging telling how the mayor had skipped town with the black-haired gypsy woman who passed through town a few weeks ago. In a way, he was doing his slain friend a favor by making him a legend. The men would all admire him, and the women folk would hang on tighter to their men lest they too suffer from another gypsy's spell. Jon R. even planned how to prevent the deathbed confessions of his silent partners. Although he was the one to pull the trigger in a fit of rage, the others did absolutely nothing to stop him. Actually, there'd been no stopping him. He wouldn't have hesitated to shoot anyone who got in his way tonight, tomorrow, or as long as he lived.

He knew he would miss the dead son of a bitch, but he knew there was no use crying over spilt milk now. What was done was done. Jon R. Ledford was certain he could make this unholy alliance work for them all. They would soon reap the benefits of the little murder club they had accidentally joined one lovely Tuesday evening in October.

CHAPTER 2

Report Card Day

Tuesday, November 13, 2007

McWhorter, Kentucky, was a place time had left behind. The population of the town was just over five thousand and hadn't changed much over the past thirty years. Big business wasn't encouraged, and the town didn't take too well to newcomers unless they were paying tourists. Those passing through would often mistake the Appalachian accents, the colorful language, and the poor grammar of some of the McWhorterians as being slow witted. A huge mistake. These hillbillies would have the last laugh while laughing all the way to the bank.

There were no franchise restaurants in McWhorter. Hazel's Diner was the eatery of choice, and it probably wasn't the place to go for those who didn't believe in eating egg centers or worried about their cholesterol. Hazel's was the place to eat real food, fried in black-iron skillets with real lard for the grease. Although Hazel had been dead for years, her son Jebidiah continued to run the restaurant using her same secret recipes.

Normally, Hazel's Diner only served dinner and supper; however, the diner made an exception and opened for breakfast for the Tuesday Club meetings. There were only thirteen people in the world who knew about the Tuesday Club's existence, and one of them was Jebidiah Moses. Providing food and a backroom for them to meet, Jeb continued the tradition in just the same manner as his momma had done before him. Neither Hazel nor Jeb was privy to the meetings. Jeb didn't really know what they met about; the truth of the matter was he didn't give a rat's hind end why they met. He just knew they were his best customers, and they kept competitors away so Hazel's would be the only source of dining in downtown McWhorter. The sound of his cash register ringing was all the explanation he needed.

Jeb had been cooking since four-thirty in the morning and had bacon, sausage, cat head biscuits, sausage gravy, grits, and eggs fixed for the group as they started meandering in about an hour later. The mayor was always the first to arrive. "Jeb, I smelled that bacon the minute I walked in the back door. I started salivating for your good cooking as soon as I hit Broad Street," the mayor said while he made his general inspection to make sure the meeting place hadn't been compromised in any way.

Parking his car at his office, the mayor chose to walk the short distance and then entered from Hazel's basement entrance. A nice sheen of sweat was glistening from his face due to his exertion from his morning walk. The group had their timing and entrance down to a fine science. Anyone who was stirring that early would not notice anything unusual. The storefront of the diner was dark, and the lights weren't visible from the street. No one would have any idea that an important meeting was taking place.

The members of the group were a select few men that had been born into the three or four generations of members. They secretly ran the town. All the elected officials were nothing but puppets for them. They'd been making these decisions for going on seventy years, and today was report card day, meaning the club would make decisions for the 2008 election.

Twelve seats surrounded a large table in the backroom. This meeting didn't call for formalities such as roll call or minute-taking. On the contrary, it was best that there was no evidence left about the meeting—period. No one dared to miss a meeting.

Most men had been groomed all their lives to come into their inherited rights as a member. Starting in 1938 with the original six men, the club continued to grow as each of the legitimate male heirs became old enough to join. No women were allowed.

In their eyes, women were not capable of making important decisions—only good for cooking and sex. The club members knew their very lives depended on never, ever breaking the code of silence. This club was a privilege in some respects, but in others, it was a ball and chain. There was no walking away from it alive.

After the men finished eating, the mayor, the chief deputy, the county clerk, the banker, the criminal, the county judge executive, the town drunk, the preacher man, the lawyer, the farmer, the coroner, and the protégé got down to business.

The mayor was almost giddy as he explained for the benefit of the newest member of the group, the protégé, the significance of report card day. Only recently meeting the rites of passage, the protégé was being initiated as a full-fledged member of the group. "Report card day's the day when we review our elected officials and make decisions for next year's election. We won every election, we sat out to win last Tuesday!" the mayor excitedly explained.

The group members were patting each others' backs and giving high fives to one another. The mayor continued, "Just as we'd expected, we had some close ones, but we were victorious in the end. That's where it counts, right?" he asked as he lifted his pudgy hand to the group. "We had some good friends who helped that we don't need to forget. But we had some enemies too, and we don't want to forget them either."

The town drunk was having a hard time keeping his head up, partly because of his hangover, but also because he knew too well the pain involved when an untimely accidental death or injury caused the election to sway in the group's favor. Silently, he thanked the good Lord above that this election went the way they wanted without anyone paying for it with his or her life. When no one was looking, he emptied his flask into his coffee cup.

Taking the floor, the county clerk explained what positions would be up for election in the coming year. The first on his list was the sheriff. Looking to the chief deputy, the mayor asked his opinion regarding whether the chief deputy was ready to take up the reins of the public office or not. "As long as he lets me fill his seat on the board of election commissioners, then I'm just fine where I'm at for the time being. The way I see it, the sheriff gets all the headaches, and I'm free to take good care of our business and run after loose women in my spare time. Yep, I'm happy just the way it is," said the chief deputy.

The criminal seconded the chief deputy's assessment. "I think all the proof you need that our chief deputy is keeping the sheriff out of our business is in your bank accounts."

"How's our latest little venture in the underworld?" the mayor asked the criminal.

The smirk on the criminal's bearded face told them a lot. "Still a work in progress, but I'm bringing my cousins from Tennessee to teach us the fine art of making crystal meth."

No other member commented. Although the members knew about and readily accepted the ill-gotten gains they received from the Tuesday Club's drug business, it was much easier to turn a blind eye to it when they didn't speak openly about it. Talking about drug dealing somehow made several of these Bible-wielding men uncomfortable.

Moving right along, the county clerk mentioned the next office on the ballot was the mayoral race. "Anyone heard if someone's gonna run against our esteemed mayor?"

"I heard the Baptist church is a tad upset about the mayor not allowing them to expand their building. I heard they might be looking to run someone against him," the preacher man bellowed in his big preaching voice.

"Um…um…that doesn't sound too good," the mayor looked troubled as he said this. "That Baptist preacher has a big following. Let me see what I can do. I may be able to give them a little slack with that building code after all. Let's see if that takes care of the situation before we react and stir up a hornet's nest when we don't have to."

Wasting no time, the county clerk continued. "The circuit court clerk is up for election next year. Anybody have any problem with our current circuit clerk?"

"Why, I think ole Lillard's done a right nice job," the lawyer stated.

The mayor interrupted him and said, "I'm not too sure about him. If you ask my opinion, I think he's gotten a little too big for his britches." Remembering Lillard's smug attitude toward him last week still went up his craw crossways when he thought about it.

Initially nodding in agreement with the lawyer, this same group of men suddenly turned a complete about face after the mayor spoke against Lillard. Very conveniently, the men seemed to remember times that Lillard Edwards had high-hatted them as well. None of the men would ever think about going against the mayor to his face. If the mayor had looked up, he wouldn't have been happy with the knowing looks that two of the members gave each other.

The meeting continued as they made decisions about each elected official as to whether they stayed or had to go. After they determined the fate of the office and chose a logical replacement, then they decided on an election strategy for each race. They had this election business down to a fine science, even knowing what the weather would mean to each election. This group of men knew how to win elections and the importance of winning these elections—those controlling these offices held the keys to the majority of the jobs in the county. The elected officials also controlled the purse strings belonging to the joint city and county government. Rockford County, Kentucky, was the only county in the state that didn't have a separate governing body for the city. The mayor was the highest official in the county and ran both city and county. This was made possible by bribes made by the Ledfords in the state's capitol over the years.

Small town politics is big time business in McWhorter. By looking at the rag-tag assortment of men, one wouldn't realize the average net worth of each member was over three million dollars. The members' wives had no idea how much money they had in their bank accounts. The banker kept close tabs on each of the member's special accounts and would transfer the money to various offshore accounts when the amount became large enough for auditors to start asking questions. Each of the members enjoyed his wealth and wasn't deprived of pleasure; he just had to be cautious and not flaunt it. At death, this money bypassed the widow and the daughters and was passed directly to the sons. If the member didn't have a male heir; then, the money and land were disbursed evenly to the current members.

The club wasn't being greedy, just cautious. The group couldn't afford a grieving widow to start asking questions. Deathbed confessions to cleanse the soul were not an option. They would have to take it with them to the afterlife and confess it personally, or their family would suffer. Most didn't have a shot at heaven anyway.

For all intents and purposes, report card day was deemed a success, and the group left as inauspiciously as they'd arrived. The smell of sausage was the only remnant of the meeting.

CHAPTER 3

Monday, Monday

Monday, March 10, 2008, 10:00 a.m.

Albert Dean Smith took to selling drugs like a duck took to water, but today, he was kicking himself for agreeing to meet this new customer. Initially he'd said no, but the crying and pleading of the caller convinced him to go ahead and take the chance, but he was damn well going to make this druggie pay for the inconvenience and risk.

Choosing the Jenkins Road location to make the transaction, Albert Dean felt safer since it was one location that gave him all the advantages. His plan was to hide behind the trees near the creek bank until he could make sure it wasn't some kind of trap. If he got cold feet, then, he could make an easy escape through the woods. Having arrived over an hour early, he waited patiently to exchange his OCs for some cold hard cash. He heard one strange sound, and before he could turn around, the bullet ripped through the back of his head. His body landed face down on the ground. The ground all around him soaked up the blood like a thirsty drunk.

12:00 PM

Daniel Brooks glanced at himself through the window of his cruiser. The trademark brown curls that the town had watched bounce in rhythm with the basketball during his hero days had been replaced with his trooper haircut. Looking into the side mirror of the car, he could see a more serious and determined squint had replaced the carefree, mischievous gleam of the eyes of his youth. Daniel wouldn't be apologizing to his town for his transformation either. He'd moved on; the town hadn't. McWhorter was still the same town he left ten years ago.

The smoke hanging in the air at Hazel's was so thick during lunchtime that it could be sliced with a knife. Daniel left his jacket in the cruiser because he wanted as little of his clothing violated by the smoke as possible. Looking through the main street window, he could tell the place was packed with the normal lunch crowd.

Knowing he was a little early for his lunch date, he changed his mind about waiting inside for her. Instead, he walked around Main Street and found himself grinning to think of the illusion that McWhorter gave to outsiders. The streets were litter free. Each storefront's soft pastel colors matched and complimented the other stores. The tulips and flowering pear trees planted in the town square were spectacular to view; however, when these outsiders ventured out of their vehicles and strolled through the appealing town, they would soon realize the town actually reeked of cigarette smoke.

The town's attitude toward smokers and second-hand smoke upset Daniel. Actually, he blamed the town for their nonchalance toward smoking as he continued through the various stages of grief. He recently watched his father suffer and die a traumatic death from lung cancer. There had been absolutely nothing he could've done to prevent it either. Forced to watch his dad wither down to nothing, he saw firsthand how the sinister cancer could eat away at a person's insides as well as his dignity. No one else in town seemed to care about his dad's untimely death as they continued to puff on McWhorter's number one legitimate cash crop.

Feeling the hunger pains gnaw at his backbone, Daniel held his breath as he entered the diner. Daniel had been away for ten years and only recently transferred to this area during his dad's illness, yet the town had never forgotten his game-winning basket in the state basketball championship game. Even after all these years, the townsfolk still reminisced about this claim for fame, and Daniel Brooks was still the hometown hero. Daniel's action photograph as he shot the game-winning basket still hung by the cash register at the diner, but he was more interested in the smaller photograph located next to the larger one. This picture was one of the last photos taken of him with his dad. Daniel and Tinker Brooks stood side-by-side in the photo as they celebrated his graduation from special operations training through the State Police Academy. Daniel felt his loss all over again.

The lunch patrons noticed him and called out his name. In other counties, he could eat at any establishment with or without his police uniform and not cause much of a ruckus, but he could tell he was the topic of conversation at the majority of tables at Hazel's. He forced a smile on his face and looked around the diner for a place to light.

He loved everything about being a state trooper. The calling on his life was strong, and he knew his desire to be a police officer was more than just a phase. By the age of ten, he also knew that he would marry Ms. Caroline Ledford. At that age, it didn't even matter that she was two full grades ahead of him and wouldn't give him the time of the day. She was the girl of his dreams.

"Here ya go, Daniel. You can have our table," Mayor Jock Ledford hollered across the room bringing him back to the present. "Caroline should be here any minute."

"Great! Thanks, Mayor," Daniel said as he looked down at the ground so he didn't have to make eye contact with Caroline's father.

Sheriff Osborne, the mayor's lunch partner, jokingly asked, "Danny, when're you gonna marry that pretty Caroline and start giving Jock here some grandbabies?" He lightly rubbed Jock's head.

The color drained from the mayor's face. Not only did Jock have an aversion for having his Grecian formula died hairdo messed up, he also didn't like the sheriff meddling in his daughter's affairs. It didn't help that the sheriff was hitting an exposed nerve regarding the fact that his thirty-year-old daughter was still single. "Leave the boy alone. Willie. They'll figure it out sooner or later, and they don't need any help from the likes of you." At that exact moment, Jock pondered that the Tuesday Club should possibly rethink their decision on keeping him as sheriff.

Undeterred by the mayor's reprimand, Sheriff Osborne waited until Jock was out of earshot and in a serious, hushed tone said, "Danny boy, come by and see me when you get some time. I could use a little of your expertise on a case I'm working."

"Sure thing, Sheriff," Daniel's soft voice answered after him.

Taking a whiff in the air, Daniel smelled her perfume before he actually saw her. Caroline was wearing her signature fragrance of Oscar, and it seemed to part the smoke-filled air as it made its way to his nostrils. Not only did Caroline Ledford, attorney at law, smell heavenly; Daniel was pretty sure she was the closest thing to an angel this town had ever witnessed. She was dressed in classic black slacks, a light blue cashmere sweater, high-heeled boots, and her long black hair was pulled back at the nape of her neck. Both Caroline and her mother always had a way of looking elegant and timeless in a town that had never heard of the likes of Dolce and Gabbana.

After Caroline made it to his table, she bent down and gave him a short hello kiss. The kiss was wet and sweet, and Daniel could still feel the effects of it even after she sat down across from him. "Mommy wanted to see if you were coming over this evening. She said to tell you she was fixing your favorites for supper."

"Sorry, babe, but I've already promised my mom that I would eat with her tonight."

"You can always bring her with you. Mommy always fixes enough for an army. She never knows who Jon or Jennings will bring, and you know she just adores your sweet momma and would welcome her company," Caroline encouraged.

He always cringed a little bit when she referred to her mother as "mommy." He had to admit her relationship with her parents was unnatural. It bothered Daniel to hear both Caroline and her brothers calling their parents mommy and daddy like they were still children. Caroline was one of three children belonging to Eleanor and Jock Ledford. It also disgusted him that all three of the children still lived at home. Caroline would soon be thirty-one, and her brothers were stairstep in ages to her.

"I'm sorry, sweetie, I'll have to take a rain check. I've already promised mom that I would be over right after my shift is finished. I really need to spend as much time with her as I can right now. She's still having a tough time of it."

Knowing Daniel was right, she wanted to change the subject quickly before he started thinking about his dad. "That's okay. What're your plans for after dinner," she said emphasizing the word *after*. They managed to eat their meal, but it wasn't easy. The diners felt an obligation to stop by their table and speak to the returning hero and beautiful attorney.

Caroline was feeling a lot of pressure about the need to get married. Her daddy kept reminding her daily that her biological clock was ticking. She was going to be thirty-one years old soon. Her daddy didn't understand, and for that matter, she didn't understand either as she asked herself the question that continued to haunt her. "Why hasn't Daniel asked me to marry him yet?" Originally, he'd asked her to marry him when he was ten and she was twelve. Looking back, she wished she'd agreed then instead of hitting him with her purse. She thought that marrying Daniel was a given. Now, she was definitely beginning to wonder.

"How about coming over to my house about nine?" Daniel playfully asked as he walked her out of Hazel's. He couldn't resist putting his arm around her waist and pulling her close knowing the women were all saying "How sweet!" and the men were thinking what a lucky son of a bitch he was. While at her car, she gave him a kiss that gave him a taste of what to expect later. He had a good mind to jump in the car with her and drive to some secluded spot right now; however, the jingle of the brass on his uniform brought him back to reality. Caroline quit torturing him and drove away in her Lexus.

He didn't smell the cigarette smoke on his clothes because all he could smell was that delicious smell of her perfume that clung to his uniform like a bee clings to a flower.

CHAPTER 4

The Ledfords

Wednesday, May 4, 1977

Jock Ledford said all the right things when he saw his newborn baby girl. Any observer would've thought Jock Ledford was the happiest man alive as he looked through the nursery's viewing window at his daughter. Jock's wife of one year, Eleanor, wasn't so convinced. She knew Jock had been praying for a son to follow in his footsteps; however, after twenty-eight hours of hard labor, Eleanor Ledford was too tired to care about Jock's happiness at the moment. Personally, she thought Caroline Morgan Ledford was the prettiest baby she'd ever seen.

Instead of thinking about his daughter's beauty, Jock was thinking about his new strategy. Johnny Clarence "Jock" Ledford could strategize and talk with the best of them. Jock used his gifts wisely as a politician. When he went door-to-door electioneering for votes, he would have a Bible in his hand, a flask of whiskey in his back pocket, and a wad of fifty-dollar bills in his wallet. Armed with his election tools, he would leave each house, one way or another, with the promise of a vote in the upcoming election.

Jock learned all about politics from his father, Clarence Ledford, and Clarence had learned from his father, Jon R. Ledford, the founder of the Tuesday Club. One of the Ledfords had been mayor since 1938. On one hand, the citizens of Rockford County loved the Ledfords; but on the other hand, they knew enough to fear them as well.

Jock could see the family resemblance in his new baby daughter, but he knew his legacy in the Tuesday Club would be destroyed without a male heir. Jock took a long draw from his cigar and calculated the number of days before he could impregnate Eleanor again.

Saturday, May 7, 1977

The sandman and the little white sheep had avoided Jock Ledford for three entire days. He was truly worried. Without a male heir, all the work his daddy and granddaddy had done would go down the drain. He was completely shocked when his firstborn turned out to be a girl. Ordinarily, everything came easily to Jock, and he just knew that his first child would be a male. His grandfather's first child was a son, and he was Clarence's first and only legitimate child. Knowing fate would smile on him as well, he had been ill-prepared for his luck to have run out. Deciding it had to be Eleanor's fault, he began to question why he chose her as his bride in the first place. He thought back to the first time he saw Eleanor.

Eleanor was a looker and came from the wealthiest family in Hyden, Kentucky; they owned the only car dealership in Hyden. Jock thought she was classy and could fit the bill for the image needed to help him build his empire. What convinced him to marry Eleanor was nothing but pure lust. She wouldn't bed him without the ring on her finger.

Jock was the epitome of happiness when he chauffeured baby Caroline and Eleanor from the hospital. Eleanor's mother came to help with the baby. Mrs. Garland had planned to stay at least a month so she could help her only daughter recover from the difficult childbirth. On the outside, Jock was most appreciative, but inwardly he was counting the hours he could be shed of his meddling mother-in-law. Of course, he was very good at keeping his thoughts and his actions separated.

Jock could tell his daughter was going to be a real beauty with her big brown eyes and pouty little lips. Jock was thinking about another little Caroline in the arms of her daddy, only this daddy was holding his daughter in an oval room. "Yep, little girl, I may have some use for you after all," Jock cooed to his daughter.

Insisting his mother-in-law sleep in the extra bedroom, he slept on the living room couch for the first few nights so as not to disturb Eleanor's rest. After Eleanor was able to maneuver around the house a little better, he went back to his bed. On the first night of his return to the bedroom, they slept in each other's arms. The next night, he placed his hands on Eleanor's large milk-filled breasts only to be scolded by his wife saying her breasts were sore. It was at this time she explained that Dr. Grant didn't want her to be doing any of her wifely duties for at least six weeks so she could heal. Jock made a mental note to self, "Make sure Dr. Grant's son isn't awarded any of the county's construction work he's bid on." Didn't Doc realize he didn't have six weeks to waste? Jock didn't sleep at all that night as he seethed with anger thinking that Eleanor and Dr. Grant were depriving him of his son. Instead, he lay awake working on his strategy.

The very next day, Jock awoke early to carry out his plan. After cooking a big breakfast, washing the dishes, and diapering baby Caroline, Jock convinced his mother-in-law and his wife that he had things in control. That afternoon, he drove his mother-in-law over the mountains to her eastern Kentucky home.

Eleanor was happy to see her wonderful husband return from the trip, not realizing she was about to learn the first of Jock's very important and valuable lessons. Jock wasted no time to begin teaching his wife lesson number one. He placed the screaming baby in her crib; her cries and Eleanor's protests fell on deaf ears. Jock soon placed his own hand over Eleanor's mouth. She looked at Jock in horror when he ripped her gown off her body before using his fist to insure her further cooperation. In the middle of the living room floor, he violently penetrated her sore and swollen body. Her mouth was filled with a dish rag causing her cries to be nothing but muffled gasps until the pain rendered her unconscious.

Later, Eleanor contemplated killing her husband while she cleaned the blood from the carpet after the rape but realized this was not an option, and she instead took the path of least resistance. Without her fighting him or even uttering any protests, she allowed him to continue to violate her unhealed body as some perverted punishment until she finally conceived. She knew Caroline needed her, and she knew both of their lives depended on her never depriving Jock of anything again—especially a son.

As soon as the doctor confirmed that his seed took, Jock started sleeping in the guest bedroom because he wanted Eleanor to get plenty of rest. He never slept a full night again with his wife, only visited her as needed. Once again, he became the wonderful and loving husband Eleanor had fallen in love with two years ago.

Dr. Grant was not happy Eleanor had conceived before she had officially healed, but was even unhappier about the financial impact facing his son due to the loss of the county work that had been promised causing his son, Edward, into looking for road work in other states.

Eleanor was able to rest again, but Jock was far from physically deprived, as he would have had her imagine. Jock had hired a pretty little secretary that was very creative about finding new ways to please him both professionally and physically. His secretary was a young girl from a large family that lived up a holler. She was one of a string of secretaries that had serviced the Ledfords over the years. For the time being, she served Jock's purposes well, but he knew the day would come when she would become a risk to him. He'd already been to the high school to pick out his next secretary, another poor little holler girl that happened to be the best business student at Rockford County High School. If his young secretary caused him no problems, then she would be transferred to a job with another one of the club members; if she wasn't careful, she could instead receive a demotion to work at the church as the church secretary. Most of his girls would choose wisely because they didn't want to work for the perverted preacher man.

The mayor knew his pool of secretaries was one of the many perks of being in his club. These loyal, hard-working, appreciative young ladies also served as nice informants. By infiltrating his girls into the town's workforce, he could keep tabs on the pulse of McWhorter, including his club members. Not only rewarding the girls for good behavior, he also gifted their families for their loyalty and silence. These girls were well aware of how important their silence and loyalty were to their very lives; they knew they were very disposable and could easily disappear without a lot of fuss.

Jock and his town were riding high right now. Jock counted his blessings daily. He was the most powerful man in McWhorter. Eleanor, his lovely and gracious wife, was thriving in her second pregnancy; and Caroline was the most perfect little girl in the world. Jock attended church every time the church doors opened so he could pray that the next child was his heir to the throne of McWhorter.

CHAPTER 5

Best Laid Plans

Monday, March 10, 2008, 2:00 AM

Inside the glove compartment of Daniel's cruiser, a diamond solitaire ring waited patiently to be placed on just the right finger. He had planned to give Caroline the ring last fall, but Tinker's sickness put a hiatus to the proposal. Tinker had been gone for a few weeks, and part of him wanted to go ahead and ask Caroline to be his wife, but he just couldn't fathom the thoughts of being alone with Mayor Ledford to ask for her hand. Between his grief and the secret distaste he felt for Jock Ledford, the ring continued to wait patiently in his vehicle.

Daniel mentioned his problem to his best friend and law enforcement brother, Deputy Joseph Mattingly Sizemore. Joe Matt, as his name had been shortened, was practically a brother to Daniel. Growing up, they had been like peas in a pod and were always together. Unfortunately, college and career paths separated them; Daniel chose to leave McWhorter for his education and experience, whereas Joe Matt started as a deputy sheriff right out of high school. Daniel knew that Joe Matt would've preferred to go with him but didn't because he couldn't leave his momma all alone.

Just as he'd predicted, Joe Matt laughed and made light of Daniel's little problem. He kidded Daniel. "If you don't hurry up and ask Caroline to marry you, then I'm going to have to take her away from you. You know she's secretly in love with me, don't ya?"

That conversation had taken place some time ago, and the ring continued to take a backseat to his other priorities. The view of the sheriff's office brought Daniel back to the matter at hand. Daniel was always happy to go to the Rockford County Sheriff's office. When it came to the line of duty, there were no finer law enforcement officers anywhere than the sheriff and his chief deputy.

Sheriff Osborne was somber when he met Daniel at the door and quickly ushered him to his office before locking the door behind him. He wasted no time in telling him about an arrest that one of his deputies made a few weeks ago. "After finding a joint on the young driver, he then searched the car where he found a trunk full of marijuana. The boy insisted he'd been blackmailed into hauling it by none other than, get this, Jennings Ledford." The sheriff lowered his voice when uttering the Ledford name like saying it in this context was some act of sacrilege.

Daniel's jaw dropped. The understanding for the privacy made sense now. Jennings was Caroline's youngest brother. He was a better-looking version of his older brother, Jon, only a little rougher around the edges. Daniel thought the Ledford brothers were mischievous but harmless. Now, he wasn't so sure. This revelation felt like a bomb that detonated in his gut. Daniel exploded, "Sheriff Osborne, why in the hell would you drop this on me? Best I can tell you're the high sheriff."

"I know. I know. I've really put you in a bind, but you're one of the few people I can trust. After all, you have Tinker Brooks' blood coursing through your veins. That makes you trustworthy in my books. God rest his soul. Did you know that Tinker saved my life not just once, but twice? He saved me from drowning when we were kids over at Cromer Lake, and then over at Nam, he saved me once again.

Daniel was upset about the position the sheriff had placed him in, but mentioning Vietnam piqued his interest. He knew very little about his dad's military days and would like to ask the sheriff more about what his dad was like back then, but refrained.

"Hell, I don't know what I thought you'd do, but I have a bad feeling about this and wanted you to know in case something happens to me. I guess I also wanted you to know what you're getting yerself into if you marry into this family. I feel I owe your daddy that much."

Just as Daniel was about to respond, a knock on the sheriff's door broke up his thought process. "Sheriff, you've got a visitor," Joe Matt hollered through the locked door.

"Keep this between us until I have a plan. I have a feeling my life may depend on it," he said as he unlocked and opened his door.

Daniel wasn't prepared for what happened next. "Hello, sheriff, remember me?" came the melodious sound.

"Why, my little Matilda Sue Grant!" the sheriff said as he grabbed her in a bear hug.

He stopped hugging and pulled the small woman out an arm's length so he could look at her. "Oops, somehow I don't think I'm supposed to hug big bad FBI agents."

"That's okay, Uncle Willie. Us big bad FBI agents allow hugs from uncles on Mondays."

"Daniel, allow me to introduce you to my niece, Special Agent Matilda Grant." Sheriff Osborne squeezed her tighter. "You may remember her as one of the twin grandchildren of ole Doc Grant? My sister married Doc Grant's only son. May he rest in peace," he said with his eyes reverently lowered.

Daniel had to force his jaw shut as he looked into the blue eyes of a fairy tale nymph. She was tiny, but not fragile. Her short blond hair had curls going in all directions, which Daniel found oddly appealing. She was dressed casually in jeans and was wearing a Reds t-shirt. Daniel didn't notice how tanned she was until she opened her mouth; her smile almost blinded him. "I think I remember playing in the creek with you and your brother," Daniel stammered like a schoolboy.

"Danny Brooks? Yeah, I remember you too. Trevor and I would beg Granny and Pa to take us to your house so we could catch salamanders and crawdads. By the way, the last person who called me Matilda died a horrible death. Call me Tillie." She smiled. As quickly as her eyes lit up, the sadness seemed to overtake them. "We used to love our visits to Kentucky. Now these visits are so hard."

"I heard about Mrs. Grant. How's she fairing?" the sheriff asked.

"Alzheimer's is so unfair. She started having some dementia right after she lost my dad in that accident. Then, when Pa died, she went downhill fast. Hospice nurses say we just need to make her comfortable. It's a matter of hours. Trevor's sitting with her now. I just had to get out of the house for a few minutes, or I was going to lose my mind."

"So did you and Trevor leave Quantico in one piece?" Sheriff Osborne asked his niece as he attempted to change the subject.

"Let's put it this way, I'm sure the Bureau will think twice before they put twins in the same academy class again."

Seemed like every deputy in the office found reason to come to the sheriff's office to catch a glimpse of Tillie and listen to her stories about her Quantico experience. She ended up staying a couple of hours, and Daniel, like the other deputies, couldn't manage to pull himself away. He was just as enamored by her musical voice and bubbly personality as the other guys.

Tillie thanked everyone for making her afternoon a little brighter as she graciously said her good-byes. Daniel was silently pleased when she gave him a quick hug instead of a departing handshake as she did the other men in the room.

He noticed that Caroline's perfume had been replaced by Tillie's earthy, clean smell.

8:50 p.m.

Daniel was confused not only about the Ledford boys' involvement in the drug business, but also about his strange reaction to Tillie

Grant. For someone contemplating engagement, his heart sure beat a tad faster every time he thought about Tillie. As a police officer, he was accustomed to the uniform chasers throwing themselves at him; they didn't interest him. He remembered his dad saying, "Why settle for hamburger when you have steak waiting at home?" Daniel had to admit that Caroline was definitely the filet mignon of women. Just as he thought about this particular cut of steak, it dawned on him, "What if my favorite meat isn't steak, but short ribs?" he asked himself when Tillie crossed his mind once again.

Grabbing a beer from the fridge, he knew he had to get Tillie Grant out of his mind before Caroline came over. Caroline Ledford was beautiful and was as good in bed as she was pretty. Most of their sexual experience had been with each other since they learned about sex in the back of her daddy's Buick when she was seventeen and he was only fifteen. Since that time, he had remained fairly faithful to her if he didn't count the time with the Matney twins. No man in his right mind could have resisted those girls. Also, the times during college when he woke up with some naked girl in his bed didn't count as unfaithfulness since he couldn't exactly remember what had transpired. Thoughts of sex seemed to do the trick. Caroline was now in the forefront of his mind, rooting out the blond FBI officer from his thoughts.

Thinking about Caroline made him conjure up his earlier conversation with the sheriff about Caroline's brothers. When moving back to McWhorter, he knew he would have run-ins with family members and people he knew. He just didn't think it would be the Ledford boys and so soon. He knew the boys well enough to know that if one of them was involved with the walk on the dark side—they both were involved. Caroline's devotion to her brothers remained steadfast. He knew Caroline would be devastated if she found out about any problems with her younger brothers. Or on second thought, would she be surprised? Caroline was smart and was very tight with her younger brothers.

Daniel looked at his watch. Ten till nine. He knew Caroline would show up any minute because she was never late. Sure enough, he could hear her SUV pulling in his driveway. The engine was just loud enough to announce her arrival. Her Lexus purchase was a source of contention with her daddy, but a source of hope for him. Caroline had her heart set on buying this Japanese-made car, but her daddy forbade it. Jock Ledford was all about American-made vehicles; anything sold by the local Chevy dealer was fine by him. Caroline's defiance in purchasing the Lexus gave Daniel hope that she could eventually break away from the mayor.

Smiling, he watched Caroline let herself in his small rent house. She was attired in her most serious lawyer getup, complete with the little cat-eye glasses. Her hair was pulled back in a serious bun. Daniel would bet money that she wore nothing underneath her skirt and jacket. Her black heels were a good four inches tall, and he knew they would remain on even when everything else came off her body. Daniel remained seated while Caroline reached behind her head and let loose her gorgeous mane of black hair. As she began to remove articles of clothing, she seductively sauntered in his direction. He didn't think any more about the Ledford boys or blue-eyed nymphs.

CHAPTER 6

Not on a Tuesday

Tuesday, March 11, 2008, 5:00 AM

An empty chair around the Tuesday Club meeting table was never a good way to start a meeting because the members could not concentrate for worry about what travesty caused this member to miss a crucial meeting. No one made reference to the absence, and the mayor continued without ever mentioning the criminal's empty chair.

The club members knew the primary election was less than two months away, and they had a few big elections at stake. The circuit court clerk election wouldn't really matter during the primary race because the incumbent was a Democrat, and the female opponent was a Republican. "No sense in wasting our time on the circuit court race until fall," the mayor gave his opinion. He also didn't want them to lose focus over a little whore. He didn't think women had any business in politics. Deciding to focus on the more pressing elections, he explained the most recent act of subterfuge. "Boys, we've been thrown a curve ball by our commonwealth attorney. It pisses me off that Gene Lester decided not to discuss his early retirement with us before announcing it in the newspaper. At this late stage of the game, we're definitely behind the eight ball. We can't have Lowell Evans as the next DA, or we're ruined. We've got to act fast because Lowell now has a jump start on us, and he's got Gene's backing. Gene will definitely pay for this! We've all been very supportive to him and now look at our pay back. We'll take care of Gene later, but right now, let's concentrate on how we can salvage this position."

"What about Tom Whitaker?" the drunk asked in his brain cell-deteriorated slur.

"He may just work out perfectly," added the banker. "You see, I may have some leverage there too since Tom's mortgage is close to being in default."

Slapping the banker's back, the preacher man said, "Hallelujah, the Lord has come through for us once again!"

The mayor tried to stop fidgeting because he knew it was time to discuss the election that was causing him to lose sleep. Nonchalantly, he opened the floor for discussing the mayoral election. The mayor would never admit it out loud, but he had a bad feeling deep down in his bones about this election. Something didn't feel right. The fact he was facing his first empty chair at a meeting in twenty-eight years also seemed to be an omen for impending doom.

"I tried to appease the Baptist Church about their building expansion, but it seems that my efforts were a little too late. Geneva Vaughn had taken a taste from the holy grail of politics and decided she liked it, and she's got the whole congregation working day and night. Hell, Geneva's one of the nicest ladies I know, but you know it's a proven fact that women have no damn business involved in politics. The only decision a woman can make without a man's help is what she's cooking for supper. Also, it seems someone always gets hurt when these so-called nice people decide to run for office," said the mayor as he worked to keep his emotions intact.

Feeling the need to intercede the county judge said, "Now, don't you fret, Mayor. We'll get a decoy running, and you know, decoys always help the incumbent. I think it's time to see exactly what Saint Geneva's made of. Maybe if she sees that politics is a tough and shitty business, then she'll back out gracefully."

The county clerk grinned as a thought crossed his mind. "Geneva's got a mighty sweet little sixteen-year-old granddaughter that my cousin just sold a bright, canary yeller, little, sporty-looking car to a few months ago. I heard she's pretty hot-to-trot."

The mayor could see where the clerk was going with this, and he liked it. "It wouldn't look none too good for Geneva if her granddaughter was tainted in the eyes of the county, now would it, and I know who we can enlist to help us out with Little Miss Canary Hot Britches."

Finishing their meeting on a strong note, the mayor was beginning to breathe a little easier. Many side conversations were taking place before they parted in their covert separate ways. The farmer was bragging and showing pictures of his prize bull just like a new papa shows pictures of his new baby boy. The coroner, protégé, and lawyer were laughing at some joke the coroner had been saving for the meeting. The banker, preacher man, and county judge were whispering in hushed tones as they compared notes about their secretaries' sexual abilities.

The group paid homage to Jeb, the king of breakfast, and exited through the various doors as usual with one exception.

"Mayor, can I talk to you in private?" the chief deputy asked the mayor.

"Sure, son. What's on your mind?"

"It's about the sheriff. I think he's doing some things behind my back. He's changed the locks to the evidence room, and just the other day, he had a closed door meeting with your future son-in-law," the chief deputy reported.

"Interesting. How long was Daniel in the sheriff's office?"

"Not long, sir. They were interrupted when the sheriff's little FBI niece paid a visit."

The mayor's hair stood straight up on its ends with the mention of those three letters together. He rubbed his chin as he said, "Hmmm, FBI. I suppose you're talking about Dr. Grant's granddaughter? Someone said the twins had gotten in to the Bureau."

"Yep. Her and her twin brother both are now bona fide agents, and I do believe that Danny boy may have been a little smitten by the little blond police bitch," the chief deputy added the curse word for good measure.

If the mayor had a bad feeling during the meeting, it had escalated to being a downright sick spell. He felt and tasted the sausage gravy as it rose up his throat.

11:58 PM

Tillie sat on one side of her Granny, Mrs. Roscoe Grant, and Trevor sat on the other side of her. Mrs. Grant's caregiver and best friend, Julia Hopper, sat inside the room by the door giving the family their final time with their grandmother. Julia had already said her good-byes and made her promises months ago before Mrs. Grant slipped into that empty chasm in her mind.

The twins each held one of her hands as she was taking her last breaths. Trevor was still shaken by the events of the afternoon. The nurse had kept their Granny sedated, but today she was allowed to wake up slightly. Mrs. Grant had not recognized anyone or spoken a rational word in months, but the hospice nurse wanted her to be able to at least look into her grandchildren's eyes for the last time, if possible.

At one point during the day, she looked into Trevor's eyes and called him by his father's name and asked him what day it was. Trevor was so surprised that he looked around to see if someone else had entered the room. When he realized it was his granny speaking and she was waiting for him to answer, he stuttered as he answered that it was Tuesday. She shook her head in agony, and her last words ever spoken were as articulate and rational as ever as she said, "Dear God, please not on a Tuesday!"

Mrs. Grant then closed her eyes. Trevor was not sure he hadn't dreamed the incident.

Mrs. Grant's breaths became fewer and longer in between until she didn't breathe anymore. The nurse recorded the time of death as 12:15 a.m. on Wednesday, March 12, 2008.

CHAPTER 7

Murder on Jenkins Road

Thursday, March 13, 2008, 10:00 AM

"Eight-two-seven, what's your ten-twenty?" came the call from dispatch over the radio.

Daniel keyed up his mike and replied, "I'm on Raccoon Mill Road. Over."

"We've got a body located at 224 Jenkins Road."

Daniel's adrenaline kicked in as he responded, "Ten-four, I'm in route." Since he had been assigned to work the Rockford County area, his job had been pretty boring. Boring was good in some aspects as he continued to heal, but it also gave Daniel a lot of time to think—too much time in his opinion. Right now, Daniel didn't want to think. He wanted to respond and let his body and his training take over so he wouldn't have to waste a brain cell on thinking about his dad, his promises to his dad, or the Ledfords.

The location was easy to find because there were a whole slew of cars and trucks lined up and down the creek bank. The first action Daniel took was to clear the area as he made his way under the bank to personally witness the crime scene. He could smell the rotting flesh before he actually saw it. The body was turned face down, and the Caucasian male had been shot in the back of the head. The caliber of gun blew a hole in his head that at exit left no traces of what used to be the man's face. There would be no facial identification of the body, but the man's billfold was still in the back pocket of his pants. The driver's license belonged to Albert Dean Smith.

Daniel was taken aback by the identity of the man, and the fact that Albert Dean was a professional criminal with rumored ties to the Columbian drug rings complicated matters. Knowing the Columbians had all kinds of styles of assassinations, Daniel couldn't rule them out, but what bothered him about that theory was that they usually needed a reason before they come after you. That didn't make a lot of sense to him. If Albert Dean was smart enough to stay under the radar of local and state law enforcement, then surely he was smart enough to stay under the drug lord's radar as well.

Sheriff Osborne and Joe Matt walked to the scene. Daniel had already roped off the entire area and called for the state police's special investigation unit to sweep the area for evidence. "I can't help but believe that whoever did this had a personal vendetta," he explained to his fellow police officers.

2:00 PM

The mayor and the county judge were busy looking through the obituaries, a task they performed behind closed doors every Thursday afternoon. As elected officials, it was important to pay their respects to the dead. The duo had attended plenty of funerals over the years, but the men had a more self-serving reason for conjuring up the dead on Thursdays. By reading the obituaries, they would find out what local died and then do some research. If the deceased owned property, then they would secretly assess it for coal, oil, and gas since Rockford County was chocked full of its fair share of minerals and fossil fuels. They would give it a couple of weeks, and then, they would pay a visit to the surviving family of the deceased and offer to help them out by taking the property off their hands. The men only targeted the most vulnerable. Each of the members of the Tuesday Club had many acres of land—thanks to their little Thursday afternoon game.

The judge executive and mayor were reviewing the prospects when they were interrupted by a knock on the door. The mayor's secretary peeped her head through the small opening in the door and said in her deep Kentucky accent, "I'm sorry to interrupt you all, but there's a call on line two that I really think you need to take."

The mayor didn't waste any time. "Hello. Mayor Ledford speaking." The color drained from Jock's face. "Jon, Jon, now you listen to me. You and Jennings get your asses back to the house and don't you leave again until you talk with me. You sure it was Albert Dean? Well, okay. It's gonna be okay. Now, listen to your daddy. Don't you worry, you hear?" Jock hung up the phone then directed his next statement to the judge. "Well, the mystery's solved. We now know why Albert Dean didn't show up to our meeting on Tuesday."

"What'ya mean? What's going on, Jock?"

"Albert Dean's dead. His head blown clean off his shoulders, and Jon and Jennings are scared. The boys have a big shipment scheduled, and Albert Dean had the money."

The judge puckered his lips and made a squishing noise with them before saying, "Who ya think killed him?"

"Hell, if I know," Jock answered. He was beginning to have that weird feeling again. "I've got to get home to the boys and try to calm 'em down."

CHAPTER 8

The Wake

Friday, March 14, 2008

Caroline had insisted on accompanying Daniel to Mrs. Grant's funeral visitation, which was out of character for her because she hated funeral homes. He drove Caroline's Lexus so she wouldn't have to ride in his dad's pick-up truck. Dressed in his khakis and a black pullover, Daniel was a little hesitant about seeing Tillie again, especially when he was with Caroline. He felt that his initial reaction to her was just a fluke, and there would be no butterflies in his stomach again. He would just concentrate on Caroline. Wearing her traditional black suit, Caroline looked the part of a McWhorter mourner.

For a Friday night, there was a big turnout at the viewing. The Sizemore Funeral Home was a large white building with antebellum columns that gave the funeral parlor a regal appearance, one befitting the last viewing of Mrs. Roscoe Grant.

The funeral home smelled of roses mixed with mothballs. One second, the smell was pleasant, and then, the more medicinal smell of the embalming chemicals would overtake the olfactory system. The couple signed the sympathy book and then found their place in a long, slow-moving line down the center isle leading toward the closed bronze casket with yellow roses cascading over the top.

Daniel recognized Tillie standing on the right side of the casket, and a blond man, who he assumed was Trevor, was standing on the left side. Tillie was hard to miss in her bright orange sweater and skirt. She looked taller than he remembered; he understood the reason for her growth spurt when he noticed the orange spike heels she was wearing. She stood out in the sea of mostly black-clad mourners with her bright ensemble. He figured her clothing choice must have been a California thing.

Trevor, on the other hand, wore more traditional clothing. His short hairstyle screamed that his vocation was either military or law enforcement. His muscular frame could be recognized regardless of his fitted navy suit, white starched shirt, and yellow striped tie. Daniel could still see enough of the boy that used to traipse up and down the creek to recognize him.

He could tell that Tillie had been crying; her blue eyes were puffy and red. She looked much different today than she had the other day. Her wild curls were replaced with a sleek hairstyle. He couldn't imagine the work that had gone into taming those locks. He felt those same butterflies zooming around in his stomach as he did on the day he saw her in the sheriff's office.

Caroline turned around just in time to see the look on his face as the butterflies fought round two in his belly. Giving him a look of disapproval, she turned back around just in time to be her gracious self as she offered her condolences in the form of a handshake first to Tillie and then to Trevor. Daniel noticed Caroline's handshake seemed to have pumped some life back into Trevor. He seemed much more appreciative and interested in Caroline than he did the previous mourners.

While Trevor was talking with Caroline, Tillie reached up and grabbed Daniel by the neck. She buried her head into his chest and began to cry softly into his sweater. Daniel stood very still and let the young woman cry. After what seemed an appropriate amount of time, Caroline broke up the moment by offering Tillie some tissues. Slowly unwrapping her arms from Daniel's neck, Tillie managed to take the tissues from Caroline. Daniel noticed there were tears rolling down Caroline's cheeks as well even though she had never carried on a conversation with Mrs. Grant. The next thing he knew, Tillie had grabbed Caroline, and both women were sobbing together.

Daniel couldn't help but compare the two women as they stood embraced in front of him. The only thing they had in common was the fact they were both very attractive women. Caroline was not big by any standards, but she towered over Tillie's petite frame. Caroline's dark, classic good looks were a stark contrast to Tillie's bright, blond stunning looks.

Finally, the two ladies separated. Tillie apologized over and over until Caroline convinced her it was okay. Daniel and Caroline again offered their condolences and moved on to give other mourners a chance to pay their respects.

Daniel waited until they were seated in the Lexus before he questioned Caroline about her crying outburst. He didn't much more get the words out of his mouth until Caroline started sobbing again. Completely dumbfounded, Daniel didn't know how to react. In all these years, he had never seen Caroline cry like this before. Gently, he reached over and brushed her hair out of her tears before he hugged her tightly. He allowed her to cry just as he had allowed Tillie to cry earlier knowing his sweater would never be the same.

CHAPTER 9

Soul Bartering and Secrets

Saturday, March 15, 2008, 11:00 a.m.

Caroline heard the light taps of her Mommy's shoes as she headed toward her room.

"Sweetie, that was Daniel on the answering machine. That's about his fifth message today. Why don't you just talk to him?" Eleanor tried to reason with her.

Caroline whined, "Mommy, you don't understand! I can't talk to him, and I can't see him right now. Look at me! I feel myself falling to pieces. My whole life is falling apart before my eyes. I can't have him see me like this. Not to mention that I made a complete fool of myself at Mrs. Grant's funeral visitation last night."

The mention of Mrs. Grant's name made Eleanor automatically tense up. If there were a heaven, she knew Dr. Grant was there waiting for his wife. Mrs. Grant had always been polite enough to her, but she didn't consider her to be a close friend. On the other hand, she considered Dr. Grant as one of her very best friends; she and Dr. Grant shared a secret.

Eleanor shook her head as if she could just shake those thoughts away like a dog shakes off fleas. "You'll heal up and be good as new in a day or two, and Daniel will be begging you to marry him. You just wait and see if your Mommy isn't right. Now let me get you some ice for your eye."

Caroline knew her chances of marrying Daniel were slim to none. She always thought Daniel loved her, but now she wasn't so sure. Daniel Brooks had never looked at her the way she caught him looking at Tillie Grant last night. Caroline knew she had lost him even before Daniel knew it. "It's just a matter of time before he figures it out," she thought. Just when she thought she had no more tears left in her body, she felt them start again. She reached for her mother's familiar and comforting arms.

"Now, now, it's okay. I'm so sorry how your daddy treated you. He's just worried right now about the election. I'm sorry you got the brunt of his frustration. I don't know why he is so set on you marrying that boy," Eleanor said while she stroked her daughter's black hair.

Caroline's emotions were running the full gamut as she went from soft tears to anger. Raising her voice, she said what was really on her mind, "If Daniel doesn't ask me to marry him, then, Daddy'll never let me marry anyone else! I'll die an old maid!"

Eleanor knew she should have warned her daughter not to come home last night. She saw it in Jock's eyes. He had that same wild look she came to know and fear when he was in one of his teaching moods. She knew that in his mind, Caroline was due a lesson. She didn't know why Jock was hell bent on Caroline marrying Daniel Brooks. Daniel had always been a great kid, but there had been great boys everywhere. Caroline could have her pick of the litter.

She remembered when Jock took Caroline into his office and had one of his many closed-door talks. Caroline bound out of the office and straight to her arms, saying that there was no way she could date a freshman. She was convinced she would be the laughingstock of the entire school. Eleanor wanted to talk to Jock about her concerns but knew once his mind was made up, there was no talking to him.

Jock must have seen something special in Daniel years ago. For whatever reason, Jock was fixated on the two of them marrying. He had been plotting and planning with the two young beautiful lives as his chess pieces for over thirteen years.

A few years back, Caroline had an epiphany and finally made a little sense out of Jock's desire for her to marry Daniel. She said Daniel was incorruptible and couldn't be bought, and her Daddy had sensed his good nature. Everything was a competition with Jock. Jock always found a way to win. Caroline said she felt she'd become his only barter for Daniel's very soul. Eleanor cringed and wondered if she still had a soul or if Jock had bartered it away years ago.

Saturday, October 20, 1979

Eleanor Garland Ledford was a realist and a survivor. No longer the naive bride, she now had been married for three years and had three babies to show for it. She was never head over heels in love with Jock, but he once stirred up feelings that made her think she loved him.

She remembered the day Jock Ledford strutted into her daddy's office at the car lot. Sensing that Jock was different from all the other boys she dated, she couldn't take her eyes off him. Even though he was ten years her senior, she didn't even mind the age gap. Actually, it made him all the more appealing. Granted he had nice brown wavy hair and distinct brown eyes, but he wasn't necessarily good looking. His head was rather large on his short body, and he wasn't but an inch or so taller than her 5'7" frame. He wasn't overweight, but he was stocky. She could tell he probably wouldn't age well, but she didn't care because when he opened his mouth, his defects and his ordinary seemed to go out the window. His smile made her weak at her knees. It was more than just his teeth. When he smiled, his whole face transformed. Not only did his smile captivate her, his voice was like music to her ears. She didn't want him to ever quit talking. She felt like one of those cobras in the basket swaying back and forth to his hypnotic voice.

To say that her view of Jock had changed over the last three years was a gross understatement. She woke up from her trance.

She was certain her feelings for him would not be considered love anymore but rather survival instincts. She had learned to adapt to her disappointments. All was not lost though, overall, Jock was a good provider and an attentive father most of the time.

She learned never to say no or deny him anything. If he became hungry at midnight, then she would get out of bed and fix him whatever he wanted to eat. Her job was to be ready to satisfy any craving he had with no fuss. There would be months he would be most generous and made no unreasonable demands on Eleanor. Then like a switch was flipped, he would change into this controlling, rough, impossible man. Much like passing a test, it was as if he would work all day to dream up things he could demand Eleanor to do. She would pass the test, and the switch would be flipped off. The evil Jock would lay dormant for a while.

So many times, she thought about packing up her babies and going back to the mountains; however, there were several problems with that scenario. First of all, how would she explain the reason for her unhappiness to her family, and would they believe her? He had bought her father years ago, and he was the same as in Jock's hip pocket. Even if they did believe her, the bigger question was would Jock ever let her leave? She knew the answer to this question, and the answer was no! He would search the world over to find her, and he would make her pay. Even if she didn't care about her own life, if she valued her daughter's life, then Eleanor knew her unhappiness would be one of the crosses she would just have to carry for her daughter's sake.

It was at this time that Eleanor learned about Valium and the corners in her mind—the places she could bury the unpleasant thoughts until she was able to think about them. These corners served her well.

She was a natural born mother and delighted in her children. Her second pregnancy, being so soon after her first one, made for a more difficult journey, but the joy in giving Jock the son he craved soon made up for the pain. Jon Weston Ledford was a beautiful and healthy little boy. Eleanor was the milk provider for baby Jon, and that was about it. Jock was at his bedside the minute he whimpered. It with as if he stood guard over his young protégé.

The time period after baby Jon's birth was as close to bliss as possible. Jock was ecstatic. He had his Caroline and Jon-Jon just like his idol, President Kennedy. Jock was always bringing Eleanor presents—some pricey jewelry purchases and other smaller gifts like candy. Of course, she knew some of his gifts, like the new house with the two-car garage, were more about image than actual gifts for her. It was important that he was rich enough to stand apart from the majority of the McWhorter citizens but not so rich that the citizens would resent him.

Jon-Jon's visit to the hospital to treat an ear infection signaled the bliss stage was officially over. It was then Jock decided he needed a second son in case something happened to his first one. Without a son, Jock was convinced he would be incapable of creating his empire.

Jennings McKinley Ledford was born by emergency caesarean surgery on January 28, 1979. Eleanor almost died. It was touch and go for days. Unfortunately, she survived, and she knew a secret Jock would never know. Eleanor knew baby Jennings would be the last child she would ever conceive or deliver. She would go to her grave before she would ever utter the plan she and Dr. Grant conjured up to make sure a fourth pregnancy would never occur. Her secret was safe with Dr. Grant.

Chapter 10

a clue

Wednesday, March 19, 2008, 9:30 AM

Driving down the small country road gave Daniel time to think about life's recent turn of events. He was very concerned about Caroline. She hadn't been to work all week long, and she wouldn't talk to him. According to Eleanor, Caroline hadn't been out of her room in days. For the life of him, he didn't understand what happened at the funeral that triggered this kind of reaction from Caroline.

Daniel was also concerned about the homicide investigation he was working. A bullet had been retrieved. He sent the slug to his buddy at the state's crime lab for ballistic testing. He had a sick feeling Jon and Jennings Ledford were involved. From what he could tell, Albert Dean pretty much had a monopoly on the county's drug activity, and he felt the Ledford boys either worked for him or were his competition. Daniel didn't want to be involved with anything that spelled out motive against Caroline's brothers.

Daniel and Joe Matt had a meeting scheduled to speak to Albert Dean's only living relative, his younger sister. Joe Matt was already there when he pulled up to the ramshackle of a large old farmhouse. What once was a well-maintained home on a sprawling farm was now a dilapidated house on a farm that was more weeds and underbrush than farmland. "What the hell happened here?" Daniel questioned Joe Matt just as soon as he stepped out of the cruiser. "I thought Albert Dean took care of his sister."

"Word is they had some falling out a few years ago and haven't spoken to each other since," Joe Matt replied. A lot of words weren't usually necessary between Daniel and Joe Matt due to the sixth sense they shared with each other. The officers were very similar in many ways. Both were tall, conservative, good-looking men in uniform, with the gray and tan colors of their uniforms being the largest difference.

The sound of the car door shutting had caused about ten dogs to go wild as the motley bunch of mongrels came out of various locations to examine the intruders. Daniel felt his side to make sure his sidearm was ready just in case he had to shoot a couple of dogs. He sighed in relief as Joe Matt started calling the dogs by name. "Come here, Tater. Quit that jumping, Fido! I see you too, Cheerio," he said to the dogs as he made his way to the house.

Daniel and Joe Matt didn't have to knock on the door. Waiting at the door, Ms. Smith stood emotionless. She was immaculately groomed in a floral print dress and was wearing pantyhose, pearl jewelry, and a pair of sturdy heels. The inside of her house was marked by the olive and gold of the seventies. Although dated, it was impeccable, a stark contrast to the outside of her home. Just as all good southern ladies had been conditioned to do, she offered them something to drink.

"I'll take some of that sweet tea of yours, if you have any made up?" Joe Matt responded. "I've gotten pretty used to her good tea. She's had a lot of prowlers on her property lately. So now when I get thirsty, I send someone over here to scare her right good," he kidded.

She smiled politely, but it was apparent she wasn't much in the joking mood. Instead, she got right to business. "How can I help you boys find Albert Dean's murderer?"

"Can you start by filling me in on the prowlers? When did it start? What did the Sheriff's Department find out?" Daniel fired the questions at her without giving her a chance to respond.

Joe Matt began filling Daniel in on the specifics. "It started back in December when her dogs would go crazy during the night, and she would see lights in the barn. They'd always be gone by the time we'd get here."

Redirecting his questions to the woman, Daniel added, "Anything unusual occur recently?"

"No, it's been a month since I've called the police, but I did have a—" she stopped mid-sentence looking as if she didn't know what to say next.

Joe Matt encouraged her to continue.

"It may be nothing, but a couple of weeks ago, a boy claiming to be Dr. Grant's grandson came by the house asking about Albert Dean. I thought it was strange since it was Dr. Grant that—" The words got stuck in her throat and choppy sobs were all that would come out.

Daniel's intrigue had intensified at the mention of the Grants. "What were you saying about Dr. Grant and his grandson?"

"Albert Dean's dead now, so I might as well tell you," she uttered before she took in a long deep breath. "You may've heard that me and Albert Dean haven't talked in seven years. I've never told nobody the reason we fell out, but it's high time I did." She paused to clear her throat. "Dr. Grant came by the house asking me if I knew why Albert Dean was in California on the same day that his son, Eddie, was killed in that accident." She paused and smiled when she said, "Albert Dean couldn't lie worth a crap to me. I always could tell if he was lying and that just killed him. If he was lying to me, he would start getting red splotches. As soon as I mentioned California and Dr. Grant's name to Albert Dean, sure enough, his neck turned bright red. I told him if he had anything to do with Eddie Grant's death I'd kill him with my bare hands!" Trying to keep her composure, she paused before she said, "I told him I never wanted to see his sorry face again, and I didn't."

Joe Matt was the first to respond, "So, you think your brother had something to do with Eddie Grant's death?"

"I'm not sure if he actually killed him, but he was involved. He may not have pulled the trigger, but his neck told me all I needed to know."

"So, what exactly did Dr. Grant's grandson say to you?" Daniel questioned.

She recounted their conversation before she completely broke down. She appeared to be crying seven years worth of pent up tears.

Daniel had already seen enough tears in the last few days and was not eager to see more. He left Joe Matt in the living room consoling the distraught woman.

Before the dogs realized he was leaving, Daniel was in his cruiser backing out of the driveway. They yapped at his tires as he sped away. He didn't pay attention to the dogs. His mind was on his next destination.

Secretly glad for an excuse to see Tillie Grant, Daniel drove straight to Dr. Grant's house. He knew he should've called first to announce his professional visit, but didn't want to remove the element of surprise. He rang the front door bell expecting to see a short blond, but was sadly disappointed when a redheaded older woman answered the door instead. He didn't know her name, but recognized her from his boyhood visits to Dr. Grant's office.

"Ma'am, I'm Officer Brooks, and I need to see Trevor Grant," Daniel said in his most professional law enforcement voice.

"I'm sorry, but Mr. Grant's not here. Only Ms. Grant is here, but she's very busy." the caretaker grudgingly said in a definite northern accent.

"I need to speak with Ms. Grant, ma'am. I would be much obliged if you would let her know I'm here," Daniel stated.

Making a sweeping gesture with her hand, the caretaker invited him to come into the front foyer. A dainty upholstered chair to the right of the foyer was where she pointed for him to have a seat and wait before she turned and headed up the stairway.

"Tillie, dear, there's a policeman here to see you." Julia was breathing hard from climbing the stairs.

Tillie wrinkled her nose before asking, "Did you catch the officer's name?"

"I believe he said Officer Brooks?"

Tillie couldn't help but smile at the mention of Daniel's name. She ran her fingers through her hair and did a breath check as she came bounding down the stair steps.

Daniel checked out every piece of furniture and photograph in this room as he tried to put it to memory while he waited. His memorization exercise was interrupted as he heard what sounded like an elephant stampeding down the wooden staircase.

She began speaking as soon as she made visual contact. "Danny, what do I owe the pleasure of your visit?" Tillie asked with a huge smile on her face. She was barefoot and her toenails polished in a bright shade of pink. She was wearing sweatpants and a t-shirt. Her face actually had a smudge of dirt on it, and her curls were going in all directions. She was lovely.

Her smile was contagious, and he gave her a smile to rival her own dazzling one in return. "Actually, I'm needing to talk to your brother, but since he wasn't here then I thought you could give me his contact information," he explained.

"Trevor? He went to check on Mom in California. He's coming back this weekend. Is there anything wrong? Anything I can help you with?"

"I'm trying to understand why your brother would've visited a lady a couple of weeks ago inquiring about the whereabouts of a man named, Albert Dean Smith?"

Tillie's face gave nothing away. At first, she was stoic, but her arched eyebrows and tilted head gave way to a more inquisitive expression.

"Albert Dean Smith was murdered on the night of March 12, and he wasn't the pillar of the community." He tried to fill her in on the hometown drama. "He reportedly had connections with some heavies in the drug trafficking world."

Daniel thought Tillie was an excellent actress, or she truly was clueless about her brother's visit to Ms. Smith's solely based on her calm demeanor.

"I vaguely remember hearing about a murder in McWhorter but really didn't pay much attention. I've been very busy over the last few weeks. Are you sure it couldn't have been a case of mistaken identity? I can't imagine why Trevor would have an interest in the man." She paused as she appeared to be contemplating her next words. "Danny, give me your phone number, and I'll have him call you."

He slowly called off his phone number. After placing his hat on his head, Daniel reluctantly prepared to leave. An awkward silence engulfed them until Tillie broke it by saying, "I've been going through Granny and Pa's attic today. I feel like a kid in a toy store. You have time to come up and take a look?"

Daniel knew he needed to get back to work, but he wasn't ready to leave Tillie yet and couldn't resist taking a peek in Doc's attic.

The brass on Daniel's uniform jingled while he tried to keep up with her pace as she raced up the stairs. Neither was out of breath as they ran up the three flights. "Wow!" was all he managed to say as he looked at the Grants' attic. He was expecting the Victorian styled home to have an attic that was dark and scary. Instead, a splash of color hit him square in the face when his head reached the height of the attic flooring. The sun rays bore through the large stained-glass window resulting in multiple colors ricocheting in all directions. This room was anything but dreary. It was a colorful, large, and organized treasure chest. Each shelf of the floor-to-wall bookshelves was filled with all kinds of collections from old books to University of Kentucky memorabilia.

"Pretty awesome, huh?" she asked. "I don't know what in the world Trevor and I will do with all this, but I can't imagine how we could part with any of it."

Just as Daniel was heading toward a table, he heard her holler, "Think fast!"

Used to being on high alert, instinctively Daniel swung his body in the direction of Tillie's voice and caught the basketball seconds before it hit his head. He then bounced the ball back to her. He noticed she caught the ball like a natural. Then using a two-hand chest pass, she whizzed the ball toward his midsection. His fingertips stung; he was impressed with the force coming from such a tiny person. Out of habit, he began to dribble the ball. Next thing he knew, she was in a defensive pose with her hands and body just inches from him as she guarded him waiting for the opportunity to steal the ball.

Inwardly, Daniel laughed as he thought, *She doesn't really think she can take the ball from me, does she? Doesn't she know the legend of the hometown hero?* He moved to the right, and she moved effortlessly with him. Just when he was about to dribble the ball between his legs, he realized she had anticipated his move and had stolen the ball. He laughed in disbelief and was about to show her a thing or two about basketball when he heard over his radio, "Eight-two-seven, we have another body."

Tillie stopped dribbling and listened intently as Daniel conversed with dispatch.

"What's the ten-twenty?" Daniel asked.

"Big Goose Creek Church off Miller Road."

"I'm en route," Daniel said.

Tillie stated, "Another dead body in McWhorter, Kentucky? Unbelievable. You need any help?"

"Help from a girl? No way," he joked.

In mock outrage, she responded, "Girl! Hopefully your policing is better than your basketball playing!"

He answered her with laughter as he jingled down the stairs.

Tillie waited until she heard the front door slam before she yelled in her best Ricky Ricardo voice, "Oh, Julia, you've got some s'plaining to do! What have you two done?"

CHAPTER 11

Wednesday's Woes

Wednesday, March 19, 2008, 6:00 AM

Pastor Bartholomew Smith had been an early riser all his life. He made it a habit of being at the church by six each morning, and he went to the Gas and Go at eight o'clock for some breakfast and conversation with the boys. He was definitely a creature of habit.

His house was within walking distance of the church, but Pastor Bart didn't want to tempt the good Lord to strike him dead with a heart attack, so he chose to drive the short distance instead. Pastor Bart was a good hundred and fifty pounds overweight and suffered a serious heart condition. His futile attempts at dieting were dismal failures because Pastor Bart was a weak man, and there were just too many good cooks who attended his church for him to resist. With visions of biscuits from Darryl and Doyle's Gas and Go filling his head, he kissed his sleeping wife on the cheek before he drove his Chevy Suburban the length of a football field to the church house.

"Bringing in the sheaves, bringing in the sheaves, we will come rejoicing, bringing in the sheaves!" Pastor Bart was singing in his big voice as he unlocked the church house door. He flipped the light switch to the on position as he had done every morning for twenty years. "Huh?" he said when nothing happened and then flipped it again. Deciding that a breaker had blown, he trudged back to his vehicle to get his flashlight. Letting the stairway banister and the flashlight guide him, he paced himself as he walked the thirteen steps to the basement floor. He was whistling the same hymn as before when a noise made him stop dead in his tracks. The noise came from the snake room. This was one room Pastor Bart refused to go in at all because of the timber rattlers and copperheads in cages there. Some of the older members insisted on keeping these snakes in case the spirit moved and someone felt led to play the deadly faith game with them. When he didn't hear anything else, he figured it was just the wind. No longer in the whistling mood, he instead started quoting part of the 23rd Psalm: "*Yea though I walk through the valley of the shadow of death, I will fear no evil, for you are with me,*" he managed.

Cautiously opening the door to the breaker box room, he let the flashlight circle the room before entering. Satisfied the room was in order, he shined his flashlight on the metal box on the wall. He calculated it would take him only seconds to walk the distance to the box, find the thrown breaker, and fix it. "I will fear no evil," he mumbled under his breath. He took two steps when he felt the wind of the door slamming shut behind him. As he whirled around, his flashlight caught a blur of movement.

He felt a warm sensation over the top of his right shoulder, and he turned around to see the whites of eyes staring directly in front of him. The eyes were all he could see because the intruder was clad totally in black. "I'm glad to hear you're not fearing death today, you sick son of a bitch," the voice mocked as he threw something at the pastor. A dark colored rope landed with a thud on the pastor's large shoulder. Pastor Bart turned his head just in time to see the rope lunge at his face. When he felt the sharp pain on his jaw, he realized the rope had teeth.

Pastor Bart screamed and urine ran down his legs when he realized the rope was a large snake. He regained his composure enough to shake the snake off his person and ran as fast as his stumpy legs would carry him toward the door. He made it about four steps before he couldn't take another one. Grabbing at his heart, he felt a gripping pain in his chest. He collapsed in a heap on the floor. His short little limbs were unsuccessful as he reached for the treasures in his pocket—his cell phone and nitroglycerin pills. His body shook unnaturally like Jell-O as each fat roll bounced off each other. Pleading for mercy, he hissed, "Pllleeaaassse."

The concrete floor was vibrating as the obese man was rolling and writhing in pain and desperation. The smell of death loomed in the air as Pastor Bart's heart exploded in his chest.

After he checked the man's pulse, the intruder whispered, "Have fun in hell." He then flipped the breaker switch to the correct position. The harmless Kentucky black snake slithered in the darkness trying to find a quiet place to rest and the black-clad avenger left after making sure the good preacher man could never hurt anyone else again.

1:00 PM

"Wake up, Princess Caroline," Jon Ledford chimed to his sister as he climbed in her bed from the right side.

Jennings, the younger brother, joined in from the opposite side of the bed and said, "Rise and shine, darling. It's after one o'clock."

Caroline moaned and put the pillow over her head. "Please, just kill me now."

"Get up and go brush those nasty teeth. Hellfire, Caroline! How long's it been since you cleaned up?" Jon was fanning his face with his hand.

Jennings added, "Breath, hell, your room smells like Ole Widow Vandy!"

Rousing reluctantly from her bed, Caroline did as she was bid knowing it was no use to protest. She could tell her brothers were on a mission, and they wouldn't take no for an answer. She passed the mirror on her way to the shower and gasped, "Oh, my goodness!"

Jon examined her face and said, "He worked you over good this time, didn't he?"

"He went too far!" Jennings ranted. "Just say the word, and I'll kill the fat bastard!"

Caroline breathed in sharply at his words, "Jennings!"

"Don't play your little innocent, straight-laced princess routine with me." Jennings countered. "You know I can kill him. I could actually kill him with my bare hands, or I could make it look like a very convenient accident. You choose."

"Really, it's okay, guys. It's nothing that a little make-up can't hide." Not wanting to discuss her problems, she instead took the offensive stance. She arched her eyebrows, lowered her chin, crossed her arms against her chest, and gave her best glower. "Are you two in trouble? Is the person that killed Albert Dean going to come after you?"

"Shhhhh," Jon's forefinger was placed on his lips. "Everything's okay, darling."

Undaunted, she continued, "You boys know how much I love you, and there's not a day goes by that I don't worry about you," she whined.

"We have a very good attorney," Jennings mocked. He then opened a window, not so much for the fresh air, but rather to conceal the smell of the joint he was lighting. "Just what the doctor ordered," he said as he passed the marijuana to his big sister.

Ordinarily, Caroline would have protested and preached to her younger brothers about the danger of drugs, but today she needed something that could take her mind off her worries.

12:30 PM

Daniel made it to the church parking lot in ten minutes flat. He and his family were members of Believers Baptist on McWhorter Street, but he'd visited Big Goose Creek Church many times with Caroline. Eleanor played the piano on occasion, and Jock was in charge of the Sunday School program.

Big Goose Creek didn't have an official affiliation with a particular religious faction but rather considered the title of non-denominational to be more fitting. They combined different beliefs and practices from various affiliations to come up with something that made everyone happy. Of all the church's practices, socializing and eating were the most emphasized.

Daniel's dad never cared for the preacher at Big Goose Creek. Pastor Bart had always been nice enough to Daniel and had actually been a big fan of his during his hero days. He could always remember hearing his loud voice cheering him on at the ballgames. His voice box's volume switch must have gotten stuck on the loud setting early in life.

Looking around at a full parking lot, Daniel realized he was one of the last ones called to this party. There were several sheriff's cars, an ambulance, and about a dozen other cars and trucks parked sporadically in the church lot. Recognizing the mayor's Buick, he rolled his eyes and cursed under his breath. He was not looking forward to seeing "his highness."

As he got closer to the front door of the church, he realized Coroner Jimmy Sizemore was acting as the greeter. "How old is the geezer?" Daniel asked himself. He knew Jimmy was an old man twenty years ago. "He must have been injecting himself with embalming fluid," Daniel thought, when he looked at the man's wrinkle-free face.

"Sad, sad day in McWhorter," Jimmy said, barely concealing the grin in his eyes. "Pastor Bart will definitely be missed."

Thanks to the coroner, Daniel at least knew that whatever happened had happened to Bartholomew. He was relieved when the first person he met in the basement was his friend, Chief Deputy Sizemore. Unfortunately, the mayor followed close behind his friend. Both men were coming out of a room at the end of the hallway. "What happened to Pastor Bart?" he asked.

"Not sure, but Jimmy thinks it looks like a heart attack," Joe Matt said while Jock just shook his head in disbelief.

Daniel questioned his friend, "No foul play?"

"Don't think so. Jimmy seems to think it was natural causes. He had a few bumps and bruises, but all that could have happened as a result of his fall to the ground with the heart attack. The coroner figured it happened sometime between six and eleven this morning. The church's secretary found him a little after eleven."

Daniel prepared himself for death as he entered the corner room. Looking death in the eye was something one never became accustomed to regardless of the number of cases worked. The air was dense due to the wall-to-wall bodies that managed to squeeze into the small room. He could hear some crying and snubs as he entered. He excused himself as he maneuvered among the first responders, the mourners, and the spectators to get a better look.

Pastor Bart was not a good-looking man while he was alive, but Daniel couldn't come up with words to describe him in his death. His pale face was contorted and his mouth gaped wide open. Elongating his normally round face, the weight of his fat jowls caused them to actually touch the ground.

The one person who knew the truth of Pastor's Bart's untimely death was in the room and noticed that a convenient roll of fat had nicely concealed the bite mark on the side of Bart's face.

CHAPTER 12

Wednesday Words of Wisdom

Wednesday, March 19, 2008, 7:00 PM

The phone rang twice before Tillie decided to answer it, knowing in all probability it would be her dear, deceitful brother on the line. She could spit nails because she was so angry with Trevor. As soon as she took one look at Julia's face, she knew that Trevor had been to see this Smith woman, and she was pretty certain it had to do with her dad's murder. Why would Trevor and Julia intentionally keep this secret from her?

Tillie ever so slowly picked up the receiver and placed it next to her ear before she grunted, "Yeah," into the mouthpiece.

"Yeah, to you too, my darling sister. What's wrong with you?"

"Trevor, what do you think I am? Chopped liver. Do the words Special Agent Grant not give me some credentials in your eyes, or am I the little sister that you don't trust?"

Trevor's jovial mood changed. "What are you talking about?" he cautiously asked.

"For starters, does the name Albert Dean Smith mean anything to you?"

Her question was met with complete silence on the other end of the line.

"How dare you keep something of this magnitude from me? The reason we went into law enforcement in the first place was to help us catch our dad's murderer together. Then you get a lead and don't even bother to tell me! All I've got to say is two can play this game!"

Realizing his dilemma, Trevor interrupted her tantrum. "I'm sorry, Sis. I wanted to tell you, but you were having such a hard time with Granny's sickness that I didn't want to upset you more. I promise I was going to tell you as soon as I got back. " Trevor explained.

"Oh, good excuse! I guess you know that Albert Dean was murdered, and due to your little secret visit, you are now a suspect," she said trying to sound angry. Tillie had a hard time staying mad at Trevor for any length of time. She guessed it must be a twin thing.

Trevor was cornered and knew he needed to explain enough to get her off his back. "Someone called a couple of weeks ago and told Julia if we wanted to know what happened to our dad that we should talk with Albert Dean Smith. The more I found out about him, the more I'm sure he had something to do with our dad's death. We all know it was not an accident that caused that front loader to crush him, but what I don't know is why Albert Dean would have anything against our dad. He was a drug dealer, and I know our dad couldn't have been involved with any dealer for any reason. Have you had any luck finding Granny and Pa's journals?"

"Nope, I've found enough jewelry, antiques, and stock certificates that we can retire now," Tillie mentioned.

Undaunted by news of their newly found wealth, Trevor encouraged her to keep looking for the journals. "Julia said granny would lock herself in her room for hours each day and would write in her journal. Think Special Agent Grant! Where would they be? After all, what did you say you were?" he paused. "Oh yeah, you're the FBI. You're the top shit of law enforcement."

"You're a creep," she coolly replied.

"Gee, thanks," he got the last word in and grinned as he closed his phone knowing that hanging up on her would really piss her off.

9:00 PM

It was 9:00 PM, and Daniel was restless. Each time he closed his eyes, he saw either the bloody mess of Albert Dean's body, the fat rolls of Bartholomew's jowls, Tillie's laughing face, or Caroline's sad eyes. He didn't know which vision was worse.

Finding himself replaying the attic basketball game over and over, he couldn't keep from smiling. He still couldn't believe he let a girl steal the ball from him. Sure, he was physically attracted to her, but it was more than just that. He really liked her. He was afraid he was falling for her, and he wasn't sure that was what he wanted. After all, Caroline Ledford was the one he had planned to marry. Or could plans change? Could he deal with Jock Ledford being a permanent part of his life?

If he could see Caroline, then maybe it could help get Tillie out of his mind. He changed his clothes then drove the short distance to the Ledford's house. Daniel parked at the bottom of the Ledford's hill and sprinted to the back of the house. Using his special knock, he waited for Caroline to respond at the same window that had served as his entrance and his fast escape route over the years. Her bedroom was decorated completely in white. Her designer bed was an invitation to climb in to the cloud of softness. Daniel felt it was definitely befitting the royal princess of McWhorter.

Soaking in her large marble garden tub, she heard a light tapping at her window. Recognizing the familiar taps, her heart beat a little faster. She immediately grabbed a towel and stepped out of the bathtub leaving a wet mess as she headed toward the window.

Caroline was relieved the room was dark and would conceal her bruises, but she was so happy to see Daniel she didn't care to take the risk. She kissed him hello through the window. The kiss was very sweet. "Well, aren't you going to invite me in?" he asked.

Letting her towel drop from her body, she asked, "Do you want the invitation embossed?"

Pulling himself through the open window, he gently grabbed her hair and pulled her toward him. His lips moved from her neck to her shoulder then down her back as he continued to lightly kiss her in places that made her shiver. Caroline was putty in his hands by the time he kissed her hard on the mouth. She began to undress him as they made their way to the bed.

Drained, limp, and completely satisfied, they stretched out diagonally in the bed, lost in their own thoughts as their breathing slowed to steady breaths. After several minutes, Caroline turned to face him, hoping the dimly lit room would conceal the greenish-yellow tint of the bruise on her cheek. If he noticed, he didn't mention it. She gently ran her fingers through his short hair. She breathed in his manly scent and rested her head on his shoulder. Knowing she desperately needed answers, she remained silent, hesitant to break the moment until she just couldn't keep quiet any longer. She took a deep breath before she asked, "Daniel, when are you going to take me away from here? What happened to our plan?"

"What?" Daniel asked, stalling for just the right words to come to his mind.

"I'm not getting any younger. I want a husband, a family. I want you," she voiced.

Daniel sat up in the bed, "Caroline, I've loved you since I was ten years old, and I will always love you. The question is do you truly love me?"

"Of course I love you."

"Do you love me enough to give me a couple of months to sort things out?" He asked but didn't give her time to answer. "I thought I had things all together, but since dad died, I'm not sure of anything right now. Will you give me two months to get my head on straight? My dad's death haunts me, and I'm in no shape to make decisions about the rest of my life right now," he explained.

"Daniel Lee Brooks, I don't have two months to wait!" she challenged knowing her fragile emotional state couldn't take two more months of her daddy's displeasure.

"You've waited all these years. Now, you can't give me two months?"

"Honestly, I can't wait. I especially can't wait knowing a certain blond FBI agent's in town," Caroline countered.

Treading carefully, Daniel was slow to respond as he posed his answer. How could she know of his attraction to Tillie when he'd never breathed his inner thoughts about Tillie to anyone? Actually, he wasn't ready to think about his feelings toward Tillie yet speak to his girlfriend about them. Daniel's wit didn't fail him. He replied in a very serious tone, "Why does it matter if Trevor Grant's in town? Now that you mention him, I noticed he was all goo-goo eyes for you at the funeral home. Is Trevor what this is all about?"

"You're impossible!" Caroline gritted her teeth and clenched her fists. "You know good and damn well which blond I'm talking about!"

Changing the subject, Daniel laid his true feelings on the line. "Caroline, here's the deal. I would marry you tomorrow if you and I could leave McWhorter and never come back, but you and I both know that's not possible. You, my dear, come as a package deal. When I marry you, then I marry your entire family. Right now, I'm in the middle of a murder investigation, and your brothers have been mentioned several times in it. How would you feel about me if I have to arrest your brothers?" He paused to let her digest the information before he softened his tone and said, "We could possibly overcome some of these challenges, but the main problem is your dad. It's one thing for Jock to run your life, but I will not have him running my life too."

"I promise it won't be like that. Daddy will be so happy that I'm married that he will leave us alone." Caroline squirmed as the lawyer in her tried to think of something more convincing to say to support this promise.

"Come on, Caroline, give me a break. You've never made one decision about your life. Your daddy has told you what he wanted you to do, and you did it. Jock Ledford decided your college, your major, your law school, and I bet he even chose your bedroom furniture. Look at you, Caroline. You're almost thirty-one years old and living in the same house as your parents. Don't you find that a tad unnatural?" Sensing her anxiety, he changed his approach. "I love you, but, Caroline, there's a point when love's just not enough. I've been independent for years. If you can tell me right this moment you would not let Jock influence you after we're married, then let's elope tonight."

She stammered, "It's complicated. There's more at stake than you realize."

"Exactly! I don't want the love I feel for you today to turn to hate when I realize I've been swept into Jock Ledford's venomous web of deceit and can't get loose. So I think this is a good time for us to take a break and think about what we really want," he said realizing this painful conversation was giving him the chance to verbalize what he's been feeling as of late.

"You mean you want to take a break as in a ... break-up?" she stammered.

"The choice is yours. We can take a couple of months for both of us to get our lives together and then re-evaluate what we want for our future. You've got two months to choose who it is you want to spend the rest of your life with—your daddy or me."

"I can't live two months without you."

"Well, pack your clothes right now, and we'll elope."

Her face twisted in terror as she contemplated packing her bag. Every fiber in her body ached to get up and pack, but she knew it would come with too painful of a price to her or to her family. She knew Jock wanted loyalty at all costs and would see her elopement as a form of betrayal. Jock would punish her even if it meant hurting her mommy or her brothers. Jock was counting on a large, vulgar wedding. It was all about show with Jock. She knew she would just have to find the strength to live without Daniel for two months. Refusing to look at him, she hung her head as the tears picked up momentum.

"That's what I thought," Daniel replied to her silence. He knew he better leave now before he changed his mind. He kissed her on the forehead and hugged her tightly one last time.

"You know, it would be much easier for me to just kill him," she said with much boldness.

Making sure he heard correctly, he did a double take and looked into her face. The look in her eyes told him she was serious—dead serious. "Now, how could we spend the rest of our lives together if you're in prison?" He tried to make light of her comment.

Caroline smiled nervously. "I'm just kidding. I ... I ... I know it's not an option," she stuttered in horror realizing her thoughts had spewed out of her mouth. Unintentionally, she had let Caroline number three loose with her thoughts. This was not good. She had to make sure she kept that Caroline tucked firmly inside her, or she was convinced no good could come from number three. Caroline number one was the weak, submissive woman that resided in this bedroom and emerged only in order to exist in her home life. The persona most people knew was Caroline number two, the personable and capable lawyer and daughter of the ruler of McWhorter. Caroline number three was the persona that was capable of most anything—even murder. Keeping number three locked inside kept getting harder and harder to do.

Daniel dressed rather quickly and started toward the open window. "Of course you know you're welcome to come by my house any night for conjugal visits," he said as a joke while he crawled out the same window he entered earlier. "She must not have liked my joke," he thought, when he felt the sharp pain of something hitting him in the back of the head.

Undeterred and a free man, he left the Ledford home. He was absorbed into the night as Caroline watched him disappear from her life for at least two months. "Two months wasn't that long," Caroline number one whispered. Caroline number two tried to formulate an elopement plan that would keep her mother safe. It had to be Caroline number three that told her she better watch out for the Grant girl, or she could kiss Daniel goodbye forever.

CHAPTER 13

The Public Forum

Monday, March 24, 2008, 2:00 PM

Jock Ledford surveyed the room and was pleased with the turnout. "Don't look a gift horse in the mouth," his daddy, Clarence Ledford, had repeatedly told Jock over the years. Jock couldn't help but think Pastor Bart's death could be the gift horse his daddy had been talking about.

Each primary election season, the local Kiwanis Club sponsored a public forum where each candidate had a chance to address the crowd in between cake auctions. The public forum was usually held at the courthouse, but Jock wasted no time in convincing the Kiwanis president to hold the annual fundraiser at the Big Goose Creek Church in memory of Pastor Bart.

Bartholomew had been one of Jock's best friends for many years, and he had every intention of using his death to his advantage. His emotionally charged speech was prepared, and he even had plans to muster up some tears for dramatic impact. Perched on the high rise of the pulpit, he could see everything going on below. He smiled without showing teeth when he realized all his crew was in position. Catching the eye of his oldest son, he nodded to him as a signal. Jon and Jennings were standing at the entrance way where they could greet or intimidate each person who walked through the doors. Itching to start the show, the Kiwanis president asked those still walking around to find a seat. Jock's smile widened when he realized Saint Geneva Vaughn hadn't bothered to show up. "Just maybe she finally wised up," he thought.

Shortly after the doors of the church had been shut, the church doors sprung wide open, and Geneva Vaughn led her supporters into the large open room. Jock gasped when he saw as many as one hundred people following his newly found nemesis into the sanctuary. The Kiwanis Club members scurried around in excitement trying to locate folding chairs to supplement their limited number of pews.

Seething inwardly, Jock saw this attention-grabbing stunt as an act of defiance against him. Of course, no one knew the extent of his anger because he was still all smiles and goodwill on the outside. When he realized Jennings had Saint Geneva's granddaughter cornered near the vestibule, he finally relaxed. "Yep, there is a Ledford God," he chuckled to himself.

After welcoming everyone to the event, the Kiwanis President turned the podium over to the auctioneer. Starting with a dried apple stack cake made in honor of Pastor Bart, the auctioneer began to rattle a stream of words. Assessing the cake to be worth five hundred dollars, Jock planned to make his presence known early. After all, it was customary for a Ledford to buy the first cake and was even more appropriate since this cake was made in honor of his best friend. This Ledford tradition was well known, and no one usually bothered to bid against Jock except for the person he planted in the audience for dramatic effect.

"Who wants to start this auction off with fifty dollars?" asked the small-statured auctioneer dressed in jeans, a big belt buckle, and sporting a cowboy hat.

Before Jock could speak up, he heard Geneva's voice beating him to the punch.

"Fifty!" Geneva hollered out.

"Do I hear sixty, sixty, who gives sixty?'

"Sixty!" countered the mayor.

The match continued like a ping-pong game as all heads bobbed first to the mayor who was seated on the platform then to Geneva Vaughn seated near the back of the room. The mayor had planned on buying the first cake, but when the price jumped up to two thousand dollars he re-evaluated his decision. It was apparent Geneva wasn't going to back down, and Jock reasoned that two thousand dollars could be used to buy at least forty votes. Reluctantly, he stopped bidding at two thousand.

"Sold for two thousand five dollars to our mayoral candidate, Geneva Vaughn!" the auctioneer exclaimed as the church house erupted in hoots and hollers.

Jock's heart sank when he realized he'd just broken a Ledford tradition. "Let 'em have their cake and eat it too," he thought as he fought off the feeling of impending doom.

Three more cakes sold with Jock buying a German Chocolate cake made by Bartholomew's widow for three hundred dollars. Then, the Kiwanis president introduced Mayor Ledford to the crowd and told him he had a total of fifteen minutes to address the crowd.

With his game face on, Mayor Jock Ledford walked to the podium knowing just what he needed to say to win this audience. "It's such a privilege to be here today and a privilege to have served you for the last thirty-five years as your mayor. Standing here at this podium where my good friend, Pastor Bartholomew, Smith spoke for over thirty years is also a very emotional time for me, but if he were here today, he'd say, 'Tell it like it is, Jock. Just tell it like it is.'" Jock paused to make sure everyone recognized one of the departed preacher's favorite sayings.

"So, I'm going to tell you like it is. McWhorter's my home. I'd gladly lay down my life for this city because of my love for this place and for these people." His eyes scanned the crowd and his hand gesture suggested he was talking about everyone present. "It's not easy being the mayor. I've had thirty-five years to learn. Now, that learning has paid off, and McWhorter has reaped big dividends for it. We have one of the most beautiful towns in the state, thanks to the town renovation that I got us funding for. Our unemployment hasn't increased in ten years, and we haven't lost nary business during this hard economic time. Crime continues to be low, and our schooling continues to improve as testing scores increase each year. I've been here for each of you no matter what time of the night. Now, I've known Geneva Vaughn for years and think she's one of the finest ladies I've ever met, but I'm gonna tell you like it is, just like what Bart would tell me to do. Geneva has no experience running a county, and it would put the life you know in jeopardy. You have your choice. It's up to you on May 6. Do you vote for a nice lady with no experience in government, or do you vote for Jock Ledford, a tried and proven leader who would lay his life down for this town? Folks, the choice is yours. I'm just telling you like it is." Jock then gave his toothy smile as he used his handkerchief to wipe the tears falling down his cheeks. Using the same handkerchief, he blew his nose as he walked away from the podium not wanting the church to see his happy reaction to the deafening applause he received.

The Kiwanis president thanked Jock and then turned the podium over to Geneva Vaughn. Many in the crowd eyed each other, wondering how Geneva would be able to top the mayor's sentiment-filled speech.

Taking the stand, Geneva pulled out a stack of papers of various sizes and colors and laid them on the podium. The crowd hushed. Geneva's red dress and gray hair stood out in the sea of blue carpet. If she were nervous, she didn't show it. She looked around the auditorium and slowly began to address the crowd. "I truly appreciate the mayor's kind words about me and can respect his concern for my lack of experience, but today I'm going to lay those fears to rest as I challenge Mayor Ledford on some of his practices. I agree wholeheartedly that we have a beautiful town, but that's the only thing I'm not going to challenge. Yes, it's true our unemployment rate hasn't changed in ten years. It hasn't changed because at 18.6 % it remains one of the highest unemployment rates in the state. We have had no new businesses in this town for the past twenty-five years, and we have spent no government money to attract any businesses to come to this town. Fifty percent of our entire high school graduates move from McWhorter in search of jobs soon after graduating—presuming they do indeed graduate." She paused giving the crowd time to digest what she had just said.

"Crime continues to be low? Come on. Where's Jock been keeping himself? Recently, we had one of our own citizens murdered. I don't know about you, but that doesn't give me a warm and fuzzy feeling. Also, our schools have some of the poorest test scores and highest dropout rates in the nation. When you're at the bottom, you have no place to go but up. I have the last ten years' comparisons if any of you would like to see for yourself instead of taking our fine mayor at his word." She waved the support papers in the air as proof.

"I, too, agree with Pastor Bart. I believe in telling it like it is. The only difference is that I have facts to support what I'm saying. I don't know about you, but I want my grandchildren to stay in McWhorter and not have to move to find jobs. I want to live in a town where I feel safe. I want my grandchildren to have the advantage of the best free education possible. I want to see new business and industry come to this part of the state. We're like a town that's lost in a time warp. I'm sure that Jock Ledford loves this town, but I'm telling you, he's the one killing it. It's time to revitalize not just the storefronts but also the way our local government works. It's time for a change that will bring us into the twenty-first century. If you want to see this type of change, then I'm encouraging you to vote for Vaughn and vote for this much-needed change!" Geneva's supporters were on their feet, screaming and cheering her on as the mayor's supporters scratched their heads realizing this fine lady was a force to reckon with.

Jock had to hand it to her. He'd never had an opponent that had the balls to out and out challenge him. He actually thought he was going to enjoy destroying such a worthy opponent.

11:00 PM

Knowing McWhorter was about to feel the mayor's fury, Woody Ledford needed to escape from McWhorter, even if it was a temporary escape through a drunken stupor. Geneva Vaughn caused quite a stir this morning when she challenged the mayor's ability, integrity, and livelihood. He never knew anyone who did this to Jock and lived to tell about it.

Woodrow Clarence Ledford was a blood cousin to Mayor Jock Ledford, which gave him the distinction of being in the inner circle of the club solely based on his DNA. His dad started grooming him for the club when he was just a pup. The mayor recognized Woody's dad's loyalty and rewarded him by having him perform the dirty deeds they couldn't trust any of the other members to perform. "The dirtier, the better" was how Woody's dad liked it, but Woody took after his mama's people and had a kind soul.

Recognizing Woody's good heart and nature, his dad decided he was going to change him even if he had to beat his nature out of him. Woody remembered when he was seven years old and couldn't bring himself to shoot a little defenseless squirrel. Its little nose wiggled, and his brown eyes met his. There was no way he could kill something so cute. However, his cuteness was short lived. His dad had no problem pulling the trigger; then, he broke Woody from his reluctance by making him eat the raw innards of the squirrel. When he hesitated before putting the guts in his mouth, his dad remedied that by beating him within an inch of his life. After that day, Woody learned how to close his heart, take aim, and shoot whatever needed shooting.

Every bad deed Woody was forced to perform took a toll on his life. He did what he had to do, but he didn't enjoy it. It would break his mama's heart if she knew what her husband and son had been responsible for over the years. Wild Turkey was the only prescription for what ailed him. This wonderful substance dulled his pain. Still breathing in and out, Woody gave the appearance that he had some semblance of life left in him, but Woody knew he had been dead inside for years. He was literally a dead man walking.

Woody couldn't help but smile when he thought about his poor little mama. There wasn't a kinder, gentler soul in this world, and he had no doubt she was resting in heaven in her Master's arms. He sure missed his mama. Thinking about her made him happy for a brief moment, and then, the yearning to see her would turn the brief moment of happiness to sharp pains of longing. A stout drink was his only cure, and he was on his way to the bootlegger's house as fast as he could drive the curvy gravel road to obtain just what the doctor ordered.

Just as he was certain of his mama's whereabouts in the hereafter, he was just as certain that his daddy didn't join her there. He figured his dad would have wanted to be with the other Ledfords anyway, so it was just as well they rot together in hell.

Woody would sure like to see his mama again, but he knew any public confession to cleanse his soul would result in the deaths of his sister, ex-wife, and daughters. He hadn't been active in any of their lives in a long time, but he couldn't bear for them to suffer because of him. He really wouldn't care to die today if it meant he could see his mama again. He wasn't afraid of hell either. He was fairly certain McWhorter was similar, and Jock Ledford was a demon straight from hell.

In a cold sweat, Woody felt his foot push the gas pedal harder in attempts to get his fix sooner. The curvy road was intimidating after dark. He was a regular customer to this Sasser Springs bootlegger because of his generous supply of Wild Turkey.

Starting to tremble, Woody realized he was about to become violently ill. He promised himself he would drink just enough to take away the sick spell. He didn't dare think about missing the meeting. After all, tomorrow was Tuesday, his favorite day of the week. Fiddling with the radio dial, he turned the radio to a country music station to take his mind away from his shaking. Woody was singing off key with the radio and trying to concentrate on the few curvy miles left to drive. Lost in his misery, the sound he heard didn't immediately resonate with him. In a delayed reaction, Woody looked in his rear view mirror just in time to see and feel the truck behind him strike the back of his car. "What the hell?" Woody yelled as his head bounced off the headrest causing his forehead to nip the top of the steering wheel. Thankfully, he was able to right the vehicle. He thought initially the truck's bump had to have been accidental, but he was wrong. The bump had not been accidental. The next thing Woody knew, he and his car were falling down the one hundred foot cliff, and his whole worthless life was flashing before his eyes.

Woody cried out his last words, *"Jesus, please save this sinner and let me see my Momma!"*

He died with a smile on his face and completely bone sober when he met his Maker.

The car landed with a thud at the bottom of the deep ravine where the thick foliage absorbed the vehicle into its bosom.

Only after making certain that justice had been served on the drunk, the driver followed the winding road back to reality feeling a load had lifted.

CHAPTER 14

Technology

Tuesday, March 25, 2008, 5:00 AM

Jebidiah had never seen his favorite patrons so discombobulated. They barely touched any of the food he'd prepared.

The mayor made a mental note to talk to Jeb about setting only ten chairs in the room for future meetings. It was painful for him to look around and see two empty chairs. It was too bad that neither Albert Dean nor Pastor Bart had sons that could fill their empty seats. The mayor gave a silent prayer of thanks he not only had one son, but he even had a spare.

He was just about to open the meeting for business, when he realized there were three empty chairs instead of two. "Hell's bells! Do ya reckon Woody was too hungover to make it this morning?"

The county judge replied, "It's not like Woody to miss a meeting even if he was hungover."

Huffing in disgust, the mayor called the meeting to order. "Well, let's get started. We don't have any time to waste, but Woody's gonna have hell to pay. It's gonna cost him. Speaking of cost, let's start with our bank accounts." He looked to the banker to supply the details.

The banker gave each member a piece of paper with their personal account information listed. The men noticed the large increases in their accounts, thanks to Albert Dean's and Bartholomew's shares being split evenly between the surviving club members. Stock market, inflation, and other economic factors didn't impact the club. The money from their illegal activity offset any gains they would have yielded from playing the market.

The banker had become an expert at international banking. The majority of the funds were protected in their offshore, nameless accounts. Their money was as safe as the passwords. The club didn't worry about the banker stealing because they knew he was too afraid of the mayor to even attempt to siphon from these accounts. He had their account numbers and passwords committed to memory, but kept a copy hidden in a secret compartment of his desk. For emergency purposes, the account numbers and passcodes were also locked tightly in a safety deposit box with the banker having one key and the mayor having the other.

The farmer whispered to the banker asking him to stick around after the meeting to discuss withdrawing some of his Tuesday Club money. He wanted to buy some bulls to start a new farming venture. The banker nodded nervously that he would stay.

The mayor looked at the somber group and decided to provide some comic relief. Placing his hand on his hip, he sashayed around the room twisting his hips and throwing kisses to the club saying, "Vote for change!" The more the men laughed, the greater the gyrations of his hips, and the more he mocked his opponent.

After the mayor tired of the tomfoolery, he began his tirade. "I don't know about you, but I'm already so sick of hearing Geneva's 'Vote for Vaughn' slogan that I could puke." His face now somber, he took his seat and in a more serious tone brought his point home. "Now, I don't have to remind you what could happen if I lose this election. Many of your family members will lose their jobs 'cause Geneva will put in her own people." He paused for effect. "Let's not forget what happens to the other elected officials throughout this room if they get their hands on the mayoral office. Why, our daddies and granddaddies would turn over in their graves if we piss on this wonderful gift they gave us."

The county clerk interrupted the mayor by saying, "Now, don't get so worked up and piss on our heritage just yet. It's early, and we have a lot of tricks up our sleeves, but it's gonna be costly ."

When the mayor heard the word costly, he realized the county clerk had an idea. "Let's hear it," the mayor demanded.

"Let's just say I don't think you have a thing to worry about," the smiling clerk smugly proclaimed.

"Now, don't play with us. You're gonna have to tell us more so the mayor'll be able to sleep," said the protégé as he patted the mayor on the arm.

"Now, boys, I've been overseeing elections for many years. It's my responsibility to make sure these here voting machines are working just right. From time to time, I have to call a repairman to come and fix 'em. Let's just say the boy who repairs them has been trained and certified by the manufacturer and can make them machines talk if he wants to. For the right amount of money, the election will be over before the first person votes. We can make it as tight or as runaway as we want it. Yep, you heard it, boys, the Tuesday Club has gone high tech!" The county clerk pounded the table in excitement as he finished his speech.

"I thought those machines were tamper and hack proof," the chief deputy contributed. "Are you sure you're not being setup?"

"Oh, yea of little faith," the county clerk spoke condescendingly. "I think you should let me take care of the machines, and you worry about making some kind of pretense to electioneer, and it's important that we select the right people to serve as the election workers. We can't have anyone that's computer savvy."

The room engulfed in chatter as each of the members excitedly talked about the possibilities that the county clerk's plan had today and in the future.

"Why, with this kind of technology on our side, we can impact other county and state elections. Think of the unlimited potential this has unleashed," the county judge dreamed aloud.

The mayor viewed the clerk's secretive action as an act of espionage that would have to be punished after the election. He had always realized the clerk and chief deputy could team up and possibly oust him from his leadership position if they put two and two together since they oversaw the elections. They had never been a threat before, but this new technology made the clerk a potential adversary. The clerk would be dealt with later, but for the time being, the mayor sighed in relief.

The meeting was adjourned, and the mayor walked out of the meeting a changed man. He no longer had the foreboding of doom, but the feeling of power oozed from his pores. It was 6:55 in the morning, thanks to the daylight saving time, he still had plenty darkness to conceal his exit. He walked at a brisk pace, the sooner he would get to his office, the sooner he could reward himself with the cat head biscuits and sausage gravy that Jeb had boxed up for him. He noticed the piece of paper wedged into the door facing. *"Vote for Vaughn, Vote for Change,"* the paper read. He wadded the paper into a small ball and aimed at the garbage can ten feet away.

Out of the corner of his eye, the mayor noticed something yellow on his precious Buick. On his windshield placed neatly under his wiper blade was the same "Vote for Vaughn," election ad that had been in the door. When he reached to pull it out, he noticed the handwriting on the back of the paper.

Happy Tuesday! Better watch your step, 'cause we're watching you!

Jock froze in place and a million questions started zooming through his mind. "Am I being followed? Did they see me go into the secret meeting? Is our meeting place compromised?"

He didn't throw the paper away as he'd originally intended. Someone was going to be very sorry. He unlocked his office door and entered his sanctuary when his phone began ringing. He knew before picking up his receiver that he wasn't the only one with the note. Impending doom once again loomed over him.

CHAPTER 15

The Confession

Wednesday, March 26, 2008, 7:00 PM

Julia Hopper was grateful Trevor was back in McWhorter. She was very fond of Tillie, but Trevor was her favorite. She made a conscious effort to treat them both the same, but Trevor just tugged at her heartstrings. He reminded her so much of the little boy whom she lost so many years ago. Maybe she would tell Trevor about her son one day, but it wouldn't be today. She'd put off sharing important information with the twins as long as she possibly could. Today was the day she chose to give them their granny's letter and journals. She heard them talking as they came toward the kitchen.

"What the heck?" Trevor exclaimed when he noticed Julia's luggage neatly stacked in the corner of the room. "What's going on Julia? Where're you going?"

"We've got to talk. Trust me. You probably will be ready for me to go after I tell you all that I've been withholding from you." Her tone made them take notice.

Tillie glanced at Trevor, and she knew he was thinking the same thing she was. They were certain Julia had information regarding their father's death.

"I'm not sure you know my feelings toward your grandparents. I owe my very life to them. There's nothing I wouldn't do for them. Do you hear me? Nothing. I'd kill for them. If it hadn't been for their loving care; then, I'm not sure I would be here today." Julia stopped talking. The twins sat motionless as they waited for her to continue. "When I came to McWhorter, I didn't actually have my nursing degree, but I had some medical office experience. They set me up in the apartment over the medical office, and as you know, that's where I called home until I moved in here with Mrs. Grant after Doc passed away." Julia paused to check their recall and continued only when she saw their nods of remembrance.

"Doc took good care of his patients. He knew secrets about his patients that went to the grave with him. Every precaution to protect their privacy was taken. He had some records he only trusted me to look after. These special files were locked in his office. I made a mistake with one of these files that I'm certain cost your dear father his life. It happened on June 17, 1993. I remember the day just like it was yesterday." Julia closed her eyes as she relived the mistake of her life.

Thursday, June 17, 1993

Julia Hopper felt right at home in her office uniform. Dr. Grant had insisted all the staff wear the same tan colored scrubs. The younger girls all complained because they preferred the printed smocks with cartoon characters. Secretly, Julia applauded the Doc's stance on the uniform, partly because she preferred professionalism over trend, but also because she felt tan was one color that accented her red hair and sky blue eyes. She knew she probably looked her very best when she wore her scrubs, which was a good thing, since it made up the majority of her wardrobe. Creeda Maggard, a summer intern, also looked good in the tan uniform. Actually, Creeda would look good wearing a feed sack. She was a tiny little thing, and her sad eyes were as big as half dollars. If possible, the tan coloring of the uniform made her eyes look that much darker and larger. Cherokee Indians used to inhabit this region of Kentucky, and if Julia were a betting woman, she would bet Creeda had a whole lot of Indian blood in her. Her movements were graceful and ghostlike as she glided soundlessly throughout the office.

Dr. Grant wasn't a big fan of Creeda's and didn't want to hire her. Julia, on the other hand, took an immediate liking to the girl which was completely out of character for Julia. The sadness she saw in the young girl's eyes was deep and heavy. Regardless of the reason for wanting to help the young girl, Julia felt compelled to convince Doc to give her a chance. When Julia explained that Creeda had worked at the mayor's office and as a church secretary, the Doc was more convinced not to hire her. Julia wasn't sure why he changed his mind, but she finally wore him down, and he finally agreed to hire her on a trial basis provided she watched her like a hawk.

Julia had been pleased her instincts were right about Creeda. Creeda didn't chitchat and did exactly as she was told and never complained. She did, however, ask a lot of questions and was especially inquisitive about the medical codes and terminology of the files. Making Creeda her pet project, Julia taught the young girl to read medical code during their slow periods.

Attention to detail was Julia's strong suit; Julia found comfort in detail and in routine. The first duty she did each morning was to check the list of appointments. After pulling the files, she prepared the patient rooms for Dr. Grant.

On June 17, Julia noticed that Eleanor Ledford, the mayor's wife, had an appointment scheduled at eleven. When she couldn't find Mrs. Ledford's file with the other medical files, she realized it must be locked up in Dr. Grant's office. She was right. It was there. She couldn't resist taking a peak into this file deemed special by Dr. Grant. Some of the special files told stories of infidelity, incest, and poor hygiene. Her brief review of Mrs. Ledford's file showed nothing scandalous, and she thought Doc must have filed it in his office by mistake. She placed the file in order of appointments with the other files on her desk.

The morning was busier than usual, which caused them to get backed up. Dr. Grant's patients were loyal and didn't seem to mind waiting. Eleanor was no exception. Eleanor Ledford definitely looked and played the part as the mayor's wife. She was perfectly dressed, not a hair out of place, but when she spoke in her sweet southern voice, she appeared very down to earth. She talked about housework, cooking, gardening, canning, and freezing—the official language of the McWhorter women. Ever the professional, Julia explained to her, "Mrs. Ledford, it may be forty-five minutes or so before we can get you back to see the doctor."

"That's okay. I brought a good book, and I don't mind to wait," Eleanor kindly replied as she pulled a paperback out of her pocketbook.

Julia had readied the files for the ten thirty and ten forty-five appointments and placed the files neatly on the doctor's desk. When she looked at the next file, she realized it was Mr. Martin's file, and his appointment was not until eleven fifteen. "Huh? Where's my eleven o'clock file?" Positive she'd pulled Mrs. Ledford's file, she frantically began to search her desk for it. Nothing. Not ready to alarm the doctor or the other girls, she retraced her morning steps. The file was nowhere to be found. Before she asked for assistance, she decided to look on her desk one more time. Low and behold, the missing file was the first file on the stack on her desk. Suspiciously, Julia looked around the room to see if someone was pulling a prank on her. No one's actions seemed out of place, so she decided to discount the episode to her age. Business was as usual for the rest of the day.

Wednesday, March 26, 2008, 7:30 PM

The twins noticed the transformation in Julia's demeanor as she relived that day. She acted as this revelation was earth-shattering news, but the twins were even more confused.

"I'm not sure I'm following you?" Trevor said in question form.

"You see, Creeda didn't show up the next morning. She called later in the day and explained that the mayor had offered her a full-time position with benefits. She was very apologetic. I was very sad and took her quitting as a personal failure. It was later in the day before I was able to tell Dr. Grant about her resignation. In some ways, Dr. Grant was relieved, but I could tell her quiet efficiency was growing on him too. When I told him she was going to work for the mayor, I saw pure panic in his eyes. He walked the short distance between us very slowly and calmly. He then kneeled in front of me and placed a hand on each of my shoulders."

Julia's speech slowed and her facial expression changed as she articulated each word in much the same fashion as Dr. Grant would have stated when she mimicked him saying, "Was there any way Creeda could have seen Eleanor Ledford's medical file?"

After a brief pause and personality change, Julia back to herself told the twins, "I explained what I could remember about Mrs. Ledford's file coming up missing. His face was ashen. He said that we needed to pray that it was just a coincidence and that Jock Ledford didn't know what was in that file. He asked me to make up a reason to call and check on Mrs. Ledford."

Not following the significance of the situation nor how it pertained to her, Tillie interrupted by saying, "Julia, you have completely lost me."

"I didn't understand until much later either, but after I did understand, it was too late. We are convinced that the information in the file was the reason for Edward's murder. Truthfully, it doesn't make much sense when you try to see into the mind of a mad man. Jock Ledford is mean and crazy. Of course, he hides it rather well. Only those who are closest to him understand his true vindictive nature. You see, a doctor comes to know his patients pretty well. I don't know all the specifics, but from what I've gathered, the mayor was desperate for a male heir to carry on his name and the family tradition. So desperate, that he abused his wife in effort to obtain these sons. Mrs. Ledford had three children in a matter of thirty-one months, and it just about killed her. Dr. Grant performed a secret tubal litigation on the mayor's wife. The two conspired to do this procedure without the mayor's knowledge or blessing. Eleanor knew her husband would never agree for her to have her tubes tied, and Doc knew she would never survive another delivery like her last one. She needed time to heal. Doc swore on his life he would protect this secret."

Trying to rationalize what he had just heard, Trevor asked, "So you think the mayor had our father killed over a woman having her tubes tied?"

"I know it sounds crazy, but Jock Ledford is a very complicated man with many issues, and when people cross him, whether real or perceived, he punishes them. Doc knew he was taking a big risk but felt it was worth it. This secret had been protected for many years until I unknowingly unleashed it by not guarding that file. Edward died a month after the file went missing. Dr. Grant always felt that Jock was behind his death, but initially couldn't tie him to it."

"What happened to Creeda?" Tillie asked.

"I don't know. I never saw Creeda again. She vanished like the wind." Wiping her eyes, Julia left the kitchen and headed down the hallway.

Trevor and Tillie just looked at each other trying to make sense of how a woman having her tubes tied could have had anything to do with their dad's death. They were still conversing when a red-eyed Julia re-entered the room. In her arms, she carried a large brown accordion-style file folder. She placed the file on the table next to the apple pie. "In this file, you will find your grandparent's journals and their investigative work as they tried to uncover the mystery of their son's death. What they uncovered was much more than they bargained for. Evidently, there's an unholy alliance by a group of men that has to be stopped. I have continued their work, and I guess you could say I've put things in motion for you. I think you'll find what you need to finish our work. We're not sure the identities of all the men involved. We know they refer to their alliance as the Tuesday Club, and we know that Jock Ledford, Albert Dean Smith, Woodrow Ledford, and Pastor Bart were all involved. We suspect others such as the chief deputy, county clerk, and judge executive but haven't found the proof we need yet," Julia stated.

In a state of shock, the twins didn't say a word while they digested the information.

"I'm going to California and stay with your mother so the two of you can both stay here and use your special training and connections to finish your grandparent's search for the truth."

After she laid a small linen envelope on the table, she said her goodbyes and left. They opened the envelope.

Dearest Grandchildren,

The fact you are reading this letter means I'm finally back home with both my husband and my son, and we are feasting at our Savior's table. This has been a homecoming that I've longed for ever since Edward and Roscoe left me. I know my mind is slipping more and more each day, and I have an overwhelming urge to get my household in order while I still can. I want you to know that I trust Julia Hopper with my life. I have entrusted her to give you our journals at the appropriate time. Knowing you are reading this letter now means that now must be the right time for you to finish what we started and make McWhorter the place that it could be.

When Roscoe and I chose to make our home in Rockford County, we truly thought we had found a little piece of heaven. I guess we were wrong.

It all started when Katherine Gail Ledford was on her deathbed. Her husband, Mayor Clarence Ledford, insisted she remain at home and wanted very little medical intervention. Roscoe didn't know what to make of it when she whispered to him that Clarence was killing her, and the "Tuesday Club" had to be stopped. Roscoe thought the woman was delusional. Mrs. Ledford died a few hours after she spoke these words, and unfortunately, Roscoe didn't follow up.

Something similar happened a few years later when another patient asked Roscoe to protect his family from the mayor and the Tuesday Club before he died. Roscoe thought this was too big of a coincidence—two people mentioning this Tuesday Club on their deathbeds. Again, he didn't have time to pursue it; however, Edward's death changed that.

As you know, we have all believed the way Edward died was very strange, and we couldn't understand why Edward would have been at the construction site by himself in the first place. It was your mother who gave us our first clue that Edward's death possibly had ties to McWhorter. Several months after Edward's death, your mother called and wanted to know what ever happened to Albert Dean Smith. She said that Edward had mentioned seeing him in California shortly before he died. He said if it wasn't Albert Dean, then, it was a dead ringer for him.

Roscoe then knew what he always suspected was true—Jock Ledford was somehow responsible for our precious son's untimely death. Roscoe and I both made a pact to find out what really happened.

When we started unraveling the town's gossip line, what we uncovered was a lot bigger than either of us had realized. The only thing we know for sure is that we can't trust anyone in this town; too many ties exist. We know Jock Ledford is the leader of the group, and his followers are a group of men who silently run McWhorter. We also know Jock has spies infiltrated throughout the county and knows anything and everything that goes on. So be very careful who you trust.

I'm sorry we've hidden this from you for so long. We thought it was best. So, my dear grandchildren, in the files Julia's given you, you will find limited records, dates, etc., that we have managed to piece together. It's enough of a start that I'm confident you can finish the task. Again, please be careful!

I place my trust in each of you and in my Lord and Savior. I pray you will place your trust in him and then one day we can all be together again. Won't that be grand?

I will always love you,
Granny

CHAPTER 16

Matter of Trust

Wednesday, March 26, 2008, 11:00 PM

It was fortunate that Trevor and Tillie could afford to take an unpaid leave from their jobs. They knew settling their grandparent's estate would be entirely on their shoulders. The extended time off work would afford them the extra time needed to unravel the McWhorter mystery.

Thinking about their father was painful, but the memories they had were also so sweet. Edward Grant was a big bear of a guy who understood how to be a dad, husband, son, and boss. He was a civil engineer with a business degree—all the necessary tools to be a successful contractor. His job came second to his family. He knew that located at home were the ingredients needed for his recipe for happiness—his family. Every day was an adventure. They camped, hiked, beached, and stayed very active. Eddie was the rock that the family built their lives around. At the impossible age of fifteen, the twin's life as they knew it came to a crashing halt. Their mother didn't know how to live without her husband, and the twins became more of a parent to her than she was to them. Life had been tough for them with the occasional visits to and from their grandparents as their only reprieve.

Gleaning what they could from each of their grandparent's investigative documents, they realized they needed help. It was too big for just the two of them. Trevor looked at his watch and couldn't believe it was almost one in the morning. Making an executive decision, Trevor dialed Uncle Willie without asking his sister's opinion. As he was waiting for his uncle to answer the phone, he wondered why his grandparents hadn't shared this information with the sheriff already. His uncle answered the phone before Trevor could change his mind and hang up. Too late. Thanks to caller identification, Trevor had to continue. He apologized for calling at this hour. He asked his uncle to come over.

Sheriff Osborne entered the house about thirty minutes later and was unusually attentive for the wee hour of the morning. The three law enforcement officers spent the entire morning reviewing the journals and research material. Trevor felt much better about his uncle when he saw the panic in the man's eyes as he reviewed the documents. "I knew Jock was shifty and all, but, my Lord, it looks like he's capable of anything. You reckon we could get any help from the Bureau? We need more than the three of us to bring 'em down."

Inviting the bureau's involvement meant the twins wouldn't be allowed on the team due to their personal connection—this was not an option. He felt Albert Dean had been justly punished, but justice needed to be served on the rest of the club as well. Trevor wanted to be part of this justice, even if it was in some vigilante role. In an effort to stall the inevitable, Trevor countered, "I'm sure many of these allegations may violate federal law, but we probably need the state's involvement before alerting the FBI. Don't you think?"

The sheriff chewed on this before speaking. "Good idea. I'll call Daniel Brooks. He's a state trooper," Sheriff Osborne stated while pulling his cell phone out of its holster.

"Whoa, wait a minute!" Trevor stopped the sheriff. "How could you trust a man that's dating the daughter of the person named most in these documents?"

With the phone still in his hand and without any hesitation, the sheriff explained, "The Daniel Brooks I know would arrest his own mother if she violated the law."

Trevor noticed how his sister's eyes lit up when Daniel's name was mentioned. "I'm sure my little sister wouldn't mind having him around. She had such a crush on him when we were little. She followed him around like a ... owww!" Trevor was suddenly hushed by the ripple of pain shooting up his left arm.

"Do you trust Daniel?" Tillie asked her uncle.

"Yep, I trust him with my life."

This was all the convincing she needed. "Call him," she ordered.

Thursday, March 27, 2008, 5:00 AM

Silence. Daniel opened his eyes thinking he would see a dog fight like none other, but instead he was met with the darkness of his bedroom and heard an annoying ringing sound coming from his cell phone. "Damn it," he said, but sighed a breath of relief.

He reached for his phone and saw the time was 5:12 a.m. and knew instinctively that calls from dispatch at this time of the day were usually not pleasant. After recognizing Sheriff Osborne's phone number, he sleepily responded, "This better be good!"

"Trust me. It is! Get dressed and come to Doc. Grant's house, but don't tell anyone."

Daniel showered and quickly threw on a pair of jeans and a sweatshirt. Thanks to his short haircut and fast clothing choice, he was on the road at 5:35. Daniel was anxious to hear what the sheriff had to say and also felt a little excited at the prospect of seeing Tillie again.

Tillie met him at the door with a quick hug, and he followed her to the kitchen where the others had congregated. She was dressed in those soft cotton cheerleading shorts and a college sweatshirt. Her legs were as brown as biscuits and as toned as they were tanned. He even liked the fact that her toenails matched the red of her sweatshirt.

After he finally managed to take his eyes off Tillie, he noticed the table with papers in various states of disarray strewn across the eight-foot dining table. The look in the sheriff's eyes told him to run, but the warmth of Tillie's nearby body held him spellbound. "What's going on?" he finally asked.

Trevor's dark circles under his eyes were dead giveaways that he was sleep deprived. Tillie, on the other hand, was bouncing all around and her hair was as wild as ever. She had a large mug of hot coffee in her hand that she extended to him.

After grunting some form of greeting, Trevor got right to the business at hand. "Thirteen years ago our father was killed in a construction accident. A front loader crushed him. Although his death was ruled an accident, Granny and Pa felt that his death had to do with McWhorter. Now, we know their suspicions were correct. We know Albert Dean Smith and Woody Ledford traveled to California the week before our dad's accident. Our Pa felt that this was a hit ordered by the mayor as a way to even a personal grudge against him."

"Wait a minute! Is this the reason you were asking about Albert Dean Smith?" Daniel asked wondering if he now had motive for his only lead in Albert Dean's murder investigation.

"Actually, we didn't know any of these details until tonight. As I told you over the phone the other day, I was only following up on a phone call. Our friend, Julia, asked me to talk with the Smith man after she received a call saying Albert Dean Smith needed to meet with me. I was only trying to hunt him down to see what he wanted. I thought he needed my professional help or something." Trevor defended.

"Where is Julia?" Daniel asked suspiciously.

Trevor was quick to answer that she was headed toward California.

Changing the subject, Daniel questioned, "Why would the mayor have a grudge against Dr. Grant?" He couldn't imagine anyone having a problem with the good Doc. He thought Doc was practically ready to be canonized.

Trevor wasn't sure if he wanted to go into a lot of these personal details about Daniel's future mother-in-law just yet, so instead he read an entry from his pa's journal.

Tuesday, July 5, 2005

I've trailed Jock Ledford many times over the past few months and managed to remain undetected, but not so sure about today. At three in the morning, I settled in my truck across the street from the City Hall. I dozed off sometime between four and five. I was awakened by the sound of the slamming of a car door. I watched Jock get out of his car, pull out an umbrella, and walk down Broad Street. I slipped out of the car, followed him from a distance, and saw him disappear down an alleyway.

I was contemplating my next move when I had to drop to my knees and hide behind a shrub as I watched the county judge go in that same direction. In the Broad Street parking lot, I recognized both Pastor Bart's big Suburban and Woodrow Ledford's car. I knew Bartholomew couldn't walk too far, so I knew they must be going in Hazel's basement entrance. Right when I was about to get brave and take a closer look, I literally ran into Albert Dean Smith. Playing it off, I told him the best cure for insomnia was a brisk walk in the early morning. I don't think he believed me, but he laughed and countered, "My doctor advised against early morning walks. He told me they were dangerous for my health. Told me that they could even kill me."

Trevor stopped reading and placed the journal on the table. "This was Pa's last entry. He was found dead by what was ruled to be natural causes the following morning. Pretty big coincidence, huh?"

Daniel was hooked. He had to know more for his own dad's sake. Sheriff Osborne left shortly after he got there. Trevor, Tillie, and Daniel remained at the dining room table and continued to sort through the information. Trevor announced he couldn't look at another piece of paper and went to bed leaving Daniel alone with Tillie. Finally!

Tillie moved around the table so she was seated next to Daniel. Her hand lightly brushed his hand, and he felt an electric charge shoot through his body. He startled at the reaction. Instinctively, she drew her hand back as well. Daniel had to know more about this conspiracy theory, but even more important was his need to understand why Tillie's touch was electric to him.

Tillie was bright-eyed and bushy-tailed one minute, then, the next time he looked at her, her eyes were closed. He couldn't give Doc's journal full attention for listening to the sounds Tillie was making. She was even cute with her mouth positioned in that weird shape as she snored little grunts. Pulling her close where her head was resting comfortably on his shoulder, she snuggled into his body making herself right at home.

If he would have looked out the window, he would have noticed a cream-colored Lexus driving slowly by the Grant's house.

CHAPTER 17

Cromer Lake

Thursday, March 27, 2008, 10:05 AM

Daniel carried Tillie to the couch in the sitting room. It was past ten o'clock, and he needed to go on patrol. He situated her on the sofa before he placed a creamy, yellow chenille throw over her tan legs. Lightly, he sneaked a feel of her legs while strategically placing the blanket to cover them. Wanting to know more of her, he ran his hands over her cheeks as he studied every facet of her sleeping face.

He radioed dispatch and let them know he was ten-eight. He no sooner went on duty until he was called to another crime scene. This time the crime scene involved a dead body that had been pulled out of Cromer Lake. He looked heavenward as he contemplated who would be the owner of this body.

Daniel wasn't sure what to expect after he trudged first through thickets and then slid down a twenty foot embankment to arrive at the scene. Only a handful of people were gathered where the water met the slate-colored mud of the bank. The body was half on land and half in the shallow water. Long dark strands of the victim's hair bobbed with the movement of the lake water. Although swollen and discolored, he could still tell the body belonged to a young female. Without touching the corpse, Daniel completed a visual. He couldn't tell if it were a homicide or not just from looking at the condition of the body. Her body could've hit a log or one of the many tree stumps that made Cromer an excellent place to fish.

Recognizing his friends' chatter before he actually saw them, he knew help arrived in the form of the chief deputy and the sheriff. Hanging onto branches to keep upright, Joe Matt mostly slid down the muddy bank with Sheriff Osborne cautiously following a few feet behind. By the look of horror on Joe Matt's face, it was apparent he knew the identity of the young lady as soon as he laid eyes on her.

The chief deputy knew this was very bad. He took his can of Skoal out of his back pocket and put the snuff under his lip. The dead body belonged to Ruth Ann Vaughn, the sixteen-year-old granddaughter of Geneva Vaughn. He remembered her being a topic of discussion at a Tuesday Club meeting, but he couldn't fathom in his wildest dreams that the mayor would take it this far.

"Who is she?" Daniel asked.

Daniel didn't have to wait long before he received his answer. Sheriff Osborne exclaimed, "Holy shit! That's little Ruthie Vaughn, Geneva's granddaughter!"

"Holy shit is right," Daniel shivered as he felt the evil of the situation. He knew that this was no accidental drowning. Her large fixated glassy eyes spoke volumes of the untold horror she'd recently faced. The Pandora's Box had been opened; Jock Ledford and his Tuesday Club had to be stopped. "He's gone too far."

"Yes, he has." Joe Matt verbally agreed.

11:00 AM

Geneva Vaughn had been door-to-door campaigning until late last night, and the fast pace was starting to wear her down. She looked at the clock on the nightstand and couldn't believe she slept until nearly eleven o'clock. Dreading to unravel out of the warm covers to start what she knew would be another hectic day, she allowed herself two more minutes to adjust to reality before rousing. She had forty reasons to drag her weary body out of the bed—forty precious days to rid McWhorter of Mayor Jock Ledford. Geneva didn't necessarily jump out of bed. It was more like a slow creep. Not bothering to make any pretense of making her bed up, she left it just as it was.

In the past, she and her husband, Glenn Dale, had always supported Jock Ledford. It was only after Jock started messing with her church's building permit that she had a change of heart. Not wanting to make a hasty decision, she and Glenn Dale spent a lot of time on their knees praying before she ever signed her petition to be a candidate for the mayoral office. She didn't hear God speak audibly to her; it was more like it felt right.

Thoroughly convinced she was doing the right thing, she was still unsure of the reasoning she was the appointed vessel. Nevertheless, Geneva was an obedient servant. She knew Jock would be hard to beat, but she also knew she had strong allies when she had the Father, Son, and Holy Ghost on her side.

It was only after she announced her candidacy that the citizens of McWhorter started trusting her enough to confide in her. Every day she became more convinced that Jock Ledford had to be dethroned. Day after day, someone would come to her or Glenn Dale in confidence telling how Jock had been involved in cheating them out of their land or money. She wasn't even surprised when several residents told stories of how their loved ones had suffered a horrible accident after crossing one of the Ledfords. The more she heard, the more determined she was doing the right thing. She knew it was going to be tough, and Jock was going to strike like the serpent he was, but she also knew what happened to the serpent in the Garden of Eden.

Geneva finally made it to the kitchen and was waiting for her coffee to perk. Out of habit, she glimpsed out the kitchen window to see if she could tell if Ruth Ann's car was still in the garage or not, but all three of the garage doors were shut. The sheen off the bright yellow car could be seen from her kitchen window had the doors been opened and the car still there. She smiled as she thought about how Ruthie loved that yellow car of hers. Ruthie had a special spot in Geneva's heart. She and Glenn Dale had actually raised Ruthie since she was four years old. Her oldest son could never get it together after his wife picked up and left both Ruth Ann and him for a married truck driver.

Emptying her coffee mug, she rinsed it in the sink before she headed toward the washroom. It was then when she had her first inclination that something wasn't right. Ruth Ann's schoolbooks were still lying on the counter top. "How odd." Geneva thought out loud.

She opened the door to Ruth Ann's room. It was then when Geneva flew into a full-blown panic. Ruth Ann hadn't slept in her bed. The lavender comforter and the white islet throw pillows were in the same location as they were yesterday morning when Geneva made the bed.

Geneva ran to the living room. The bone-tired weariness replaced with an adrenalin rush as she practically hurdled the ottoman to get to the telephone. Starting to press the buttons of the telephone, she stopped when she heard the knock at the door. She put the cordless phone on the counter and walked slowly and calmly to the door as Pastor Ables, Sheriff Osborne, and Trooper Brooks entered and explained the reason for their visit.

The sound of her scream reverberated throughout McWhorter.

1:00 PM

Geneva went through every emotion possible, but the only one she could remotely deal with at this time was rage. Geneva Vaughn was mad. Every fiber in her body called out that Jock Ledford was somehow behind her precious Ruthie's death. She just knew it.

"I wanta see her!" Geneva demanded to the sheriff.

"Geneva, why don't we wait until Glenn Dale can get home?" reasoned the sheriff as he tried to rationalize with the woman. He knew she was ill-equipped to handle seeing her granddaughter's swollen black and blue corpse.

"Dear Lord, please tell me my baby isn't anywhere near Jimmy Sizemore!"

"Yep, she's at the Sizemore Funeral Home," the sheriff answered.

"No! You get her out of there now! I mean it! Jimmy'll destroy whatever evidence they find. I don't want him to touch my baby." Her demands changed to pleading. "Please, I'm begging you. You can't possibly understand. Jimmy and Jock are in some type of secret club together. They would do whatever it takes to cover up any evidence that pointed toward Jock's involvement."

Daniel said very quietly so only the sheriff would hear, "Does everyone in McWhorter know about the Tuesday Club?"

The sheriff only nodded at Daniel before he started throwing out orders, "Daniel, go ahead and call Joe Matt and see if the coroner will sign off on moving her."

1:30 PM

Jock had a headache. He knew that sex was a quick remedy for what was ailing him; he self-diagnosed his condition as having too many sperm in his body. Knowing men produced millions of sperm on a daily basis, it just made sense that by continuing to produce them day after day without any outflow would cause a man to surely burst. He had no plans of bursting any time soon, not when he had sweet Sissy around. His big-breasted secretary was one of his best finds yet.

Just as Jock's forefinger was ready to press the intercom button and only minutes from relief, he was startled by hearing Sissy's heavily accented voice booming from the same little box located only inches from his face. "Mayor Ledford, the judge is here to see you."

The judge executive entered his office and wasted no time in getting to the crux of the matter. "I'm kinda worried 'bout Woody. No one's seen or heard from him since Monday."

"Now that you mention it, it wasn't like Woody to miss the meeting on Tuesday. He's not been acting right for the past few months. I hope he didn't wreck off one of those bluffs and kill his fool self. I'll call Joe Matt and see if he can check around."

1:40 PM

Joe Matt entered the coroner's office and made the call to the mayor. Joe Matt Sizemore and Coroner Jimmy Sizemore shared the last name, but that was about all they shared. Joe Matt was creeped out by his cousin's office. The office furniture was dark mahogany, and the walls were painted in a manly shade of brown. Jimmy had spared no expense in decorating his sanctuary. Dealing with death every day, one would think the old coroner would want his office to be a place of refuge from death. In contrast, it was hard not to think about anything but death when there were as many as twenty dead animals hanging on the walls, perched on shelves, or lying in the floor.

It was hard to look at this old man and imagine him owning a weapon, let alone using it to take down some of the scariest animals in the world. Jimmy's only son, on the other hand, seemed unscathed by the dark world his father and his grandfather created. Jimmy put Joe Matt in the mind of the Joker from *Batman*. It appeared that Jimmy had been experimenting with those embalming chemicals and the funeral parlor make-up; he had a permanent grin on his face.

Joe Matt tried to quit thinking about the creepy old man and instead think about his phone call. He knew he couldn't waste any time. The coroner needed to know what the mayor wanted them to do. "Sissy, this is Chief Deputy Sizemore. I need to speak with the mayor."

Jock's intercom was getting a full workout. "Joe Matt Sizemore on line one," Sissy said as she announced the call.

Jock and Jack looked at each other knowing something was amuck for Joe Matt to be calling. "Mayor Ledford," Jock said as he put the receiver to his ear.

"It's not good," Joe Matt started.

"You found Woody?" Jock asked.

"Nope. We found little Ruth Ann Vaughn floating in Cromer."

The mayor placed his hand over the receiver and relayed to the judge what Joe Matt had just said. Jock had to work at controlling his emotions.

He put his mouth back to the receiver, "Does Geneva know yet?"

"Yep."

"Any signs of foul play?"

"Too soon to tell. She's pretty banged up, but that could have happened after she drowned. I don't really know much of anything, and Jimmy hasn't had a chance to look at her. Based on my call from the sheriff, it doesn't look like he'll be performing a full evaluation either. The Vaughns are insisting we take her straight to Frankfort."

"Shouldn't that be our coroner's say whether she goes or not?" Mayor Ledford sucked in air a little too fast. "She's just a little girl who drowned. How hard would that be to rule her death as an accidental drowning?"

"I don't know. I'm just telling you what I've been told. Any reason to be worried?"

"Why, of course not," the mayor feigned disbelief Joe Matt would even ask the question. "Keep us informed, you hear? Poor ole Geneva. I'm sure she's heartbroken."

The judge studied Jock and tried to read him. His poker face didn't give anything away. "You okay?" he asked after he'd ended the call.

"Why wouldn't I be okay? That lake's a dangerous place, and you know how those young teenyboppers are."

"Isn't March a little early for them to be congregating at the lake?"

Acting as though he didn't hear his last statement, he paid him no never-mind. He picked up the paper and started looking for the section where the obituaries were listed.

CHAPTER 18

Bacon Creek Drive In

Thursday, March 27, 2008, 6:30 PM

Tillie and Trevor just sat in unbelief while their Uncle Willie and Daniel told them about the death of Geneva Vaughn's granddaughter.

"Do you honestly think Jock Ledford did this? Is he that evil?" Tillie asked.

"Is he that stupid?" Trevor added.

"I wouldn't put anything past him. It'd be just like him to think he could get away with this murder just like he's gotten away with everything else over the years," the sheriff explained. "I definitely think Jockie Poo's messed up this time. He's underestimated Ms. Geneva. He probably thought she'd turn tail and run then he'd be a shoo in as always."

Daniel interjected, "I think Jock Ledford better hope Geneva doesn't have the power of Elijah. He's pretty much asking for a firestorm to rain down on him, if she does."

"Actually, maybe we're the firestorm." Trevor had a look in his eye that made Daniel think Trevor could be capable of murder.

"I just realized I'm starving," Tillie announced as she changed the topic of their conversation. "I think a hotdog from the drive-in over at Bacon Creek sounds good." Tillie, usually the healthy eater, made exceptions to her diet when it came to the Bacon Creek Drive-In. The drive-in had always been a special treat for her as a little girl.

Daniel struck while the fire was hot. "Now that you mention it, a good ole Bacon Creek foot long sounds mighty tasty."

Tillie threw a lightweight jacket on one arm as she headed out the door. "Trev, Uncle Willie, you want us to bring you something back," she asked.

"Count me out. I've got to head home and eat supper or Brenda'll quit cooking for me," said Sheriff Osborne with a laugh.

Trevor thought his sister was playing with fire by being alone with this man, and his tone voiced his protectiveness when he made his order. "Bring me back a foot long with chili, onions and mustard, some of those crinkled fries, and a root beer float. Make it snappy. I'm hungry."

"Got it!" Tillie said. Trevor's message wasn't lost on Tillie, but she didn't let it deter her.

Daniel headed in the direction of his truck until he realized Tillie wasn't behind him but had instead ventured toward the garage. Completing an about face, he followed suit.

He watched Tillie slip into the garage and disappear into the darkness. Daniel was feeling around the wall trying to find a light switch when he felt her presence. He felt her fingers lightly touch his arm. The shiver started at his head and made its way down to his toes.

Before she could slip away, he grabbed her arm and pulled her toward him. She tried to resist, but Daniel was too strong or so he thought. Just as suddenly as he had her in his grasp, she'd twisted around and out of his grip.

"Two can play this game," he thought as he put all his police training to work. Adjusting to the darkness, he was on her trail. He could see her silhouette and was ready to claim his prize. Just when he thought he had her, he felt her twist his arm behind his back.

"Daniel Brooks, you have the right to remain silent," she quoted the first line of the Miranda.

"And you, darling, have the right to be—" Daniel stomped on her toe causing her to lose her grip. He was going to put an end to this game and do what he had wanted to do for days.

Now facing her, he could feel her sweet breath on his face as they leaned against Dr. Grant's old Ford pickup. Bending his large frame closer, his lips had no trouble finding hers. There was no resisting on her part either, instead her lips parted as an invitation for his lips to continue their quest. It started as a sweet kiss, but neither made any attempts to break it. After what seemed like an eternity of exploring each others' mouths, the couple came up for air. Words didn't come to either of them as they stood entwined and slightly embarrassed. Breaking the silence, Tillie began to laugh softly. He loved hearing the sound of her laughter. The only way he could describe it was to imagine the sound a spring tulip would make if it had a voice, breezy, colorful and, sincere—a pure symphony of woodwinds.

He silenced her with another kiss, and his hands began to explore her body.

Finding the sensation of the movement of his hands combined with the longing in his kiss to be more than she could stand, she broke the kiss.

Instead of protesting, Daniel pulled her tightly into him for a quick hug then kissed her on the top of her head before saying, "Trevor's going to be calling out an APB on us."

"Trevor's always spoiling my fun," she joked as she stomped her foot in a mock tantrum.

His eyes having adjusted to the dark, Daniel walked toward the Grant's older model Volvo and opened the driver's door for Tillie before he walked toward the passenger's side.

Tillie carefully backed the car out of the garage, closed the door with her remote control, and then, she headed the car down the street as expertly as Daniel could have maneuvered it. She didn't seem the least bit nervous. "I'm interested in knowing why you're going to the hotdog stand with me tonight and not with your black-eyed beauty? Are you engaged?" she asked.

When safely out of the city and on a straight stretch of a county road, Tillie goosed the gas pedal letting the overdrive kick in, which caused Daniel's head to be forced against the headrest. After he found his voice from the shock of the blastoff, he answered her, "No, I'm not engaged, and to answer the first question, I'm hungry and like hotdogs. My relationship with Caroline is very complicated, and I'm sure you know your recent bombshell about the Tuesday Club didn't help the matter."

"So I'm confused? Did you just cheat on her by kissing me in the garage?"

"Caroline and I agreed to take a break."

"Humph. How convenient!" She wasn't sure how she felt about this but wasn't going to question it further. Truth was she had it bad for Daniel, but she wasn't going to let him know.

"You might as well know now that I'm not very good about expressing myself, but here it is in a nutshell. I'm at a point in my life where I'm going to have to make some very important decisions. I care deeply for Caroline, but sometimes caring deeply just isn't enough. Of course, you do realize there are many complications about us forming any type of relationship too. What can I say? I'm a complicated kind of feller," he joked.

"Complicated or crazy?" Tillie teased while looking straight ahead as she drove. She couldn't risk looking at him, or she wouldn't be able to conceal the large smile that was fighting to take charge of her face because he'd mentioned forming a relationship.

Daniel was relieved to see the hotdog stand up ahead. The hotdog stand was in Bacon Creek, the next town over from McWhorter and had been there as long as he could remember. It was a drive-in of sorts, but had no stalls or speakers with buttons to push to place the orders. A curb girl would come and personally take the order. Tillie parked her car in a dark corner, isolated from the other cars. They placed their order and got back to their conversation.

"So what's it like to be a twin?" Daniel asked.

"I don't know what it's like *not* to be one. What's it like being an only child?"

"How'dya know I was an only child?"

"You're not really asking me that now, are you? Does FBI not mean anything?"

"Let me see. *F* could be for your pretty face, he said as he lightly touched her face with first his finger and, then, his lips while he took his time working his way from the face to the back of her neck. Tillie felt the magic of his touch, and every nerve ending was alive and tingling.

If they'd been paying attention, they would've noticed the driver of the Chevy truck parked caddy cornered from their vehicle wiping tears from her eyes.

8:30 PM

Resembling a madman, Jennings paced the floor only stopping occasionally to punch the wall or to use a stream of grunts and expletives that were guttural and unintelligible. "Atmothafriksonab," Jennings cried out before he landed in a heap on the floor.

Feeling Jennings' pain, Jon didn't care what his daddy said or thought as he took his brother in his arms to comfort him. Jon knew Jennings was the most athletic and best looking of the two brothers, but felt not one iota of jealousy. Never had. He loved both Jennings and Caroline with a love that was hard to explain; it was like they were extensions of one another and could feel each other's pain. It was hard to tell where one ended and the other one began.

This crying outburst didn't fit the persona Jennings had created for himself. Jennings, the Casanova of the Appalachians, had the wild animalistic magnetism that appealed to the women, but he was a man's man as well.

Jon didn't know if Jennings was upset because he was scared or mad because he lost a new lover. All he knew was he had never seen his brother in this kind of shape. "It'll be all right," Jon whispered low in Jennings ears so his daddy wouldn't hear.

This kind of emotional crap made Jock queasy to his stomach, but he waited until the soap opera performance played out before saying anything. Finding a lull in the drama, Jock chose to take the opportunity to speak. "Settle down, son, and tell me exactly what happened to the little Vaughn girl. Tell me the truth, did you kill that little girl?"

Jennings lifted his head from his brother's chest and ran his fingers through his wild locks as he tried to gain composure.

"Absolutely not! I left her alive and with a smile on her face. She met me at the lake cabin, and we had a nice little time. Then I got a call from one of our runners and had to leave. End of story."

"Runner? Which runner?" Jon asked. Ordinarily, the runners called him first with any problems. He thought to himself, "Why would they start calling Jennings, and why start on this particular night?"

"It was that new Lewis boy. He just had a case of cold feet about driving through Georgia and needed a little encouragement. We drank a few beers, and it seemed to calm his nerves." Jon smelled a rat. Something wasn't right with this picture. He mentally made a note to talk to Mr. Dewey Lewis. Thinking Jock would surely smell the same rat, he waited for Jock to ask more questions about the runner. Strangely enough, Jock didn't ask any more questions. "Very odd," he thought, but he didn't voice his concern.

"Son, did you, uh…uh…leave any evidence, if you know what I mean?"

"I told you I didn't—"Jennings clearly perturbed as he began to defend himself until he realized mid-sentence what evidence Jock was talking about. "Let's see, Daddy. Wasn't it you who told me I was to impregnate Ruth Ann so Geneva would lose focus? Best I remember those little swimmers won't swim upstream with a rubber on."

The sound of the slap echoed across the room as Jock reminded his son who was still the boss. Jennings, not in the mood to placate his daddy, lunged for Jock. Jon grabbed Jennings before he did something they would all regret.

Turning on and off his charm like a water faucet, Jock said in a syrupy sweet tone, "Now son, your daddy loves you, but I've got to know everything so I can help you. I feel some sick son of a bitch is trying to hurt me through you. Who knew you were with the Vaughn girl?"

"You and Jon were the only ones I told."

"What about her? Who'd she tell?" Jock questioned.

"Nobody. She swore to me she wouldn't tell a soul."

"Hellfire, boy, are you retarded or something. To a sixteen year old girl, not telling a soul means only telling five other little whores instead of the whole junior class," Jock explained the intrinsic details of sixteen-year-old females.

"But, Daddy, Ruth Ann wasn't your ordinary sixteen-year-old. Actually, I liked being with her. She really was different," defended Jennings as a tear slid down his cheek.

Jon asked, "Daddy, who do you think did it? Are they trying to set us up?"

Jock didn't comment. He was doing what he knew best—trying to figure out how to turn a bad situation to work in his favor.

CHAPTER 19

Pilgrimage

Tuesday, April 1, 2008, 7:30 PM

It was Tuesday. The sun was settling in nicely behind the foothills of the Appalachians, and a group of men were antsy to get a particular meeting underway. After the little note incident that happened last Tuesday, the mayor decided that a change of venue was necessary. Several carpooled to the secluded dirt road that was on the far north side of the county and a good thirty minutes from city limits. Their vehicles hidden, they headed toward their meeting place. Unlike their solo entrance routine for their normal meetings, the group made their trek to this meeting place together. The trail leading to the secluded spot was difficult even for the younger members as they wound around hills, crossed over rocky creek beds, and fought through thickets. They took their time and had little to say during their journey; they reserved their lungs instead for deep breaths.

The group usually met at the special meeting place once a year as a commemorative gesture to the club's founding fathers. The seventy-year-old unmarked grave of the fallen Mayor of McWhorter was a nice secluded backdrop for the Tuesday Club meeting. The group felt Hazel's had definitely been compromised and was no longer a safe place to meet. This spot in the deep forest represented privacy. From Jock's point of view, the location also served as a reminder of the group's need to be loyal to him at all costs. The gravesite looked like an ordinary campsite complete with a fire pit, rough-hewn benches, and tiki torches.

Jock wanted to laugh when he looked at the judge. Judge Jack Brown had no skin other than his face showing. He was surprised he didn't have mosquito netting over his face to complete his ensemble. "Not taking any chances on getting a bug bite, are you there, Judge?"

"Damn it, Jock. You know how allergic I am to stings. Why, a few mosquito bites can hospitalize me, and I don't even want to think what would happen if a wasp or bee stung me this far out. I've come prepared, though. I'm armed with these here pens that ort to do the trick. Someone be sure and stick me if I go limp or start swelling up like a big balloon."

The chief deputy joked, "Why, I'd be honored. Hand me one of them little pens. I've always wanted to stick the shit out of you anyway." The others quietly sniggered but were still a little too unsettled in their surroundings to joke around much. The group had nothing to say as they watched the fire spit sparks of colors in all directions.

The chief deputy broke the silence when he asked the farmer. "You find out what's killing your cows?"

"Nope. I've lost four heifers so far and—"

The lawyer interrupted before the farmer could finish. "That prize stud of yours okay?"

"Yep, Bocephus Boone's just fine. I'm working on installing the equipment to harness his manhood for artificial insemination purposes." This struck the men's funny bone; the farmer talked about semen collection like it was a household topic. The once somber group was now laughing.

The farmer's icebreaker was just what the group needed. It was during this friendly banter that the mayor felt the club's loss the most. The laughter was too quiet.

"Is it coyotes?" the banker asked after the laughter subsided.

"Could be, but I don't think so. It would take a pack of coyotes to bring one of my big cows down, and I've only been finding one big set of paw prints. I figure it's a mountain lion or a panther."

"Panther?" This piqued the coroner's interest. The coroner was ordinarily very reserved during these meetings, only speaking if necessary, but he practically yelled the word *panther* while he craned his neck toward the farmer, waiting anxiously for his reply.

"Yeah, I heard a panther sounded just like a woman screaming," the protégé added. The farmer nodded in agreement. "Is that right? That's what it is then. The first time I heard it, I thought it was Ethel screaming."

"Ah, fellers, you know there ain't no panthers in these parts," the mayor stated as an authority on Kentucky predators.

"Maybe not. I've yet to lay my eyes on the culprit."

If the glow of the embers had been brighter, the group would have been able to see a transformation had taken place in the old coroner's face. He added just one very articulate sentence to the conversation, "I've never killed a panther before."

The chief deputy cautioned, "I've heard they're deadly sons of bitches."

The old man didn't hesitate before answering. "So am I." His normal funeral home smile was gone, and in its place was a very wild and bewildered look.

All heads turned toward the old man. He had to be close to eighty years old, and the group had never seen him dressed in anything except funeral attire. Even now, he was wearing a suit jacket with his starched white shirt and dark paisley tie. The only exception to his outfit being the Merrell hiking boots he had on his feet. The old man showed no signs of fatigue; he wasn't even breathing hard from the recent hike.

The mayor thought this panther mumbo jumbo had gone on long enough. The Tuesday Club had two members dead, another one AWOL, someone knew about the club's existence, and he was facing his toughest opponent yet. Listening to these men carry on about a fictitious panther was more than he could take. "Dear Lord, what's happened to us? Don't you see we've got some serious problems, and all you men can do is chitchat like women about Pete the Puma? Do I need to remind you that we've inherited a special gift, and I'm not gonna let you forget it? We need to come together and quit trampling on our father's graves."

It worked. The mayor now had the group's undivided attention. He applauded his leadership skills. As was typical of his behavior, he softened his countenance and his tone, and he brought the meeting to order by asking the question: "Do any of you have any idea where we could find poor Woody?"

The chief deputy gave a run down. "We've been to every bootlegger, every one of his properties, his cabin, the old slut up Stella's Branch, and all his kinfolks' houses."

"You don't reckon he would go in a drunken stupor and tell everything he knows, do you?" the county clerk asked.

The mayor contemplated the clerk's question before answering. "That's crossed my mind, but he's been drinking a long time, and he's never compromised our club before. Why, his daddy was the most loyal member to ever set foot in this club, and I know he raised Woody right."

The judge executive asked, "What about Ruthie Vaughn?"

The mayor turned his venom on the judge just as fast as a rattlesnake would strike. "What about her?"

The judge could feel the heat of the mayor's eyes penetrate him even though the dim glow of the small campfire prevented him from seeing the mayor's face clearly. "You don't think they're going to try and blame you for the murder now, do ya?"

"Murder! Why no one murdered that little girl. My guess is she had all she could take with this election and decided to end it all," the mayor seemed outraged as he spoke. "I really hate a little girl had to die in order to get her granny's attention, but as you know, I've got an election to win, and we need to use this in our favor. We need to get the word out that Ruthie committed suicide because she was tired of her granny spending so much time away from her. By supper time tomorrow every woman in McWhorter will turn their backs on Geneva."

"Don't forget about the autopsy," Joe Matt reminded him.

"Good point. We need to have our banker get us some money so Joe Matt can throw a little money up in Frankfort."

"You always told me that money talks, sir," the chief deputy answered but tried not to laugh. The King of McWhorter was playing a new ballgame, one where he didn't own the ball and make the rules. Joe Matt knew the preliminary results were in and by all indications, the autopsy spelled out homicide. No amount of money was going to help now.

Trying to reassure the mayor, the clerk said, "You do realize you have the election in the bag."

The mayor smiled and gave a fist pump in the air, but it galled him to think he was leaving the outcome of his election in the hands of this greedy bastard. He liked winning the election fair and square. (Although winning fair and square to Jock meant buying votes, having crooked election officers, and having dead citizens vote.)

The club continued working on their strategy for a couple of hours as they drank a few beers. The coroner remained fixated on his panther all night. If the group had paid any attention, they would have also noted that another member of the group was lost deep in his thoughts as well.

CHAPTER 20

The Dream

Friday, April 4, 2008, 2:00 AM

Geneva Vaughn had been overweight as long as she could remember, and now her clothes seemed very loose due to her recent weight loss. After Ruthie's death, Geneva didn't know how to function. She had an enormous hole in her heart that nothing could fill, not even her favorite comfort foods worked their previous charm. She refused to play the "if only" game. If only, I weren't running for mayor, then I would have noticed the change in Ruthie; or if only I had checked her room that night, then maybe I could have gotten to her in time.

Not knowing which way to turn, she picked up her Bible and read and reread it looking for answers. Sometimes she felt her prayers were only going as far as the ceiling then bouncing right back down to earth. Feeling spiritually dead, she didn't know which was worse: the heartbreak of losing Ruthie or the loneliness without feeling the Lord's presence.

All that changed overnight when she finally received a word from the Lord. It was while she was sleeping that she heard the Lord whisper in her ear, "*This kind of spirit can only be removed by praying and fasting.*" She sat up in the middle of her bed and declared a fast.

It was amazing how much better she felt once she started fasting. She feasted on the word of God.

She knew Jock Ledford was behind Ruth Ann's death, but so far, there was no evidence linking him or anybody to Ruth Ann's murder. The word around town was that Ruth Ann committed suicide because she didn't want Geneva to run for mayor. Of course, Geneva could see right through the mayor's handiwork on that one. Anyone who knew Ruth Ann knew she was her mam's biggest supporter. It was going to take more than a rumor for them to be desperate enough to put him back in the office. Besides, she knew something the mayor didn't—she knew the results of the preliminary autopsy. Although it was just preliminary, the findings supported death due to strangulation, not drowning. Even worse, it showed she had been brutally raped.

Desperate for answers, Geneva knew someone had to have them., and it was only a matter of time before God revealed them. Only after she started to fast did the Lord seem to put things in motion for her. It started with a dream.

Geneva had a dream that was as vivid as if she was actually there—a real out of body experience. No, she didn't see herself flying or anything of the sorts, but she could see the scene unfold before her as though she was watching it at the movie theater, only complete with smells and three-dimensional sight. In a t-shirt and skimpy underwear talking on the phone, Geneva saw Ruth Ann's best friend, Gabby McKinley, sitting Indian style on her bed. A clock with large digital numbers in fluorescent green blared that it was 10:34 p.m. The room smelled a lot like Ruthie's room, all sweet with lotions and perfumes. Yellow and orange pillows were heaped up behind her. There was an open magazine in front of Gabby, and as she turned the pages, she would occasionally squeal and say, "No, you did not do it. OMG, I can't believe it!"

"Neeva and Glenn Dale would shit if they knew who you were out with at this time of the night, not to mention—what you've been doing," said Gabby as she threw her head back and laughed.

It was only then when Geneva realized this dream was a gift from God; he was letting her see through a window back in time. It had to be the night of the murder, and the person on the other line with Gabby had to be her Ruth Ann. She tried to scream at Gabby for her to let her talk to her granddaughter. She and Glenn Dale both woke up to her screams.

"Get up and get dressed," she ordered Glenn Dale. "We need to pay a little visit to Ms. Gabby McKinley. She knows who Ruth Ann was with that night," she said as she hopped out of bed and started rummaging through her drawers.

"Neeva, its two o'clock in the morning. Have you lost your mind?"

"Nope, I've found it."

8:30 AM

Thinking about Caroline was painful for Daniel, but his thoughts somehow managed to always turn to her. She'd always said they were the perfect pieces of life's puzzle. As quickly as he thought about Caroline, his thoughts turned back to Tillie Grant. Tillie made him smile. She was so funny, independent, and they had so much in common. She craved physical activity, and he enjoyed running with her. "Hmmm. Perfect puzzle pieces or kindred spirits, which one's the most important?" he wondered out loud.

The vibrating of his cell phone interrupted his thoughts. "Officer Brooks," he said as he opened the phone and placed it to his ear ending his daydream session.

"Danny boy, you into anything right now?" Sheriff Osborne asked.

"Just finishing up with some paperwork. Why? What's up?"

"Can you meet me at Geneva's house? She called and said there was someone that had something they needed to tell us."

"I'll meet you there in thirty minutes,"

9:00 AM

Caroline Ledford's mental state was deteriorating at a rapid pace, and mundane things were difficult for her to perform. She noticed her navy shoes didn't match her black slacks but didn't bother to change before she walked out the door. Her thoughts revolved around Daniel Brooks and Tillie Grant. "Basketball, why hadn't I played basketball with him?" she asked herself when remembering Tillie playing ball with Daniel at the park. As far as she could tell, he wasn't spending the nights with Tillie. His truck was normally parked at his house by midnight each night.

"Too bad he couldn't get a bee sting, or something that would prevent him from being able to have sex," she thought out loud. Then voila, it came to her. "Poison ivy!" She felt the demons she had carefully chained in the pit of her soul break loose and work their way upward as she laughed maniacally. She knew she was losing control, but in a way, it felt so good.

She turned her SUV around and headed toward her daddy's closest farm. Luckily, Caroline and her brothers were immune to poison ivy as far as they could tell. She'd tried to become infected by poison ivy several times before. One of her friends in grade school had used poison ivy to write her boyfriend's initial on her stomach. Caroline was so jealous. Try as she might, no bumps would appear on her. She could lie down in poison ivy. To prove the point to Daniel, she actually laid in a patch of the three-leafed menace completely naked. Just as she predicted, she didn't have a reaction; however, Daniel ended up at the emergency room because he had a reaction from the casual contact with Caroline. Caroline smiled at the thought of a miserable Daniel covered from one end to the other in calamine lotion. "Serves him right!" she spat.

After she'd picked an armful, she headed toward Daniel's house. Revenge was so sweet. It was at this particular time she realized she just might have some of Jock's blood flowing through her veins after all. She turned on the radio and started singing along. Her singing was as off-key as it was loud, but Caroline didn't care. She sang all the way to Daniel's driveway.

Using her key, she let herself in Daniel's house and carefully made her way to his underwear drawer. Daniel's house had the look and feel of a military home. His bed was made, and she would bet his corners were perfect.

Opening his underwear drawer, she removed the three top pairs of underwear. She put the boxer briefs to her nose and inhaled the clean smell of Daniel's washing detergent before she carefully rubbed the inside of them with the ivy. Caroline giggled each time she started on a new pair.

Driving to work, she felt like she was a different person. Actually, she kind of liked her blue heels with her black slacks. Her new motto was, "Don't get mad, get even!" Her thoughts turned from Daniel to her daddy. "Watch out, Jock," she thought as she decided she would never allow him to hurt her or her mommy again. She opened her glove compartment and transferred the small .38, her daddy's sixteenth birthday present, to her purse.

9:15 AM

Sheriff Osborne and Trooper Brooks arrived at the Vaughn's house at the same time. They were both anxious to know what evidence Geneva had discovered. Daniel had been to Geneva's house so many times over the past ten days that he didn't bother going to the front door but, instead, went around to the kitchen door, which was usually left unlatched. Ringing the doorbell to announce his visit, Daniel then pushed the door open as he hollered for Geneva.

"Daniel, that you?" Glenn Dale called from a distance.

The sheriff shouted back, "Daniel and me!"

They met Glenn Dale as they rounded the end of the kitchen. "Come on in, fellers."

They sounded like a herd of horses as they clicked their way down the hardwood hallway and followed Glenn Dale into Ruth Ann's room. There they found a distressed Gabby McKinley lying on the carpet with her head in Geneva's lap. Gabby's mother was sitting on the floor with her back next to the wall. Not only were her eyes red, but her whole body was shaking. Her cigarette was vibrating in her mouth as she inhaled the carcinogens.

Gabby had tightly clutched in her arms a pillow from Ruth Ann's bed. Her long red hair cascaded over Geneva's lap, and Gabby would frequently place the pillow to her nose and take a deep breath. Daniel wasn't sure if she was trying to get away from her mother's smoke or if it was in an effort to obtain the memory of Ruth Ann's scent.

Ever the observant one, Daniel noticed Geneva's face was not as full, and she looked more at peace than he'd seen her in a while. Glenn Dale was sitting on the bed, and although his face was gaunt, he seemed calmer as well. Clearing her throat, Geneva broke the silence and began to speak. "The Lord revealed to me that my little Gabby here had been keeping a secret. Me and Glenn Dale paid her a visit early this morning, and she told me she didn't know what I was talking about. After we left, she must have had some kind of breakdown and had to come and tell us the truth." Geneva quit talking and looked lovingly at the teenager. The young girl put her head in the pillow and sobbed. Geneva hugged her tighter and said, "It's all right, baby girl, it's all right."

When Gabby didn't start to speak right away, Gabby's mother took up the slack. "Gabriella hasn't been right since Ruthie turned up missing. She's been sleeping with me ever since the uh…accident. I thought it would get better, but…uh…it's only gotten worse. When Geneva and Glenn Dale came knocking on the door this morning, I thought Gabby was going to come out of her skin. She swore to them she had no idea who Ruth Ann was with that night. It was only after they left this morning that she had a complete breakdown, and the only way I could get her to calm down was to bring her to Neeva." She stopped talking long enough to take a long draw from her cigarette. She held the smoke in her lungs, and as she started talking again, the smoke exited her lungs with each syllable. "Now go ahead, baby girl. Go ahead and tell them everything."

"ShesbeenseeingJenningsLedford!" Gabby managed to blurt out; her words blended as she tried to say them all in one breath.

"Whoa, slow down, darling," The sheriff softly said.

"Jennings Ledford is the best-looking thing in McWhorter, and Ruth Ann was in love with him from the time she talked to him at the public forum. He understood what it was like to have a parent running for election. They just hit it off from that day. He's been calling her and was so sweet to her. She's been sneaking out and meeting him for over a week before she—" Gabby stopped short, because she couldn't bring herself to say her friend was dead.

Other than the cigarette smoke, the air had now been cleared, and all was silent. Daniel used this lull in the conversation to think. He knew Jennings wasn't perfect. He was a lover, not a killer, but then again, he was Jock's son.

Gabby made eye contact with the tall officer. Daniel's eyes seemed to see straight through her. They were the only truth serum she needed before words started spewing from her mouth uncontrollably. "I just can't believe Jennings would hurt her. They were going to marry and everything!" She clamped her hand over her mouth before she said more.

"Good Lord! How old is Jennings Ledford? He's gotta be ten years her senior," the sheriff enlightened the group.

"Ten years don't mean nothing when you're in love," Gabby said.

Daniel had to wrap his mind around this. "Did you ever see Ruth Ann with Jennings?"

"Oh, no. She made me swear on my life I would never tell a soul about it. She said no one would understand because of the election and all."

"Is that the reason you didn't tell anyone after she died because you didn't want to break your promise?" Daniel asked.

Gabby's mom interrupted. "Lord, honey, this child's been plum scared to death," she said as she handed the officer the note that had been left on Gabby's car shortly after Ruth Ann's body was found.

Daniel read the note that had been printed in bold handwriting with a red marker.

You'll be next if you tell a soul!

Reading this, Daniel could understand why she would be scared. He took hold of one of her small hands and promised, "I'm sure you've been very scared. I would've been scared too, but you're doing the right thing. I promise we're not going to let anyone hurt you. We're going to take very good care of you."

Gabby spoke her mind, "I know that it wasn't Jennings who did it. It had to be someone else. You see, she called me right after he left and told me all about it." Peeking out the corner of her eye at Geneva, she made sure her talking about "it" didn't upset her. She continued when she realized Geneva seemed okay. "They had been meeting at some lake cabin."

Daniel had carnal knowledge of this lake cabin because he and Caroline had used it as a rendezvous point. "Caroline! Dear Lord, what will this news do to Caroline?" he thought.

"Ruth called me, and she was still in seventh heaven about their...uh...you know, experience. I know he was gone, or else she would have never risked calling me. He was very serious about her keeping their relationship a secret. She called me after she saw him drive away. She was all excited and said Jennings had told her he was in love with her and wanted her to be the mother of his babies. She wanted to tell me more, but her battery was about to go dead. She was horrible about forgetting to recharge her phone."

She showed them her text messages from Ruth Ann. There it was in black and white, Jennings Ledford's name, typed by the dead girl's own fingers. It didn't look good for Jennings. Daniel knew Jock wouldn't be able to easily fix this problem for his baby boy.

Daniel put in a call to his captain requesting around-the-clock protection for Gabby. He was dreading making his next call.

Geneva pronounced, "God has allowed things to go on in McWhorter long enough. He won't allow his name or his church to become a mockery."

CHAPTER 21

JHJF—I Think

Friday, April 4, 2008, 10:30 AM

Jon realized how very little he knew about his employee, Dewey Lewis. It was almost like Dewey showed up one day, and they accepted him without question. It was probably because no one wanted to challenge Albert Dean. They knew Albert Dean would've invited the devil in himself if he could teach him how to make crystal meth. As soon as Albert Dean died, they let Dewey run dope for them since they weren't interested in making meth.

Jon paid a visit to his rent house occupied by Ms. Tillery. Marveling at the quaint little house with the picket fence, he smiled thinking someone involved in illegal activity lived in the little white house with black shutters. A pot of pansies adorned the front porch near the white porch swing.

Thumbing through his collection of keys, he finally found the key to Mary Jane's house. He and Jennings had twenty or more houses they bought cheap and fixed up. They had a nice little legitimate rental business that supplemented their drug business. Come to think about it, he sincerely doubted Mary Jane ever paid rent on this house. Of course, Jennings probably took it out in trade. With that thought, a nauseating feeling came over him as he wondered if Dewey was the jealous type. "What if he was trying to set Jennings up because he was jealous over Mary Jane?"

Jon gave one quick warning knock before he entered. The house was every bit as neat on the inside as it was outside. No one was stirring, so he made sure to make plenty noise as he walked down the hall. He knocked before opening the door to Mary

Jane's bedroom. Mary Jane sat straight up in bed and attempted to cover her breasts. He noticed how her long blond hair only served to accent her naked chest. Remembering the business at hand, he forced himself to look elsewhere. Dewey didn't startle until Mary Jane elbowed him. Rubbing the sleep from his eyes, Dewey slowly rose and just as slowly stated, "Well, hello, brother Jon. You come here to play with us this morning. My Mary Jane here likes them. Now, what's that fancy word for them three ways you keep talking about, mango-twal or something like that?"

"Sorry, I'm not a group sex kind of guy," explained Jon. "Actually, I'm here to talk with you."

"Have I done something wrong?" Dewey questioned while pulling up his britches. At the doorway, both men turned in time to catch a glimpse of Mary Jane as she removed the covers from her naked body, stood, and stretched in a provocative pose. "Damn, ain't I the luckiest sumbitch in Kentucky!" exclaimed Dewey with a big lopsided grin on his face.

Jon couldn't argue with that. After they settled at the kitchen table, Jon spoke about his concern. "About the other night when you got cold feet and called Jennings, I was wondering why you didn't call me instead of him."

Dewey scratched his head. "What're you talking about? Cold feet about what?"

"Cold feet about driving through Georgia fully loaded. Remember, you called my brother Jennings the other night?"

"I ain't never called Jennings in the day or the night. Ain't sure I even have his number," declared Dewey. "You all right?" he said when he noticed the color of Jon's face.

"I'm not so sure," Jon stated while he tried to figure out who was lying to him, Dewey or Jennings.

11:30 AM

Caroline grabbed the phone, looked at the caller identification, and a smile automatically formed on her mouth followed by a look of terror. Had Daniel already discovered she'd broken into his house? Her heart came up in her throat while she tried to find the little button on her phone—the only current obstacle standing in her way of talking to Daniel. Not able to think clearly, she pushed buttons until finally pressing the right one. "Hello," she managed in her most professional voice.

"Hello, yourself," he chirped then followed with a more solemn, "You doing okay?"

A wave of relief flowed through her body. She knew he wouldn't have been chipper had he discovered her crime. "I'm okay," she lied. She had to be smart. Did she let him make the first move, or did she confess her love for him?

Before she had time to choose the right words, Daniel explained the reason for the call. "Listen, Caroline, I'm sorry to be the one to tell you, but your little brother is in a big heap of trouble."

"What?" This was the only word she could summon. No apologies or confessions of undying love? Was this a professional call? Anger bubbled to the surface. She'd give him professional! "What has Jennings done now?" She asked, her voice void of any emotion.

"What if I tell you Jennings was with Ruth Ann Vaughn on the night of her murder?"

Caroline dropped the phone. The phone landed in the floor; the battery went one way, and the phone went the other way. "Damn!" she exclaimed as she pulled her desk phone closer to her and left the mechanical carnage on the floor.

With shaking hands, she managed to dial Daniel's number using her desk phone. As soon as she heard him pick up, she started speaking, "Daniel, please tell me today is April Fool's Day, and this is a sick joke. You know Jennings could never hurt a girl."

"I wish I could, babe, but it's serious. You need to get to Jennings fast, and make sure he cooperates. He needs to come in for questioning."

"You know he didn't hurt that little girl, don't you? You know he couldn't or wouldn't have hurt her! You know him too!"

"It doesn't matter what we think. I'm worried someone's working hard to make sure we think it's him."

"I'll call him now."

"Caroline?"

"Yes."

"I miss you."

"Me too. I don't think I can do this."

11:45 AM

Ordinarily, Caroline would have called her daddy before she made a move, but those days were over. She knew her daddy had to be behind Jennings dating the little Vaughn girl in the first place. It didn't take rocket science to figure Jock's connection and motive. Jock probably thought if the girl turned up pregnant then Geneva would forfeit the election.

Suddenly, a ball of fury rose up in Caroline's center that made her see red. Curling up her fingers into a ball, she pounded her mahogany desk not caring about her perfectly manicured French tips. Her daddy had crossed the line this time! She was not going to sit back and let Jennings pay for it. She regained her composure before she called her brother, Jon.

"Hey, Sis," he answered the phone knowing it was Caroline on the other end.

"Why didn't you tell me Jennings was screwing the little Vaughn girl?" she screamed into the phone. "Was it because daddy didn't want anyone to know?"

"Lordy mercy, I didn't think you would be interested in knowing about our little brother's love life. How much time you have? Because it'll take me a long time, actually, it may blow your mind to know how many of your friends and even the mothers of your friends Jennings has screwed."

"You know what I mean, you asshole. I just got a call from the police wanting me to bring him in for questioning. You need to get him, and meet me at the State Police Post in an hour. I believe he's in big trouble."

Jon asked, "Do you think Jennings could have killed her?"

After a long pause, she finally said, "Maybe, if daddy told him to."

Jon was afraid she would say that.

1:30 PM

Wasting no time, the entire Ledford clan met in the parking lot of the police post. Immediately, Jock started giving his crew his marching orders. Noticing Caroline was acting strangely, he put his arm around her back. "It'll be okay, just listen to your daddy. Have I ever let you down yet?"

Repulsed by his touch, Caroline slipped from his grasp and said as she put distance between them, "Surely, you don't expect me to answer that, do you?"

Jon and Jennings eased between the two. They both knew what their daddy was capable of doing to their sweet sister for offering those defiant words; they felt the need to protect her.

"Why, you little ungrateful whore!" Jock hissed then whispered so only she could hear, "You want me to break your mommy's heart and tell her all about our little office chats?"

Caroline grabbed for her purse thinking she would rather be in jail than spend one more day having to look at her despicable daddy.

Having an idea what was in her purse, Jennings grabbed it away from her, "Here ya go, Sissy, let me help you with your pocketbook."

Visibly shaken, Jock felt that not only was he losing control of his Tuesday Club but was also losing control of his own family. Realizing he was in the parking lot of the State Police Post, he knew he couldn't lash out. He had to use a different tactic.

"Look at me, Jennings," Caroline said as she grabbed him by his shoulders. "Tell me exactly about your involvement with Ruth Ann."

Jennings told her the same story he'd told Jon and Jock earlier.

Jon interrupted, "Are you certain it was Dewey Lewis who called you that night?"

"Yep, I'm sure, all right. He called me, and then I met him at the garage. Come to think of it, he was acting kind of weird. Here, if you don't believe me look at my phone. See, here's the number he called me from." Scrolling down his phone records, he handed the phone to his brother when he found the right phone number. Jon proceeded to call the number and got a recorded voice about reaching a disconnected phone number.

Jon wrote the number down and wanted to believe his little brother, but knowing what Dewey had told him earlier, he knew it didn't look good. Dewey didn't have a reason to lie. On the other hand, Jennings could lie with the best of them. Only problem with that, Jennings could never lie to him.

"Listen, son, just tell the truth. Remember what the good book says, 'the truth will set you free,'" Jock advised his youngest son while the others just looked at him in disbelief.

Jock observed the group. They may be mad at him right now, but he knew they came from his seed, and he had made them what they were today regardless of how ungrateful they were acting at this very moment. They were his greatest creations, even better than the downtown renovations. He knew in the end they would understand him better than anyone and would side with him— after all it was in their blood, and blood was thicker than water.

Noticing the Ledfords in the parking lot, Daniel thought they looked like they were having some kind of party. He stuck his head out the door and yelled, "Everything all right?"

Jennings answered, "Hey, Dan, you're right on time. Daddy's getting ready to preach."

The group headed through the doors and followed Daniel into the area reserved for questioning. Two detectives were waiting for Jennings. "Sorry, guys, but only Jennings and his attorney can be in the room while we question him," the older detective said.

While in the questioning room, Jennings stuck to his same story. Against Caroline's objections, he even admitted to having sex with the minor. He knew it was only a matter of time before they had the proof anyway. His only variation in his storytelling involved Dewey Lewis. Not being able to explain in full detail about their drug running business, he told the detectives Dewey had called him with a work crisis.

Daniel felt a little better about the situation since Jennings' story matched the little McKinley girl's story to the "T." In theory, Daniel knew Jennings could have left the cabin then doubled back to commit the crime. Somehow, he didn't think so, but he was determined to find out. Best he could tell Dewey Lewis had Jennings' life in his hands. He needed to get to Dewey fast.

Grabbing Caroline by the hand, Daniel put it up to his lips and gently kissed it. Her hand was so soft, and she smelled so incredibly wonderful.

Caroline thought her heart was going to stop. She didn't want this moment to end, but it ended anyway as Daniel walked away from her for the second time. Her heart ached, and her anger resurfaced. Caroline number three began to count the number of hours before Daniel would be showering and putting on his clean underwear.

3:30 PM

Mary Jane Tillery was frightened when she saw the gray police cruiser sitting in front of her house. "Dewey, please tell me you've not been cooking meth in the outbuilding again?"

"I told you I gave that up after Albert Dean died. You've completely reformed me," he said before he wrapped his arms around his girlfriend.

The pair was interrupted by the sound of the knock on the door. Daniel and Joe Matt stood on the porch waiting for someone to answer. Daniel observed a very inviting home with a porch swing that would be perfect for late evening beer drinking. "The only thing missing with this front porch is a cold glass of sweet tea or a six pack of beer," Daniel told his fellow officer.

Before Joe Matt could say anything, the door leading from the house to the porch opened. Mary Jane gave the boys her most inviting smiles. Joe Matt was prepared to see Mary Jane, but from the looks of Daniel, it was definitely a jaw dropping experience as Daniel personally experienced one of the miracles of McWhorter. Having not been around for a while, Daniel had no idea little Mary Jane Tillery grew up to be an anatomically correct version of Malibu Barbie.

Inside the small house, an overgrown boy was waiting in a recliner in the living room. Dewey Lewis had just turned twenty, a good six years younger than Mary Jane.

Mary Jane, ever the hostess, was happy to get the boys something to drink. She explained, "Mountain Dew's all Dewey will drink besides Budweisers. I have to limit his Buds until dark, or he would stay drunk all the time," she said as she headed toward the kitchen.

It was Dewey's turn at hospitality. "Boys, now tell me how would you like to come home to that every evening? I don't care if I ever drink another Bud as long as I can tap that every day," Dewey bragged as soon as Mary Jane left the room.

Daniel wanted to remain professional, but he understood where this man was coming from. What he couldn't understand was why Mary Jane would settle for this bozo. Dewey had a baby face, but a man's body. He would have passed for a teenager in the right setting. He stood a little over six feet tall, had dirty blond hair, was unshaven, and, in Daniel's opinion, was very ordinary looking. On the other hand, Mary Jane was the most beautiful woman he'd ever seen.

"Fellers, what can I do for you?" Dewey asked.

Getting right to the point, Joe Matt stated, "We need to understand where you were at around eleven p.m. on March 26th."

"Hell, I don't even know what night was the 26th? I've slept a little since then."

Daniel answered, "It was a Wednesday."

"Let's see. I believe if I'm not mistaken, that was the night me and Mary Jane went on a double date with her sister and her boyfriend. We ate at the hot dog stand then went to the drive-in movie place over in Bacon Creek to watch that movie. Now, what was the name of that movie?" He studied hard trying to recollect the name of the movie before calling out to Mary Jane for help. "Honey, come here a minute!"

The men heard a commotion in the room next door before Mary Jane reappeared.

"Honey, what was that movie we saw with your sister? You remember? It was the one with that movie star named Matthew that you like so good."

"Fool's Gold," she answered without hesitation.

"Isn't she the smartest thing? Damn, if she's ain't only purty, she's smart too. Come here, baby, and give me a kiss for that one."

Mary Jane walked over and bent down where the officers had no trouble reading the large PINK written on the back of her sweatpants. She gave Dewey a kiss that left both police officers a little weak in the knees.

After they were through with their smooching, Dewey said, "Mary Jane, what night did we go to the movies?"

"It was Wednesday. I've still got the ticket. It was the first time we did it at a drive-in, so I kept the stub. You want me to go get it?" Without waiting for an answer, she rounded the corner.

"How well do you know Jennings Ledford?" Daniel asked Dewey.

Dewey took his time before he answered Daniel's question. "Well, he's one of my bosses, but Mary Jane knows him a lot better than I do. You see, he's nice enough to let my Mary Jane live in this house rent-free. My cousin, Albert Dean Smith, had me doing odd jobs for him, and after he died, then I started working for the Ledfords." He was careful to leave out anything about the drug business.

"Do you remember if you spoke with Jennings on Wednesday?"

"Nope, I didn't have no reason to talk with him."

"Do you have a cell phone?" Daniel asked.

"Yep, you need to see it?" he asked as he reached in his pocket to retrieve it.

Daniel wrote down his cell phone number, his home number, and Mary Jane's phone number as Dewey called the numbers out loud in a slow, deliberate tempo.

"Have you ever used 545-9897?" asked Daniel.

"Nope." Dewey didn't hesitate before answering.

"Do you know anyone that has a phone with this number?"

Shaking his head, he said once again, "Nope."

Daniel didn't like the way this interview was going. It wasn't going well for Jennings—that was for sure. Why would Jennings lie about Dewey calling him? Then, on the other hand, why would this couple lie? He had Mary Jane's tickets in his hand, and it matched their story.

Finished with their initial questioning, the officers thanked the couple and headed toward the front door. As soon as they were out the door, they heard Mary Jane holler, "Dewey, talking with good-looking cops makes me want to play with handcuffs!"

Hearing the sounds of footsteps running in the direction of her voice, they heard him calling to her, "Don't start without me. You promise not to hide the key like you did last time?"

Laughing at the couple's antics, Daniel said when they were safely out of earshot, "Only in McWhorter would the redneck hook up with the gorgeous nympho."

"Gotta love Rockford County!" Joe Matt agreed as he stepped into the passenger side of the cruiser. On a more serious note, Joe Matt added, "I think your boy's in big trouble."

"Don't you find it strange Jock didn't buy Dewey's silence?" Daniel asked.

The chief deputy countered, "Wasn't it convenient they still had their tickets?"

"Too convenient. But damn! I believe if I did it at the movie with her, then I'd want to hang on to my ticket as a memento too. By the way, what does her sister look like?"

"You're not interested in the Tillery sisters are you, Danny boy? Rumor has it, you now have two women at your beck and call, and here you're talking about adding a third. You trying to gain a monopoly on the McWhorter women or something?"

Daniel didn't respond verbally, but he let his middle finger do the talking. The men rode the rest of the way to the sheriff's office in silence. Both men were caught up in their own thoughts and fantasies.

CHAPTER 22

The Hunter and the Avenger

Friday, April 4, 2008, 10:30 PM

The night was clear, but the native Kentuckian could feel rain in the air. This same gut feeling also told him tonight was the night the old coroner would choose to hunt the elusive panther. He hoped his instincts were right in both instances; they needed rain, and he needed to avenge innocent blood. The avenger and his accomplice had been planning this night ever since the club's last meeting, and just as the avenger knew rain would be forthcoming, he also knew that Jimmy Sizemore would panther hunt tonight.

The avenger wasn't the only one whose body told him tonight was the night for a panther sighting; Jimmy Sizemore felt his heart beating a tad faster all day. Killing a panther would mean more than a trophy to the old man; it would somehow vindicate his granddaddy. His granddaddy took him on his first hunt and instilled the love of the kill in him. It was this same granddaddy who had actually seen a Kentucky "painter" as he called it in his native mountain language. Mimicking the sound of a panther's death screech, he would begin to tell about the night he ran for his life.

Jimmy, an impressionable youngster, latched onto every word that came from the old man's mouth. Others felt the old man was a brick shy of a full load—the butt of a joke. Not Jimmy. He just knew his granddaddy was telling the truth about his encounter with the panther. He thought, "Yes, I'll kill the black panther, and the joke will be on the town." The coroner smiled a real smile before he morphed, body and soul, into a dangerous hunter.

———◦◦◦———

The borrowed, large, black Labrador and Rottweiler mix dog was more apt to lick someone to death than to hurt him. Although in the dark, the avenger felt the dog could pass for a large dangerous predator. Anxiously awaiting the signal, the avenger was in position holding the leashed and muzzled dog with a death grip. The normally docile canine sensed danger and lurched at every noise. There was no holding the dog back when he heard the eerie, high-pitched scream coming from the cliff's edge. This was his accomplice's signal that it was show time.

———◦◦◦———

The sound Jimmy heard was a cross between a woman giving birth, and the sound his grandmammy used to make when the spirit moved her during a revival service. Trembling, the coroner went into action as the sound resonated deep in his soul and pulled at him to follow. Sniffing the air like a feral animal, his heightened senses could smell blood. He liked to think of himself as the ultimate predator. There it was again. "Sounds like it's up on Turkey Ridge," he thought to himself. Knowing that timing was critical, the coroner reacted as fast as his body would allow him. That panther was fast. He would make his kill and, then, be out of the area like lightning. Thankful for the moon and stars to guide him, he headed toward the sound. His precious baby, Winnie——his .300 Win. Mag. Rifle—was secured in his shoulder sling.

Hearing a cow bawling in the distance, he stopped and listened again trying to discern which direction to take. He narrowed his eyes while he tried to get in the head of the animal. He'd spent the last week studying the habits of this particular feline and knew that after the cat got his fill, he would head to the safety of the cliffs.

The cat screamed again. Impossible! The noise was now behind him. Earlier, he was certain the cat's position was in front of him. Then the cat in front of him answered with another loud cry. "I be damned! There's two of 'em!" he whispered to himself. Two black panthers—he didn't know whether to be excited or scared at the prospect of having two targets.

The cat in front of him sounded again as the two animals communicated back and forth with each other. Continuing to trudge straight ahead, Jimmy knew the cliffs would be the obvious choice. The panthers probably had a den with cubs located snugly in the cliff's rocky hiding place, and the springtime would be the right time for birthing. He climbed through the rugged forest terrain and headed toward his prize.

The avenger and the accomplice were surprised by the second panther sounds, but played along with what was obviously the real McCoy. The accomplice would play the predator sound that echoed loudly through the battery-powered sound system near the cliff's edge. Then another scream would come from the pasture down below. Not only did they have the black dog masquerading as a panther, but they were about to see a real live one as well.

The coroner was light-headed by his fast ascent up the mountain, and his mouth felt like cotton. Hearing the sound of a low throaty growl to the left of the ridgeline, he came to a complete halt as he tried to survey the landscape for the owner of the growl. He knew he didn't want his back toward the cliff's edge. This could be treacherous. One wrong step could cause him to free-fall a football field length to the rocky bottom.

"Do panthers growl?" he asked himself when hearing the growl again to his left. The growl sounded more canine than cat. He heard more noise to his right, then a tiger-like roar from the same direction. "Now, that sounded more like it." He looked from left to right.

Bringing his gun up to firing position, he readied for the perfect shot. Out of his peripheral vision, he saw the shadow of a huge animal to his left and could hear the growls again. He turned his gun toward the sound to the left, then, back to his right when he saw greenish-yellow eyes glaring at him in the dark. The eyes looked to be about twenty feet from him and closing fast. Changing his rifle's direction, he took aim at the animal gaining on him from his right. He pulled the trigger only to hear a click, and the cat kept coming. Immediately, he grabbed the bolt to recharge the weapon only to hear the firing pin not hit its mark again.

The coroner realized something was terribly wrong; Winnie had never let him down in the past. The panther was closing the gap between them and was almost on top of him. Nowhere to go but down, he stood his ground.

The avenger was holding the leash of his muzzled animal with all his might and watching in the moonlight as a large black cat was closing in on the coroner. Having a sudden feeling of remorse for removing the gun's firing pin, he thought about letting the dog loose but changed his mind when he remembered the many wrongdoings that Jimmy had helped the Ledfords cover up over the years. This was out of his hands now. He was not the only avenger. The Almighty was the Great Avenger, and it appeared he was giving him confirmation that he was doing the right thing. One hand held onto his weapon, the other hand held onto the dog's harness with a death grip.

The coroner was trapped. He had no place to go. The large cat was five then four then three feet from the hunter. The hunter had become the hunted. As he looked death in its greenish-yellow eyes, a splash of calm came over him as he realized his destiny. Death whispered in his ear, and he welcomed it. The black panther symbolized death to the Choctaw, and it was only fitting it would usher him to his just reward. The panther pounced. The old man fended him off with his gun as the two predators—one man, the other beast—fell the three hundred feet to their deaths, both fighting each other on their descent to the rocky ground below.

The avenger and accomplice marveled at the old man's tenacity. They moved swiftly as they dismantled their sound system and let the dog guide them to safety off Turkey Ridge in the dark of the night.

CHAPTER 23

Saturday Morning in McWhorter

Saturday, April 5, 2008, 8:00 AM

The group agreed to get an early start and arrived at the firing range in two separate vehicles. The Kentucky sun was just peeping over the mountain, and the horizon had a sepia dreamy look to it. Whipping around like a feisty dominatrix, the early April wind had a moist nip to it. The firing range was a typical outdoor range with concrete slabs poured at different shooting increments, the longest at twenty-five yards. The eight six-foot wooden target frames were waiting for the paper targets to be inserted and were inviting the trio to unleash their inhibitions safely into the mounds of dirt at the end of the line. This range had been built on what looked like an old strip mine with large high walls exposing the inner workings of the earth with various veins of dirt and rocks.

Daniel stapled the paper targets into three of the wooden frames at the end of the rows, and Tillie couldn't help but admire him from a distance. For whatever reason, Daniel knew her eyes were on him so he put on a show as he stretched and bent.

Feeling Trevor's eyes on her, she realized she was busted. Trevor caught her ogling Trooper Brooks's muscular backside as he stretched to staple the silhouettes into place. Embarrassed, she looked away and made herself busy. She made sure all four of her magazine clips were full with the forty-caliber rounds.

Feeling especially playful this morning, Daniel gave Tillie a short peck of a kiss on her lips while at the same time, he very competently disarmed her. He then discharged her weapon first into the left side of her wooden frame seventy-five feet away and then again straight into the heart of the target without ever taking his eyes off Tillie.

"I believe your gun shoots slightly to the right. Here, you try it," he said as he handed the gun to Trevor for him to shoot in confirmation.

Trevor traded weapons with Daniel and proceeded to unload Tillie's weapon three times directly into center mass. "Doesn't look like there's a problem to me." Trevor smugly said as he gave the gun back to his sister.

"Mind if I try yours?" Daniel asked Trevor.

"Knock yourself out," Trevor replied. The men exchanged weaponry and both stepped into an empty firing lane and began firing their competitor's duty weapons.

Again, Daniel's first round went awry, but this time it went high and lodged into the top of the wooden frame in the same lane he had fired Tillie's weapon. The next two rounds followed Trevor's shot into the heart of the paper target. "I'm thinking about getting me either a Ruger .380 or a Sig but can't make up my mind. Think I can try your little Ruger, Tillie?" Daniel asked.

"Sure. Let me go to the car and get it." She ran to her granny's car to get her personal weapon. Deciding they may need more ammunition, she popped the trunk to get another box of shells. Hearing the tail end of the boy's conversation about the pros and cons of the Ruger, Tillie came back from the car carrying a gun in each hand. "Trev, when did you get this little Smith and Wesson? I don't remember seeing it," she asked.

Trevor casually explained, "Oh, that gun. It's a gun that Julia and I found at Granny's house. I wanted to check it out."

Daniel grabbed both guns from Tillie, and before Trevor could protest, he shot the Smith and Wesson in the tree to the left of the range.

"Sorry, couldn't resist," he said as he handed the Smith and Wesson back to Trevor. He then began to shoot Tillie's Ruger into the target in lane three. "I really like the feel of this little Ruger," he said after firing three times into the target's sweet spot.

The playful banter was gone as the three professionals secured their earmuffs and began firing their duty weapons, starting first at the twenty-five yard mark, then, easing their way to the fifteen, and finally to the ten-yard mark. The sounding of the discharge and the *ping ping* sound of the bullets slamming into the mounds of dirt were all that could be heard for the next hour. There was no clear winner as the centers of the paper targets had large gaping holes staring back at them, clearly indicating the expertise of the group.

Yep, Tillie thought, *he has passed all my tests. He may be the one.*

Daniel took his time while walking to the targets to remove the paper from the forms at the end of their shooting session. Tillie followed Trevor to their granny's car to remove her backpack for their outing. Daniel carefully used his knife to dislodge the two bullets he had purposely fired into the frame. Careful to keep the two bullets separated, he placed each in a separate plastic evidence bag. He would come back later for the bullet in the tree. He planned to send the bullets to his buddy at the lab for ballistic comparisons with the bullet that was found in a tree near Albert Dean's dead body. He couldn't take any chances.

9:00 AM

Deep in thought, Eleanor stared at the wall in front of her. She was concerned for both Caroline and Jennings; she knew Jock would make Caroline pay the price of his retribution for her acts of disrespect. Jennings. Something wasn't right at all. She asked herself, "Why isn't Jock trying to help our youngest son?" He was acting all helpless and distraught. She knew better; he had a plan. The loud ringing of the kitchen telephone brought Eleanor out of her trance and back to reality; however, her body was unable to respond in like time to her brain's commands, and as a result, the answering machine beat her to the draw. Hearing Jock's footsteps, Eleanor knew she was in trouble when he entered the room just in time to hear the click of the recording device. Recognizing the voice of their attorney, Roy Allen Jones, Eleanor cringed.

"Jock, you're never going to believe this. They found Jimmy's dead body lying next to a two hundred pound black panther this morning. Call me when you get this message." Another click signaled the message was over.

A pasty-faced Jock stumbled toward the kitchen table trying for the safety of a chair before his knees gave way. "I'll be damned!" was all he could muster as Eleanor brought him his morning coffee. He wasn't sure if he was more amazed by the fact there really were panthers in these parts or troubled by the fact his club members were dropping like flies. Including Jimmy, he was now down four members if he counted Woody.

Eleanor knew better than to comment. It only took a few hard slaps across her face for her to learn when to speak to Jock and when to keep silent. Now was not the time for her to comment about the news. Acting as though she heard nothing about Jimmy Sizemore or a panther, she placed her husband's bowl of oatmeal and toast in front of him.

When Jock didn't immediately begin to eat, only stared at her, she realized her mistake. She had forgotten the strawberry preserves. She ever so painstakingly began spreading the preserves over the toast so that no white was showing. Jock ate in silence.

10:00 AM

On a beautiful Saturday morning and in the safety of their garage office, Jennings, Jon, and Caroline discussed Jennings' plight. Jon reluctantly recounted his visit with Dewey Lewis.

"That sorry lying sumbitch! I'm gonna beat the truth right out of him!" Jennings fist met the metal of the garage wall with a loud thunderous boom. "I swear it was Dewey Lewis who called me, and as God is my witness, I left the cabin and met the lying sumbitch right here at this office. We even drank a few beers. I bet I can even find the damn bottle he drank out of. I swear to you he was sitting right there in that chair where Caroline's sitting, wearing that dumb ole orange hat with the 'T' on it he always wears. You've got to believe me!"

"Do you think he's the jealous sort?" Jon asked his brother.

"Jealous about what?" Jennings was clearly confused.

Sighing in disgust, Jon spelled it out for his brother. "Are you, or are you not, still banging that Tillery girl? You know, Dewey's so-called girlfriend?"

"Well, I'll be damned! Is that what you're worried about? Why, Dewey doesn't have a jealous bone in his body. He likes watching just as much as he likes participating," Jennings grinned at Caroline when she wrinkled up her nose in distaste.

Jon explained, "According to Daddy, Dewey gave this same statement to Joe Matt and Daniel, too. He has a pretty airtight alibi. Mary Jane even produced the ticket stubs showing they were both at the drive-in together on that particular night. It's too late for us to throw any money their way. They can't change their story now since Daniel's involved. You know how Daniel is."

"No way! I'm screwed!" Jennings shook his head. "What's Daddy saying?"

"Not a word. He just shakes his head like he doesn't have a clue what to do."

"Bullshit! I'd like to see the day Daddy doesn't have a clue what to do!" screamed Caroline. "Jennings, I want you to think very hard about who knew you would be with Ruth Ann on that particular night?"

"I'm not stupid. The only person besides Daddy who knew about Ruth Ann was Jon."

"I beg to differ about your stupidity. Please tell me how Daddy convinced a grown man to commit statutory rape on the minor granddaughter of his opponent." She paused, but before he could answer, she added, "You do realize even if we can prove you're innocent of murder, you confessed to having sex with a minor, which would be a class C felony in itself."

"Ahh, Sis, I had to tell 'em. You know it was only a matter of time before that autopsy would've come back with the DNA. As for the idea, let's just say Daddy gave me the idea, but it didn't take too much convincing after I saw her. Sissy, I don't claim to be perfect by no means, but I have a hard time passing up these little sixteen-year-old girls. These young girls ain't like they used to be. Why most of them shave their cooters by the time they're in eight—" Jennings stopped as he dodged the pen Caroline hurled at his head.

Choosing to ignore Jennings' comments, she instead directed her questions to Jon. "Jon, did you let it slip to anyone? Did you know he was going to be at the cabin?"

"I knew he was going there, but I didn't tell anybody."

"Can you think of anyone at work you would've told?" she asked Jennings.

"Like I've already told you, I didn't tell a soul 'cept Daddy and Jon."

Caroline reasoned, "Let's think about this logically. As far as we know, Ruth Ann's death hasn't been ruled a homicide yet. Before we overreact, we need to find out what the autopsy report states."

"She was murdered as sure as I'm sitting here. I know she wouldn't have killed herself. She was too happy when I left her. Her plan was to get her clothes on and leave so she could sneak back in the house before Geneva ever knew she was gone." Jennings stopped in the middle of his thought. "Where's her car? Was it still at the cabin?"

"Good question," Jon and Caroline said in unison.

"We've got some homework to do. We need to get a tail on Dewey Lewis and Ms. Mary Jane Tillery. We need to understand why they're lying. We need to find out everything we can about this mysterious Dewey Lewis. Why did he come to McWhorter? But most of all, we need to find out why our precious Daddy is suddenly quoting scripture, preaching, and now clueless at a time when his son's freedom's at stake. Something sounds fishy to me." She wouldn't utter this heresy to anyone but her brothers. "Let's meet back here on Monday morning."

CHAPTER 24

Curvy Roads

Saturday, April 5, 2008, 10:00 AM

"Breathe in, breathe out, show no fear, show no weakness, breathe in, and breathe out," Tillie repeated in her mind. The same ritual that helped Tillie get through the Quantico training was now helping her car sickness. She hated being wimpy.

Daniel chuckled when finally looking at his pale passenger. "You're looking a little green around your gizzard."

"I'm okay," she lied through her teeth.

"Sorry, I'll slow down. I'm just excited for you to see this place."

"Do you think you can at least tell me where we're going?"

"Do you like authentic Italian pizza?"

"You know I love pizza, but at this moment, it's best for me not to think about food."

"What about snakes?"

"Pizza and snakes! I get it. You're luring me with the pizza to take me somewhere to kill me. You're a cruel guy, Daniel Brooks—" Stifling her last words as she felt the rumblings in her stomach, she clamped her mouth shut.

Daniel was thoroughly enjoying seeing this tough little FBI turning a nice shade of chartreuse. Daniel braked hard and pulled off on the side of the road into an empty church parking lot. After she appeared to recover, he grabbed his pale little friend and kissed her until she had some color in her face. "You drive," he ordered knowing that it should cure her carsickness.

It seemed to work. She drove the curvy roads, and all seemed well with her. Eventually, the curvy back roads opened up to a four-lane highway as it led the couple to the Natural Bridge State Park. The small town of Slade with its Red River Gorge became Daniel's weekend refuge during his college days. He could expend his test anxiety on physical activities like hiking and rock climbing.

Daniel had booked them a time at Torrent Falls Climbing Adventure. He also planned a romantic ride up the sky lift at the Natural Bridge and had a picnic safely tucked in the back of his truck. The Natural Bridge was pretty awesome in itself. Although he had a full day of activities planned for Tillie, it was the night's activities that were on his mind. Just thinking about the possibility of sex with Tillie made him have a tingling feeling in his loins. It was almost like he had an itching sensation.

Shutting off the Caroline valve in his brain, he was determined that this weekend was all about Tillie as they continued to learn things about each other. He enjoyed the easy flow of conversation he had with her, and he genuinely liked her as a person. He needed to see if they were compatible as a couple.

Realizing Tillie was being unusually quiet, he saw that she seemed mesmerized by the scenery passing them by as they sped up the open road. Daniel felt the itching sensation again, and he knew there was no way he could wait until tonight. He placed his hand on her thigh. Tillie's eyes became increasingly larger as his fingers began heading north.

Sucking in air, Tillie knew it was too late to turn back now. Daniel's hand was inciting tingling sensations she had never felt before. She had to start her breathing technique. "Breathe in, breathe out, concentrate, focus!" she told herself.

Daniel said in a low, sexy whisper, "Turn off on the next road." She was too weak to protest as she turned onto a gravel road. The wheels crunched over the gravel as she increased her speed. Tillie thought she might burst if she wasn't able to stop this truck soon. Tillie's breathing now was labored, and her vision was blurred by the activity going on under the confines of the steering wheel.

As soon as the truck was safely parked, Daniel didn't waste any time as he began to undress her. He started with her top as he unbuttoned her flannel shirt, one button at a time, kissing the bare skin he had exposed inch by inch. Impatient, she decided to help him, but her efforts were met with resistance.

—◦◦◦—

Daniel was thankful he hadn't waited until tonight to make love to Tillie. Not only did his itch get satisfied, but his eyes were able to feast on Tillie's perfect little body; a view the subdued light of night would conceal.

Wet with sweat, Tillie collapsed into his chest, and he held her tightly. He could feel both of their hearts racing when he first heard the voice. It was only one word, but he could recognize Caroline's voice anywhere. "Daniel!" His eyes flew opened expecting to see Caroline peering through the window. He turned his head to look to the right, then to the left, and then sighed in relief when he realized he and Tillie were still alone. Just as he was about to relax, another alarm went off in his head. He realized he just experienced wonderful, unprotected sex with an FBI agent. He thought, "Should I be concerned?"

"Yes." Caroline's voice sounded again in his head, and he even smelled her perfume.

CHAPTER 25

The Banker's Dilemma

Saturday, April 5, 2008, 10:30 AM

Rupert E. Jones, the President of Rockford National Bank had a sleepless night, and morning couldn't come soon enough for him. Dressed in banker casual, a Ralph Lauren Polo, khakis, and Italian tasseled loafers, he drove his Mercedes to the bank as soon as dawn broke.

Rupert's sleepless night was caused by the resignation of his secretary of ten years. Ordinarily, this shouldn't cause any sleep deprivation, but Mayzella Wooten was not an ordinary secretary. Although he was a happily married man, part of the reason for his happiness was his secretary. Mayzella had not only been his secretary and lover but his wife's best friend as well. He felt sure he could replace her duties as secretary and mistress but knew finding a replacement for his wife to befriend was not going to be easy.

Elizabeth Jean Mayfield Jones was a gracious hostess, a smart lady, and a beauty queen—all the major banker's wife prerequisites. Although she had a chemistry degree, she never put her degree to use. She preferred to stay home and be a token banker's wife. Although Mayzella was not of Lizzie Jean's same social stature, someone not familiar with Mayzella's circumstances would think she'd come from good family stock and had a college education by the way she dressed and spoke.

Definitely not the beauty queen Lizzie Jean was, Mayzella's pieces and parts fit together attractively. Thankfully, not too attractive or else Lizzie Jean would have been threatened by her.

If Lizzie Jean was satisfied then Rupert was happy because her happiness or unhappiness was contagious.

Mayzella and Lizzie Jean seemed to be best friends and confidantes, but Rupert knew it was all an act on Mayzella's part. She never actually told him this in so many words, but he knew he could count on her to slip into his office, shut the door, and completely rock his world before she would have any luncheon encounters or frivolous shopping trips with Lizzie Jean. If that didn't mean she hated his wife, then, it meant something close.

He tried to talk Mayzella into staying by offering her a raise, a promotion, a new car, and even a new house. Lizzie Jean tried too. Mayzella's reason for leaving with no notice was because she said she met someone and was moving to Fort Lauderdale to be with him. She explained she wasn't getting younger and thought she'd better strike while the iron was hot.

After Rupert was over the initial shock, he felt her leaving was probably for the best. He was fairly certain Mayzella had fallen in love with him. She should have known he would never leave Lizzie Jean for a trailer trash secretary regardless of how good she was in bed or in the office.

Mayzella couldn't have picked a worse time to leave, though. He had examiners from the Office of the Comptroller of Currency coming in on Monday, and there was always a lot of work needing to be done in preparation for the audit. Smart like a fox, Rupert concealed his wrongdoings rather well. It wasn't out of necessity that caused him to embezzle money from the bank, but he stole for much the same reason he cheated on his wife—he liked the thrill of the game. The feeling of being able to outsmart so many people was better than any orgasm.

Having several items on his morning agenda, he entered his office with his first line of business to call Jock Ledford. He needed to call the mayor to talk about the transfer fees for Jimmy's money and to ask his aid in finding a new secretary.

Jock's pool of secretaries was well-trained, efficient, and relatively good-looking. It had initially repulsed Rupert to think Mayzella had sex with the mayor, but it didn't take long for the repulsion to ebb away. He couldn't help but be a little excited by the prospects the unknown may bring, and he remembered the thrill of the interviews. He would ask these young girls dressed in their Sunday best why he should choose them over any of the other candidates for the job, and then they would show him all their finely-honed skills. "Whew," he said as he wiped the sweat off his brow.

He didn't have time to fantasize about young girls. He had a lot to accomplish in order to prepare for the examiners, mainly concealing his fiduciary misconduct which included fictitious loans, added fees, and incorrect interest amounts. Before he became engrossed in this preparation, he decided to log into the offshore bank account so he could check on the amount in Coroner Jimmy Sizemore's account. He knew this would be Jock's first question. When Jimmy's account showed a zero balance, he was baffled. "Humph, I must have entered a wrong number," he mumbled. Thinking he may've entered an old account number, he removed the false bottom of his desk drawer and felt for the envelope containing all the Tuesday Club account information. When he couldn't feel the envelope with his fingers, he actually bent down and peered into the dark hole under his custom made desk. He felt the panic rise in his chest when he realized the envelope wasn't there.

Turning his attention back to the computer, he found the account balances of all the Tuesday Club members had been wiped out as well. Over thirty million dollars were gone. Vanished. His heart was beating so hard he could feel each heart squeeze as a throb in his temple. Beginning to sweat profusely, his vision began to blur. He then logged into the bank's system and sighed in relief that his bank accounts at Rockford National were all still intact. With over a half a million in his personal accounts, he wasn't totally busted, but it was still a far cry from the $5,365,000 he had in his offshore account.

His relief was short-lived when he tied Mayzella's sudden departure and the missing envelope together. She had to be the one behind this. He had to find her. If he couldn't find her, then his death was imminent. Jock Ledford would hunt him down and kill him if he didn't get the money back. Of that, he was certain.

12:00 PM

The large two-bedroom condominium was on the tenth floor of the building, and Mayzella loved sitting on the balcony. Seeing the blue of the sky meet the blue of the ocean was almost a religious experience for her—that is, if she had any religion left in her.

The ocean was everything she hoped it would be. The water was a dark blue in some points, but lightened to a blue-green shade as it came closer toward the shore, and still even lighter, almost white, from the white foam caps of the waves as they came crashing onto the shore. She now knew what her uncle Buddy was talking about all those years ago when he said the ocean was alive. He said the ocean actually breathed in and out. She thought it sounded magnificent and had dreamed of going to Daytona Beach since that day.

Actually, Uncle Buddy was her mom's uncle. Technically that made him her great uncle, but regardless, he was one of her only relatives that had escaped Crow's Creek. Every section of Rockford County had a name, and this name reflected on the people from that area as well. Hailing from Crow's Creek didn't win anyone any favors. Her uncle Buddy was her hero for making a life outside of Crow's Creek and because he was the only person that paid any attention to her for the right reasons. Fascinated, she sat on the trailer's front stoop listening to his stories of a life outside of her Appalachian prison, knowing one day she would escape to this distant place in Florida.

She had no remorse for lying to Rupert and Lizzie Jean about her planned destination being Fort Lauderdale or about meeting the man of her dreams. She knew it was only a matter of time before Rupert put it all together and came looking for her. Thankfully, she had a head start.

She knew when she accepted the mayor's offer of employment twelve years ago that it was going to require more than just typing. Sex was going to be part of her life one way or another—a means for survival. She thought she might as well use it to help her have a better life. In her opinion, the mayor and his buddies smelled a heap better than the boys on Crow's Creek.

Growing up on Crow's Creek was a harsh upbringing, and she grew up feeling like a green bean in a potato sack. Her family seemed content to bring a used trailer onto their papaw's property and live off the government. The boys were taught all the tricks to pass the crazy test so they could sit home all day, drink beers, and watch television while the government issued them a check because of their disability. The girls grew up knowing just as soon as they got their period they needed to start having babies. A bastard baby meant they could go on the draw; every time they added another one, they increased their monthly check. In some ways, this life was so brilliantly simple she could understand how families could fall into this lifestyle. This life, however, would never work for her mainly because she didn't like babies. Dreading to see the bump on her momma's belly, she knew what it would mean to her. Her momma would add a new kid every year to their illegitimate horde, and Mayzella, being the oldest, would be the one to take care of the infant.

Jock Ledford saved her from a life of babies and poverty. When she signed on to work for Jock, the deal was sealed in blood. Her blood. She knew she would be paying for this particular favor for the remainder of her life. At this minute, she felt it had been worth it. Here, she was smack dab in the middle of Daytona Beach and the proud owner of a brand new beachfront condominium. She thought Jock did a nice job of choosing this place for her. Sitting on the balcony and looking at the ocean was a great place to think. She mostly thought about what a fool she'd been. Rupert had never once told her he loved her and never made any promises to her. She then felt the suck of wind coming from the sliding glass door before she heard her new lover's steps approaching her.

Deek was a far cry from Rupert Jones, but at least, he was hers for the taking. He'd pledged his undying love for her and that was more than the reaction she received from Rupert. Actually, she wasn't sure if Rupert was capable of loving anyone other than himself. He was wired differently than the average man. On the other hand, Deek was wired all right—wired from the effects of his marijuana habit.

"Did you mail both packages?" she asked her new lover.

"Yep, one to Lizzie, and one to the comprehensive something," Deek proudly stated.

"Comptroller, you knuckle brain," she corrected him.

"I sure hope you kept one of those DVDs. I wanted to watch it again."

Mayzella wished she could be a fly on the wall and watch Lizzie's expression when she realized that she didn't always win. "I'm ready for that ride down the beach," she said. Deek's little yellow car was not Rupert's Mercedes, but at least it had a sunroof.

CHAPTER 26

Research, Repent, and Relapse

Saturday, April 5, 2008, 12:30 PM

Trevor Grant had been mad all morning but had no right to be angry. Tillie was a grown woman, and if she wanted to go off with a man for a night, then, he couldn't tell her she couldn't, or could he? Daniel Brooks seemed like a nice enough fellow, but he'd never seen Tillie so gaga about a guy before. He didn't like it.

He decided to exert some of his pent-up aggression in the form of a daily run. He wasn't sure if it was his protective instincts kicking in or sheer jealousy. In all probability, his little sister was going to have sex, and here he was stuck in McWhorter living a celibate lifestyle. His celibacy wasn't by choice, but pickings were mighty slim in McWhorter. Most of the single women in McWhorter were still in high school, and the words statutory rape didn't appeal to him. The only woman in McWhorter that remotely interested him was Caroline Ledford, and under the circumstances, he didn't think she would be his best option.

He ran by the *Rockford Sun Newspaper* office and thought this morning would be the perfect time to look through their archived editions. The morning had been the perfect temperature for a run. He used his shirt to wipe his brow before entering the newspaper office. The light cream two-story building with a teal-colored awning and matching shutters had the look and feel of the town's coordinated effort to create the look of a quaint little beach town, only in the foothills of the Appalachian.

He expected the newspaper office to have the same chipper interior as the outside. He wasn't prepared to walk back in time, but that's how he felt as he went through the door—like he'd been sucked into a different era. The room was dark with the shades drawn on all windows. The decades of ink and smoke penetrated his senses as he stepped foot onto the entrance's concrete flooring. Thinking someone should have heard the jingle of the bell on the front door signaling his arrival, he waited for what seemed like an appropriate amount of time before he took further action. He finally pressed the bell sitting on top of an old desk. "Brrrriiinnng," it called out.

An older woman with her gray hair pulled through the back of a baseball cap came bouncing through the doors to the right of the foyer exclaiming, "Sorry, sorry, sweetie. Hope you haven't been waiting long. Just trying to finish Coroner Jimmy Sizemore's obituary. Isn't it a shame about poor old Jimmy Sizemore? He's been our undertaker for as long as I can remember. I'm afraid Barry, Jimmy's only child, won't be able to give the same kind of service Jimmy did. Jimmy went right by the book on funerals and was a professional all the time. Lordy, I would turn over in my grave if Barry wore shorts or something inappropriate like that in the funeral home when I'm laid out." She finally stopped for air but was still shaking her head about poor Jimmy.

Normally, this woman's ranting would have penetrated Trevor's last nerve, but as soon as she mentioned Jimmy Sizemore's name, he latched onto her every word. "What happened to Jimmy?" He mainly was interested because Jimmy Sizemore's name had been linked to the Tuesday Club.

"He fell off one of his cousin Bobby's cliff tops," she said as matter-of-factly as one would talk about the foods they'd eaten for dinner. "He'd been hunting a panther. Can you believe that a man his age was out by himself hunting a dangerous animal like that? I wonder if he had a tie on?" She tilted her head back and chuckled as she imagined the spectacle. "They said the panther was found dead only a few feet away. Barry's gonna get it stuffed and put it in his dad's office. That gives me an idea. I think I'm gonna write about Jimmy and his hunting adventures," she said as she talked herself right into the idea.

"I'm sure Jimmy would've liked that," Trevor said before he extended his hand. "By the way, my name's Trevor Grant. I was wondering if I could take a look in your archive room. I need to do a little research about my family tree."

"Why, you're one of the Grant twins," the newspaper editor said while she studied him. She looked first this way then that way as she completed a full examination on Trevor. Evidently, he passed her inspection as she quickly turned from looking at him to a different direction as she motioned for him to follow. "The archive room is in the basement. I'll forewarn you. It's a mess. We have some of the papers on the microfiche, some on microfilm, and some in hard copy. The librarian from the public library wants to help us organize them, but truth is we've not had time to fool with her yet," she explained as she gave Trevor a whirlwind tour of the newsprint office on the way to the stairwell.

The basement was a pure nightmare. There were two large tables on either side of the room and stacks and stacks of newspapers everywhere. On the far side of the room, there was a makeshift rack where the newspapers had been kneaded through the stick hangers and were dangling like pants hanging in a closet.

The old lady showed him how to work the machines and the general direction to look for specific dates. Satisfied that she'd given him all the information he needed, she bounced up the stairs like a youngster. He was grateful she left the door opened. Making sure it was still there, he felt for the gun placed in the built-in compartment of his undershirt. He may have to use it to shoot any rats or boogie men that lived in this dungeon.

Deciding on the time frame to start his search as the early forties, he settled in for a while. He wanted to find anything he could find about Jock Ledford's grandfather and acquaintances. If he could associate names with the Ledfords, then, he thought he could figure out some of the other members of the secret club. He thought to himself *I may just wait around long enough and all the Tuesday Club members will be revealed because it appears they're all dying.* Somehow, this didn't set well with him. He wanted justice to be served, but thought a more public mass hanging would be his idea of fair dealing.

He used a scratch pad and started writing the names of the Tuesday Club members he knew:

- Mayor Jock Ledford – alive
- Albert Dean Smith – shot in the head
- Woodrow Ledford – MIA
- Pastor Bart Smith – dead by a heart attack
- Coroner Jimmy Sizemore – dead by a hunting accident
- Judge Jack Brown – alive

He found himself chuckling about some of the newsworthy articles and even found himself touched by the stories of the fallen WWII soldiers. "Bingo," he said and slowed the film down when spotting a picture with a man that was a larger version of Jock Ledford who was surrounded by several other men. "Well, hello there, Mr. Ledford," Trevor spoke to the photograph. To Jon R.'s right was Leroy Brown, and to his left was Gillie Bean Smith. He read the names on the bottom of the photograph and started jotting down the last names of all the men pictured: Osborne, Ledford, Smith, Adams, Brown, Brooks, Bowling, Clemmons, George, Young, Peacock, Blair, Clinton, Martin, and Jones. He needed to research each of these men. As far as he knew, all the men listed in the photograph could be a part of the Tuesday Club.

He circled the names Osborne and Brooks. Was it possible that both the sheriff and Daniel were part of the Tuesday Club? He looked back in the names to see if he overlooked the Sizemore name. He couldn't find it. "Interesting," he spoke out loud. He was slightly relieved. Based on everything he read, he knew with certainty Jimmy Sizemore was part of the club. Knowing the Sizemore name wasn't on the list gave him a little comfort. He tried to recall conversations with Daniel and his uncle Willie regarding the Tuesday Club, hoping he hadn't messed up by confiding in the fellow policemen.

He was going to church tomorrow, for sure. He felt he was going to need some divine direction as well as redemption.

1:30 PM

Caroline drove by all of Daniel's favorite haunts and couldn't locate his truck anywhere. Surely, he was smart enough not to go out of town with that little blond hussy. While driving, Caroline had a sinking spell, and her vision was fuzzy. She pulled her vehicle to the side of the road. "I'm just hungry," she said as she tried to think of the last time she ate. Putting her Lexus in drive, she pulled away from the curb and continued through town in the search of food.

She was losing weight like crazy. She could pull her skirt band out two inches from her waist. "I know. I'll run by and let Jeb fix me a bite to eat," she spoke in a whisper. A grilled cheese sandwich actually sounded like something she might be able to keep down. She had no idea how hard a break-up would be on a person.

Knowing she didn't have time for her own worries, she decided instead to think about Jennings. He was in a heap worse shape than she was. She knew in her heart her little brother didn't murder that girl. She just knew it! If he did, then, he had to have an accomplice, and Jennings would never trust anyone other than his brother to have his back. Someone had to do something with the girl's car. According to Joe Matt, there was no trace of the little yellow Cobalt. He said there had been an all points bulletin issued the day after the murder, and they had divers check all around Cromer Lake to see if the car was there. The car couldn't have disappeared into thin air. Someone knew exactly where that car was located, and they just needed to push the right buttons until they found out who knew.

Thinking about disappearing made her once again contemplate the location of Daniel. "Stop it!" she ordered herself. "Stop thinking about Daniel!"

Driving a little over the town's speed limit, she was lost in thought heading down Elm Street. She noticed, in her peripheral vision, a man clad in gym trunks and a sweatshirt. She realized who the toned blond man was; an idea was born. "There's always more than one way to skin a cat," she thought. She stopped her Lexus in the middle of the street and waited for the blond runner to reach her.

"Hey there!" she said loudly using her sweet and sensuous voice.

Trevor Grant didn't want to stop because he knew exactly the temptation that waited for him in the little SUV. He threw his hand up in acknowledgment but kept running.

"I'm heading to Hazel's to get a bite to eat. You hungry?" She asked as she eased her vehicle forward at his same pace.

Trevor was so hungry he could have eaten half of the beautiful arm dangling through the driver's window. "A little," he answered, "but I've got a salad and sandwich waiting for me at Granny's." He was proud he was able to resist her invitation.

Caroline wasn't ready to give up that easily. "I love salad. You got enough for me?"

Trevor was in a bind. *How do you say no to that?* he thought as he crossed the road and entered in the passenger side of her SUV. He was in the clutches of the devil's daughter. No amount of church was going to save him now.

11:30 PM

Tillie thought if she died this very minute, she would die a happy woman. If she had any doubts about her feelings for Daniel Brooks before, they'd been washed away along with her inhibitions. She'd experienced the best day of her life.

She even enjoyed going to the Reptile Zoo and watching the owner extract venom from a black mamba. "Who would think this primitive setting would be home for one of the nation's largest venom suppliers?" she repeatedly asked Daniel. She had to admit she was a little surprised when the zoo owner invited Daniel to assist him with wrangling the large puff adder into the clear plastic tube. Explaining the tube was for the snake's protection, the owner further explained to the rest of the group that he ordinarily didn't allow assistance from spectators; however, Daniel was special. It was pretty evident Daniel knew the process and looked right at home around the snakes. Daniel later shared with her that he used to spend a lot of time volunteering at the zoo and had developed a deep respect for the reptiles.

Yes, she would say the day was perfect, but for one small thing. Of course, she could have dreamed it, or it could have been the way the light was shining on him; but for a brief fleeting second, she noticed a look on Daniel's face she'd never seen before. It happened while he was holding the poisonous snake. His whole countenance changed, maybe it was from fear or an adrenaline rush, but it was a Daniel she didn't know. It was the same look Trevor had on his face when he was ten years old, and he used a fork to hold her hostage in a bathtub full of hot water. Every time she would try to step out of the scalding water, he would poke her with the fork. Trevor wasn't so smug after she threw a punch that busted his nose. The best way to describe both Daniel and Trevor's expression was bloodlust. Then as quickly as it came about, it was gone. There was no trace of the foreign Daniel as he looked down at her from his elevated position with a grin that was more goofy than sexy. He was back. She must have been mistaken. Just to be on the safe side, she couldn't get him out of the zoo fast enough to suit her for fear the look would return.

The Daniel she was falling for had re-emerged as they shared pizza from a small yellow, hiker's haven pizza place. The pizza was every bit as scrumptious as Daniel had promised. She would be satisfied if they could stay together in this gorge forever. She didn't want to share him with anyone. She loved feeling his arms tightly around her. The outside setting was just icing on the cake. They chose to camp instead of staying at the lodge. She realized she'd been waiting for Daniel all her life. She never felt lonely before, but now that she had Daniel, she realized just how lonesome she'd been.

Replaying the events of the day in her mind, she was grateful for the brief time she had to reminisce by the campfire light. She could feel her face turn red as she thought about making love to him. He kept telling her he had the itch for her. Earlier, she didn't understand his comment, but now she thought she may have an itch of her own. She turned over so she was now facing Daniel and started kissing his neck. Later, the entwined couple fell asleep watching the embers of the campfire change from the bright yellow inferno to a soft red glow. They snoozed in the forest for some time until Daniel woke himself scratching his abdomen. He was itching uncontrollably and could feel the culprits—the tiny bumps. He noticed Tillie was scratching in her sleep as well. Daniel knew the feel of poison ivy and was fairly certain this was his problem. He gently nudged Tillie awake, "Are you allergic to poison ivy?" he asked.

"I don't know."

The couple spent the rest of the night at the emergency room of the nearest hospital being treated for a very embarrassing case of poison ivy.

Sunday, April 6, 2008, 7:30 AM

Jock was up early on Sunday morning studying his Sunday School lesson about the Ark of the Covenant. He couldn't understand why the Almighty struck that boy down for touching the ark. After all, he was just trying to steady it. "Here, the good Lord let 'em have harems and multiple wives, and then killed the boy dead for touching this gold suitcase thing." He just shook his head in disbelief, not understanding the significance of the lesson.

Jock knew the Bible as well as anyone. He could twist it and shake it and make it his own without another thought. For some reason, he felt like parts of the Bible applied to everyone but him. Jock heard the jingling of the telephone. The phone rang twice before Eleanor was able to stifle the sound. Clearly in a good mood this morning, he smiled thinking how well-trained Eleanor was. He heard the pitter-patter of Eleanor's heels as she brought the telephone to his office. He knew exactly who was calling and was surprised he hadn't heard from him before now.

Eleanor covered the mouthpiece of the phone and silently mouthed in exaggerated form, "It's Rupert Jones from the bank."

Jock took the phone and motioned for his wife to close the door behind her. He waited until the sound of her footsteps was far enough away before he said, "Hello, Rupert."

Rupert's voice sounded about three octaves higher than it normally did, "Jock, buddy, I'm sorry to bother you so early on a Sunday morning, but we've got real problems."

"Settle down, son. Now what kind of problems do we have when the good Lord has given us such a beautiful Sunday morning?"

Inhaling deeply, Rupert then spit it all out before he lost his nerve, "You see, Mayzella quit on Friday, and you see, now all our off shore accounts have been wiped out completely. You see ..." He paused and gulped before coming to the conclusion, "The Tuesday Club is busted." Rupert's confession was met with complete silence.

Jock finally filled the empty air, "Now, Rupert, son, you've been working too hard. You know we had our system foolproof with you being the only living soul knowing the account numbers. There's no way some little whore secretary could have gotten to our numbers. It must be some kind of mistake?" he baited Rupert.

"Sir, it's no mistake. The money's gone, and so is the envelope with the passwords."

"So, you're telling me you got too friendly with my little Mayzella and let your guard down enough so she was able to bypass all that fancy-smancy security protocol you promised me, was—what was that word you used? Foolproof!" Jock wasn't baiting now.

"Yes, sir," was Rupert's only reply.

"Where is she?"

Rupert somewhat composed said, "She said she was moving to Fort Lauderdale. I've hired a private eye, and he's there now looking for her."

Jock lowered his voice. "You better find her, you smug, big feeling, SOB. Do not—you hear me—do not breathe this to another living soul!" Jock said as he pressed release on the handset of the phone. Jock placed his hands behind his head and leaned back in his big oversized office chair, clearly reveling in the experience. He smiled. He loved it when a plan came together. He knew they would never find his sweet Mayzella in Fort Lauderdale. He would give Rupert a day or two to sweat before he told him he had all the money in safekeeping. This would teach Rupert boy a valuable lesson about trusting these little whores. Rupert was getting a little big for his britches anyway. He thought he was so hot to trot dealing with these offshore accounts. He needed a way to keep Rupert honest, and he was pretty sure he found it.

He had to hand it to Mayzella. She played it off just fine. He always knew she was a smart one. He figured the money he had to pay her up front was well worth it. At least, worth it for the time being. He figured he could put his new condo to good use later.

He went back to studying his Sunday School lesson like no conversation had ever taken place between him and the banker.

11:00 AM

The Big Goose Creek Church hadn't been the same since Pastor Bart's death. Various preachers had been trying out for the job. Jock took an instant dislike to the old man in the pulpit today and wondered who in the world had invited him to tryout. He almost thought he knew this man. There was something very familiar about him. This preacher was an old feeble man in a tired gray suit. His t-shirt was visible through the dingy, threadbare, yellowed shirt he was wearing, and his large boxy tie had been in style twenty, maybe thirty, years ago.

The old man walked humped over taking baby steps as he walked. Jock was afraid the frail preacher would kick the bucket before he got two sentences out of his mouth. He wasn't big as a minute. Noticing the large veins in the man's hands, he watched the blue blood pump, weaving a trail up his hand toward his forearm.

Taking the podium, Jock confidently gave his weekly Sunday School report then took his seat by his wife in their normal pew. Today it was just him and Eleanor seated in the pew; none of his children saw fit to attend which agitated him. Between looking at the irritating little man and his agitation toward his children, his chest began to swell and pains ran across his upper torso. He refused to give into the pain, but instead ignored it.

After singing all five verses of "Blessed Assurance," the old man hobbled to center stage. He grabbed each side of the podium, and from Jock's ringside seat, the grip looked like a death grip. He was holding onto the podium with his head bowed and his eyes closed. Everyone was looking around at each other wondering if someone needed to call 911 when all of a sudden, the man sprang to life. His eyes opened; his head jerked up in one swift motion. Looking around, the preacher's eyes seemed to penetrate the very souls of those seated in the congregation. He removed his hands from the podium and straightened his rounded back, which appeared to gain him several inches in height. Walking around the pulpit, he still hadn't uttered a word.

The entire church was spellbound by this transformation. The old hunkered-over man was now walking around the pulpit in an upright position. He smiled, and his false teeth were coffee stained and looked too big for his mouth. Repulsed by the brown teeth and the uncomfortable familiarity, Jock was ready for this man to finish and be on his way.

After having properly sized up the congregation, the old man wasted no time with small talk as he pulled out his Bible and asked the flock to turn to Deuteronomy chapter 32. His smooth baritone voice had a crystal clear resonance as he pronounced each syllable with no Kentucky twang. He didn't sound southern, hillbilly, and thank the Lord, he didn't have the nasal sounding Yankee dialect, either, Jock thought. He had to admit the old man had his attention, and he too turned the pages of his daddy's Bible to the chapter he mentioned.

The old man gave the perfunctory time needed for the congregation to find their place, and then began to quote the word.

> "Read with me verses one through six. Give ear, O heavens, and will speak; and hear, O earth, the words of my mouth. Let my teaching drop as the rain, my speech distill as the dew, as raindrops on the tender herb, and as showers on the grass. For I proclaim the name of the Lord: Ascribe greatness to our God. *He* is the Rock. His work *is* perfect; for all His ways *are* justice, A God of truth and without injustice; righteous and upright *is* He. They have corrupted themselves; they *are* not His children, because of their blemish: A perverse and crooked generation. Do you thus deal with the Lord? O foolish and unwise people?"

The old man paused and looked around the room again. He once again took hold of the podium and lowered his head. If Jock didn't know better, he would think there was some type of power source in that podium he was plugging into in order to regenerate his battery. Not a lot of time had passed, but when Jock looked at his wristwatch he realized over fifteen minutes had ticked off the clock since he had given his report. When he looked back up, he felt somebody was messing with him. The bright overhead lights had dimmed, and it looked like another light had been placed directly behind the man which illuminated him from head to toe. He looked at the light switch to see if someone was messing with it but saw no one around it.

The old man once again raised his head and walked around the stage looking each person in the eye. Many of the members looked away when his eyes rested on them, not wanting to take any chance in giving away their dark secrets. Not Jock. He refused to look away, and the man locked his eyes with Jock's eyes, just as two bucks locked antlers as they battled. A stare down contest was taking place with neither Jock nor the preacher blinking or looking away. Finally, the old man had seen enough and looked away. Smiling smugly, Jock felt he emerged the victor.

The old preacher man began to speak once again quoting the scripture from the big black ragged book he was carrying around. "Skip down to verse nineteen," he kindly ordered. He began reciting the word, only this time he would say one sentence with the emphasis on one particular word, and then he would pause so the congregation could soak in the word of God.

"And when the Lord *saw* it." (Pause.)

"He *spurned* them." (Pause.)

"Because of the *provocation* of his sons and his daughters." He paused, but he said the next cadence in such a manner that each word was articulated perfectly and equally emphasized in slow and deliberate measures. "And *He* said: 'I will hide My face from them; I will see what their end *will be*, for they *are* a perverse generation, children in whom *is* no faith.'"

The old man moved to the left of the stage and began speaking directly to old Sister Potter as if in conversation. "Verse twenty-one says, they have provoked Me to jealousy by what *is* not God."

Sister Potter answered him by finishing the verse, matching his rhythm, word for word, only in her country accent by saying, "They have moved Me to anger by their foolish idols."

Giving another rare smile, the preacher seemed pleased. Someone from the amen corner hollered out an "Amen!" in support of Sister Potter.

The old man went back to his task and recited verse twenty-two, "But I **will** *provoke* them to jealousy by those *who are not* a nation; I *will move* them to anger by a foolish nation. For a *fire* is kindled in my *anger!*"

The preacher now was fired up, and he said the next words of verse twenty-two with such intensity Jock felt the little hairs on the back of his neck prickle upward. "And shall burn to the lowest hell; it shall consume the earth with her increase, and set on fire the foundations of the mountains. I will heap disasters on them."

The old man looked around. There were no sounds, even the babies didn't dare cry out as they all listened to the perfect word of God that spewed from the man's mouth.

Jock had removed his arm from around Eleanor's shoulder and was now sitting straight up in the pew. Now, he was sure someone was intentionally messing with him because he began to see a mist gather around the pulpit at the man's feet.

The big black book was shut and placed neatly on the podium. The next words were not from Deuteronomy, but were said with the same authority as he had exhibited when quoting the Bible, only in a much lower pitch. The words were stated like he was warning a friend. "Be prepared. God is taking over this city. You will know I'm speaking the truth when you see his wrath fall on this city in the form of sleet, ice, and hail," the man stated. "Remember, even the winds obey his voice. Take heed and remember this warning."

Jock wiggled around not sure whether to get up and challenge the man or if he needed to run out of the building as fast as his legs would carry him. It didn't matter what he wanted to do because his feet were fastened to the floor, and he was unable to move them at all.

The old man took a drink of water, and he ended his sermon by quoting Deuteronomy 32:35. "Vengeance is Mine, and recompense; their foot shall slip in *due* time; for the day of their calamity *is* at hand, and the things to come hasten upon them."

Jock knew the sermon was over because just as the lights had dimmed earlier, they now shone brightly. The haze had lifted, and the old man once again gripped the podium with his head bowed. Transformed from the empowered man of God back into the feeble old man, he shuffled back to the seat provided for him. The pianist took his seat at the piano, and the choir scurried back to the choir loft.

The congregation began singing the invitational hymn "Only Trust Him" with much vigor. Jock stood and was finally able to move his feet. He sang as loudly as he could as his mind thought of the debauchery that he would do to this man for making a spectacle out of him in the church his family had built. While the church was singing, the old man slipped silently out the door leading from the choir loft.

3:00 PM

Pastor Ables sermon was titled "Mustard Seed Faith." Geneva thought there wasn't much better food in the early spring. She'd planted mustard greens before, so she was well aware that the mustard seed was very tiny. Hundreds of mustard seed would fit into one greasy bean seed. She was humbled. Just to think if she had faith the size of one of those little mustard seeds, then she could say to the mountain, "Move," and it would move. This was more than she could comprehend. According to her pastor, the key to having mustard seed faith was to believe.

"Neeva, you ready to go to your election committee meeting?" Glenn Dale asked in his sweet dating voice.

Geneva knew she was the luckiest woman on this earth to have such a catch as Glenn Dale Vaughn. "I'm ready when you are," she replied.

Her heart wasn't in the election, but she had thrown her free will away when she gave her life to the Lord. He had truly become her Lord and Master twenty some years ago when she realized there was a difference in Jesus being her Savior and in Jesus being her Lord. She just said, "Here am I, Lord. Mend me, mold me, and I'll follow you wherever you lead me." She just had no idea when she said this that he was going to lead her and her family in such dangerous territory. She had so many mixed feelings. She couldn't believe her little Ruthie had lost her virginity to that Ledford boy after her many talks about keeping herself pure. That sin had cost Ruthie her life but not her soul. She knew she was in heaven and would see her once again.

She and Glenn Dale had decided not to open her grandbaby's battered body to the public last week at the funeral. On the night of Ruthie's viewing, she noticed Jennings Ledford staring at the picture of Ruth Ann sitting on a table by her closed casket. It looked as though his intent was to memorize every feature of her pretty little face. Jennings Ledford was guilty of robbing her granddaughter of her virtue, but he wasn't guilty of taking her life. Of that, she was fairly certain. She couldn't say the same thing about his daddy, though. When Jock Ledford came by to pay his respects, it was all she could do to shake his slimy hand. His palm was cold like a reptile, and his face and soul matched his hand. He said all the right words, but his eyes didn't match what he was saying. Standing at full height from her seated position, she looked Jock in the eye and said, "Rest assured. Your sins will find you out." That's all she said and all it took to get Jock's dander up. His face and neck plumped up like a big toad frog. Jock Ledford was speechless.

She thought, "No wonder the Lord's not going to release me from this election."

CHAPTER 27

Monday Madness

Monday, April 7, 2008, 7:00 AM

The winds had changed in McWhorter and had blown the beautiful April weekend to a distant foggy memory. Joseph Mattingly Sizemore had to wear his winter uniform jacket, the one with the brown furry collar. It wasn't much to look at, but it sure did feel good when the wind started nipping at his neck. Joe Matt was a product of practicality. He never owned a brand named article of clothing in his life unless his momma picked it up from a yard sale. Edna Mattingly Sizemore had been raised hard and knew the value of a dollar. When Joe Matt failed to turn the light off when he left a room, she chastised him and told him how she grew up in a house with eight children, no electricity, and no running water. God forbid, he stay in the shower too long; she would be knocking on the bathroom door telling him how much money it took to heat the hot water he was wasting down the drain.

Joe Matt's dad had left Edna enough money to live on comfortably for the rest of her life, but he doubted she ever dipped into any of Big Joe's money. Instead, she lived on her meager paycheck she made working at the Laundromat. He couldn't bring himself to leave Edna just yet—even if it meant taking quick showers and enduring her lectures. She held some invisible ties that trapped him in the same little two-bedroom clapboard-siding house he had lived in all his life.

Edna had worked outside all weekend cleaning her windows and taking advantage of the beautiful spring days. She had always talked about April being such an unpredictable month for the weather. Edna was prepared when overnight, the weather dropped thirty degrees. Joe Matt awoke to a nice cozy fire roaring in their wood burning stove.

Joe Matt hated he couldn't share anything about the Tuesday Club with her. "What would she do if she knew her only child was a millionaire several times over?" He dreamed of one day running away from McWhorter and the Tuesday Club, and he was determined to make arrangements to take care of Edna for just that time.

Living with Edna had its advantages. Not only did she have a breakfast plate on the table ready for him after his shower, but also his winter coat had been laundered and laid out on his bed with the rest of his uniform. She could put his uniform together better than he could.

Big Joe was good enough to Joe Matt and Edna, but he wasn't the kind of dad or husband that caused his son and wife to grieve unmercifully over his death. Big Joe's death occurred at a bad time in his son's life. Thankfully, Joe Matt had Tinker Brooks around to help him during this impressionable time in his life. The only other male influence Joe Matt had growing up was Jock Ledford. Interestingly enough, Big Joe had never mentioned anything about the Tuesday Club to Joe Matt. He found out about the club when he was sixteen-years-old from Jock Ledford. Jock threatened his very life if he told anyone. This had to be a hard task for any adult, but at sixteen it was almost impossible. After he was ushered into the club at an early age, he clung to it as a newly found refuge. He had a lot of questions, and Jock was the man with all the answers. His relationship with the mayor had always been a love-hate relationship. He was just as nice as he could be to Joe Matt one minute, and then in his next breath would berate or threaten his life.

Joe Matt grieved and mourned more when Tinker Brooks died than he had mourned for his own father. Tinker Brooks recognized Joe Matt needed some direction and felt it was his obligation to give it to him. He taught him to play sports as well as the intricacies involved in fishing and hunting. Tinker could shoot a tick off of a dog's back. He never talked about his time in the service, but he and Daniel speculated he must have been a sniper. Just like his dad, shooting a gun or a basketball came natural to Daniel as well. On the other hand, Joe Matt had to work hard at anything he did. It infuriated him that everything came so easily to Daniel. Lashing out, Joe Matt's jealousy would sometimes get the best of him and would result in regular fistfights between the two friends.

Driving on autopilot, Joe Matt poked along Main Street. His cruiser was warm as toast and his furry collar felt good around his neck. The sky opened up, and the rain came down. He heard an occasional ping of the ice as evidence the temperature was decreasing. Sighing in relief, he was grateful that the schools had let out for spring break this week. He knew he better make sure he had enough men to work the roads today as the ping sounds became louder and more frequent.

8:00 AM

If the *Rockford Sun* had a vote for the most eligible bachelor in Rockford County, then Roy Allen Jones would definitely be in the running. Roy Allen was the baby boy in a house of five sisters. Roy Allen didn't come out of being raised in a house full of women unscathed. He had the unique advantage of understanding the make-up of being a woman. He knew all about makeup, break-ups, and Midol.

Roy Allen was the best-dressed lawyer in town, and it didn't hurt he drove the town's only corvette. He had two close calls with the altar; the first one was a short-lived shotgun wedding. Thankfully, it ended up being only a false alarm. Getting a case of cold feet a week before the wedding, his second fiancé left him permanently scarred.

Figuring he had plenty of time to settle down, he earmarked forty as the age before he really needed to get serious about a family. Waiting until he was forty gave him two more years to make Caroline Ledford forget Daniel Brooks and instead fall in love with him. Two years used to sound like an eternity, but now he was thinking two years were only a blink of an eye. Now, the main question on his mind wasn't regarding matrimony, but instead, he was asking himself if he would live two more years or two more days for that matter. What if God were punishing the Tuesday Club and what if he were next on the list?

Expecting a nice day, he was instead met with an arctic blast when he opened his garage. He decided to change into more suitable clothing for cold weather. He chose his L.L. Bean look for such a turbulent day and left his corvette in the garage. Instead, he revved the engine of his Jeep Cherokee to let it warm. He backed out of the garage and turned around in his wide driveway. He was glad he was driving the jeep. The rain was turning to sleet fast. "Damn it!" he exclaimed as he looked at the hand on the gas gauge pointing at the "E." He hoped he had enough to make it to D & D's Gas and Go. The gas station was the only one in town and was owned by the Spivey brothers, Darryl and Doyle.

Pulling into the gas station, he also saw the chief deputy at one of the four gas pumps. Joe Matt threw his free hand up in greeting to Roy Allen. Roy Allen reciprocated. They had been cautioned over the years to never appear too friendly with the other members of the club for fear of rousing suspicion. Joe Matt and Roy Allen finished pumping their gas, and both men headed for the warmth of indoors both making a beeline toward the coffee pot. Those Spivey boys sure knew how to brew good coffee. Many folks in McWhorter didn't own a coffee pot, but instead went every morning to the Gas and Go to warm up to a good cup of coffee and conversation. Both men left at the same time with their steaming Styrofoam cups.

Before Joe Matt had a chance to close the cruiser's door, Roy Allen placed himself between the door and Joe Matt then said, "Buddy, I'm not sleeping too good. It seems like every week the Tuesday Club loses another member. I'm afraid God's finally showing his wrath for all our fathers have done over the years."

Joe Matt took one look at Roy Allen and realized he wasn't playing him. He was legitimately scared. "Get in. Let's talk a spell," Joe Matt ordered his elder club member.

9:30 AM

The ache in Caroline's heart was still there, but maybe the pain wasn't as severe as it had been a day or two ago. She had to admit that Trevor Grant was a nice way to occupy her time plus he served as an informant. He let it slip to her about Tillie having poison ivy. This news was bittersweet. It was funny on one hand, but on the other hand, she now knew Daniel had been intimate with someone else. She had to admit the pill was a lot easier to swallow knowing she had inflicted her revenge in places where it had to hurt.

"How long will it take Daniel to figure out I was behind his agony, or will he even suspect me?" she worried to herself. On the same note, she also wondered how long it would take Tillie and Daniel to figure out how Trevor had been spending his time. Caroline number three smiled knowing that Daniel would never expect this from her. "Did he think I would just dry up and be a celibate old maid for the rest of my life? Did Daniel really think he could let me go or that I would give up so easily?"

Stepping outside, Caroline shivered; the wind chilled her all the way to her bones. She couldn't believe the change in the weather. It kind of unnerved her to one day be driving with her windows down, and on the next day, she had to use her four wheel drive feature because of the slick roads. Her life was just as unpredictable as the weather.

Some things in her life had been grand, but the highs in her life could never make up for the lows. Jock Ledford was as low as one could get. She had never allowed her mind to think about all the forms of punishments and lessons she had endured over the years. Some of the things were locked so tightly in her head she wasn't sure if she could crack the code where the painful memories were stored or if she would ever want to unleash them. Once unleashed, she was sure the thoughts would surely kill her, or… Caroline number three would kill somebody.

She really had to watch her step. Jock Ledford was a volcano of emotions waiting to erupt, and it was taking everything in him to keep from ripping her to shreds. Taking her mommy's advice, she took many extra precautions from installing new locks, changing alarm codes, and installing security cameras.

She knew her daddy was behind little Ruthie's murder. It was almost as if Jock wanted Jennings to be blamed. He could have made this all go away long before now. Now, Jennings's alibi looked like a joke. She'd like to have a nickel for every time she heard her daddy call her brothers his heir and spare. "Why would he throw away his son like that?" she asked herself. Then, like a ton of bricks it hit her, and she said out loud, "Dear Lord, is he using Jennings to punish me for losing Daniel?" She knew her recent actions toward her daddy not only put her and her family in harm's way; she also jeopardized Daniel's life as well. She pushed the speed dial on her telephone.

"Hello my fine, Caroline," Daniel answered.

"Hello, Daniel, I was just calling to check on you."

"Doing okay, other than a bad case of poison ivy. How 'bout you?"

She was at first silent as she decided how to answer. Caroline number three took care of that as she took over the call with her voice dripping with sympathy. "Poison ivy. Imagine that!"

Caroline's false sympathy must have resonated something within Daniel. He was silent for several seconds before he loudly exclaimed, "Please tell me you didn't do this to me!"

"Didn't what?" The bad Caroline used her sweet innocent voice before the laughter tumbled out of her mouth uncontrollably.

"Damn it, Caroline! It's not a bit funny!"

Her laughter ceased just as easily as it had started. With no emotion, she answered, "No, Daniel, having the love of your life break his commitment to you is not a bit funny." She wasn't going to stick around to hear his feeble attempts of denial so she hung up. Shaking, Caroline number one didn't know whether to laugh or cry. She wondered how long it would take him to find out about Trevor.

7:00 PM

Tillie was delighted about Daniel's invitation to dinner. He was going to fry fish and hush puppies. She didn't have the heart to tell him she wasn't crazy about fried fish, but decided instead she would force herself to eat every last fat gram. She was going to look good doing it too. She took pains with her hair, and she even threw on a little mascara and lip-gloss that had a hint of pink coloring. She chose a pair of GAP jeans, a pink J. Crew sweater, and her black boots. She thought her pink calamine lotion matched her clothing selection perfectly.

She hated leaving Trevor alone, but realized he was a big boy and could fend for himself. Oddly enough, she had a strange feeling he may have met someone. He was acting all secretive since she got home from her little excursion, but laughed until he cried when she told him about their trip to the emergency room.

The shot she received at the hospital helped dry her poison ivy. She thought she was going to die of itching if something didn't work.

Reluctantly, she admitted to herself that the Tuesday Club and her dad's murder had taken a backseat to her infatuation with Daniel Brooks. He was all she could think about during the day and night. She felt like a giggly teenage girl with her first crush, all warm and tingly inside, even if right now she was a tad pink and itchy.

10:00 PM

The McWhorter ground temperature was still warm from the seventy-degree weekend; however, the April ice storm still wreaked major havoc. The county's first responders worked through the night. Treacherous as it was, the ice storm had a magical effect on the town's appearance. The streets glistened, and the pear trees along both sides of Main Street sparkled. It looked like the town had been coated in a layer of diamond dust.

The ice facade fit right into McWhorter's public image; the ice-covered beauty was actually dangerous and deadly. The weight of the ice on the power lines was causing them to snap, leaving many in Rockford County without power. This was a real problem because most of the citizens didn't have any firewood or fuel left for their heaters. They had seen no need in replenishing their supply since winter had been officially over for seventeen days.

Jock kept his old Chevrolet four-wheel drive for bad spells like today. The truck's heavy body kept it from slipping and sliding. Driving slowly, he knew stopping and starting were the trickiest parts of driving on ice. His elderly passenger was "oohing" and "aahing" about the beauty of the ice-encrusted scenery, but he noticed she was still holding onto the armrest like her life depended on it. "This is sure strange weather. I've never seen the likes of it in all my eighty years," the old woman stated as he pulled into the parking lot of the church's makeshift emergency shelter. The truck came to a slow stop only feet from the church's salted sidewalk. He delivered her safely to the welcoming committee.

The words of the weird preacher man about ice and sleet kept coming to his mind regardless of how hard he tried to repress the thoughts. He knew the weather today was nothing but a coincidence, and it played right along with Geneva's plan of attack. He had to hand it to his opponent; he only wished he'd thought of it first. "What better way to convince voters to vote for her than by showing them that I'm crazier than a loon?" he thought. She was trying her doggonedest to drive him crazy.

Several people had to have been involved in her Sunday morning hoax. He figured one person was causing the lighting effects, another was operating the fog machine, and a third person had to be operating some kind of magnet from the basement that prevented his feet from moving. For fear of playing into Geneva's antics, he didn't dare ask anyone else about the funny business at church. Geneva would love for the town to think he'd lost his mind. On the contrary, call it divine inspiration or not, but the old man and now the weather had helped him to find his way.

Jock Ledford had been to the radio station earlier in the day and recorded an emergency message telling the good citizens to stay indoors and explained what to do if they had an emergency. Hearing his recorded message at least hourly, he grew fonder of it each time he heard it. Of course, Geneva wasn't going to be outdone by him, so he was sure she was the one who orchestrated opening Believers Baptist Church as a refuge to the folks without power. Again, she outfoxed him. So he decided if he couldn't beat her, then, he would join her. This was when he and his boys decided to put their Chevy trucks to good use. Jock and Geneva both capitalized on this unfortunate turn of the weather. Geneva Vaughn and her cronies were serving up optimism in the form of piping hot potato soup, corn bread, hot chocolate, and coffee.

Weary to the point of exhaustion, Jock felt better today than he had in weeks. It felt good to be out there and hearing his people praising him. "Bless your heart, Mayor Ledford. We didn't know what we'd do without Homer's oxygen," one lady said adoringly. He heard similar comments all night long as they promised him their vote come primary.

He liked being worshiped by the good citizens of McWhorter. The Ledford's had ruled and been idolized in McWhorter for a long time. His people had always gone out of their way to be good to him, but for some reason in the last few months, it seemed the tides had changed. He heard less and less of the "Bless yous" and noticed more people avoiding him or whispering when they thought he wasn't looking. He knew it was all because of that witch, Geneva Vaughn. It was all her fault. Clearly, he had underestimated her tenacity because he thought for sure she would tuck her tail and run after the unfortunate death of her little grandbaby. Even extending the olive branch of peace to her didn't work but rather resulted in her throwing the olive branch back into his face. He had to hand it to Geneva; she was a gutsy broad. "Too bad she would have to die," he thought.

Making his rounds in the shelter, he made sure everyone was comfortable before he headed out in search of some other desperate soul. Suddenly, it dawned on him that tomorrow was Tuesday and there was no way they could meet at the secret meeting place in this weather. "Where're we gonna meet tomorrow?" he thought in a panic.

County Judge Jack Brown was at the shelter spreading goodwill as well. Jock saw the judge executive in the kitchen. Jock motioned for the judge to come to him. The judge handed his ladle to his wife and did as his leader requested.

"What's up?" the judge said in a low voice.

"With all this wild weather, I had plum forgotten about the meeting tomorrow. You know there's no way we can meet at the woods, and I'm afraid to meet at Hazels knowing someone's watching us there. You got any ideas?" Jock asked.

Jack's facial expression remained unchanged until the light bulb went off in his head. "You got the keys to your church house?" Jack asked.

"I sure as hell do! Good idea. Why didn't I think of that? That's a perfect place. We can even park around back so people can't see our cars from the road. I knew you were good for something." Jock pounded the judge's back in gratitude.

Jack was all smiles knowing he had pleased the mayor and said, "I'll get on the horn and get it organized. Why don't you see if Jeb can cook in the church's kitchen? I've sure been missing those biscuits of his," the judge stated while he licked his lips.

"It's the sausage gravy I've been hankering for. Why, Jack, I believe you came up with another excellent idea. You're just full of 'em today." Jock placed his arm around his friend as a gesture of triumph.

Jock left the church on his way to pick up another of his loyal voters. The tides seemed to be turning, if it weren't so slick, Jock would have felt like jumping up and clicking his heels together.

CHAPTER 28

Foolproof

Tuesday, April 8, 2008

Smiling from ear to ear, Jeb kept refilling the gravy bowls. He could tell he'd been sorely missed. The majority of the Tuesday Club members ate like they'd been plum starved to death. "My, my, if I hadn't fed you this morning, you fellers would sure 'nuff dried up and blowed away," he joked with his customers. The cook was glad for the business and actually missed the buzz of excitement that preparing the secret meal created for him. Cooking for the smaller group was a little easier, but he thought it was strange that in such a short time this breakfast club had dwindled from twelve down to only eight.

As he washed the dishes, he noticed one plate hadn't been touched. It was the plate belonging to the banker. It didn't look like he did anything but move his food around a bit. Jeb wasn't the only one who noticed the banker's lack of appetite. Realizing he should go ahead and confess to the man about the money, Jock couldn't bring himself to say the words because he was having too much fun watching him squirm. "Served him right."

"Did you bring the money?" Jock asked the banker.

Rupert answered by nodding his head. Taking over fifty-thousand dollars out of his own bank account, he reluctantly brought it to the meeting so they could distribute to use to buy votes and election officers. This bought him time to find Mayzella. The election officers had always been a critical element to their strategy. They were the eyes and ears of the election. According to the clerk, they would be even more important at this election.

They would be the ones who'd have to inspect the machines at the beginning and, then again, at the end. They would also be the ones who were responsible for making sure the tally tape from the actual votes would be illegible so no one could verify the results. Instead, they would have to depend on the doctored tapes with their desired results.

Jock called the meeting to order after he belched a compliment to the chef. "Lawsy, Jeb, if you hadn't fed us this morning, I was going to pine away to nothing." The mayor pulled the top of his britches out from his waist to show he had several inches of play in his waistband. Other members told how much weight they"d been losing too. Though, none of them let on about the real reason for the weight loss—they were afraid their chair would be the next one empty. Some of the men had whispered that Woody had been on a rampage to kill them. Others feared that God was striking them dead as a punishment for the sins of the Tuesday Club.

The mayor called the meeting to order by proclaiming, "We've got a lot of work to do this morning. Before we get to the meat and potatoes of the meeting, let's start with some side items. Roy Allen, you got someone to buy up unpaid property tax and front our TC Inc.?"

"Sure do. It wouldn't look none too good on us if the citizens knew we were the ones behind buying up our good citizens unpaid property taxes."

The protégé wasn't following the significance of what they were talking about. "That sounds like we're doing a good thing, right?"

Rolling his eyes before he spoke, Roy Allen knew this rookie had a lot to learn. "After three years of paying the property tax, the property belongs to us. We've made a lot of money over the years, and it's perfectly legal."

The protégé asked, "What happens if they decide to pay before the three years are up?"

"If they decide to pay before the three years are up, then they pay the property tax to us at a hefty penalty. It's pretty much a loan at a very high interest rate. TC Inc. will be buying up property tax in Rockford County as well as twenty other counties."

"Yep, it's been a good money maker for us over the years, and just like our good lawyer said, it's one hundred percent legal." Jock reiterated as he took back over the meeting. "Joe Matt, you got that list of workers ready to review."

The chief deputy rose from his seat and passed out the proposed list of workers he and the county clerk had recommended.

Silently, they reviewed the list. The farmer broke the silence. "Why the hell do you have Zuri Martin on this list? She's a pure saint, and no amount of money thrown her way would make her cheat at a game of hokey pokey, let alone a major election."

The county clerk took the floor and stated, "I'm glad you noticed that Bobby. We decided we would only rig eight machines. That way it won't look as suspicious. You know Geneva's guard will be let down when she sees we have Zuri Martin and other salt of the earth folks like her as officers."

The mayor digested what the clerk was saying, and he had to agree with him. Only, he didn't like the clerk being the one with all the best ideas, and he didn't like the fact the clerk and the chief deputy had been making decisions behind his back.

Roy Allen Jones, the lawyer, asked the group about the commonwealth attorney's race.

Again, the clerk being the expert on all things pertaining to elections piped up and said, "I'll tell you that Lowell Evans is out there working his ass off every day."

The mayor wasn't thinking about the race, but instead was still focused on what was said earlier. "How can you be sure what the tally will be when you only have eight machines rigged? Looks to me like you'll have to have them all rigged, or you've left us exposed?"

The clerk and chief deputy looked at each other, both willing the other one to speak. Finally, the clerk broke the silence. "Actually, the rigged precincts account for seventy percent of the votes. We'll also plant officers at each of these other precincts, and if it looks like we're in trouble, then we'll go to plan B."

"Plan B? Humor me." The mayor strummed the table in anticipation of their response.

"Before the election, we'll run a test with these machines. We'll keep the tabulations. If the race gets out of hand, then our planted officers will destroy the real tabulations and use the doctored ones printed during the trial run," the county clerk answered.

"I thought the reports were time stamped," the mayor said still poking holes in their plan.

"They are, but it's amazing what a little iron heat will do to that paper," the clerk countered smugly.

"Boys, lately I've been hearing about this being foolproof and that being foolproof. You've been making decisions without my consult, and you're playing with my very livelihood. I've humored you all long enough. Look here at poor Rupert. He couldn't even eat his breakfast, now could you, son?"

Rupert knew where he was going with this conversation, and he didn't open his mouth. Instead, he just nodded his head once.

"Yep, Rupert insisted he take care of all our money. It wasn't good enough we left our money in the bank or put it in a safe, but Rupert, here, talked us into hiding it into multiple offshore accounts. He assured us his system was foolproof, and our money was safe, but it wasn't. Was it, son?"

Again, Rupert slightly shook his head up and down.

"You see, Rupert let a little whore into his safety zone. Boys, what've I told you over and over? You can't let your tally wag do your thinking for you."

Rupert closed his eyes expecting a bullet to enter his brain any minute, but instead he felt the clap of the mayor's chubby hand land squarely on his back. "I'm your leader for a reason. I've got to look out for all our best interests. Now, don't you fret, Rupee boy. Mayzella may not have been loyal to you, but she was loyal to me. I now have control of all the money since you can't be trusted."

Not knowing whether to laugh or to cry, Rupert was too choked up to speak at the time. Once again, he only nodded.

"Now just think, boys. If I didn't have the foresight then that little gal would be over thirty million dollars richer, and we'd be nothing without that money, and McWhorter would go to hell in a hand basket without us." The mayor took a swig of his coffee before continuing with his point. "Now, I'm real proud of you boys for thinking this vote rigging system up, but don't you try to blow smoke up my ass. You understand? You boys come and talk to me about your plans involving the Tuesday Club. Let me make it very clear. I'm in charge here, and I don't want any more surprises at this meeting. No more of this foolproof shit, you hear?"

After the mayor made a few revisions to the plan, the cash was distributed, and the meeting was adjourned.

Making small talk, the men questioned Joe Matt about the investigation into the Vaughn girl's death. The chief deputy told them what little he knew.

Leave it to the farmer to reduce the tension when he said, "Boys, my love rocket should be delivered next week."

The protégé asked, "What the hell's a love rocket?" He then sized Bobby up as he spoke. If cousins could be extreme opposites, then Joe Matt and Bobby Sizemore were just that. Bobby was a slight man, and his long face sort of resembled his beloved Holsteins. Looks aside, the farmer was witty and very likable, but rumor had it he beat his wife every time he drank hard liquor.

"A love rocket is just another name for the semen collection contraption. It's actually an electro-ejaculator for my prize bull, Bocephus Boone. If it works like I think it will, then it may change my whole approach to farming. Me and Ethel've been getting up at four in the morning and milking twice a day, seven days a week, three hundred and sixty-five days a year. If I can get me a few more studs like my baby Bocephus and sell their semen, then I can make as much money from selling them baby makers from a few bulls as I can by selling milk from one hundred Holstein cattle. Can you believe some bull semen goes for as much as a million dollars?"

The men listened to Bobby intently and didn't say a word until he was finished. As if on cue, they all burst into laughter. Making crude comments about not forgetting the Vaseline, the guys left the church house.

CHAPTER 29

Examiners, Mailmen, and Cougars

Tuesday, April 8, 2008 7:00 AM

Waiting for his entire body to quit shaking, Rupert Jones sat in his Mercedes until he was fit to drive. He was relieved Jock had the money but was angered he let him worry for four days. Now that he didn't have to worry about the money, his thoughts turned to the examiners. He had been too preoccupied to pay much attention to the examiners on their initial arrival. Other than briefly speaking to the head examiner in the hallway, Rupert hadn't been in contact with the group. Now that he was back in his right mind, Rupert thought it would be wise for him to pay a little visit with them this morning.

Not sure if it was his imagination, but something didn't feel right to Rupert when he walked through the bank. Call it paranoia, but Rupert had a funny feeling something was going on in his bank that he didn't know about—a party he hadn't been invited to. He decided he needed to find out exactly what loan files the examiners had requested just to be on the safe side.

Walking past his empty secretary's desk, he went straight to his office and placed a call asking for a complete list of the examiner's requested files. Shortly, a loan clerk was at his office with two sheets of paper in her hand. Rupert motioned for her to enter, but didn't utter a word, afraid his shaky voice would give him away. She handed him one sheet of paper. "This was the original list they requested," she explained.

Rupert reviewed the list, and it looked like a random list of loan files. Thankfully, he didn't see any of his doctored loans on this list; he sighed inwardly.

"Here's the list they requested late yesterday evening," she said as she handed him the second sheet of paper.

Rupert couldn't say a word. He only nodded at the loan clerk. He wasn't sure how long she stayed at his desk. His vision went blurry. All he knew was when he finally was able to focus, he was alone. The second list contained all the loans he had siphoned funds from over the years. The list was as complete as if he had prepared it himself. "Dear Lord, Mayzella's struck again!"

10:00 AM

The mailman was over an hour late. She realized the roads were bad, but it still aggravated her that he was late. Unbeknownst to the mailman, she used him to set the pace of her daily workout routine.

Lizzie Jean worked out in her physical fitness room from ten until eleven each morning. When both kids left for college, Lizzie Jean turned to exercise as a way to occupy more of her time. Her husband Rupert was ultra conservative. He always played it safe even if it meant being on the side of dull and routine. This was a trait she hated about him yet loved at the same time.

Saving the elliptical cross trainer workout until the end of her session, it was during this exercise she could look out the window to see the mail truck which signaled it was time for her to start her cool down. She wasn't sure how long she worked on her elliptical before she realized ten forty-five had come and gone many minutes ago. "Where is that damn mailman?" She'd gone thirteen minutes over her time limit because the mailman wasn't on time.

After showering she began to work on her hair and makeup. Her hair wasn't cooperating. Of course, it was the mailman's fault. She now had a scapegoat to blame anything that went wrong with her day. "Oh well, we all can't look perfect every day," she softly admitted to herself.

Lizzie Jean's long blond hair had been part of her so long she had an anxiety attack just thinking about parting with it. Compromising with her stylist, she cut several inches of her hair so it laid a couple of inches past her shoulders, but that was the best that she could do. After all, she needed it long enough to pull up in a ponytail. She absolutely refused to give up her ponytail regardless of her age.

Choosing a pair of her favorite jeans, she then tucked a blue tank top into the top of her britches before she finally heard the mailman's brakes squeal. She looked at her clock and noted it was noon; the mailman was over an hour late. Looping one of her favorite belts through the loops of her jeans, she then chose a white long sleeve blouse to finish her ensemble.

When Lizzie Jean was fully dressed, she went out the front door to fetch her mail. She wasn't the kind of woman to go out the door in her housecoat. As the wife of the town's bank's president, she had a certain image to maintain. Noticing the melting icicles hanging on the power lines, she guarded her head with her hands as she hurried to the mailbox.

Tuesday was not a big day for mail, so she was surprised to see her daily paper had company—a small package addressed to her. Instantly recognizing the writing on the package, she was excited to see what Mayzella had sent her.

Safely inside, she tore into the small package like a kid opening a Christmas present. She was disappointed there was no letter or note from Mayzella, only a single DVD enclosed in a plastic case. Placing the DVD in the player, she sat back on her leather couch and settled in to watch whatever it was Mayzella had sent her. The television came raring to life with a familiar background—the interior of her husband's unoccupied bank office. She thought the large expensive desk was overpowering for the room. She tried to tell him this, but he just loved that desk. She smiled as she saw her husband enter the room. She wondered what in the world possessed Mayzella to send her a DVD with her husband in his office. She continued to watch the screen for some revelation.

Never in her wildest dreams did it occur to her to doubt her husband's fidelity, and even as she watched the DVD, she was clueless. She and Rupert had a good marriage and an entertaining sex life, plus Rupert had practically stood on his head to win her over during their courtship. He asked her to marry him a total of three times before she relented. He was damn lucky to have her, and she let him know it on a daily basis.

When Mayzella came into view on the screen, it was only instinct for Lizzie Jean to size up her appearance as mediocre at best. It wasn't until Rupert smiled at Mayzella before Lizzie Jean realized something wasn't quite right. When Mayzella began to undress in front of her husband, she finally understood. Lizzie Jean was in shock and couldn't move a muscle. She was fixated on the television screen as she watched Mayzella have sex with her husband on the large desk. Guess the desk's size had a purpose after all.

The screen went black, and just as Lizzie Jean thought she could actually breathe, it started playing again. This time the camera was in a different location in the office and on a different day. Lizzie Jean watched one sex scene after another, her husband and her best friend in the starring roles, until her eyes would no longer focus and her head became woozy. She didn't even feel the pain when her head collided with the coffee table as she crashed to the floor.

3:00 p.m.

Rupert worked alone in his office until late in the afternoon focused on coming up with his strategy. Deciding indignation and outrage would be his first responses when confronted of wrongdoing, he would then give the appropriate amount of time before he realized the coincidence between this issue and the sudden departure of his secretary. He would say, "Now, it all makes sense," like a huge mystery had been solved for him. After all, Mayzella was the employee who drew up all the paperwork as well as the one who closed all the loans in question. These examiners would have to understand the wrath of a jealous lover; this would at least buy him time. Of course, if this plan didn't hold mustard, then plan B would be to find which examiner was most receptive to bribery. He wouldn't go down without a fight. That was for sure. "Mayzella, the game's not over yet. I'm going to make you sorry you ever heard my name after I get finished with you."

Knowing he needed his wife as an ally, he thought it best for him to go home and let her know that Mayzella had set him up. If he knew one thing, it was that he could count on Lizzie Jean to support him.

3:15 p.m.

Lizzie Jean regained consciousness and had a throbbing headache. Feeling around on her head, she just knew her pump knot had to be the size of a goose egg. "Oww!" It was. She managed to clean up the mess her fall created before ever so slowly walking to the kitchen, each step causing a sharp pain to shoot through her entire body.

Needing to review the damage to her face, she headed down the Mexican tiled hallway to look in her large decorative mirror. When she looked at her reflection, she didn't recognize the stranger looking back at her. Of course, the woman looking back at her had the same blondish hair and the same blue eyes she remembered, but she could tell the woman looking back at her was not the same Lizzie Jean of an hour ago. In a matter of sixty short minutes, Lizzie Jean had a complete makeover of her soul. The crying wimpy version of the old Lizzie Jean had been replaced with a steel heart and soul of a psychopath.

Lizzie looked deeper into the mirror trying to find that young girl who was once full of dreams and full of life, the same girl who wanted to make a difference in the world. Slowly turning the pages of her life in a backward motion, she found herself thinking of the time before she compromised her life and married the dull banker. It was the time when she was the life of every party, the belle of the ball, and the tiara-toting beauty queen. She was pretty special if she had to say so herself. She dated a lot of different fellows but it was mainly the chase that intrigued her. As soon as she had them where she wanted, she moved on to the next conquest. Of course, that was before she met Professor Workman.

She fell hard for her chemistry professor. Professor Workman was in his early thirties, and she was convinced he was her soul mate. He was handsome, but her biggest attraction to him was his contagious passion for life.

She didn't even mind he was married. Confident in her abilities, she knew he would come to his senses in good time. She had to hand it to him; he wasn't an easy conquest. She had to work hard. His original interest was strictly platonic, and his intentions were extremely honorable. The more honorable he was, the more she yearned for him. It only took one taste of her forbidden nectar in the back of the supply closet for him to be hooked. They were very good together, and together, they planned on conquering the world, one chemical compound at a time.

This bliss was short-lived, and her world fell completely apart when her parents received wind of her unholy relationship with the married professor. They pulled her out of college. She became a prisoner in her parent's mansion. Placing her professor on the back burner, she waited for just the right opportunity to plan her escape, knowing he would be there waiting for her.

Convinced that lulling her family into a false sense of security was her best bet, she knew then she could make her move to run away with her professor. She met Rupert Jones at this very vulnerable time in her life. She was sorely against going on a blind date arranged by her father, but knew there would be no better way to gain their trust than to appease them with this boring banker. Rupert Jones was nice looking, sweet, and so very predictable. She bet he never did one spontaneous thing in his life. She had to hand it to him; he was tenacious if he was anything. Too bad her heart belonged to one man.

With her parents' guard down, they made the mistake of leaving her alone with a telephone. It was the worst day of her life. It was this day when she found out that her precious professor had not only left the college but had left his wife as well. Just as she and her lover had originally planned, he had moved to Africa with her lab partner instead of her. Supposedly, the couple was married in a tribal ceremony. Something in Lizzie Jean died that day, and she truly became her mother's daughter. Her dating Rupert Jones made her parents very happy. He just kept coming back to her until he wore her resolve down. Finally, she relented, thinking he was a safe choice for her and truly the path of least resistance. She immersed herself in this new frivolous life and never let herself think about Professor Workman again—until now.

Lizzie Jean re-entered her current life and thought, "What a fool I've been!" She tried to contemplate what to do. She thought first about packing her bags and leaving, but she decided that wasn't her style. Finally, she knew what she had to do—she had to make him pay. After all, he was supposed to be the safe choice, and marrying him wasn't supposed to have caused her this kind of pain. In a matter of minutes, she had formulated her plan.

4:00 PM

Ordinarily, Jock Ledford could make the drive from his office to his home blindfolded. It was a good thing too because he was basically driving on autopilot as his truck slowly rounded the curves. He was literally jolted back into the real world with his initial thought that he was being electrocuted until he realized he had turned his cell phone on vibrate mode. "Damn computer gadgets," he said before he stated his normal greeting. "Mayor Ledford."

"Mayor, this is Joe Matt, and I wanted to let you know the preliminary results of the autopsy are in, and it doesn't look good," the chief deputy calmly stated.

"Doesn't look good?"

"Nope, it's being classified as a homicide, and the sheriff and the prosecuting attorney's been behind closed doors all morning about your boy."

"Is that right? What do we need to do?"

"I don't know, other than find that yellow car," Joe Matt answered.

The mayor lied, "I only wished I knew where to start to look for that yeller vehicle."

4:30 PM

The house sitting on the cul-de-sac on 321 Rosebud Lane was the best looking house in the neighborhood. Its very presence from the dignified shade of red brick to the black of the shutters shouted that the president of the bank lived there. Inside, the home was immaculate as always, and Rupert heard the soft music playing as he entered from the mudroom. He could tell the music was coming from the kitchen. Lizzie Jean was preparing dinner in nothing but high heels and an apron. "Damn, I'm feeling better already!" he thought.

Lizzie Jean lay down her mixing spoon and practically ravaged Rupert as he entered the room. "Whoa, now hold on, honey," he stated as he tried to peel her off him. "What's come over you?" he said with a big grin on his face.

"I don't know how to explain it, but have you ever had one of those days when you woke up and felt like making a change in your life? I feel like a courageous cougar," she purred.

Placing his brief case on the floor, he hastily picked her up and carried her to the bedroom. "Cougars are cats, and you know how I like a little pussy," he laughed.

She stifled her laughter by burying her face into his chest. *Yes, she now knew all too well this particular fondness*, she thought as she began unbuttoning his stuffy banker's shirt.

They made love for over an hour. Their lovemaking went from sweet and sensual to animalistic. Lizzie Jean was insatiable.

Lost in their thoughts, they both lay on the bed as they regained their strength. Neither said a word until Rupert broke the magic by leaving their love nest and heading toward their bathroom. The room was accented with red and black towels, candles, and other matching wall decorations. The bathroom was as large as many bedrooms. Lizzie Jean's garden tub was separate from the shower and used mainly by her. Rupert's shower was a large walk-in he'd designed himself so it would spray at different angles.

Rupert had been in the shower for several minutes before noticing through the fogged glass shower door he had company. His naked wife had entered and was at the sink located directly across from the shower stall. He smiled thinking about their recent romp. He thought he may not have to replace Mayzella's position too soon if he could come home every day to this type of treatment. He smelled them before he actually saw them. Lizzie Jean looked like she had some cleaning supplies in her hands. He had long ago accepted she was more than just a neat freak. The bathroom looked sterile to him, but he wasn't about to express his opinion to Lizzie, so he turned his attention back to his showering.

He heard the bathroom door shut; he knew he was once again alone in his thoughts. Sniffing, he noticed the cleaning chemicals had a very strong odor. His chest began to constrict, and he was having difficulty breathing. His nostrils and eyes were now stinging from the strong stench of the chemicals. The steam from the spray of the jet seemed to carry the smell. He thought he was going to die if he didn't get some fresh air soon. He reached to turn the water off, and he found himself struggling as he tried to remember the right direction to turn the faucet handle.

He tried to open the shower stall, but it wouldn't open. He wasn't sure if the inside door handle was broken or if it wasn't working due to his disorientation. He was trapped. Trying to muster enough strength to yell for Lizzie, he couldn't make a sound. His lungs felt like they were made of lead. He couldn't breathe. His vision was blurry. Feeling the bile of his empty stomach in his throat, he crumpled over in the shower. The last thing he saw in his mind was Mayzella's smug face before the room went completely black.

Meanwhile, Lizzie Jean was in the kitchen putting the finishing touches on Rupert's favorite meal.

CHAPTER 30

Hell's Bells

Wednesday, April 9, 2008, 7:30 AM

Researching the process of bull semen collection had taken more time this morning than the avenger had originally anticipated. It was a rather interesting procedure. He heard the thud of the roll of newspaper hitting his front door. Deciding his research could wait, he opened the door to fetch his paper.

The avenger was shocked when he saw the headlines, "Bank President in Critical Condition." He read the short article explaining that Rupert Jones had been found unresponsive in the shower. According to the newspaper, no one knew what caused Rupert to collapse. He was in critical condition. The newspaper article quoted his wife asking for prayers as her husband battled for his life.

Reaching for his wallet, the avenger pulled out a small to do list and marked the banker's name off this list. First, the criminal was shot, and now, the banker has fallen ill with no help from him or his accomplice; this just confirmed they were doing the right thing. He looked heavenward and gave silent thanks for the help. He felt no remorse because all he and his accomplice did was act as catalysts to put some things in motion. The Lord was the one who made the final judgment. Poor Woody, he was a victim of this club and had never been on their list; the avenger sure hoped Woody would come straggling in anytime now.

He wasted no time calling the accomplice to talk about the recent turn of events about the banker. They spent the rest of the conversation discussing the farmer's love rocket and making their plans to avenge more innocent blood.

7:45 AM

The county judge executive and the county court clerk were sitting in their vehicles waiting for Jock's Buick to pull in its rightful parking space. They both were in an uproar and were going to demand Jock do something to protect them. Jock pulled into his parking space and was met by the two-pale-faced politicians. "Damn it!" Jock was upset because he had taken his little blue pill this morning, and he didn't want to embarrass himself. Now, it looked like Sissy would have to take a back seat as he met with these old codgers.

"Have you heard?" were the first words he heard when he opened the car door.

Slowly placing his feet on the concrete slab, Jock made sure they landed on solid surface. "Heard what?" the mayor asked perturbed because evidently they once again knew something he didn't know.

"About Rupert being in critical condition at the hospital," the judge explained.

"Mercy sakes! What happened?" the mayor asked in a high-pitched squeak.

The clerk explained, "They're not sure, but they know it happened in his shower."

"Hell's bells!" was all the mayor could manage as he did the math in his head. If Rupert didn't make it, then he was down five members. This news definitely affected his libido. Huffing he finally said, "Come on in, boys, and tell me all about it."

CHAPTER 31

A Woman's Scorn

Thursday, April 10, 2008, 11:00 AM

Mayzella Wooten was very nervous. She called the bank to see if the rest of her money had been wired into her account. Nothing. "Damn him!" She knew better than to have trusted the mayor. She was beginning to smell a double cross. Jock told her the deed to the condo would be mailed to her and explained her only job was to keep Deek out of trouble for a little while. He gave her fifty-thousand dollars in cash the night she left McWhorter. He told her he would wire the rest of her money once she had a new account set up in Florida. The account had been opened days ago, and she made sure Jock had all the information to make the wire.

Fearing the mayor was capable of something like this, she was glad she took some extra liberties when she helped him transfer the money into the new offshore accounts. Looks like she and Deek were going to need it after all.

She hadn't met Deek until she picked him up in Knoxville, Tennessee, on the night she left her job, her lover, and her old life behind in McWhorter. She left her car in the storage unit Deek had rented and rode the rest of the way to Florida in Deek's little yellow sports car. Deek was several years younger than she was and was very good for her ego. Each time Deek looked at Mayzella, he declared she was the most beautiful woman in the world. At first, she enjoyed his compliments and boyish charm, but his goofball routine and his fixation on making crystal meth grated on her nerves. Thankfully, he didn't partake in the meth, only considered himself an expert in cooking it. According to Deek, anyone could cook meth, but making crystal meth was an art form.

"Hey, Zella, come hyere!" Deek hollered to her from the deck.

Mayzella cringed. Her first instinct was to ignore him, but on second thought, she was afraid he would shriek again, and she didn't want her neighbors hearing his hillbilly, off-key, goose honk of a voice. She walked out on the deck where Deek was reclined on the chaise lounge wearing only his Dale Junior NASCAR boxer briefs. He had a pair of binoculars in his hand which was not unusual as babe watching had become his favorite past time. She was expecting him to point out some big breasted woman, but instead he passed her the binoculars and said, "Look over to the right, and see if that there man with the blue hat looks familiar to you? I could swear he keeps looking right back at me through his binoculars. There's something common about him that makes me think I've seen him before."

The color drained from her face when she recognized the mayor's friend. He was dressed as a vacationer, but she would recognize him anywhere. Most people had no idea of his close association with the mayor, but she was one of the very few people who knew of their true relationship as well as this man's sexual perversion. The mayor asked her to have sex with the man as a favor to him, and it wasn't something she ever hoped to repeat. She shivered as she thought to herself, "He's one mean and kinky bastard!" She'd always thought him to be a fine Christian man, as did most of the other folks in Rockford County. Now, she believed him to be more akin to the devil than to God.

She knew they were in serious trouble. "Get ready, we've got to get out of here," she ordered.

"Zella, you're not serious? We just got hyere."

"Dead serious! Now, get a move on if you want to live through the day."

Deek may not have been the sharpest tool in the shed, but he could tell by the look in Mayzella's eyes she wasn't kidding.

Mayzella headed toward the bedroom, grabbed a small overnight bag, and started throwing only necessities into it. She picked up her cell phone and dialed the number to the only person in the whole world she trusted. She knew she needed help.

1:00 PM

According to Jock Ledford, funeral homes and hospitals were two of the best places to campaign. Jock insisted his eldest son, Jon, accompany him to the hospital to check on Rupert during their dinner break. He felt Jon needed to get his face out there more if one day he were going to follow in his political footsteps.

They found Lizzie Jean sitting in a small wooden chair staring into space in a private room inside the intensive care unit. Her long blond hair was pulled into a ponytail, and her face had a scrubbed clean sheen to it. The mayor gave her a nod when he walked in the room. His eyes went from Lizzie Jean to the lifeless form in the hospital bed. Rupert's face was as white as the sheet that covered him. He had tubes going in every direction from his body. Rupert's eyes opened briefly, but Jock could tell they were unseeing. He had an apparatus over his mouth and nose that was pumping life into his body.

Startled, it took Lizzie Jean a minute to realize she had company. She bid the men to sit down on the other side of Rupert's bed.

"You holding up okay?" Jon asked.

"I'm okay," she stated. "I'm just not sure if Rupert's going to pull out of this or not."

The concerned mayor asked, "What's the doctor saying?"

"Not much."

"Do they know what caused this? Do you think someone could have slipped in and done this to him?" Jock had to know.

"I don't think so. He was still in the shower when I found him. An intruder would've had to come past me in order to get in or out of the house. They think his condition was caused by a couple of things. When he fell in the shower, he must have hit his head pretty hard, but their biggest concern is the damage to his lungs. I'd just cleaned the bathroom when he showered," Lizzie Jean stated in a dry, matter-of-fact tone.

"Cleaning chemicals?" Jock countered.

Large crocodile tears slid from Lizzie's eyes and slowly made their trek down her cheek. "Rupert always fussed at me and called me a clean freak," she said the last two words in broken syllables through her sobs. She tried to pull it together as she finished her thought, "And now, it looks like my fanatic obsession on cleanliness may have contributed to his condition."

When she started crying, then Jock was ready to fly the coop. His parting words were, "Lizzie, darling, I know you've got to be plum tuckered out, and we didn't mean to bother you. We just wanted to check on you and see if you're fairing okay. You know that your man here is a close personal friend of mine, and I would do anything to help him. Now, you know I'm just a phone call away, don't cha?"

Lizzie Jean didn't look up at Jock; she just nodded her head and said, "Please pray that he comes through. I don't know what I'll do without him."

Jock and Jon left the sterile room before they made their way down the long tiled hallway. Jock was troubled about something, but he couldn't quite put his finger on it. It sounded like it was another accident for another Tuesday Club member. "Too many accidents," he thought. By looking at Rupert, Jock knew short of a miracle—he would not recover. He could see the worry in Lizzie Jean's eyes and the sincerity in her comments. He just couldn't put his finger on what was bothering him about the scene. Something was definitely nagging at him. Something wasn't right.

Only after Jock entered his car and saw his bottle of Listerine lying on his seat did it dawn on him what was wrong with the picture. "Jon, I believe I remember old man Rupert bragging about Rupert Jr. marrying a chemistry major. Now, wouldn't a chemistry major know better than to mix certain chemicals together?" Now, it all made sense to Jock. He could sum it up in one word. Mayzella. Not only did Mayzella take revenge on Rupert by reporting his crooked ways to the OCC as he'd instructed her, but sounds like Mayzella also wreaked a little havoc on the home front as well. "Son, you've heard the saying that 'hell has no fury like a woman's scorn.' Take heed, my son, to mind your *P*s and *Q*s when it comes to your extracurricular activities, or it could be you in that hospital bed."

He hoped he hadn't underestimated Mayzella. Speaking of the smart whore made him remember that he needed to make a call to see if his loose ends had been tied up. He shook his head as he thought, "Mayzella is a smart little whore. She knows way too much. She and Deek were too big of a risk to keep alive."

CHAPTER 32

Sleeping with the Enemy

Friday, April 11, 2008

Trevor Grant found comfort in researching the history of McWhorter. The more he learned about the people of McWhorter, the easier for him to understand their ways. He found a strange new kinship with all he met. It seemed as though all the family trees had various branches that interlinked with the other trees in McWhorter's small forest. The newspaper cellar became his refuge.

Today, Trevor insisted Tillie come and help him, not necessarily because he needed her help, but more as a way to pull her head out of the clouds. She'd settled into Daniel's routine and was too comfortable with it. It seemed both Tillie and Daniel had lost all interest in the Tuesday Club. The only other person that seemed the least bit interested in his research was his uncle Willie, but he still seemed pretty sidetracked as well. He hadn't been able to talk with the sheriff in a couple of days. He tried to call him a few times, but his phone must have been messed up because it would go straight to voice mail. He thought if he didn't hear from him today he needed to check on him.

Trevor settled onto the seat with the microfiche machine and started with 1961. He kept coming up with three common last names that were associated with the Ledfords: Smith, Sizemore, and Jones. He jotted down on a piece of paper all the people of Rockford County he could recollect with those last names. His list was comprised of Joe Matt Sizemore, Jimmy Sizemore, Bobby Sizemore, Albert Dean Smith, Bartholomew Smith,

Rupert Jones, Rufus Jones, and Roy Allen Jones. "Tillie, what do you know about Joe Matt Sizemore?"

"Not a lot. I know he's Danny's friend, but Danny doesn't talk a lot about him. Why, what'dya find?"

"Nothing really. I just find the names Sizemore, Smith, and Jones associated with the three Ledford mayors in the past."

"We need to talk with Danny and find out what he can tell us about these families."

Trevor rolled his eyes at his sister. She couldn't say two sentences without bringing Daniel Brooks name into the conversation. They worked in silence for the rest of the hour.

"Oh, my goodness!" Tillie's voice raised three decibels with each syllable a higher octave than the previous one.

Leaving his chair in one fell swoop, Trevor was at his sister's side. "What is it?"

Tillie didn't answer, instead just pointed at a picture of three young shirtless boys. The boys looked to be in their early teens, and all were grinning ear to ear as they held up a catfish as large as they were. Trevor recognized Jock Ledford as the shorter boy in the middle right away. It took him a minute to realize that the boy on the right with the large ears and lopsided grin was none other than Sheriff Willie Osborne.

Tillie tapped her pink polished index finger on the photo of the third boy. "Do you recognize him?"

There was something definitely familiar about the face, but he couldn't place it until he read the name in the caption below. "Tinker Brooks?" It was then he realized Tillie's squeal was more about this third boy in the photo than about their uncle Willie being childhood friends with Jock Ledford.

"Granny's letter warned us about trusting anyone." Trevor lowered his voice just above a whisper.

Tillie's voice was loud and clear. "There's no way Daniel's involved. Now let's be rational, just because these boys went fishing together when they were young, doesn't mean they're part of the Tuesday Club. I don't think Uncle Willie would be involved, but I know with all my heart Danny would never ever be part of this madness."

"He's been part of Jock Ledford's world for a long time. You do remember Caroline Ledford was his girlfriend for many years? What if you're sleeping with the enemy?"

Tillie didn't answer with a comeback immediately. She chose her words very carefully, "Hmmm. Interesting question you pose there, brother dear. If Caroline Ledford is the enemy, then, I guess I could ask you the same question. You really didn't think you could hide things from me, did you? Now, let's talk about just which one of us is sleeping with the enemy?"

CHAPTER 33

Crunch Time

Saturday, April 12, 2008, 3:00 AM

The phone rang only twice before the mayor answered. "Where the hell are you?" he said knowing the caller could only be one person.

"They're gone," the hit man stated emotionlessly.

The mayor, groggy and in a state between sleep and awake, couldn't think straight. "What?" he asked.

"It's like the rapture. They've vanished. The yellow car's here, but there's no sign of 'em."

"I thought I told you to take care of those loose ends as soon as you got there? But no, you had to take care of your tallywag, didn't you? They must've seen you. Now you listen here, and you listen well. You find 'em! You find 'em today and discard what's left so a gator or a shark can get rid of the evidence." Not holding anything back, he slammed the receiver back on the set then he grabbed a cigarette and lit it. The room was pitch black with the amber glow of the cigarette, the only light. The light of the cigarette would grow brighter as he sucked on it, and then would fade as he held it between his two fingers and thought about his strategy. "Now where would that little whore go?" he contemplated out loud.

He took one last long drag of the cigarette before he tapped the life out of the fire altogether. He cradled the back of his head in his hands. He smiled when he figured out exactly how he could track her down. He had to hand it to Mayzella Wooten. She was one smart little Crow's Creek whore, but thankfully, he couldn't say the same thing about ole Deek. Deek was so dumb he didn't know his asshole from a hole in the ground. He would lead him right to them.

4:30 AM

Mayzella liked the feel of the steering wheel of the white Range Rover. She chose this particular vehicle not because she knew it was Lizzie Jean's dream car, but because it was rugged. She realized she needed a vehicle that could handle rough terrain. Admittedly, she did experience a thrill wondering what Lizzie Jean would think about her new ride.

The new smell of the tan leather seats was sweeter than any of those perfumes Lizzie Jean had insisted she test during their shopping sprees. She had inherited an extra sensitive sniffer from her momma. Her momma could sniff out a man from a mile away. She said it was the aftershave she could smell, but half the men her momma fooled with had faces that hadn't seen a razor in a good long time.

Thankfully, the mayor had taught her a few things. He taught her to trust no one, especially him. That extra half million she had wired earlier in the day of her departure had sure come in handy and, hopefully, would help to save her life.

"Wake up, lover boy," she said as they crossed over the Tennessee line into Kentucky.

She was on her way back to the area she had only days earlier escaped from. She decided her best defense was to take the offense.

5:00 AM

The early morning air was heavy in Tillie's lungs as she grasped to find her running rhythm. Every labored breath was visible as the mist from her expended moisture hung in the air like a ghost. Blowing out generously, she liked seeing her breath as a thin veil of smoke.

The streets of McWhorter were empty which made her daily run easier. She hadn't planned on getting up so early, but old habits were hard to break. Plus, she had a lot on her mind. The *splat splat* sound of her running shoes hitting the concrete sidewalk was comforting. It was downright cold this morning, and she wore her navy bureau-issued fleeced sweats. Underneath her oversized sweatshirt, she wore a special made undergarment with a pouch that fit her Ruger .380 perfectly.

She remembered a time when she felt McWhorter was the safest place in the world. Now, she thought she would rather take her chances in any big city than in this little town. The sickening sweet hospitality of the people in McWhorter unarmed her and gave her a false sense of security. She found she had to peel many layers off the good citizens of McWhorter before she could really see their true nature. Though she was certain there were many good Christian people in McWhorter, it was hard to tell the difference between who was genuine and who was faking. The mayor was a perfect example. Each time she visited McWhorter as a child, the mayor gave Trevor and her bubblegum or a piece of butterscotch candy. She thought he was the nicest man ever but, of course, look how that turned out. He was the antitheses of nice.

Thinking about the mayor made her thoughts turn to the mayor's daughter. Tillie could not believe Trevor had been seeing Caroline Ledford. Trevor didn't deny it, but he didn't own up to it either. He just didn't say anything at all, which was all the proof she needed. She didn't like it. She didn't like it at all. She didn't think Daniel would like it either. Her heart dropped a little in her chest when the thought occurred to her, "Would it make Daniel want to run back to Caroline?" She knew how to remedy that. She just wouldn't tell him, and she would make sure Trevor didn't either. If Daniel found out, it would have to come from Caroline herself.

"How well do I really know Danny? Is he only letting me see what he wants me to see?" she asked. In one way, she thought she knew him, but then she remembered how he acted that day when he was around the snakes. Could she really say she knew everything about him? "Could he and Uncle Willie be fooling us?" she asked herself. "Daniel Brooks was a good guy. He had to be!" She'd guarded her heart all these years waiting for just the right person; she couldn't be wrong about Danny. She just couldn't! After all, it was just a photograph of three boys fishing. Just because they fished together as boys didn't mean the sheriff and Daniel's dad were as corrupt as the mayor or belonged to any secret club. Kids grow up and make their own adult choices.

The sound of a car engine in the distance brought Tillie back to reality. She immediately took a defensive posture and began scanning the fog-shrouded horizon for intruders just as she had been trained to do. She felt for her gun from her pouch and kept her hand on the gun in case she needed to use it. The chill of the metal on her flesh made a shiver run from the top of her head down to her toes. An older model farm truck made its way down Main Street. The old man waved at the runner. Relieved, Tillie waved back while still holding the gun tightly with her other hand.

Later, she heard the steady rhythm of another set of footsteps in the distance. She put her hand back on her weapon. Her unease turned to joy as she recognized the runner. She stepped up her pace from a brisk jog to a dead sprint as the adrenaline coursed through her body.

It didn't take but a minute or two before the couple breached the distance between each other. She leaped into his arms. The weight of her sudden lurch caused Daniel to stumble, but he was able to steady himself just in time for her mouth to find his.

"Well, good morning to you, too," Daniel managed to say before their lips locked again. They found a place between two of the storefronts that was away from the prying eyes of

Main Street and explored each other's bodies in the cool mist-shrouded morning.

They walked the remaining distance to the Grant's home. Deciding to probe a little, she asked, "Do you feel like you really knew your father?" she pried.

Daniel didn't see the question coming, and it hit an exposed nerve; however, he answered anyway. "I'm sure there're things about him I didn't know, just like I'm sure I didn't let him always know everything about me, either." Daniel answered. He conveniently left the part out about the madman that emerged in his dad's last days when he told him things that were both cruel and horrible. The doctor assured him it was from the lack of oxygen getting to his father's brain, but he wasn't so sure if there weren't some truths buried in his outbursts.

"What about you? Do you feel you know everything about your parents?"

"Actually, I was just thinking how little I know about my mother. She never talked much about her parents or even Uncle Willie for that matter. Now, it's too late."

Daniel couldn't help her there, and he didn't know how to respond about her mother's illness, so he created a diversion. "Speaking of the good sheriff, have you heard from him in the last day or two?"

"Trevor spoke with him last night. He said he took Aunt Brenda on a little vacation before the election season consumed them and would be back in a day or so."

10:00 AM

The Ledford's independent investigation was hitting brick walls as they searched for answers about the murder of Ruth Ann Vaughn. They were meeting in Jon's office at the garage.

"How did Dewey take it when you fired the bastard?" Jennings asked his brother.

"He didn't seem upset at all, more relieved than anything. Seems the pot-smoking meth cooker has turned plum Christian on us. Told me he was real sorry about what was going on with you, but insisted he didn't meet with you that night and wouldn't say he did because that would be a lie. What did you find out about him?" Jon looked at his older sister for answers.

"I haven't gotten the results yet. I can't believe you boys hired Dewey in the first place. He's a foreigner. Didn't our good daddy preach that interlopers are dangerous?"

"Hell, Sis, he wasn't an interloper. He was Albert Dean's cousin. Albert Dean brought him into the fold. Throwing the boy out on his ass after his cousin was murdered wouldn't be very Christian of us, now would it?" Jennings defended their actions.

"Okay. We're getting nowhere with Dewey Lewis, so let's start with Albert Dean then. How exactly was Albert Dean related to Dewey?" Caroline asked.

Jennings said, "I'm not really sure how they're related. Now that you mention it, his sister's the only relative I know about."

"Brothers, let's talk about your little—" she cleared her throat, "side business. Help me understand what happened to Albert Dean. I know Daddy told Mommy you boys were in a heap of trouble over something involving Albert Dean?"

"We have no frickin' idea what happened to him. One day he was here, then the next he wasn't. We helped him with his local operation, but he worked with some heavyweights all on his own. He was always looking for ways to diversify his business. We just sell pot and pills, and he knew we weren't interested in going any deeper. We were worried because he had the money we needed to pay for our load coming in, but we ended up finding it in his hiding place back behind his sister's barn," Jon explained.

"Could Dewey've killed Albert Dean?" Caroline continued writing the entire time she posed the question.

The boys looked at each other, and Jennings spoke for both of them. "Your guess's as good as ours?"

Caroline leafed through the pages of her notebook. "Okay, let me see if I have this right. Albert Dean brought a boy into the midst of your business who he claimed was his cousin, but you don't know for sure if they were related or not. Then Albert Dean died, and you kept this boy working for you. Now, he's our only hope for Jennings to get out of this mess, but the problem with that is he's lying right through his teeth claiming he never saw Jennings that night. To put icing on the cake, Dewey also lives with one of Jennings' ex-girlfriends."

"I guess that about sums it up, but who said she's my ex?" Jennings draped his arm around his sister's shoulder. "You left out the part that I had the prettiest and smartest sister in the state."

"Please tell me you're not still sleeping with Mary Jane? Hold that thought. Let me put it this way. If you have the notion to hook up with Ms. Tillery, then resist your urge. Am I making myself clear?"

"Damn, Sis, a man's gotta have some fun," Jennings joked.

Caroline knew there was something they were missing. "What about the tail on Dewey and Mary Jane?

Jon answered, "Nothing out of the ordinary so far. If you can call their lives ordinary."

"Okay, we need to step it up a notch this week. Gene Lester's taking the case to the Grand Jury this Thursday." Caroline stopped talking when she felt the room starting to spin. She looked down trying to get her bearings. The boys noticed the change in their sister, and Jennings was able to get one of his hands under her back before the rest of her body hit the concrete floor.

Caroline opened her eyes to see her brothers' two heads looming only inches from her face. "What happened?" she asked.

"Hell, Sis, you're a bag of bones. When's the last time you ate anything?" Jennings asked.

"I'll be okay. I just need something to drink."

Jennings didn't like her answer. "Like hell you will. I'm taking you out right now and getting Jeb to fix you some of his good meatloaf and mashed taters."

Just thinking about greasy meatloaf made Caroline begin to taste the bile that was rising in her throat. Raising the rest of her body off the floor, she managed to crawl the distance to the trashcan.

"Caroline, you're going to the hospital. You're dehydrated. We've got to get you some help," Jon ordered.

"Get me a sprite or something. I'll be all right."

Caroline managed to sit in the chair and drink a few drinks from her sprite can. The longer she sat, the more color she regained in her cheeks. Finally, convincing her brothers she was okay to drive home, she headed out the door to her Lexus.

She was opening the door to the car when she smelled the familiar smell of Stetson cologne. She turned her head and looked directly into the eyes of a monster. Jock grabbed her free arm and twisted it behind her back. She knew better than to resist. She quit fighting many years ago.

"Who do you think you are? I helped bring you into this world, and I can take you out, you little ungrateful whore!" he whispered into her right ear while twisting her arm harder and harder behind her back. Standing perfectly still, she dared not to move a muscle knowing her arm was going to break any minute. She had learned years ago any resistance made it ten times worse. Of course, that was before he ruined her world by destroying her chance to marry Daniel. Thinking about Daniel gave her all the courage and strength she needed to make her move. With her high-heel boot, she stomped as hard as she could on his left foot, then she took her free elbow across the right side of his face using every ounce of energy she could muster. Bulls-eye! She heard the crunch of his nose, and felt it give way under the force of her hit.

Jock was taken back by Caroline's attack. He loosened his grasp just enough for her to pull the gun from her purse with her good hand. "Daddy, remember who taught me to shoot this little thing?" she asked as she placed the steel barrel of her gun in the midst of his fat gut.

Automatically, Jock took a step backward when he felt the hard object poking his midsection. He knew he could probably disarm her, but he didn't want to take any chances she'd accidentally shoot him. Instead, he backed away. After all, he was a patient man. She would eat off his platter of revenge. No child of his was going to disrespect him and get by with it. Afraid to turn his back on her, he walked backward until he entered the garage. He felt the wet blood dripping from his nose. "How on earth am I going to explain a black eye just three weeks away from the election? Maybe I can blame it on Geneva. That had to be good for a few votes," he thought as he turned around and walked into his sons' garage.

Caroline got into her vehicle as fast as her shaking legs would allow her. She was pretty sure her arm was broken. The pain was intense. Even with the pain of her arm, she felt better than she'd ever felt before. She won her first battle, but she knew this meant war.

CHAPTER 34

Catfish and Moonbows

Sunday, April 13, 2008, 12:00 PM

"Zella, listen what it says in this brochure about a moonbow. It says Cumberland Falls is one of two places in the world we can see a moonbow." Deek slapped the brochure across his jean-clad leg, and the sound made Mayzella jump. "Hot damn! Let's go see it!"

"Where did you get that brochure?"

"I ... uh ... found it in the bedroom of the cabin."

Mayzella had personally checked the bedroom when they arrived, and she didn't remember seeing a brochure. The Cumberland Falls State Park was only an hour away from McWhorter and was a good place to wait on her uncle. She moved so she was face-to-face with Deek before she spoke to him like he was two years old. Slowly and deliberately, she spoke, "Deek, listen very carefully at what I'm going to say to you. Are you listening? Do I have your undivided attention?"

Deek smiled and shook his head up and down in a manner one would expect a toddler to make.

"How many joints have you smoked today?"

"Maybe two? I had to take the edge off some way, or I'm going to go stir crazy."

"Listen to me. We have a very bad man looking for us, and if he finds us, then he plans to kill us. You need to be at your senses at all times. Do you understand this?"

Again, Deek pumped his head up and down, but this time he wasn't smiling.

"Where's your phone? You can't tell anyone where we're hiding. Do you hear me? You haven't, have you? Give me your phone. I can't afford to take any chances," she ordered.

Deek reluctantly handed his phone to her. "No, Zella. I haven't told anyone."

"You can't call your momma, dad, or brother until I tell you it's okay."

"Well, you told your uncle Buddy," he reminded her in the same fashion a kid would do to justify some wrong doing.

"That's different. My uncle Buddy is coming to help us."

"Why can't my brother help?"

"Uncle Buddy can fend for himself. What about your brother?" She saw in his eyes that Deek wasn't kidding about going crazy. He was like a caged animal. She decided to take a different approach. "We're going to get through this crisis. When we do, then I will go to the falls with you, and we'll even have us a picnic. It's just not safe right now."

"I don't understand what it would hurt for us to have a little fun while we're here. I just want to see this waterfall and this moonbow. I've never seen one in real life before."

Unable to appeal to his common sense, she decided to use another scare tactic. "Well, the Cumberland Falls are over sixty feet tall. I've always heard the rocks at the bottom are as sharp as knives. Most bodies that go over the falls are never recovered. I've heard it's because of the catfish that live at the bottom of the falls. Some say they're the size of grown men," she explained. She bugged her eyes, and she stretched out her arms as far as they would go, giving Deek some idea of the size of the catfish. "We have to make sure we're not food for those humongous catfish. You understand?" Mayzella could tell by the ashen color of his face that he got the jest of her talk.

CHAPTER 35

Numbers and Manna

Monday, April 14, 2008, 9:00 AM

Geneva Vaughn's life now consisted of a series of numbers. Eighteen. Ruthie had been gone eighteen days. Twenty-two. The election was twenty-two days away. Ten. Geneva Vaughn had been fasting for ten days. Twenty-four. This was the number of pounds she had lost. The number she liked the most was two thousand twenty-six. This was the number of registered voters that had promised to vote for her come May 6th. If all these people voted as promised, then, she would easily win. Of course, she wasn't naive enough to think they all were honest.

She walked into her granddaughter's room and picked up a photograph of Ruthie. "Ruth Ann, your mam sure does miss you." Wiping her nose on the sleeve of her pajama top, she realized the longing for her granddaughter was as real now as it had been the very first day she found out Ruthie would never come home again.

Taking out her Bible, she read while she was in her granddaughter's room. Reading the Word was sweeter than her homemade chocolate cake. Every word filled her soul just like food filled her belly. Every hunger pain ceased as she devoured every word of four chapters from the Gospel of John.

After she read her Bible, she kneeled in front of Ruthie's bed. She felt closer to her Lord and to Ruthie while she was in this room. She had a lot to tell Jesus and had a lot she needed to ask of him too. She knew his promises were true. Romans 8:28 told her that to those who love God, all things work together for the good…according to his purposes. She had no choice but to trust him—no place to look but up.

CHAPTER 36

Symphony of Chaos

Tuesday, April 15, 2008, 2:00 AM

Weak bladder or not, Jock knew there bound to be something significant about two o'clock in the morning because he had been waking up at this same hour for the past few weeks. Reaching on his nightstand, he felt around in the dark until he found his pack of cigarettes and his box of matches. Jock had a-pack-a-day habit and had no plans of quitting any time soon. His granddaddy and his daddy both smoked their unfiltered Winstons up until they died. If it were good enough for them, then it was good enough for him too.

He chose to use matches over those disposable lighters. He liked the sound and the smell that the match made when he struck it to the box's rough black phosphoric surface. He sucked twice on his cigarette when he noticed some type of movement out of the corner of his left eye.

Remaining very cool and collected, Jock used his right hand to feel under his mattress for the pistol that he kept hidden between the mattress and box springs just in case of an emergency. Using the dark of the night for cover, he gently maneuvered the gun from his hiding place and placed his hand, gun and all, under the covers. He continued to act as though he'd never heard anything. Not wanting to give away his element of surprise, he cleared his throat right before he turned on his nightstand lamp. He swung the gun in the direction of the noise and was prepared to pull the trigger.

In the corner, sitting ever so patiently was the weird little preacher man. Jock wasn't one to get riled up very easily; however, he could feel his legs beginning to shake beneath the covers.

Neither man spoke a word. Jock continued to take drags off his cigarette, but never took his eyes or his aim off the man. The lamp didn't give off much light, and the man was still much in shadow. Wearing the same old suit as before, the man had his thin legs crossed at the knee, and his Bible lay unopened in his lap. Trying to wait him out, Jock's impatience was getting the best of him. He finished his smoke, then, crushed the burnt end of the cigarette in the ashtray so that it lay small and twisted in the midst of the other butts.

"What do you want from me?" Jock said in a slow steady voice.

The man didn't answer immediately. After a few seconds of silence, the man finally said one word, "Repent."

"I'll show you repentance," the mayor calmly stated as he pointed the gun toward the old man's head.

The old man seemed unfazed as he quoted from Matthew 13, "Repent, for the time draws near, when God shall send his fire to devour the weeds that have been planted within the wheat and to weed out those who do not truly serve God."

Jock had enough of this old man's nonsense. He pulled the trigger. Nothing. He pulled it again. Again, silence. Jock pulled the barrel back to inspect it. He opened the chambers. All five rounds were there and appeared to be ready to do their job when fired.

Looking back up, Jock was surprised to see the old man had disappeared into thin air. He'd only taken his eyes off the man for five seconds tops. He was tired of this hocus pocus. "Maybe, I am going crazy," he thought to himself.

Jock realized he should have gone to the bathroom earlier.

5:00 AM

"Great! April 15th and it looks like there's a red sky this morning. That's all I need! No good could come from this day," Jock said as he kicked at the cat curled at the foot of the outside door. "Damn, pole cat looking thing!" he cursed the stray black and white cat that had taken up residence at his door. Continuing toward his vehicle, he was talking to himself like the madman he was becoming. He was also none too happy he had to conceal, using makeup, the bruising under his eye caused by his daughter's attack.

It was Tuesday, and he was heading for his weekly Tuesday Club meeting. The club only met once or twice most months, but they could count on meeting at least weekly during the months of April and October. The mayor could have sworn the weather forecaster called for a nice spring day today, but now seeing the pink in his first glimpse of the morning made him highly suspicious that the weatherman was in cahoots with Geneva Vaughn too.

"Red sky at night, sailor's delight. Red sky in the morning, sailors take warning," he recited as the big Buick purred awake. The sun hadn't officially risen this morning, so maybe his eyes were playing tricks in the dark. It wouldn't be the first time his eyes failed him as he recounted his 2:00 a.m. visitor. Actually, he would have thought last night was all a bad dream had he not found his soiled underwear lying in the middle of his bathroom floor this morning. "Geneva's the only answer. She had to be behind it." He refused to give credence to the thought he was losing his mind. Just thinking about Geneva made the throb in his head pound harder. In only a couple of weeks, he could be shed of her once and for all. He couldn't wait to see her face when she realized she was beat like a drum.

No one mentioned the banker's empty seat as the mayor, chief deputy, county clerk, judge executive, lawyer, farmer, and protégé assembled in one of the empty Sunday School rooms in the basement of the church house and hastily ate their breakfast so they could get on with their business. They had a lot to cover and only a short time to do it in. The judge had known the mayor since he was just a pup, and he noticed Jock wasn't behaving like himself this morning. His eyes were bloodshot and glassy. If he didn't know better, he would have sworn Jock was wearing makeup. Deciding against calling any attention to his observation to the others, he made a mental note to check on the mayor later.

Jock called the meeting to order, only to give the floor to the county court clerk so he could give the club an update on the election specifics. The clerk began, "We'll have a secret session for our 'special' workers to explain exactly what's expected of them on the Friday before the election. Their extra payment will be *contiguous* on their ability to keep their damn mouths shut."

Interrupting the clerk's speech, Jock announced. "Damn it, Rufus, if you have to use them big words to make you feel smart, then you ort to make sure you know what they mean before you use 'em. I think the word you're looking for is *contingent*. Their pay will be *contingent* not *contiguous*, you old fool!"

The clerk shot a dirty look in the mayor's direction and continued. "As I was saying, we'll have a meeting on Friday for our special officers, and then the actual precinct worker school for all the workers will be held on the next day. My little technology friend is scheduled to pay a visit sometime the week before the election."

"Exactly what day?" The mayor interrupted again.

"We haven't pinned down the exact date."

The mayor exhaled slowly and tried to keep his blood pressure in check. His teeth were clinched together as he calmly spoke to the clerk, "I need an exact date and time."

The clerk was secretly enjoying watching the mayor come unglued. "I'll find out exactly when he can be here. I thought we would use it as an official visit when we inspect the machines."

"I want to be there," the mayor demanded.

The clerk waited a minute before he spoke. "Now, Jock, I'm not so sure if that would be a good idea. You know Geneva has her cronies everywhere, and if someone photographs you going in with me and this here Frankfort official, then she could have a reason to protest."

The mayor scratched his head. "I don't like it one damn bit!" He stood up and started walking until he was directly behind the clerk's seat.

The clerk turned only his head and looked up at the frazzled mayor giving him a polite grin. The mayor didn't smile back. Instead, he pulled his pistol out of his pocket and placed the gun's barrel directly in the clerk's temple. Feeling the cold steel against his scalp, the clerk's meager smile was replaced with a different look, a look of terror. The other men could do nothing but stare in complete astonishment at the scene unfolding in front of them.

"If you even think of double-crossing me, you knobby kneed bastard, then you'll not live through the next day." Making his point, Jock put his weapon back in his pocket, sauntered back to his seat at the head of the table, and continued just as though nothing had ever happened.

The clerk never opened his mouth again for the rest of the meeting. No one else spoke unless the mayor spoke directly to one of them. Unbeknownst to the mayor, many side conversations were taking place with the members using their eyes to communicate when Jock turned his head.

Jock Ledford decided he liked this kind of meeting. He liked seeing these men on edge. He thought, "They need to understand my sense of urgency, and if I have to manhandle them to get it done then, by hell, I'll do just that." Of course, he didn't want to give a reason for a mutiny, so he thought he would end it on a better note so that his theatrics weren't forefront in their minds when they left. "Bobby, did that thingamajig you ordered for your big stud come in yet?"

"Not yet," the farmer replied weakly.

The mayor made one last feeble attempt at ending on a positive note. "How long before UK shoves little Billie boy out the door? Why, he's made a pure mockery out of the state's finest institution."

Not being able to help themselves, the group, one by one, started chattering about their dislike for the University of Kentucky's head basketball coach. The mayor knew that true Kentuckians couldn't resist a good dose of coach browbeating.

Dismissing the group, Jock said, "I believe unless anyone has something else to say, then, we're finished."

The sound of the chairs scraping across the concrete floor was all Jock could hear; the men couldn't get out of the meeting fast enough. Jock silently followed behind them. He wanted to make sure they didn't team up together on the way out the door.

The sun had taken its rightful place in the sky, and Jock had been correct. The sky was an eerie shade of pink. The only other time he could remember seeing a sky like this was when the town suffered its one and only tornado. He went back to the kitchen and woofed down another biscuit smothered with a generous coating of chocolate gravy. Nothing like drowning one's worries in chocolate.

7:30 AM

A loud pounding on the door startled Daniel Brooks. "Who would be coming to my house at this hour?" he questioned. He grabbed his duty weapon on his way to the door. He looked out the window and saw a familiar SUV. Feeling foolish, he put his gun away.

Caroline Ledford stood at his door. She had a long coat on and high heel boots. He took one look at her, and knew he was in serious trouble.

"Well, hello, Ms. Caroline."

She didn't answer him. Instead, she stepped in the door and immediately wrapped her thin arms around his neck and kissed him long and hard. Daniel was conditioned to respond to her passion. Responding to her affection seemed like second nature to him, and he couldn't help himself.

Caroline unbuttoned her coat to reveal she was wearing nothing at all underneath.

Daniel had resigned himself to the fact Caroline would not be part of his future and was making plans in his mind to share his life, for better or worse, with Tillie Grant. In his head, he knew he needed to send Caroline on her merry way, but instead he found himself headed in all too familiar territory. At one point, he started to protest, but Caroline's ardor was just too strong. He couldn't resist, no matter how loud the siren in his head was signaling him to stop.

It was only after they were finished making love when he realized she was wearing a brace on her wrist. Something else was different. He had to admit it had been a while since he'd felt Caroline in his arms. She was a stark contrast to Tillie's petite muscular frame, but it was more than a comparison to Tillie. She was much smaller than he could remember. She was a bag of bones. He could actually count her ribs.

Daniel sat up quickly in the bed. "Honey, what's wrong with you? Aren't you eating? What happened to your arm?"

Caroline didn't answer. She knew if the tears started flowing, she would never be able to turn them off. Instead, she hugged him and said, "I'm ready to elope now."

Daniel didn't know what to say or how to respond. He just hugged her tightly. His thoughts turned toward Tillie. He could almost smell her clean girly smell in the midst of Caroline's signature Oscar de la Renta. "What do I do now?" he screamed in his head.

4:30 PM

Roy Allen Jones and Joe Matt Sizemore had plans to meet after work to drink a few beers. They'd been meeting since the day of the ice storm. They didn't want the mayor to know about their after meeting camaraderie; he would frown upon any type of fraternization that hadn't been prearranged by him, especially by the younger members. He would tell them their friendship was somehow jeopardizing the club, but in reality, they all knew the mayor didn't want them to form alliances within the group for fear they'd try to undermine or overthrow him. After today's meeting, it was abundantly clear this was exactly what needed to happen before someone else had an empty chair at the meeting.

Joe Matt was going to eat and take a run before he met up with Roy Allen. His momma had a kettle of soup beans and a pone of cornbread ready for him when he walked in the door at four thirty in the afternoon. He felt the sting of the onion in his eyes before he smelled it. His little momma had her back to him at the sink studying something through her kitchen window and didn't even budge when his big feet clodded across the linoleum floor. He didn't want to scare her, so he said, "Momma" in his softest voice. She jerked to life like a hornet had stung her.

"Lawsy day, my head was in the clouds so far, I guess the boogie man could have come right in here on me, and I wouldn't have even heard him." Edna then redirected her body toward the sink and pointed for Joe Matt to look. "I want you to look out there at that sky. Have you in all your days ever seen a sky like that before?"

Joe Matt crowded around the sink to try to see out the window. "It looks like an ordinary sky to me."

"Watch it move. The clouds are moving way too fast for my liking. It's brewing up something, just don't know what."

"Are you sure? The weatherman called for a pretty day, and it's been up in the sixties all day today."

"Did you see that red sky this morning? Son, now that weatherman will lie right to you, but them red clouds won't lie." She shook her gray head as she said, "Something's not right. I can feel it. You're planning on staying home tonight, aren't ya?" Her last words said as more of a command than a question.

"I'm going to eat these good beans and take me a little run. Then Roy Allen's gonna pick me up, and we're gonna drink us a few beers."

"Beers! You don't need to drink any beers on a night like tonight. You're supposed to be the law. How can you be the law when you're three sheets to the wind? I sure wish you'd stay home with me tonight."

Joe Matt didn't know what to say. "Well, let me eat some of your good beans, and I'll run over to Roy Allen's for a little bit. If the beans are really good, then I may only drink one beer instead of three and come back home for seconds of this good grub," he lied. He had no intention on stopping at even three beers.

"I don't like it." She shook her head, and her actions were in swift jerky movements. This was Edna's best attempt at a tantrum. Based on a lifetime of experience of living with Edna, he knew what came next. Every step she would make would be like lead hitting the floor. Cabinet doors would shut rather loudly, but not so hard that the cabinets or their contents would be damaged. If that didn't work, then the silent treatment would be his punishment for days or until she felt he'd learned his lesson. He didn't have time to worry about placating her for weeks about his latest slight, and he knew he really needed to spend some time with Roy Allen tonight. They needed to try to make some plans about what to do about the Tuesday Club. The mayor was officially losing it. Joe Matt knew he needed to distract his momma before she sullied up completely. Standing in front of an opened Frigidaire, he posed the question, "Do you have any of that good homemade chowchow for the beans?"

He could tell she was trying to stay mad but didn't have the wherewithal to be able to resist her baby boy when it came to her canning. Her chowchow had taken first place in the county fair for the last ten years. "Don't tell me we're out of chowchow!" she said in a panic.

Quickly, Joe Matt emptied the remains of the red, green, and yellow mixture from the open jar into the bottom of his soup bowl using the door to serve as his shield from Edna's prying eyes. Once his act of sabotage was complete, he poked the empty big-mouthed jar around the door to give her the proof the jar was empty.

That did it. "Now don't you worry! I've got some out in the cellar with the rest of my canning. Let me run out there and get you some. I can't believe we already ate that last jar. I could have sworn we still had enough for supper. I can't eat soup beans without some good chowchow either." The last words were barely audible because she said them as she scurried out the back door, forgetting about her efforts at being mad.

Joe Matt spooned out a large helping of the beans over his chowchow into one of the large brown bowls. He didn't dare uncover the chowchow at the bottom of the bowl. The screen door slammed, and he heard Edna jabbering. He couldn't make out what she was saying until she came into the room with him.

"Knowing when to pick your green 'mater is the secret to having good chowchow. They can't be too hard, and they can't be too soft. About the end of July's the best time to make it cause that's when your 'maters are usually just right."

Joe Matt just shook his head and said, "Is that right?" or "Well, I'll be," at the appropriate times to humor his momma.

5:00 PM

Daniel Brooks turned to physical activity when he was troubled. Today, he especially needed the adrenaline and endorphin release that came with physical exertion. Daniel sweated until he couldn't sweat anymore; then, he headed toward the shower. He took his Irish Spring soap and scrubbed every spot of his body, again, hoping to wash away any lingering scent from his morning with Caroline. He had a date with Tillie in an hour. Hanging his towel back on the rod, he also wiped down the vanity.

Dressed in a pair of jeans and redwing boots, he decided to tout his alma mater in the form of his maroon hooded sweatshirt with the letters *EKU* blaring with pride. He knew it would take a total of fifteen minutes for him to get to the Grant's house—fifteen total minutes for him to decide what to do. Should he tell Tillie about his romp with Caroline and risk the chance of never seeing her again? Or should he keep his mouth shut until he had his feelings sorted out? Actually, in his head, the decision was made. He knew what made the most sense. It was his heart he was having a harder time trying to convince.

6:00 PM

The black 2006 Corvette was an impressive vehicle by any standards, and Roy Allen felt a kinship to the car he never felt with a woman. The car had actually been better to him than any of his past girlfriends. It got him to where he wanted to go with no protest and was ready and raring to go any time he was.

Clearly shaken by the mayor's antics this morning, Roy Allen knew Jock was out of control. The mayor had always been a conniving, crazy bastard, but now, it was apparent he was headed down the path of a Jim Jones type of breakdown. This primary election was going to drive him over the edge.

Joe Matt told him he would be waiting for him behind Deaton's Garage about a mile from Joe Matt's house. No one would think much of seeing Joe Matt running alone since that was part of his normal routine anyway. It was very possible the mayor had someone watching all the club members. The Corvette's tinted windows would conceal Joe Matt once he was in the car, but they couldn't be too careful. Pulling beside the garage, Joe Matt jumped in the car and they sped off to find a bootlegger.

Joe Matt wasted no time in giving his opinion. "Puzzy Creed's be the closest place, and he keeps them in a net in the creek—they're always ice cold,"

"He charges a fortune for his liquor!"

"What are you complaining about? You get a kickback."

"True." Roy Allen hadn't thought about it as a way of paying himself since the Tuesday Club got paid to keep Rockford County dry.

Looking out the window at the pink sky, Joe Matt remembered what Edna said about the sky earlier. "What do you reckon it means when you have a red sky in the morning and a red sky at night too?" he wondered out loud.

"I'll tell you what it means. It means we definitely need to get on a good dog drunk because the end of time is near." Although Roy Allen said it in jest, it struck a chord with both men prompting Roy Allen to push the throttle harder.

6:30 PM

Daniel found himself especially in awe of the sky as he drove the distance to Tillie's temporary home. The entire sky appeared to consist of various shades of pink and purple. He was grateful the sky had occupied his mind for a total of four minutes of the drive. Montgomery Gentry occupied the rest of his time as he sang, off-key and loud, along with the duo booming from his speakers.

The knock on the kitchen door caused Tillie to redirect her attention from the recipe book to the person at the other end of the knock. Daniel couldn't help but smile as the domestic diva opened the door with a smudge of flour on her cheek. He didn't wait until he stepped through the threshold before he properly kissed her. Tillie responded with equal passion, but she broke the kiss when she remembered her dinner.

"Well, not sure I like that howdy doo." Daniel pooched his mouth out in a pout, clearly not finished with the make out session.

Tillie playfully giggled and said, "Danny, there's plenty time for that later. I've prepared you a feast.. I can't wait for you to taste it!"

Daniel sat where she instructed. She, then, presented a salad that had dark green leaves with nuts, strawberries, and squiggly looking brown things in it. He headed toward the fridge to retrieve this buttermilk and chive delicacy.

"What'cha looking for?" Tillie asked as she saw him pilfering in the fridge.

"Ranch dressing."

"No, honey, you don't eat ranch with this type of salad. Here, try this raspberry vinaigrette. I promise you'll love it."

Eyeing her suspiciously, he obeyed the little tyrant and found the ranchless salad edible. He wasn't sure of Tillie's motive for preparing this meal, but he was certain she would be on her soapbox before the night was over regarding saturated fats and triglycerides. He didn't really mind her lectures because she was just so cute when she was trying to be convincing. Her short hair was curly today; she was wearing a pair of hip hugging jeans, a short t-shirt, and her orange toenails accentuated her lack of shoes. "Orange toes? Are you serious?" he asked Tillie.

"You got a problem with it?" Tillie was fast on the defense.

"As long as you cover them up in company, then I guess it'll be okay. Some crazed Kentucky fan will mistake you for a Tennessee fan. I can't be responsible for what could happen to those pretty feet of yours if that happens!"

Her thousand volt smile made his stomach sink as he remembered his act of betrayal this morning. He truly wished he could turn back time. However, he wasn't sure if Caroline showed up tomorrow, next week, or even next year that he would be strong enough to resist her. He didn't like himself at this particular moment.

As soon as they finished the first course, Tillie beamed as she placed some type of fish sitting on top of a bed of rice in front of him. Before they had a chance to taste their fish, they heard a noise. They both turned to what sounded like someone throwing pebbles at the glass panes of the window. "What the—" Daniel let the question dangle and ran toward the living room window. "Hail!" he screamed.

"Hell, what?"

"It's hailing! Come look at the size of these hail balls!"

Like a stealthy cat, she was by his side to see what was causing the commotion. "Wow! They're as big as golf balls!"

"Golf balls my ass, baseballs would be more like it," Daniel said when he heard glass breaking on his dad's old truck. Instinctively, he placed his body in front of Tillie. Growing in size, the now softball size hail was wreaking havoc on everything it touched. His thoughts turned first to his mom, then oddly enough, to Caroline. He wasn't sure if Caroline wouldn't crumble just like the glass in the windows if one of these behemoth balls were to hit her in her fragile state. He couldn't afford to think about her right now. Instead, he pulled Tillie closer to him.

"Was that your truck windshield? Listen to that hail beating on this old roof." The sound of the storm was in a way, musical. The steady rhythm of the hail beating on the roof with the occasional crashing of the glass windows was nature playing its own symphony of chaos. "Oh no! Trevor's out in this mess!" The twin felt her knees weaken just thinking about her brother's safety.

7:00 PM

The two men heard when the rain turned from liquid to solid form as they drove toward home. Thankfully, they were only a few miles from Roy Allen's house.

"Where did that come from?" Joe Matt said remembering his momma's earlier concern about the weather. "You better floor it." Joe Matt knew hail usually preceded a tornado, and he wanted to get to cover as fast as he could. He whined to himself, "Why didn't I listen to my momma?"

Roy Allen was only a few minutes from the safety of his garage. It was a good thing too, because based on the sound of the bangs on the top of the Corvette, the hail balls were growing in diameter. Roy Allen cringed at each large thud. He could almost feel the gashes the large hail balls were making to his car.

A large grapefruit-sized ball landed in the middle of his windshield causing the glass to shatter. Both men covered their faces expecting to be covered with the glass. Luckily, the glass held in place, but it was very hard to see through the jigsaw puzzle of glass fragments. The finish line insight, Roy Allen remained focused. The force of the hail was beating his car like a drum.

Joe Matt had his cell phone to his ear. "Momma, are you okay?"

Roy Allen could only hear one side of Joe Matt's conversation, but could imagine what Edna was saying on the other end.

"I know you told me something was gonna happen. Yeah, Momma I should have listened to you. Yep, the insurance is paid up."

Roy Allen pressed the button to his automatic garage door opener and hurried his vehicle under the enclosure. Joe Matt hopped out as soon as the car came to a halt and assessed the damage to the vehicle. "I be damned!" The black Corvette looked like someone had taken a ball bat to it.

Roy Allen didn't dare open the driver's side door. Instead, he opened a beer and chugged it. He rested his head on the back of the headrest and turned his Eagles Greatest Hits CD on full blast as he downed it. His precious Corvette had been completely annihilated. The fiberglass body had holes and rips all over it. He wasn't prepared to see his car in this injured state. He was now certain his world was coming to an end. His poor Corvette would never be the same. He decided the remedy for this heartache would be beer and lots of it.

CHAPTER 37

The Aftermath

Wednesday, April 16, 2008, 8:00 AM

McWhorter's hailstorm made national news. Geneva Vaughn had been out late the night before helping her friends and neighbors cover their exposed roofs and shattered windows. Armed with garbage bags and duct tape, Glenn Dale helped with the rooftops, and she helped cover the windows of the houses and vehicles.

The Vaughn's vehicles were safely parked in their three-car garage. The yellow car's spot remained empty and left a void in the garage just as Ruth Ann's absence left a void in their hearts. The big walnut tree in their front yard must have taken the brunt of the storm. In the big scope of things, the Vaughn's had only minimal damage from the hailstorm.

The governor was trying to assess the damage the storm caused in order to determine whether to declare a state of emergency. Television news trucks lined the streets of McWhorter to get a look at the damage caused by the unusually large hail. Geneva had the television in her bedroom playing loudly so she wouldn't miss any of the news coverage while she dressed for another big day. "Only twenty more days," Geneva thought as she mentally marked another day off her countdown.

She had her pantyhose up to midcalf on one leg and was starting on the other leg when the sound of his voice caused her fingernails to rip a hole in the nylon. She looked up in time to see Mayor Ledford, in his heavy mountain accent, tell the nation about McWhorter's hail storm. He even showed them a large ice ball he'd retrieved and kept in his freezer overnight. "I have plans to keep this as a reminder to me and my town that regardless of its size or looks that one misdirected force of nature could cause such devastation to so many." His signature smile was replaced with a look of great concern as he spoke directly to Geneva through the television. "Don't be lulled into complacency. You never know when devastation may visit your house."

She answered back by throwing her ruined pantyhose toward the mayor's round face only to see the brown ball hit another target on the television. Instead of hitting her intended target, she ended up hitting the image of one of her dear friends, when the camera panned out to those around Jock. She hung her head in shame. "Yes, Lord, I know I'm not dealing with flesh, but with powers and principalities. Yes, I know that throwing things ain't the answer," she said as she repented.

11:50 AM

The mattress of the tourist cabin smelt of mildew and decades of campfire smoke. Mayzella had slept on worse smelling mattresses growing up on Crow's Creek. Actually, her most vivid smells of her childhood were of cheap liquor and baby spit-up. Mayzella was reluctant to return to her childhood home just because it took her weeks to get the stench out of her nostrils and the memories out of her head.

Mayzella checked her fake Rolex and realized it was nearly noon. She could see daylight oozing through the cracks in the heavy shutters, but had no idea half the day was already gone. Groggily, she remembered Deek fixed her a drink before they went to bed. She wouldn't put it past him to have drugged her. Mayzella gently reached her hand to his side of the bed.

"What?" was all that came out of Mayzella's mouth when she realized Deek was not in bed next to her. Sheer panic came over her as she jumped out of bed to find him. She started calling his name, gently at first, but the call soon changed to a desperate hateful tone.

She pulled his floppy sweatshirt over top her thin negligee and walked barefoot outside the perimeter of the cabin hoping to find him nearby; the sweatshirt hit her just above her thigh. The April ground was too cool to go shoeless, but Mayzella could've probably walked on ice this morning. She was only focused on finding Deek. The Range Rover was still parked in the driveway. She was hesitant to yell because she didn't want to attract any attention to herself. "Cell phone!" Mayzella remembered she'd confiscated his phone.

She jumped the two steps leading to the cabin's front porch and ran back to the bedroom. There, she found her purse on the top of the nightstand and rummaged through it until she found not only her cell phone but also Deek's phone. She sighed loudly. At least he wasn't using his phone to lead the mayor to her hideout. She wanted Jock Ledford to be in such a tizzy trying to find her that he was reckless. She knew he and his hired man were very dangerous, but she needed to have the upper hand. The battle had to be fought on her territory if she had any hope of surviving. Her uncle Buddy would be back in town tomorrow, and then, the trap could be sprung. She couldn't afford for Deek to leak the information just yet. Knowing Deek would be useless to her on the battlefield, she just hoped he wasn't a casualty. She'd grown fond of him. It wasn't the feeling she had for Rupert; her fondness for Deek was more like her feelings for a puppy dog.

"Oh, hell!" she said out loud when thoughts of Deek being tortured by the mayor's hired man ran through her mind. She knew she was going to have to find him. She pulled the jeans she'd worn yesterday onto her slim body and began looking for her boots.

Whistling, she heard the familiar hum of Deek's off-key whistling rendition of "Dixie." She didn't care if it was off key or not, the sound was like a balm to her soul. "He's safe," she whispered. She stepped barefoot back onto the porch again. "Where've you been?"

"Been 'sang hunting this morning."

"'Sang hunting?"

"You know, ginsang hunting." He raised both hands in the air much like a hunter would do to show off their kill. There in each hand were multiple roots. They reminded her of flesh colored squid as the roots hung down his hands like tentacles.

"Dear Lord, you scared me to death so you could go look for ginseng. Where's my gun? I might as well kill you now before the mayor gets a hold of you!"

"Don't be mad, baby. You wait 'til I fix you some ginsang tea. It'll make you so horny you won't know what to do with yourself."

Sex was the last thing on Mayzella's mind right now. Her heart was beating so hard she could see it through the sweatshirt. Running as hard as she could, she jumped on his back and bit him.

2:00 PM

In a matter of thirty minutes, the community of McWhorter took quite a thrashing. It looked like every window in McWhorter had plywood or plastic covering it. Caroline couldn't help but smile, thinking about how the perfect little town her daddy had carefully built was now falling apart in front of him. Barely recovering from last week's ice storm, the town now had to deal with another freak act of nature that had all but destroyed the town. Knowing how her daddy liked publicity, she was sure he'd find a way to be in front of every news camera as he told of McWhorter's plight. She figured he would also find a way to blame this on Geneva Vaughn, convincing others that she really was a witch that brewed up this hailstorm. Sad thing about it was some people would actually believe him.

The roads had been swept to remove the glass, but downtown had not resumed its business as usual status. A lot of strangers had come to town including the media, insurance adjustors, roofers, and dent repair professionals. Yes, the carpetbaggers had come to McWhorter. On every corner was a sign about paintless dent repair or roofers for hire. They must go from one hail ravaged town to the next; our tragedy is their meal ticket.

Caroline was meeting with the guy she'd hired to follow Mary Jane and Dewy. She waited for him in her car while she nursed her injured arm. The doctor said it was a hairline fracture, but the pain came from the torn ligaments. She didn't tell anyone the source of her injury, more from a lifetime of keeping secrets than protecting her daddy. Trevor Grant had accepted her explanation without question; lying to Trevor was much easier than lying to Daniel. She was fond of Trevor, but unfortunately, he wasn't Daniel. Daniel was going to see the light any day now. She just knew it!

The black SUV with tinted windows pulled next to her right on time. The private detective was a retired state policeman who'd started his own security business. He opened her passenger door and took a seat. He handed her an envelope before he said, "Mary Jane had an interesting meeting on Sunday. You can see the photos and all the information in the envelope. I'll keep someone watching."

Caroline didn't have a chance to say hello or goodbye before the detective was back in his SUV and driving away. "More than interesting!" she squealed when she saw a picture of Mary Jane Tillery getting into her daddy's Buick at eight o'clock on Sunday morning. This confirmed it. Caroline was now convinced her daddy was in cahoots with Mary Jane and Dewey. He was the one who set Jennings up to take the fall for Ruth Ann's murder. Spinning her tires, she wasted no time as she headed toward the garage to see her brothers.

3:00 PM

Joe Matt would never underestimate his momma Edna's ability to predict the weather again. He'd paid dearly for the mistake.

Not only did he have to listen to her repeatedly tell him "I told you so," he also had to babysit an inebriated lawyer. Joe Matt practically had to drag him out of the Corvette. "If I didn't know better, I would've thought it was his girlfriend who was injured instead of a damn car," Joe Matt said in frustration.

Shaken, but still able to function, Joe Matt teamed up the next day with Daniel as they helped the citizens of McWhorter regain some semblance of a life. It had been a productive day for them even if they weren't putting bad guys in jail. The two officers were driving down Bronwyn Street when they heard an explosion. The sound was behind them.

Stopping his cruiser on a dime, Joe Matt spun his car so it was headed toward the sound of the explosion. They could see the black smoke rising above the row of houses.

"What da ya reckoned blew up?" Daniel asked his friend.

"Not exactly sure, but from here, it looks like it's either Mary Jane's house or one on that same street." They followed the cloud of smoke to their destination.

The closer they got to the fire, the more convinced they were that the smoke was coming from Mary Jane's house. They could hear the sirens of the fire truck blaring from a distance behind them. Someone must have called 911 right after the detonation. The two officers were the first to respond, and Mary Jane Tillery met the cruiser at the end of her driveway. She was a mess. Her face was smudged with blood, and her blond hair had black soot all in it. "Hurry, Hurry, Dewey's hurt bad!" Her eyes were as big as saucers; the severity of the situation was evident by her disarray and the sound of panic in her voice.

In a matter of seconds, the two officers' long-legged strides made it to what once was a small building behind Mary Jane's house. The tin strips from the roof were strewn all over the yard, and the small building was engulfed in flames. Dewey was lying about ten feet from the building. He was face up and had been badly injured. It looked like Mary Jane had been able to drag him to safety, but not before he was severely burned. He was missing a hand on one arm, and the other arm had been horribly mangled from the elbow down. Blood was puddled all around him. Unable to look at Dewey, Mary Jane left to go and wait for the other emergency vehicles. Well-intentioned neighbors had congregated around the house.

"My guess is whatever exploded did so near Dewey's hands," Joe Matt reasoned.

Daniel had seen many meth labs in his career, and he knew without a doubt this explosion was a direct result of cooking the illegal substance. He also knew Joe Matt was very aware of what had been in or near Dewey's hands without actually coming out and saying it.

Dewey moaned. The sirens of the ambulance sounded close.

"Dewey, can you hear me?" Joe Matt leaned down in Dewey's direct vision.

Dewey was trying to talk. His lips were moving, but no sound was coming out. Joe Matt leaned his ear only inches from Dewey's lips.

"Bri-er rubble." Dewey's face was burned and several teeth were missing making his attempts at talking very difficult.

"Don't worry about being in trouble. Buddy, we're here to help you." Joe Matt reassured the injured man.

Dewey shook his head back and forth and moaned even louder. He then reached up with what remained of his left hand and grazed Joe Matt's face, leaving a trail of blood where he touched. "Brooder eek rouble faws elp."

Joe Matt looked at Daniel for assistance. Daniel took a stab at interpreting. "Dewey, do you have a brother?"

Dewey nodded his head just enough for them to tell he was saying yes.

"Is he in trouble?"

"Baaaad mon."

"Is your brother a bad man?" Daniel asked.

Dewey shook his head in frustration and moaned because every movement was painful.

"A bad man is after your brother?"

This time Dewey nodded in affirmation

"Who's the bad man?"

"Ma-or"

"Mayor Jock?"

Another nod.

"Where's your brother?"

"Foss."

"Floss, moss, falls? Are you saying falls like the Cumberland Falls?"

Dewey nodded. "Elp eek, elp im peez."

Mary Jane ushered the paramedics over to Dewey, and they let their training take over as they tried to save the man's life. Dewey was suddenly silent. The officers were not sure if it was because he didn't want to talk in front of the others or because he was past the point of talking.

Daniel cornered Mary Jane who looked less like a Barbie doll and more like something out of a Tim Burton movie. "Did you know your boyfriend was cooking meth in your building?"

"I told him not to, but since the Ledford's fired him, he felt he had no other way to earn his keep. He claimed he was the best crystal meth maker in Tennessee," she said all in one breath.

The stretcher rolled past them, and Mary Jane ran after her boyfriend not caring that Daniel wasn't finished with his questions.

The firefighters had the blaze under control, and the clean-up crew had been dispensed. Dewey was on his way to the hospital. The police officers felt they'd done all they could do at the scene. As soon as the men were in the cruiser, they started putting things together.

"Did you know Dewey had a brother?" Daniel asked his friend.

"I'm ashamed to say it never crossed my mind to check about his family."

"I'm going to make a call. In a matter of minutes, we'll have all we want to know about Dewey Lewis's family."

Joe Matt shook his head. "Wonder why he would bring up the mayor?"

"Well, I be a son of a bitch! It all makes sense!" The light bulb went off in Daniel's head. "What if Dewey has a twin brother, and what if that twin brother posed as Dewey on the night Ruth Ann was killed?"

"I'd say we need to get to Cumberland Falls soon because that brother will be lucky to live through the night. I'm going to call the sheriff."

"Good. I'm going to call Caroline."

Joe Matt couldn't help himself when he asked, "How long after you call Caroline before you call Tillie? Damn, it must be tough keeping two women happy?"

"Would you just call Willie already? For your information, Caroline will need to call Gene Lester. I'd say we'll need to postpone taking Jennings to grand jury tomorrow in light of this new discovery, don't ya think?"

3:45 PM

Daniel thought the sheriff acted almost elated when he read the fax out loud. "Deek and Dewey Lewis were born on June 3, 1982, twin boys of Edwin and Janet Lewis. They're identical in every way and reportedly tormented their teachers by trading places on a regular basis."

Sheriff Osborne shook his head in disbelief after tying it all together. "I could just kick myself. Why didn't I think of this possibility? No wonder Dewey could be so adamant about not being with Jennings that night and Mary Jane could produce those movie tickets so easily. I'll have to hand it to Jock. He had his bases covered as he nailed the coffin shut on his youngest son. I knew he was a mean hombre, but I thought if he cared for anyone it was his boys."

Joe Matt added to the conversation by saying, "If Dewey knew the whereabouts of Deek, then, chances are the mayor knows too. We need to get to him fast."

"Cumberland Falls State Park is huge. How in the world will we find him in that big of an area?" Daniel asked.

"We're not going to find anyone by sitting here talking about it," Joe Matt reasoned.

"Daniel, would you mind to go to the hospital. I hate to ask you, buddy, but my men worked all night because of the hail storm and are too tuckered out to be of any use against Jock Ledford. I'm afraid someone'll try to finish the job on Dewey." The sheriff said nicely before he ordered his chief deputy, "Joe Matt, you need to keep an eye on the mayor. We need to make sure he doesn't head toward Cumberland Falls. I'll take Deputy Caldwell with me and head to the falls to see if we can find them."

"*Them?*" Daniel asked.

The sheriff explained, "I doubt Deek will be by himself. I bet he's got people with him."

Daniel wasn't happy with the sheriff's plan, especially since it involved him going to the hospital instead of Cumberland Falls. He hated hospitals. He asked, "What are you going to do if you find *them?*"

In his best authoritative tone, the sheriff answered, "Why, I'll convince him and anyone with him to come back with me so we can help protect them."

"What if he's the one who murdered the Vaughn girl? Would you still want to protect him?" Daniel continued picking holes in the sheriff's plan. "Isn't Cumberland Falls in Whitley County? Ain't that out of your jurisdiction?"

"All good points, Danny boy, but don't you worry about jurisdiction. Whitley's sheriff is my fishing buddy, and he'll help me with the jurisdiction issue. After all, I'm just going there to help the poor boy. I'll call him on the way. Now, you boys best skedaddle. We've finally got Jock by the gonads. Let's not ruin it." The sheriff practically pushed the other officers out the door before he placed his campaign hat on his head and followed them. Alone.

4:00 PM

The smell combined with the hospital sounds, the light taps of shoes and the whispered conversation grated at Daniel's nerves in the same way that fingernails on a chalkboard would bother others. He hadn't been back to the hospital since his dad died. "Why didn't I just tell Willie no? After all, he's not my boss, and I'm the one who has jurisdiction in Whitley County," he verbally kicked himself.

Repressed images began foraging to the front of his mind as soon as he walked through the doors. He remembered watching his dad thrash about in pain and talk out of his head like some mad man as his oxygen-deprived body continued its fight against the foreign invader—cancer—that had taken control within. Daniel also remembered his own feeling of pain mixed with relief as Tinker Brooks slipped forever away from him.

Daniel took a detour to the restroom. Removing his hat, his brow was covered with sweat. He leaned over the sink trying to erase the painful memories. He cupped his hands under the aluminum faucet and caught the cold water in them. He poured the water over his pale face and left his hands to linger there for a minute.

The same trooper that had earlier been on the verge of a meltdown when he entered the restroom exited the facility as a composed professional. His leather boots tapped on the floor in spite of his efforts to walk quietly. He made it to the emergency room in time to see Mary Jane bent over sobbing loudly and a white sheet covering the entire body in the bed next to her.

Well-meaning nurses tried to help the grief stricken woman. Mary Jane stood with their assistance before she folded over the bed onto the lifeless body of her lover. "I'm so sorry Dewey. I'm sorry. Don't leave me. I'm sorry!" Each time she said *sorry* her voice grew louder.

Daniel was relieved to see Mary Jane's sister enter the curtain-enclosed cubby. It wasn't hard to recognize the family resemblance. He had to admit Mary Jane was a tad prettier. A tinge of guilt overcame him as he realized he was admiring these women while the corpse of a young man lay just feet from him.

Mary Jane's sister said, "Sissy's here now. You calm down." Her soft words caused Mary Jane to still. Daniel shut the curtain on their grief and decided to wait outside for Mary Jane to calm down.

When out of earshot, Daniel took his cell phone out of the holster of his utility belt. He dialed Caroline's number. It rang three times. "Hello!" Caroline answered excitedly.

He didn't want to lead her on, but he needed to let her know about the recent happenings. "Caroline, I don't have but a minute to talk. I'm at the hospital waiting to talk with Mary Jane."

"Hospital? Mary Jane? What's going on, Daniel?"

"I really can't get into it right now, but I've got something important to tell you. Did you know Dewey Lewis has a twin brother?"

"Twin brother! You've got to be kidding! So you're telling me Jennings was telling the truth all this time?"

"I'm not one hundred percent sure, but we do know Dewey has an identical twin brother who could've easily posed as Dewey on the night Ruth Ann was killed."

"That's great n—" Caroline stopped midsentence as she remembered the detective's report. "Mary Jane, as in Mary Jane Tillery?" she backpedaled.

"Yep."

"Interesting. Daddy met with Mary Jane Tillery Sunday morning. Is she all right? Did my daddy hurt her?"

"She's fine, but her boyfriend's dead. There was an explosion." As Daniel said this, he suddenly became very interested in what

Mary Jane was so sorry about. "So why do you think Jock was meeting with Mary Jane?" he questioned Caroline.

"I have no idea, but don't you think it's pretty convenient that Jennings claimed he was with Dewey the night of Ruth Ann's death. A couple of weeks later Mary Jane conveniently met with daddy, then poof, her boyfriend's dead?"

"Do you think Jock's lost his mind? How long did he think it would take us to figure out Dewey had a twin?"

"Who knows how daddy's evil mind works." She knew her daddy always had a strategy in mind in everything he did, and she knew he was adamant about not leaving loose ends. That would explain the explosion, but why frame Jennings? "I just don't understand it. Why would he set up my brother?"

"I can't figure it out either. Just hang onto your proof of their meeting, and you better call your brothers and let them know too, but tell them not to share just yet. You be careful, and take care of yourself. You hear me?"

"Thank you so much, Daniel."

"You're welcome, sweetie."

"Daniel, I love you!" she said into the receiver but quickly disconnected. She was afraid of hearing his response.

She should have stayed on the line. "Love you too," Daniel whispered. As soon as he knew he was alone on the telephone line he berated himself. "What the hell am I doing?"

CHAPTER 38

Cumberland Falls

Wednesday, April 16, 2008, 4:30 PM

Deek convinced Mayzella to walk in the woods with him. She agreed to the little excursion thinking it would help to become more familiar with the route to the river. She already felt safer since her uncle Buddy arrived. The hike was nice, but Mayzella wished she'd worn her hiking boots, her gym shoes continued to slip and slide as she climbed up and down the hills and valleys leading to the river.

Deek was extra attentive to her today; she figured it was because she'd confiscated his stash of weed. He was much more likeable when he was sober. Her heart was safe with Deek. Safe. Safety. Now more than ever, Mayzella coveted those words. She just wanted this ordeal to be over and for them to be safe even if it meant living on the run for the rest of her life. Once again, she mentally ran through the plans she and her uncle Buddy concocted.

When the cabin was just over the next hill, Mayzella was tempted to make a run for it until something shiny in the distance caught her eye. She stopped all movement then placed her finger to her mouth signaling for Deek to stop and listen. It didn't take long for her to find the source of the shine. The reflection of the sun on the man's shirt made a kaleidoscope of color appear.

"It's just the law. It's okay," Deek whispered to her.

"Take another look at the law's face. Does he look familiar, or what was the word you used in Florida? Does he look 'common' to you?"

"I be damn!" Deek exclaimed. "That's the same man that was at Daytona."

"Deek, now listen to me. I need to understand how he found us? Have you called your brother? Does Dewey know where we're at? "

"You've got my phone, remember?"

"Deek?" She gave him one of those knowing looks.

"Okay, okay. I called him on one of them pay phones when I went 'sang hunting."

Unfortunately, the damage was done; the plans had been put into motion prematurely because of Deek's stupidity. "One of these days, you'll listen to me. Just pray your brother's okay. You've got your gun, and you remember our plan, don't you?"

She closed her eyes and said a quick prayer in her head, hoping the Lord still remembered her. She then barked orders. "I'll distract the sheriff while you double back and go get Uncle Buddy. I'll lead him the long way around, but we'll end up under the falls like we planned. Got it?"

"Honey, you go get yer uncle, and I'll lead that sheriff to our trap. It's way too dangerous for you to go gallivanting in the woods with a crazy man chasing you," He said thinking he settled the matter once and for all.

"Let's stick to the plan. Don't worry about me. I'll be just fine. Now, you go on, and get Buddy." Before he could protest more, she was on her feet with her pistol in her hand. She shot at a tree that was just to the right of the sheriff's head serving as a distraction so he wouldn't hear Deek's loud footsteps.

Instinctively, the sheriff ducked his head, then, raised his hands into the air. "What the hell! I'm here to help you, Deek. You're in real danger and need the protection I can offer."

Mayzella laughed and hollered back at him, "I guess that's the reason you were at Daytona too, you sick bastard!" She fired again, but this time she made sure to tear up the gravel to the left of him. Bullet number two.

Out of gun range, Mayzella watched Deek as he disappeared in the woods behind the cabin. Based on her best estimation, she figured she had about an hour before the falls would be closed to visitors. She double-checked her pioneer moxie with her watch. She only wished she'd worn her hiking boots. "Too late now. It's show time," she whispered as she started her route. She turned to make sure the sheriff took her bait but didn't see him. Not good. Underestimating the sheriff would be a mistake, so she ran as fast and as hard as she could making sure to leave plenty of scattered leaves and overturned rocks so he could easily follow.

4:40 PM

The hospital had a small chapel located near the front entrance. The chapel was large enough to hold a couple of church benches, a podium, as well as an altar. The vaulted angled ceiling was high with a sharp pitch. Keeping his mind occupied on the room décor, Daniel waited until Mary Jane's chest quit heaving and her tears slowed to a trickle before he spoke. "Mary Jane, I need to ask you a few questions. Is that all right with you?" He spoke directly to Mary Jane, but since her head was downcast, he looked to her sister for approval.

Mary Jane nodded.

"Were you aware Dewey had a twin brother?"

Mary Jane's head rose up; the expression on her face told him all he needed to know. Clearly, she wasn't expecting this question. She didn't answer one way or another as she debated inwardly. Reluctantly, she nodded slightly.

"Do you know why Dewey was concerned about the safety of his brother?"

Her eyebrows almost touched. "How do you know he was worried about Deek?"

"He told me."

"You talked to Dewey? When?" she asked.

"He managed to say a few words to Joe Matt and me before they loaded him on the stretcher."

Stuttering, she asked, "Is that a-a-all h-h-he said? Did he s-s-say anything else?"

"Like what?" Daniel baited as he watched her already pale face grow whiter.

"I d-d-don't know. L-l-like, what caused the exploo-oooo-sion?"

Daniel definitely suspected foul play. He could tell she was nervous about this deathbed conversation. A full blown investigation into Dewey's death would follow but now he was most interested in finding all he could about the Vaughn murder.

Changing the subject, Daniel asked, "Mary Jane, when was the last time you spoke to Mayor Ledford?"

"You mean Jennings' d-d-dad?" she stammered, appearing to stall for time.

Daniel nodded his head in confirmation.

"I-I dooon't knooow." Her whole body was jumping up and down like she was freezing to death.

"What about Sunday? Did you see Jock then?"

Mary Jane didn't answer. Instead, she sobbed into her hands.

After several minutes of listening to her cry, her sister stopped the questioning by saying, "I don't think this is a good time for my sister to talk to you. Why don't we schedule another time when her *lawyer* can be here?" she said, emphasizing the word *lawyer*.

Smiling, Daniel said, "That's fine. I understand." She'd already told him enough. She was up to her eyeballs in trouble and needed the best lawyer that Jock's blood money could buy. He'd know all the answers soon enough. Anyway, he needed to get to Cumberland Falls. Something didn't feel right.

5:30 PM

Mayzella kept a steady pace as she zigzagged through the woods for over an hour just as she'd rehearsed. She rested using a pine tree to conceal her. Trying to regain a steady breathing pattern, she listened for noises telling her the sheriff had followed. Nothing! She'd run like a crazy woman for no reason! She knew she couldn't go back to the cabin for fear of running into him. She had to go forward. "Deek! Damn him! He better not have done something stupid." Sticking to the plan, she headed toward the falls praying Deek hadn't tried to get the sheriff to follow him instead of her. She wouldn't put it past him to try to bribe him. She knew money wasn't a motivator for Sheriff Osborne. He would do it for free as long as he could inflict pain. She cringed thinking about the pain he caused her in the past.

Following the plan, she headed toward the caves underneath the falls. The sun's light had already begun to fade in the dense forest. Slowing her run down to a trot, she still hit the ground hard when her right foot found a rabbit's hole. Her nose bleeding, she spit dirt and leaves out of her mouth. Slowly picking her tired body off the ground, she began her descent to the river, careful to stay concealed so she wouldn't be an easy target.

Arriving at the base of the falls—the caves—the sound of the river spilling over the falls made it impossible to hear anything except the loud static roaring of the water plummeting and crashing onto the rocks only a short distance away from her. Inching away from the powerful falls, she concentrated on keeping her back to the cool smooth rocks.

She sensed she wasn't alone; however, she couldn't see or hear anyone. Her worst fears were validated when she recognized the owner of a scream. "Deek!" she whispered as her heart came up through her throat. "So much for wishful thinking," she thought as she heard the scream again. She knew her intuition had been right; their plans had gone haywire. Holding her gun firmly in her hand, their fate was now up to her. Silently, she inched toward Deek's squalling.

The constant backlash of the water cascading over the rocks had worn the large gray stones under the base into weird shapes and sections. She finagled around the rocks to follow the sound.

Her eyes finally adjusted to the lack of light, and her body was shaking from being drenched from the spray of water.

She saw him. There lying on a large rock, reminding her of a sacrificial lamb on the altar, Deek had been badly beaten. Based on the rise and fall of his chest, he was still alive. The sheriff had his back to her as he continued to jab and hit at Deek. Deek didn't curl up or even attempt to protect his vital organs. "Not a good sign," she thought.

With her bead centered on the back of the sheriff's bald head; she cocked her gun and was ready to pull the trigger. She was distracted from her aim when she heard the sheriff say. "Ms. Wooten, I wouldn't advise you to shoot a man in the back. Just think if you missed, then you would be the one who strikes the fatal blow to your little hillbilly lover or what's left of him. You really didn't think I would fall for yer little trap, now did ya?"

The sound of his voice took her back to the time when he brutally raped her. He'd done things to her she never thought possible. She'd never told anyone because as much as she feared the sheriff, she feared Jock even more. After that night, she avoided the high sheriff like the plague.

How she wanted to pull the trigger and watch Willie's brains splatter, but she knew he was right. She couldn't live with herself if her bullet ripped the life out of Deek. She needed to think of her next move.

The sheriff slowly turned around so he was facing Mayzella. In his right hand, he held a gun pointed at Deek's head. Even in the dim light, she could see Deek's eyes were swollen shut, and his face was the size of a basketball. "Go ahead and shoot, little miss banker woman. I'll squeeze this trigger even if it's the last thing I do," he smiled as he thrust his words at her.

"How can you call yourself a sheriff? Didn't you swear to uphold the law?"

"Darling, that's exactly what I'm doing. You, my dear, are a thief to the tune of over a million dollars, and you can't deny it.

Let's not forget, Deek, here either. He's guilty of murder. I bet he didn't bother to tell you that he was on the run. Now did he?"

Sucking in air rapidly, she tried to remain focused. She didn't believe him. Deek didn't have a mean bone in his body, or did he?

He sensed he'd struck a chord with Mayzella so he continued. "I bet lover boy didn't tell you the little 'yeller' car you've been riding around in belonged to Geneva Vaughn's dead little granddaughter, now did he? Yep, I'm upholding the law just fine by ridding the world of two outlaws."

She didn't know what to believe. She recollected that Deek acting a little strange when she questioned him about the car and thought it was odd Jock wanted her to babysit Deek. Now she realized she willingly stepped into a plan that would allow Jock to have his loose ends together. "Concentrate!" she told herself. She refused to let this man get under her skin. She called for Uncle Buddy in her mind hoping telepathy really worked. "Be ready, Uncle Buddy. Please be ready!"

She had to hand it to Deek. He made sure the sheriff was in the spot they'd planned. Now, she had to do her part and make sure she was positioned correctly without giving the plan away, praying Deek hadn't already revealed it. She slowly started inching to her left.

The sheriff used his left fist to hit Deek in the kneecap; Deek's only response was a low moan. Mayzella squeezed the trigger to distract the sheriff and, also, as a signal for her uncle. The warning shot ricocheted off the rock to the right of the two men.

"Little lady, I'd be willing to make a deal with you. I'll let your boyfriend live if you'll pleasure me real good like you did last time," he lied, and the wickedness in his soul came out through the sound of his laughter.

She'd turn the gun on herself first. "Nope, I'm not going there again!" she said before she let her pistol do the talking. Once again, she squeezed the trigger. "Oh, Lord, was that my fourth bullet or fifth?" The sheriff didn't flinch. The only way she knew the bullet hit him was when she saw the blood starting to flow out of Willie's right shin.

His eyes flashed hatred before he said, "Two can play that game." He shot Deek in the same shin as his. This time Deek's scream was blood curdling.

"Please, God, let Uncle Buddy hear these shots," she prayed.

Willie laughed. "You want to play some mo—" his sentence was cut short. His mouth contorted into an odd shape like he was studying on what to say next. Then she saw the stream of blood begin to spew from the hole directly between his eyes. Her prayers worked! There really was a God, and he heard even the prayers of someone from Crow's Creek. The redeeming shot made not a sound. The only sound she heard was the sheriff's dead weight colliding with the rocky floor at the base of the waterfalls.

"Thank you, God! Thank you, Uncle Buddy!" she gave quiet praise. She'd heard tell how her uncle Buddy was a sniper in the army. Now, she saw firsthand the proof of his skills with his long-distance rifle. She maneuvered as fast as she could to reach Deek's side. She gently stroked his hair.

Deek's eyes remained closed, but he asked, "I did good?"

"Yes, baby, you did real good." She kissed his cheek.

Her bearded, mountain-man uncle wrapped her up in his big arms. He only gave her a second to cry before he said, "They'll be coming soon. We need to get out of here." Buddy dragged the corpse of the fallen sheriff to the water's edge and let him sink in the dark water. Sheriff Osborne's eyes and mouth were opened. They watched the water of the falls push him downward. Mayzella watched him sink until she couldn't see any sign left of him. She had no way to know she watched the sheriff sink in the water just the same way he and the mayor had watched a wide-eyed little girl's lifeless body sink in the blackness of Cromer Lake.

"Bon appétit!" she called to the catfish before carefully throwing his gun toward the spot where she'd last seen him.

They captured water so they could get rid of the blood. Deek was alive, barely. "I feel like part of me's missing," he said at one point during consciousness.

"No, honey. You just had a bullet to your shin, but you're all in one piece. I promise." Her words seemed to satisfy him as he drifted off. She had no way to know the significance of his statement. The bond with twins ran deep, and a very real part of him died when Dewey took his last breath.

Buddy slung Deek's limp body over his shoulder thinking not of his comfort, only of their urgent need to get on the road. Buddy field dressed the young man's wounds once they got back to the cabin while Mayzella removed any evidence of their visit. The three disappeared into the night. The Range Rover safely concealed in the back on the eighteen-wheeler's trailer of a truck that had the name "Mountain Man" artfully scripted on the large blue doors.

CHAPTER 39

The Search

Wednesday, April 16, 2008, 5:30 PM

The blue lights were flashing silently as Daniel Brooks wove through the traffic. Sirens blaring, the other cars bowed to the speeding emergency vehicle that was on a race against time. Joe Matt's knuckles were white as he clung to the cruiser's seat.

"I've got a bad feeling. I'm afraid Sheriff Osborne may be in trouble," Daniel justified his need for speed before ordering his friend to try calling the sheriff again.

Joe Matt dialed the sheriff's number, but again it went straight to voice mail.

"See if you can reach the sheriff of Whitley County." Daniel still couldn't understand why the sheriff didn't take his deputy with him like he said he would. Daniel cut his thought short to listen to Joe Matt's end of the conversation with Whitley County's Sheriff.

"You've not heard from Sheriff Osborne all day?" Joe Matt repeated for Daniel's benefit. "He went on a professional visit to Cumberland Falls a couple of hours ago, and we've lost contact with him." Joe Matt went silent as he listened to the voice in his ear. "I'd sure appreciate it." Silence again. "Okay, see you shortly."

They only had a few minutes before the state resort park would be cloaked in darkness. Daniel called his sergeant requesting additional units be dispatched to the Cumberland Falls State Resort Park. He hesitated before making his next call. Tillie answered in the sparkly voice that still caused the butterflies to stir in his belly. Thankfully, he didn't have to treat her with kid gloves; instead, he explained the situation to her giving what details he knew. He heard in her voice the precise moment when her personality changed from girlfriend to policewoman.

Daniel's passenger was clinging to every word Daniel was saying, waiting with bated breath for the call to end so he could have his say, "If that don't beat all! I'll have to hand it to you, Danny boy. You're more of a man than I am. I can't even hang on to one woman, let alone have two dangling from a leash."

"For crying out loud, it's her uncle!" he defended.

Thursday, April 17, 2008, 6:00 AM

The cloud-covered and fog-encrusted condition made daybreak a lackluster experience for the hundreds of volunteers that showed up to search for Rockford County's missing sheriff. The park covered over sixteen hundred acres in two counties. Law enforcement officers and other volunteers from all over the state scavenged the area using spotlights and dogs throughout the long dark night.

The deep excited yelps of the dogs sounded evidence they had honed into the sheriff's scent in various places throughout the wooded area of the park. The dogs sniffed excitedly around the underbelly of the falls, but without the appropriate lighting, it had been much too treacherous for anyone to search on the jagged rocks. They'd have to wait until daybreak before searching the caverns under the falls.

Tillie, Trevor, Joe Matt, and Daniel sat in Daniel's cruiser sipping hot coffee as they waited for the fog to rise. They'd purposely concealed information about the reason the sheriff paid a professional visit to the park. They didn't want the mayor to know they knew about his connection with Deek Lewis, but they didn't want to obstruct justice either. They gave just enough information to keep their secret safe.

The mayor arrived shortly after the search had commenced dressed in combat gear and trying to take charge. He may've been in charge of Rockford County, but he didn't carry a lot of clout with these professionals as they searched for one of their missing law enforcement brothers. They brushed Jock Ledford aside like dandruff.

As second-in-command, Joe Matt stepped up to the plate as he assumed the position of the highest law enforcer in Rockford County. Joe Matt sipped his coffee and studied his Tuesday Club leader strutting around like a banty rooster. He didn't think Jock was personally responsible for the sheriff's missing state, but who's to say he didn't place a call and have someone do his dirty work. With both Albert Dean and Woody—his hired thugs—gone, Joe Matt realized Jock was short on hired help. Of course, he wouldn't put anything past Jock Ledford.

By the way Jock was carrying on, one would think he'd lost his long lost brother instead of someone he barely tolerated. Jock regularly mentioned his dislike for Sheriff Osborne in the Tuesday Club meetings. Based on the way Sheriff Osborne rolled his eyes or grunted each time the Ledford name was mentioned, it was apparent there was no love lost on him either. Or was this an act? After all, they regularly ate lunch at the diner together, and the fact that he remained in his current public office for so many years also spoke volumes. "Strange?" *A question only Jock and Sheriff Osborne knew the answer to,* Joe Matt thought.

Someone fitting the description of Deek and a slim brown-haired woman had been seen near the cabin where Willie's vehicle was parked. Joe Matt knew if they didn't find the sheriff in the next twenty-four hours, the next step would be to conduct a body search in the river and with the Cumberland River swollen and at its crest; it would be very difficult to search. He was worried that not only would they find the sheriff's dead body, but possibly Deek's and the unknown woman's as well if Jock had anything to do with it.

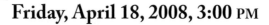

Friday, April 18, 2008, 3:00 PM

Nature's recent handiwork had caused McWhorter's rhythm of life to be off kilter. Ordinarily, the town had a pulse of its own. The two periods each year the citizens could count on to add a little zest to their lives was during the election periods—the May primary and the November general election; however, the disappearance of Sheriff Osborne caused the normal election routine to come to a screeching halt.

Many businesses closed to join the search for the missing sheriff. Even the schools let out so the teachers and students could help. News crews once again crowded into the little town so they could keep their viewers updated on the status of the beloved sheriff.

The town was still reeling from the aftermaths of the ice storm, hailstorm, the meth lab explosion, and now the missing sheriff—all in such a short time frame. Dented vehicles with plastic covering on one or more windows accounted for the majority of the vehicles on the roads. The town's residents normally would've been caught up in the excitement of the events, but now, they prayed for something resembling normal and routine. They yearned to go back to the time when the election activities were the most excitement they had all year. The churches had organized a prayer vigil to pray not only for the sheriff's safe return but to also pray for the town to find its lost rhythm.

Trevor Grant could feel the energy of the bustle of activity that was going on around him, but the faces didn't show excitement; they showed fear. The raised brows on the faces had the perpetual "what next?" look.

Trevor realized how little he knew about his uncle Willie. He'd seen him at least annually, but now was questioning Willie's absence in his and Tillie's lives growing up. He vaguely remembered what his aunt Brenda looked like. Not only had she been absent from his life, she'd also been conveniently MIA during the search for her husband. Deciding it was his family obligation to check on his long lost aunt, he drove to her house. The sheriff lived on the family farm on Turtle Branch. A lady who resembled his aunt came to the door and told him he needed to leave because Brenda was sick and couldn't be bothered. From his brief exchange with the lady, he could tell she was slow-witted, but not so slow that it prevented her from getting her point across. Not only was she adamant that her sister couldn't be disturbed, she was equally adamant that he not wait around.

CHAPTER 40

Life on the Run

Friday, April 18, 2008, 8:00 AM

The West Virginia Mountains served as a nice hidden backdrop for the fugitives. The area was beginning to come to life with new foliage, and the air was clean and crisp. Mayzella couldn't get enough of the cool air in her lungs especially after living out of a semi with two stinky men for two days.

Mayzella was finally at peace with herself. It only took fourteen hundred and thirty-six of the hardest miles of her life for her to make this journey. She now shared a bond with both Buddy and Deek she never dreamed was possible. Knowing they risked their lives for her had completely changed her.

Realizing she wasn't safe as long as the mayor was alive, she, at least, felt he wouldn't be able to find her for the time being. She figured he would have the election to keep him occupied for a couple of weeks, which should give her new little family the time to mend and to make a new plan.

They took the long scenic ride to West Virginia by way of Tennessee and Virginia. Knowing Deek needed medical attention, Buddy took him to one of his Vietnam veteran friends. Using the cover of the night to hide them, they met the good doctor at his small practice in Tennessee. Buddy carried Deek up the few steps into the office. This time, he handled him much like he would have carried a baby.

Deek was positioned on the examining table and was grimacing as his eyes adjusted to the bright fluorescent lighting. The doctor had the look and feel of money. Opposite on all fronts, the doctor sure didn't look like someone that would be friends with her uncle

Buddy. Just as the last few hours of torment had broken barriers inside of Mayzella, she could tell the time spent in the trenches of war must have broken down any barriers between the two soldiers.

The doctor didn't waste time before he assessed Deek. His movements were quick and calculated. After a thorough examination, the doctor said Deek was in bad shape but he was in luck with the gunshot wound. It was a clean wound, and the bullet had exited without doing major damage. After cleaning and dressing the wounds, he started him on a regiment of IV antibiotics and fluids. Only after the entire contents from the plastic bags seeped into Deek's dehydrated body did the doctor send them on their way and wouldn't take a penny in payment. Referring to his experience in Vietnam with Buddy, he explained, "I can never repay this big bear. Can't put a price tag on my life," Giving something without taking something in exchange had been a foreign concept to Mayzella. Now, she understood completely.

Without Deek's constant chatter, the ride was very quiet. Buddy wasn't big on chitchatting and made his words count in between his spits. "I've gotta get me some shut-eye while I can," he announced around two in the morning.

Mayzella thought for sure she wouldn't be able to sleep; however, when she laid her head on the pillow, sleep didn't take long to come to her. She dreamed of Rupert. She hadn't thought about him in a while, but ever since hearing about the fate of her former lover, she couldn't get him out of her mind. In her wildest dreams, she didn't think Lizzie Jean would try to kill him. Divorce him, maybe, but she knew Lizzie Jean was behind his collapse.

Mayzella used the solitude of the drive to think. She thought a lot about her past, her childhood, and her adult life. She thought about her family, Rupert, Deek, Lizzie Jean, the mayor, and every man who'd used her. By the time her uncle Buddy pulled the big rig into a truck stop at their final destination in West Virginia, she'd made peace with her past and had a new plan for her future—a new plan involving happiness.

CHAPTER 41

More Acorn

Sunday, April 20, 2008, 10:00 AM

In a thirteen-day time frame, Lizzie Jean had developed a new routine that coincided with Rupert's needs. At the hospital by nine each morning, she would then leave at six each evening, much like punching the time clock. After the sixth or seventh day of no improvement, the doctors gave her little hope of regaining the Rupert she knew.

A meeting was scheduled for this upcoming Wednesday to discuss the options for his long-term care. Doing her homework, she already knew the only choices would be a long-term care facility or to bring him home; neither of these choices was feasible for her. She would never be able to deal with strangers invading her home, and a nursing home was out of the question. The third option was her only option, but she wasn't ready to deal with that option just yet.

Lizzie Jean liked the routine of the hospital and liked the respect she was shown by the staff. Bringing gifts, she would make sure to reward the nurses who were especially helpful to her. It didn't matter that most of the presents she gave away had been gifts bought by the bank staff that she found lacking; they seemed to make the nurses happy enough. She also enjoyed the attention from the various men on staff at the hospital. Taking pains in her appearance, she made sure she looked her best each day. After all, she had a reputation to uphold as the bank president's wife; she planned to uphold this same standard even if Rupert would never walk back in the doors of the bank or not.

She could tell Doctor Roberts was more interested in her than just as a patient's wife. She found him very attractive. She'd always been faithful to her husband and never once considered another man until now. The doctor was dark-headed with just enough silver around his ears to look distinguished. Although somewhat slanted, his eyes were dark and mysterious. After discovering she was a fitness buff, he'd offered her a key to his office so she could use his fitness equipment at her leisure. She wouldn't have minded a nice little romp with this fine-looking man who wore no rings on his left hand until she found out his lack of rings was misleading. Refusing to hurt another wife in the same manner she'd been hurt, her interest in the handsome doctor faded when a nurse spilled the beans about his marital status.

"Mayzella Wooten," She hadn't thought about her dear friend in several days. "Yes, Mayzella would pay whether in this life or the afterlife," she said, her voice sounding as distraught and hopeless as the situation. As an afterthought, she added in a slightly aggressive tone, "On second thought, maybe I owe Mayzella a favor," she thought while contemplating how to live the rest of her life without a cheating, lying husband.

CHAPTER 42

Another Monday

Monday, April 21, 2008, 2:30 PM

The Buick followed the silver Chevy Tahoe at a distance. Jock Ledford was not trying to be discreet for the sake of those in the Tahoe; instead, he was trying to look inconspicuous to the cars following him. The Tahoe's destination was the warehouse down on Harris Street where the voting machines were stored. Today was the day the clerk's computer guru was going to make the adjustments to the machines to seal the fate of the various elections.

There it was again. The pain in Jock Ledford's chest was real. At first, he ignored the pain, but the sharp, jabbing pulse-like pains were coming too frequently for him to ignore anymore. He had Sissy bring him some of her daddy's nitroglycerin pills, which he had to admit gave him some comfort. He noticed the pains worsened each time he thought about certain topics—the missing sheriff, Mayzella Wooten, or the election to mention a few. He knew Mayzella was smart, but she should've been no match for the sheriff. After all, his nickname was Wiley Willie for good reason. He was crazy—crazy like a fox and would fight a buzz saw just for the fun of it.

"If Willie took care of the loose ends as soon as he got to Daytona like I told him, then, it would all be over with by now. But, no! The good sheriff took care of his own perverted needs first causing him to lose his element of surprise." He knew Willie was dead, or he would've found a way to have called him by now.

As sure as he was sitting there, he knew Mayzella and Deek were on the loose again. Without Mary Jane's aid, he wasn't sure if he'd be able to find them again so easily. "That Mayzella's a vindictive little whore. She's gotta go. No doubt about it."

Thank goodness, the pills started working. The tightening in his chest was loosening up some. He was able to park in the back of the warehouse's parking lot behind the dumpster. This gave him all the view he needed as he watched the county clerk, chief deputy, and a long-haired hippie-looking boy unfold out of the SUV. He wasn't sure what computer gurus were supposed to look like but figured this young man looked the part. Jock smoked a cigarette as he tried to ease the tension while he waited for the trio to secure his legacy.

4:00 PM

The stairs creaking with each methodical step gave Tillie fair warning she was no longer alone in her attic sanctuary. She already knew who it was, so she didn't bother to turn around. Call it a twin thing. She was trying to sort out her feelings about her uncle Willie. What really was bothering her was the absence of any heart wrenching pain on her part.

"Why didn't you answer me? I was beginning to worry." Trevor started out strong, but softened his harsh tone midway into his question.

She was still perturbed at him about dating Caroline Ledford, and she wasn't in the mood for his demanding tone. Her answer matched his hateful sound. "Probably because I didn't want to. Did you find out anymore about Uncle Willie?"

"Divers found a boot toward the falls that could have been Willie's, but that's about all they found. Between the many rock ledges and the murky water, the divers aren't hopeful of finding much more. The body should have surfaced by now."

"You think Uncle Willie was a member of the Tuesday Club? Could our own flesh and blood have been part of murdering our dad?"

"Your guess is as good as mine. What'd ya remember about our aunt Brenda?"

"Very little. Why?"

"I went to see her today, but some woman wouldn't even let me in the house."

"That's odd."

Trevor was silent for a few minutes before speaking, "Sis, why don't you go and pay a visit to our aunt Brenda. That woman may let you in since you're a girl. Plus, you can be charming when you want to be."

"Who do you think this woman is?"

"She looks like Brenda, only she's younger. She seems a little, you know, a little challenged." Trevor wasn't sure how to word his concern.

"Challenged? What're you talking about? Is she crazy or what?

"You know. She didn't seem just right—a brick shy of a full load. Definitely a little slow."

CHAPTER 43

Brenda Osborne

Tuesday, April 22, 2008, 5:00 AM

On this particular damp and dreary morning, the Big Goose Creek Church felt less like a place of worship and more like a torture chamber as the mayor, protégé, county clerk, county judge, farmer, chief deputy, and lawyer ate their breakfast in silence. The mayor had a plate in front of him but was only moving the food around on his plate. Actually, no one felt like being chipper this morning as they remembered what happened at last week's meeting. Jock wasn't encouraging their normal breakfast banter either. The protégé noticed the mayor had lost weight, and his eyes looked more intimidating; they looked dark and dangerous. The protégé remembered his father telling him that Jock's granddaddy had devil eyes. The protégé never understood what he was talking about until now. When looking into the mayor's eyes, he felt he was looking straight into the soul of the devil himself.

"Is history repeating itself?" he asked himself as he thought about Jock pulling the gun stunt at last week's meeting. He refused to be like the club's forefathers and sit back and watch an innocent man die. His father told him that initially the men followed Jon R. out of fear for their families. Later, they followed because of the rewards that came from being part of the Ledford's unholy club. Before long, the members got caught up in the power, prestige, and money that being a member afforded them. They either justified or turned their heads to the bad stuff that happened. Of course, the Ledfords were masters at explaining how everything, even the crimes, was done for the good of

McWhorter. Believing this malarkey made it much easier for the members to swallow.

The protégé was brought back to the business at hand when he heard the mayor clearing his throat. He looked up in time to see the mayor's evil eyes boring a hole straight through him.

"Sorry, mayor, I was a little zoned out and didn't hear what you had to say."

The silence was deafening as the men sucked air into their chest cavities and held it. No one exhaled while they waited to see what the punishment would be for the protégé's act of sacrilege.

The mayor continued to study the protégé but said nothing. Someone should have warned the protetge that the Tuesday Club's cardinal rule was to always respect Jock Ledford or face his wrath. Breathing a sigh of relief, the lawyer sat back in his chair when he realized the stare would be the extent of Jock's punishment. The attorney wondered if the protégé had been shown leniency because of his newness to the club or if it had more to do with the newest member's size and stature.

"Pay attention, son! I'm not up here whistling "Dixie." I'm talking about your very livelihood."

"Sorry, sir," the protégé said in his most polite and respectful voice

The avenger looked around at the faces of the men. He saw a wide gamut of emotion as he studied his fellow club members. In one member, he saw jealousy toward the mayor. He was certain this member was biding his time to overthrow Jock and take his rightful spot as the leader. He would be no better than the current leader if he ruled. In another member, he could see the dollar signs swimming in his thoughts. This man would side with the devil himself if it made him more money. Blind allegiance to the man who held them in bondage was all he could see when looking in the eyes of yet another member. When he saw only disgust in the faces of the other two men, he decided these men, his accomplices, would be the only ones that deserved a second chance at life—a life without the Tuesday Club. They were victims just as much as he was. The avenger knew that redemption could never come to McWhorter as long as the mayor and these three crooked men continued to walk the streets. As long as they breathed, the Tuesday Club would exist.

The avenger only half listened as the clerk spoke about the success of rigging the voter machines, the election workers meeting, and other pertinent election information. No one spoke unless being spoken to, and no one dared make a wisecrack. Even the farmer kept in check and didn't make any of his normal funny remarks.

The mayor volunteered information. "Barry Sizemore will be coming on board as soon as the primary election is finished. He asked us to give him time to take care of his dad's estate. I told him if he wanted his share of the money, he better be at the May 13th meeting."

Since the mayor brought up the subject of money, the protégé thought now would be the appropriate time to ask about their Tuesday Club money. He knew that any mention of money would really get Jock's dander up. "Do you have a new statement for us since the banker, unfortunately, won't be able to join us?"

The mayor threw daggers with his eyes at the newest member. Ordinarily, he didn't give two warnings to anyone. He started to pounce verbally on the younger man, but hesitated as he saw the same question burning in all the members' eyes. After all, the money was the biggest motivator for them to continue to follow his lead. He thought he would go ahead and pacify the money-hungry bastards by explaining, "I don't have no damn statements, but yer money's safe."

"Is our money still in our offshore accounts?" the chief deputy questioned.

"Boys, now, if that don't beat all. What kind of question is that? Did ya think I went and cashed it in—all thirty plus million of it? I guess ya think I have all of it at my house and me and

Eleanor swim around naked in it every night?" He paused waiting for them to see the humor in his statement. When no one even cracked a smile, he continued, "Well, of course, it's still in the same frigging banks!"

The lawyer didn't want to be left out in the semirevolt so using his best legal voice of reason he asked, "No disrespect intended, sir, but we've always had a back-up plan when it came to the money. If something happened to you, then we'd all be in a peck of trouble."

"Exactly!" the mayor agreed with the lawyer thinking this was the first thing said that made any sense. "More of a reason for each of you to make sure I'm kept safe."

The county judge couldn't keep his mouth shut any longer. "Hell, Jock! We ain't no doctors. What if you killed over tonight with a heart attack? All that money yer family's been putting back in these accounts will be out there and even yer own boys won't be able to get to it."

Mentioning the heart attack struck a chord with the mayor, not only because of his recent chest pains, but also because of the heart attacks the club had helped to induce throughout the years, thanks to the coroner's aid. Jock lied, "I've got it covered. If something happened to me, then my oldest boy will be able to get to the passwords. I'm not planning on kicking the bucket any time soon. Maybe, never. You hear?" He really meant it.

Ignoring the mayor's claim of immortality and changing the subject, the farmer questioned Jock about the banker, "How's our boy, Rupert, doing?"

The mayor shook his head and answered in one word, "Vegetable."

"Boys, there's worse things than death," the county clerk said just to hear his own voice.

Finished talking about Rupert, the mayor changed the subject. "We need to decide on a new sheriff."

"But what if they find Sheriff Osborne alive?" the chief deputy asked in a panic.

Ignoring the chief deputy's question, the county clerk gave his opinion on the matter. "I vote that our own chief deputy would be a good one."

The chief deputy explained the actual protocol. "Actually, the governor's office has been in contact with our office. Temporarily, the sheriff's position will be offered to Brenda Osborne."

"Lord have mercy! Poor old Brenda can't get unmedicated long enough to get out of her house, let alone make a decision about the sheriff's office. Joe Matt, you just call the governor back and tell him Brenda wants you to take the position."

"Brenda Osborne has a drug problem?" the chief deputy asked. She always seemed perfectly fine to him. Something didn't sound right.

"You mean I'm the only one who knows about Brenda's little problem. Well, trust me. She's not fit to run the sheriff's department," Jock explained.

He said all he intended to say about Brenda so he decided to end the meeting. He was tired and felt the need to put one of those little dynamite pills under his tongue. He turned to the farmer and said, "Got your love rocket in yet?"

The farmer smiled a toothy grin and said, "It's scheduled to be here on Thursday. I told Ethel I was going to try it out on her first."

No one laughed or made any comment about his intended humor. These men could have gone a lifetime without thinking about Bobby and Ethel Sizemore's love life.

7:30 AM

Joe Matt left the meeting and drove straight to Turtle Branch to see firsthand the status of his boss's wife. He arrived to see a familiar looking Volvo in the sheriff's driveway and a good-looking blond peering through the small pane of glass at the top of the front door.

Joe Matt couldn't help himself as he stared at the jean-clad backside of Tillie Grant. Looking at her sweet package made him feel a little envious of Daniel, but just as quickly as he felt the green-eyed monster beginning to set in, he shook it off. He and Daniel had been through too much for him to get a touch of the jealous bone now. Finally, he spoke up. "Hello, you purty thing!" Joe Matt greeted Tillie.

"Hey, Joe Matt," she said as she glanced backward long enough to make sure it truly was him standing behind her. Continuing to beat steadily on the door, she tried unsuccessfully to rouse someone. "I know someone's in the house, but they won't even acknowledge me."

Joe Matt joined her in her pounding efforts, and the sound the two of them were making could be heard from some distance. "We've got to get in this house!" Tillie exclaimed. "Something's wrong."

Joe Matt agreed and hollered in his most official voice, "This is the police! Open up, or I'm going to break this door down." Beginning to count backward from ten, he got all the way to three before the patter of feet could be heard through the door.

The door opened just enough for a woman to say through the crack. "Please leave us alone! My sister's really sick today."

"I want to see my aunt right this minute." Tillie's voice was harsh and unapologetic. She used the small opening as an invitation and used all her strength to push the door open, woman and all. Instinctively, Tillie headed in the direction toward what she remembered as her grandparents' bedroom. The woman protested every step she made. Tillie made it to the door frame of the room with Joe Matt close behind, both stopped in their tracks as soon as they saw the fragile person in the bed.

Had they not seen the rise and fall of the woman's chest, they would've thought she was dead. Actually, there were many corpses that looked better than this lady. Her blank eyes stared past them as she moaned softly. Joe Matt was the first one to her bedside. Noticing the discarded syringes in the trashcan, he carefully pulled Brenda's left arm out from underneath the covers to examine the soft underside of her forearm. All black and blue, it looked like a pincushion.

"Oh, my goodness! What have you done to her?" With the intention of shaking some sense into her, Tillie grabbed hold of the woman standing as a shadow in the back of the room. The horrified look in the lady's eyes was all Tillie needed to gain control of herself.

Brenda's younger sister began to cry. "You don't ... understand. If she don't get her ... shot, then she gets bad sick ... Willie told me ... I had to take care of her ... and that no one was to know about her problem!" Her words were choppy as she tried to talk between crying spurts. "She's almost ... out of her medicine, and I don't know where Willie is!" By this point, the lady was sobbing.

Joe Matt radioed for an ambulance. Brenda Osborne wouldn't live many more hours without immediate medical intervention. "Why didn't Willie get her any help?" he asked himself as much as he asked Tillie.

Wednesday, April 23, 2008, 10:00 AM

The Intensive Care Unit was full of activity as the nurses and doctors tended to the critically ill patients. Every patient in their individual curtained cubby had their own problems, and the various wires attached to their bodies fed the vital information to the monitors located at the hub of the unit. Brenda Osborne had been close to death's door, and the medical team paid close attention to her condition. Tillie and Trevor stayed by her side throughout the night. Those watching from a distance would never realize the pair hadn't laid eyes on their aunt in several years. Mindlessly, Tillie found herself staring at the hypnotic green blip as it painted a series of hills and valleys on the monitor directly above Brenda's head. Her erratic vitals were evidence of the internal battle being fought as her body craved the heroin it was used to receiving.

Brenda's sister, Luella, wouldn't leave her sister's side. Luella's devotion was without question; however, it was clear Luella was not mentally equipped to answer the nagging questions surrounding her sister's condition. She didn't think she was doing anything to harm her sister, but on the contrary, felt she was helping her by injecting the medicine. She said her sister was real sick, and the shots would make her better. Luella's devotion and loyalty were just as evident for her brother-in-law. She became quite upset when she was told he was missing and presumed dead.

Tillie knew they were all in trouble. The truth about her uncle was about to come out, meaning, they had made a horrible mistake by confiding in him. She was now certain that, somehow, he was involved in McWhorter's Tuesday Club.

CHAPTER 44

Southern California

Wednesday, April 24, 2008, 10:00 AM

The Southern California climate was perfect for those gifted with green thumbs. The air was so ripe with fragrances she could practically taste it. Julia enjoyed taking Lucille Grant through the neighborhood on their daily constitutionals. She was convinced she saw improvements in Lucille's condition after their walks each day.

As she walked, Julia found herself comparing the west coast scenery to springtime in Kentucky—each area owned its unique brand of splendor. Kentucky's redbud trees in April were usually a sight to behold. The purple-colored buds ushered in springtime and were only bested by the brilliant white and pink dogwoods blooming in all their glory around Easter time. Kentuckians referred to the cold snap after the blooming season as dogwood winter. Each cold spell that followed a particular blooming period was labeled a winter by those in McWhorter. They spoke about these winters the same as they did spring or summer.

Julia didn't own an almanac and didn't buy into many of the old-wives-tales and superstitions that had been passed down from one generation to another. It was difficult for her to believe how many—of even the McWhorter younger generation—continued to prescribe to this way of thinking. Parents in McWhorter didn't bring their babies to the doctor to be treated for thrush—a common treatable yeast infection—but rather went down to Old Man McKnight's house so he could blow inside the baby's mouth.

Julia couldn't believe it, but she was actually homesick for Kentucky. She never thought she would feel like that place was home, but more of a place for her to hide out until she was ready to begin living again. In hindsight, McWhorter had not only been a place for her to heal, but a place to find a new family and a new beginning. She was even prepared to die for her new family if needed as wrongs were now being made right. Her mistake in judgment cost her new family too much for her to ever repay, but at the very least, she now knew that Eddie's murderers had been punished.

Wiping a tear from her cheek, she slowed her pace and breathed in the fresh air. She stopped pushing the wheelchair and picked a flower that was growing on the wrong side of a neighbor's fence. From a distance, the bloom looked a lot like a fried egg. She placed the small white flower with a yellow center bloom behind Lucille's ear. Lucille lightly touched Julia's hand and turned so they were facing. When they made direct eye contact, both women smiled.

CHAPTER 45

A Ton of Bull

Thursday, April 24, 2008, 4:30 AM

B efore hearing the rooster crow, Bobby Sizemore was wide awake. Just like a kid on Christmas Eve, Bobby had the big eye most of the night due to the possibilities the next day held for him. When sleep finally came, it was short-lived due to the ruckus his dogs were making as they chased some animal away from their well-marked territory. When his internal clock struck five, he knew it was time to begin his day. He wanted to get an early start on his milking duties, so in the afternoon he could drive to Bacon Creek to pick up the device that caused his restless night. Giving a forceful shove to Ethel's back, Bobby wanted to make sure his wife was awake as well. "Get up and fix me some breakfast," he ordered.

Ethel didn't comment but did as she was told. Better looking than Bobby, Ethel still was no beauty queen. Mornings weren't kind to her either. Home perms had damaged her hair beyond repair, and this morning she looked like a cartoon character with her wiry hair going in every direction except the right one.

She added grease to the iron skillet readying it for tenderloin and eggs, and then, she placed her homemade buttermilk biscuits in the warmed oven to bake. Eyeing the time on the stove clock, Ethel knew Bobby's bowels were as predictable as the clock. She timed her breakfast so the food was on the table at the same time Bobby finished his bathroom business. Just as planned, Bobby came to the kitchen in his dingy white t-shirt and equally dingy drawer tail to eat a piping hot breakfast.

Bobby and Ethel Sizemore ate their breakfast in silence until Bobby spoke. With a mouthful of food, Bobby saw fit to tell his wife the reason for his rush this morning, "Going to the vet's office this afternoon," he said as he headed out the door.

She knew he wasn't the model husband, but he was okay as long as he wasn't drinking. Ordinarily, Bobby was witty and mild-mannered; however, with a couple of drinks in him, he would turn into a monster. Ethel had nursed so many black eyes and broken bones over the years she'd lost count. Her kids begged her to leave him, but she couldn't bring herself to do it. Bobby Sizemore and the life of a farmer's wife were all she knew. She tried her darnedest to keep him away from the booze.

Ready to start his daily ritual, Bobby slipped on his signature coveralls, pulled on his black rubber muck boots, and placed a "Ledford for Mayor" hat on his head as he headed out to milk the seventy-five head of Holstein cattle that were waiting for him. He loved his cows, but he was tired of the wear and tear the milking routine had on his body. Up before the crack of dawn, he completed his morning milking duties, and then just as soon as he ate a bite of supper, it was time once again for the same evening milking ritual. He finished around ten or eleven each night. Just like a wet nurse, Bobby's life revolved around a milking schedule since the cows' udders didn't recognize weekends or holidays.

Bobby knew picking up his electro-ejaculator was the first step in being able to phase out his labor intensive dairy business. Having his prize bull, Bocephus Boone, as well as the six bull calves he recently purchased, were also steps in the right direction. Bocephus Boone was as fine a stud as he'd ever seen; he felt sure he could charge a lot of money for his baby makers. He figured the semen collection business was all about the bloodline. He made sure the bloodlines of all his bulls were rich with milk producers on both the sire and dam's side.

Normally, Holstein bulls were ornery and hateful; however, Bocephus's mild manner caused him to be quite the exception.

Having won every contest entered, Bocephus was well thought of by all working in the bovine industry. Bobby treated his prize bull just like royalty. The seven bulls were kept separate from his dairy cattle; they had their own barn and a separate pasture.

He walked up the hill to his dairy barn. He whistled as a signal for his border collies to start rounding up the stragglers. Most of the cows lined up in the pen outside the dairy barn, waiting their turn to feed and be relieved of the milk that had painfully gathered in their udders since the last milking. Turning on the light in the milking room, he then turned the propane heater to the high setting to knock the chill off the room. The milking room was completely made of concrete with metal bars for stalls. He could milk five cows at the same time. Each milking station was just large enough for the cow's body. Once the cow was secure in the stall and udders washed, then the suction devices with tubes were placed on the cow's teats. The cow gladly exchanged her milk for the food provided in the trough.

Bobby pulled the levy that opened the stall door and allowed the cow to leave the barn. The cow left, but not before she lifted her tail and left Bobby a present of appreciation. Bobby didn't seem to mind. He was used to it. Anyway, Ethel would be the one cleaning it up.

After finishing her household chores, Ethel would help Bobby finish the milking. The excess cow manure would be pushed out the door into the manure pit. The pit was so deep that if a cow fell off the walkway into the pit, she would have a hard time swimming out from the depths of the muck.

As soon as Ethel arrived at the milk house, Bobby relinquished all his duties to her so he could be on his way to Bacon Creek to pick up Bocephus's present.

12:30 PM

Bobby dished out the eighteen hundred dollars to the veterinarian. Spending money was hard for Bobby. Even though he was a millionaire a few times over, he didn't live like one. Farmers were taught to be poor—they bragged about their cows and crops but, never about their money. It didn't set well to be a farmer who had money. If a farmer were fortunate enough to run into some money, it was a given the money was immediately supposed to be invested back into the farm. Bobby had the farmer's lifestyle down pat, and he grieved over every dime that left his pocket.

Feeling a little apprehensive, Bobby thought a beer would help him feel better about spending the money. His truck knew the way to the nearest bootlegger's house. Puzzy Creed, McWhorter's infamous bootlegger, convinced him to come in and drink some pure grain liquor with him. Against his better judgment, Bobby complied, and the clear liquid burned all the way down. It didn't take much of the pure grain before the cares of spending money were completely gone.

Carefully, Bobby made his way home. The black case holding the love rocket was placed firmly against him as he drove. He didn't even notice the vehicle following him at a distance. Relief was in sight when he saw the tip of his bull barn in the straight stretch. He could barely keep his eyes opened. He entered the long driveway that ran parallel to the state road, and pulled his truck next to the bull barn. Instead of facing his wife, Bobby sat in his truck and continued to drink from the bottle hidden in a little brown paper bag. Bobby had enough mind to know he needed to stop drinking now because he would need to be sober for his sperm collecting experiment. He forced himself to place the lid back onto the bottle. Sliding the bottle under the truck's seat, he thought a nap was in order. The inebriated farmer staggered his way to the house for a few hours of sleep. He couldn't remember much after leaving his truck. His next memory was of standing in the milk house five hours later.

10:00 PM

The last of the cows were in the milking stalls, and Bobby was pacing, impatient for his evening job to be finished so he could try his hand at semen collecting. He wished Ethel had finished milking tonight but figured that was a moot point. He couldn't remember what set him off or even the fight itself. The only reason he knew there'd been a fight was by the bleeding wound on his right knuckle. "Why did I let Puzzy talk me into drinking that pure grain?" he asked with regret in his voice. He hadn't drunk in over eight hours, yet he still had enough of the pure grain in his system that his nerve endings were numb.

Opening the door for the last cow to leave, he couldn't wait any longer to try his hand at semen collecting. The night was dark and starless as he walked the two hundred yards to the barn. His border collies escorted him silently to his destination. He listened for any panther screams as he walked the distance—a little paranoid after Jimmy's death. Relieved when he finally made it to the bull barn, he pulled the big wooden door shut behind him. He zoomed his flashlight around the pitch black barn. Bocephus Boone had a large stall to the right of the open barn, and the young bulls were in a metal pen on the other side. The open area in between had a mixture of sawdust, hay, and dirt for the flooring. The barn smells were a natural aroma for Bobby. Farming was in his blood, but it stopped there. His kids didn't want to have anything to do with the farm or with him. He knew he would have no one to keep the old farm going after he was dead and buried. This should have made him sad, but it didn't. He didn't plan on dying until he was a ripe old age, and after he was gone, he didn't care what happened to his farm.

Upon entering the barn, he could hear Bo's low snorting sounds and the bawling of the young bulls as they called out for their mothers. Music to his ears. He walked over to the light switch, flipped it, and called out to his bovine audience, "Daddy's here!"

Bellowing in protest to the sudden adjustment in the barn's lighting, Bocephus wasn't a happy camper. The farmer always felt in awe each time he was in the big bull's presence. Bocephus was a sight to behold. He weighed a ton, and his neck was muscular and thick. The spotting on his body was more black than white, but his face was mostly white with one black ring around his right eye. Bobby patted the bull's head. "Hello, boy. Me and you's gonna have us some fun tonight." It was Bobby's turn to snort as he laughed about the treat he had in store for his pet.

Bobby led the big bull by a rope around his neck to one of the three hitching posts. It was also close to the barn's only electrical outlet. He had a hard time deciding whether to purchase the electro-ejaculator or the artificial vagina. In the end, he chose the ejaculator partly because it didn't require the bull to mount and reportedly produced a larger volume of sperm. Although the main reason for his selection was because he felt he could manage the bulls by himself if he used the love rocket. He was about to find out. First, he needed to restrain Bocephus before he placed the probe in his rectum. Once the probe was in place, he would turn the dial and cause a series of short, low-voltage pulses to be applied to the pelvic nerves, causing the bull to ejaculate.

He would not collect the semen tonight, but instead would let it fall to the floor because the kit hadn't been sterilized. Tonight's rehearsal would just prove if it would work or not. The reason for his eagerness to perform the procedure tonight was not just financially motivated, but sexually motivated as well. Animal mating excited him in ways that sex with women could never fully satisfy him, and Bobby didn't want any spectators around to witness this perversion—especially his wife.

Bocephus was pawing at the dirt floor. "Hold on, Bo! Let Bobby figure this out, then both of us can go to bed with a big smile on our face," he told the large animal.

Plugging the device into the outlet, Bobby then carefully inserted the probe. Bo pranced around upset about the foreign object in his rectum. "Shhhh, it's okay, Bo. Just give ole Bobby a minute to get this figured out. Shhhh, settle down."

Used to his master's voice, Bo quit prancing and calmed down a bit, but he was still not happy. Bobby knew he needed to figure out how to turn the device on while keeping the bull calm and the probe in place.

Finally, he was able to turn the dial on the device to the on position and the response by the animal was pure mayhem as he began to hop around and bawl loudly. "Damn it! Be still, big boy!" he yelled in his meanest voice while managing to turn the device off. He now wished he was stone sober and could more clearly focus on the tasks at hand. His hands were bouncing around like he had the palsy. Just as he and his pet bull were beginning to calm down and get it figured out, the lights went out in the barn. "What the hell!" Bobby hollered. As he looked toward the light switch, his hand accidentally turned the dial on the device to the high setting.

The bull's reaction was so severe it tore the device from Bobby's hand. Due to the effects of the alcohol, Bobby's body didn't follow his brain's command. His brain told him to move right, but his body stumbled to the left. The bull reared his head, and the rope holding him to the hitching post came loose allowing him the freedom to rear up on his hind legs like a bucking bronco. Bobby's eyes hadn't adjusted to the dark. He couldn't see anything—only hear and feel the weight of the bull as his hooves landed with a thud on the barn floor. Bobby never expected the mild-mannered bull to have such a severe reaction to the device. "Damn it! I can't see a blessed thing!" he cried out. He couldn't see, but he could feel a sudden wind right before his head exploded from the force of the bull's hind leg kicking him in the face. The bull then continued to stampede and trample the farmer until he was able to shake loose the probe. As soon as the love rocket was lying safely on the floor, Bocephus calmed down like the tame bull he normally was.

The lights came back on as suddenly and mysteriously as they'd shut off, only to find yet another Tuesday Club member dead. A very shaken avenger and accomplice managed to shut the barn door. As they walked to their vehicle, they used the remainder of the steak to feed the dogs. Once again the avenger was thankful that nature finished the job he'd been called to do.

CHAPTER 46

Sleepovers and Sizemores

Friday, April 25, 2008, 12:32 AM

Tillie stayed at the hospital with Brenda until after midnight. She and Trevor decided to stay in shifts. "No use in both of us being sleep deprived," he reasoned with her. Not having the energy to argue with her brother, Tillie relented. She was tired, and a soft bed sounded wonderful. At first, she drove to her granny's house, but when she pulled into the garage she couldn't convince herself to get out of the car. The thoughts of being alone in the big house didn't appeal to her at all. Realizing it was almost one in the morning, she decided to take her chances that Daniel was at home. Alone.

She was really missing him. Although he stopped by the hospital, she could tell he was on edge. He didn't talk about his aversion to hospitals, but it was very obvious he had one. She was sure it had something to do with his father's illness.

Sighing in relief, Tillie was overjoyed to see only Daniel's cruiser and his dad's old truck parked in his driveway. Since she didn't have a key, she had to knock. Daniel let her in as soon as he recognized her voice. She laughed when she saw his Glock in his hand. "Well, I guess saying you weren't expecting me is definitely an understatement?"

Clearly not amused, Daniel sleepily replied, "You could've called first."

"But that would've ruined the surprise. I wouldn't have gotten to see you in your tighty whiteys carrying your weapon, now would I?"

Daniel smiled, but was bone tired and didn't feel like having a sleepover tonight. Of course, he couldn't tell her that.

Tillie explained her visit by saying, "Trevor's staying at the hospital, and I was scared to stay alone."

"Scared my ass, you just wanted someone to keep you warm. I've got your number, little lady. Don't you think you can fool me that easily."

"Guilty as charged," she said as she raised her hands in the air. "Mind if I take a quick shower?" She wanted to wash away the hospital odors from her body.

"No. Just make sure to clean up your mess," he said before he crawled back into his bed.

Tillie wasn't sure what to say to that. At first, she thought he was kidding, but when he didn't smile, she realized he was serious about her cleaning up after herself. "Yes, sir, your royal highness!" she said behind the safety of the running water.

"Definitely, he's a little OCD," she diagnosed him in her mind as she realized that his house was immaculate. No water was wasted in this shower. She was in and out and snuggled in the bed next to Daniel in five minutes flat. Maybe it was the late hour or the fact he wasn't expecting her, but she sensed a change in him. He definitely didn't seem interested in lovemaking tonight. She hoped it was because he was tired and not because he'd grown tired of her. She sighed in relief when she felt him pull her close to him. They slept entwined until the rude ringing noise of Daniel's phone awoke them only a few hours after they fell asleep.

Finding the phone, Daniel groggily answered it by saying, "Yeah." When he realized it was Joe Matt, he said, "I'm kinda busy right now with a pretty blond. It's okay, go ahead."

Wide awake, Tillie couldn't help but eavesdrop on the conversation. Unfortunately, Daniel's side of the conversation was not very informative.

Finally, she heard Daniel ask, "Any foul play suspected? Oh, Okay. Ethel okay? I'll be there as soon as I get dressed."

5:32 AM

Tillie was almost dressed by the time Daniel walked out of his bathroom. The familiar adrenaline rush of law enforcement had kicked in, and she was looking forward to thinking about something other than her aunt Brenda, the Tuesday Club, and her relationship with Daniel.

On first instinct, Daniel's reaction was to spare Tillie from the gore he was sure would be present at the scene until he realized as an FBI agent, she'd probably seen worse.

Driving hard on the early morning roads, Daniel was cautious. Since the call was not an emergency, he didn't see the need of turning on his top lights or sirens. It took over twenty minutes to drive the curvy country roads that led to the Sizemore's land. Using the drive time, Daniel filled her in on what he knew about the Sizemore family. "Bobby Sizemore wasn't known for his good looks, but he was a hard worker and loved farming."

"Do you think he could've been part of the Tuesday Club?"

"Possibly."

Carefully, Daniel pulled the cruiser in behind the other cars. Barry Sizemore was there with his hearse pulled as close to the barn as he could get it. He also recognized Joe Matt's cruiser, but didn't recognize the half dozen other vehicles lined up next to the barn.

The sun was just peaking up over the ridge, and Tillie was assaulted by the farms smells as soon as she opened her door. Knowing death was just feet away, she wished she would've stayed in Danny's warm bed.

The dogs took a barking fit when they entered the barn. Daniel reached to grab Tillie's hand, but she pushed it away. Her action caused Daniel to find a reason to smile at this very somber occasion. Tillie wouldn't want to be seen as weak, but he knew deep down she was not as tough as she led others to believe. He caught himself once again beginning to compare Tillie to Caroline. These thoughts were short lived. It was easy to get his love triangle out of his mind once he got far enough in the barn to see the blood splattered all over the ground and walls. A blanket covering what was left of the body.

Ethel Sizemore was surrounded by her family. He found it odd that none of them were crying. Instead, they looked toward the blanket with long faces and big eyes. Ethel was wearing her farm working apparel. Her jeans were tucked inside her rubber boots. She had on a dirty looking hat with the bill pulled down low, but the wide bill still didn't conceal a swollen and bruised eye and fat lip.

Ethel explained to the officers, "Bobby'd been drinking earlier in the day. He's not very nice when he drinks, so I didn't help him milk. I heard the milkers turn off around ten. I went on to bed. When I woke up around three, and he still wasn't in bed, then, I went looking for him. This is how I found him."

She'd just finished her story when Mayor Ledford entered the barn. Normally, the mayor was at least civil to Daniel, but today when he saw him standing next to Tillie, his eyes went dark. He didn't acknowledge either of them. Instead, he went straight to Ethel's side and hugged her. Daniel knew Jock could count on Ethel's vote in a few days.

CHAPTER 47

Sodom and Gomorrah

Saturday, April 27, 2008, 10:00 PM

Counting on both hands, Trevor Grant could count the number of times he'd seen his Aunt Brenda, yet it seemed now his life revolved around her every breath. Now, he knew exactly how many breaths she took in a minute. Out of boredom, he counted her breaths, the blips on her heart monitor, even the tiles on the floor to keep his mind occupied. He felt instinctively protective of her, just not sure who he was protecting her from. Trevor knew her induced sedation was giving her body the rest it needed in order to heal, but he wanted to shake her awake. "Talk to me!" he screamed inside his head.

He kept wondering how Brenda could've come in contact with heroin. "How would a homemaker become addicted to heroin? Did she wake up one morning and decide today was the day to get stoned on heroin?" he quietly asked. No matter how many times he mulled it over in his mind, it just didn't add up. Could she have known something on her husband, and this was his way of keeping his secret quiet? Lightly he bit his lip, arched his brows, and ran his hand through his short blond hair. "Yes! That had to be what happened! But what did she know?" Having no false illusions, he now suspected William Osborne of drugging his own wife. He also lied to him about taking Brenda on a vacation. There was no way she could've traveled then. According to Daniel, the sheriff had also lied to him about several things on the day of his disappearance too. Brenda's sister said, she and the sheriff had been giving Brenda the medicine for several weeks, but that was all she could tell them. No way around it, the sheriff was deeply involved in McWhorter's dark side.

Allowing his mind to further wander, his thoughts landed on Tillie's gory description of the trample scene that took the life of Bobby Sizemore. Based on his last name alone, Trevor knew Bobby Sizemore was part of the Tuesday Club. Using his fingers, he began to count the number of deaths and tragedies in McWhorter since their visit. "Good Lord! Am I sitting in the midst of Sodom and Gomorrah?" He would have to remember not to look back when he left this little town. Everything in him cried out for him to take Tillie and leave, but he knew Tillie would never leave Daniel just as he knew he couldn't leave McWhorter until Jock Ledford and his little club had been properly punished. Justice at all cost!

Chapter 48

The Calm

Tuesday, April 29, 2008, 5:00 AM

Sugar wouldn't melt in Jock Ledford's mouth when the chief deputy, the lawyer, the protégé, the clerk, and the judge met with him at the Big Goose Creek Church. With a big smile on his face, he greeted each man at the door by embracing him. The men had to do a double take to make sure this really was Jock Ledford. Even his dull eyes appeared to have sparks of life reflecting in them, and his rich bass voice was almost sing-song.

Jeb had prepared his normal breakfast grub but also fried some dried apple pies at the request of the mayor. Based on his saccharine filled attitude, it was evident Jock had been nibbling on Jeb's sweets before they arrived. This could be the only answer for his drastic change in personality. Or could it be because Jock brought both of his boys to the meeting with him?

Constantly baiting each of the members with questions to stimulate conversation, Jock wasn't content to let them eat in silence. They talked about every ball team in the SEC. After the breakfast plates were cleared, Jock shut the door and asked the chief deputy about the farmer's death. "There's just one thing I've got to know. I've been lying awake thinking about this. Now, son you've got to tell me the truth. I can't stand it any longer." He built up his questioning to a peak; then, he let it fester as he paused before asking the final question. "Did Bobby die with his hand up that old bull's ass or what?"

Joe Matt chuckled before he explained, "Not sure exactly where his hand was at the exact moment of his death, but yes, I did find his love rocket plugged up. I put the contraption up so no one else would know the ugly details of his death."

"Lordy, Lordy! What a way to die!" was all the mayor could muster in between outbreaks of laughter. The laughter died down, and the mayor took the floor for more serious business. "Fellers, I hope you didn't mind that I brought my boys with me today. I think we're going to have to make some changes, or our little club's gonna dry up and blow away. We're now down to six members—the same number that started the club in 1938. It's gonna take more than six of us to run this town in this day and age. Barry Sizemore'll be joining us next month, and I'm going to talk with Rupert's son when he comes home for the summer. I'll give Bobby's boys a little time before I talk with them."

The avenger hung his head. This was the last thing he wanted to hear. As far as he was concerned, the Tuesday Club had run its course and was having its last meeting. The next generation needed to be free to make their own choices and not live in fear.

During the course of the meeting, Jock passed out a list of all the people who had Geneva Vaughn's signs in their yards and another list with all her financial contributors. "I want to make sure you remember these people. These are some of the same people I've helped over the years, and now by supporting her, they've turned their backs on me." The old Jock was seeping out of his new skin as he began to rant. When he felt his chest tighten, he began softening his tone as he said, "I'm sure they felt sympathy to poor Geneva and couldn't bear to tell her no when she asked." Looking toward the clerk, he then asked, "How's the absentee voting going?"

The clerk cleared his voice and took his rightful spot at center stage. "We've had a steady group of mail-in votes, and my office has been busy all week with voters using the machine. Isn't it amazing Bobby voted shortly after he died thanks to our coroner? I'm always amazed by the great resurrection power of the McWhorter elections. Some people who've been dead and buried for years manage to turn up and vote each election. Spooky isn't it?" Several of the men chuckled.

Unfazed by the ghosts of McWhorter, Jock asked, "Did we account for these absentee votes when we rigged the machines?" Jock began to fret about yet another hole in the plan.

"Depends on how many we get," the clerk answered.

"Maybe you'll just have to conveniently lose a few of 'em, if'n it becomes a problem. If you know what I mean." The mayor emphasized the ending of his statement.

"I'm sure we can arrange for that to happen if needed." The clerk laughed with the mayor like they were best friends. He must've forgotten the feel of the gun against his temple.

Changing topics, the mayor looked toward the chief deputy and said. "Joe Matt, are we gonna keep the sheriff on the ballot, or what'da we need to do?"

The chief deputy had been slumped in his seat but straightened up and reported, "Yep. Right now we don't know if he's dead or alive, so we need to keep him on the ballot."

Satisfied with the answer, Jock went to the next topic. "Election officers on board and ready?"

"Yep, everything's going just fine. All we need to know is where you're gonna have your celebration party." The clerk again joked with the mayor.

"I've reserved Hazel's back room again this year. Jeb's gonna have fried chicken and all the works. We'll have all the food your belly can hold, and plenty of my favorite boys will be there. I'm inviting Jack, Jim, Mark, and maybe that damn Mexican, Jose Cuervo."

The judge called out, "Be sure and have a backroom ready with some of your best girls too. Nothing goes better with election parties than a little booze and a lot of loose women!"

"Why, Jack, if I didn't know better I'd think you're up to no good. You can't do nothing as long as you've got that woman of yours glued to your hip. Get rid of her by about ten, and I'll have you plenty of little whores to choose from," said the mayor.

Unable to help himself, the protégé couldn't resist asking Jock once again about the club's money. "Any news about our money?"

The mayor successfully kept himself in check throughout the meeting, but his eyes went dark and dangerous at the protégé's mention of money. He chose to make a mockery of the question. "Jon-Jon, tell them you know how to get to their damn money in case something happens to me. They're all worried half to death about me kicking the bucket."

Jon took his cue and ran with it. "Yep, Daddy's given me the combination to the safe that has the directions and passcodes for the offshore accounts. If something happens to my old man here, then I can get to the money. We can have us one hell of a wake!"

This seemed to satisfy the group, and no one else commented on the subject of finances. The mayor concluded the meeting by saying, "Boys, I've got an election to win, so if you don't mind, let's adjourn and get to work. Please be careful and don't do nothing foolish this week. I don't want to have no more empty chairs next week! You hear?"

2:20 PM

"Uhhhuhhhh ... Uhhhhuuhhh ..." Brenda cleared the cobwebs from her throat before managing to put a question together. "Whoooo ... aaare ... youuuu?"

When Tillie realized her aunt was speaking to her, she answered, "Why, Aunt Brenda, it's me, Tillie Grant, your niece."

Brenda looked around the room with wild eyes. "Where's Willie?"

Unsure of how to answer, Tillie just smiled and rubbed her aunt's hand.

Brenda wasn't satisfied with her lack of an answer so she again demanded, "I asked where my husband is."

"I have no idea."

Finally, finding her true voice, Brenda began to throw out questions one after another. "How did I get here? Where's Luella? What do you mean you have no idea where Willie's at?"

The nurse must have seen or heard Brenda and came running into her room with a syringe in her hand.

This rather inquisitive patient changed as she drawled her bended knees into her chest in a protective posture and pleaded like her life depended on it. "Please, please don't stick me! Please, I beg you not to stick me!"

Instinctively, Tillie jumped from her seat and placed her body between the nurse and the bed. "She's not going to stick you." Tillie said to her aunt, but looked at the nurse as she spoke. She then dismissed the nurse by explaining, "She's okay. Can you give me a minute alone with my aunt?"

As soon as they were alone, Tillie began to answer her questions. "You've been through quite an ordeal. Your sister's safe right now. Luella is resting at the motel down the street. Aunt Brenda, you are safe. No one's going to stick you again. Do you understand me? I'm a police officer, and I will not let anyone hurt you."

Brenda listened to her niece before saying, "You don't understand! I'm not safe!"

"If you're worried about Willie, then you probably need to know he's been missing for almost two weeks. He's presumed to be dead. Is he the one who did this to you? You can tell me the truth."

"Are you sure he's dead?"

"No. Not a hundred percent since we don't have a body, but something tells me we'll never see him again."

Brenda became agitated and started throwing her head from side-to-side on the pillow. "You've got to get me out of here, or I'm as good as dead."

"You're still very sick. I don't think we can move you right now."

"Who knows I'm here? As long as I'm alive, I'm a threat to them."

"A threat to Uncle Willie?"

"And his broth—" she stopped in the middle of her word.

When no other words followed her outburst, Tillie saw that Brenda's eyes were shut. She'd conveniently fallen asleep mid-sentence.

2:30 PM

Since Brenda had been hospitalized, Trevor had been unable to go to the newspaper office until today. Trevor hurried down the stairs to get back to his research. He'd made peace with all the ghosts residing in the basement; the odd sounds no longer unnerved him. He was at home in the midst of all this history.

Trevor began devouring every newspaper looking for anything he could find about the Osborne family—his mother's family. He found the birth notice for his mother, Lucille Osborne, without any problem, but was having trouble finding his Uncle Willie's birth announcement. He could find no announcement for an Osborne male. Birth announcements, weddings, and obituaries were important for the newspaper to print. Other than the big family Bible, the newspaper was the official record for most people in McWhorter.

He looked one more time at the newspaper dated closest to Willie's date of birth and reviewed each announcement in detail. He read out loud. "Jersey and Hershel Storm announce the birth of Gertrude Rachel Storm. Nope, not it. Here's one. Lewis and Mahala Brock announce the birth of their grandson, William Coleman Brock. Huh, grandson? That's kind of odd. Right first name, but wrong last name." He stopped his conversation with himself and wondered why the Brock name seemed familiar. "Brock Cemetery! Oh shit! Lewis and Mahala are my great-grandparents. Willie was a bastard! So, was Papaw Bill not his real dad?" he asked.

He made a copy of the two birth announcements using the antiquated Xerox machine. Wanting to share his new found information with his sister, he ran all the way to the hospital. Upon arriving at the hospital, Trevor first stopped at the water fountain and took a long gulp of water before he headed toward ICU. He couldn't wait to show his sister his findings. Wiping the excess water off his chin, he was backing away from the fountain when he felt her body collide with his. It startled him more than hurt him, and he found himself automatically starting to apologize as he turned to see who it was that hit him with the force of a small linebacker. There all sprawled out on the cold hard tiles was his twin sister. "What's your big hurry, Speedy Gonzales?"

Tillie was embarrassed by her spill, especially when she eyed people down the hallway pointing at her. As she pulled herself off the floor, she explained, "I was coming to find you before you ran me over," she joked before adding, "You're not going to believe it! Aunt Brenda woke up and actually talked to me!"

"You're kidding! Did you find out anything about Uncle Willie?"

"Only that she's very afraid of something which I presume to be him. She told me that as long as she's alive then she's a threat to *them*' Not sure who *them* are just yet though?"

"*Them* as in plural? You think her sister's involved?"

"I don't think so, but in this freaky town who knows? She started to reveal names to me but fell asleep midstream. I could've sworn she was going to say she was a threat to Uncle Willie and his brother? Only problem with that theory is Willie doesn't have a brother."

"Or does he? Let me show you what I just found," he said as he led her to the isolated waiting area and handed her the birth announcement.

Tillie started to read the announcement out loud. "William Coleman Brock?" She said with a puzzled expression on her face. "I don't understand."

"Keep reading," he encouraged.

"Lewis and Mahala Brock announce the birth of their grandson? I still don't get it."

"Do you remember the name of the cemetery where our Granny and Papaw Osborne are both buried?"

"Oh. It's Brock, isn't it? So are you thinking this is Uncle Willie's birth announcement?

"It has to be. I've looked through every newspaper, and it just so happens to coincide with his actual birthday."

"So could it be possible that Uncle Willie has a different father than our mother? And if that's the case, does that mean he could have a brother?"

Trevor finished her thought for her. "Big coincidence, huh?"

"Wow! Talk about skeletons in closets. Poor Momma. No wonder she retreated inside herself like one of those terrapins. You remember that turtle we played with at Daniel's creek that tucked its head and legs into its shell when we got close to it. Danny called it a 'tar-pin.'" She smiled as she mocked the elongated way Daniel pronounced the name of the turtle. Not wanting Trevor to know how quickly her thoughts turned to her lover, she let her thought slide and finished with her original point. "That's exactly what momma has done. Life has been too dangerous and hard for her to expose the soft interior parts of her life any longer. She's like that turtle that's tucked safely inside its shell."

Changing the subject, he pointed out, "I bet Brenda can shed some light on this for us."

"She's very scared. I'm not sure she'll tell us anything or not. Just think about it. She doesn't know us from Adam. I do believe she was drugged against her will. You should've seen her when the nurse came toward her with a needle. She cried and begged the nurse not to stick her."

CHAPTER 49

Hope

Wednesday, April 30, 2008, 9:30 AM

Eleanor drove Caroline to the doctor in Lexington, the closest metropolitan area. She told Jock she was going to Lexington to shop for something new to wear for his victory party. He handed over a wad of bills and told her to buy something pretty. If he suspected her motives were different from what she told him, his poker face didn't give anything away. Eleanor knew he was an expert at hiding his feelings. She not only had to play his game, but this time, she had to beat him because her daughter's life lay in the balance. Actually she wasn't completely lying because she fully intended to find something nice to wear today.

Eleanor diagnosed Caroline's condition a few days ago, but Caroline continued to deny she was pregnant until she couldn't deny it any longer. Learning from her own mistakes, Eleanor knew it was too risky for Caroline to see a local physician.

As they drove, Caroline's mind wandered. Having been on birth control pills since she was a teenager, she really hadn't thought much about being a mother. She'd learned her future was to be exactly what her daddy had wanted for her—nothing less or nothing more. After all, according to him, she was a product of his creation. If Jock wanted her to have children, then she would be a mother; if he didn't want her to have children, then she wouldn't have them. She'd been conditioned over the years to be nothing but a puppet with her dad holding all the strings.

Regardless of what Jock wanted, she was pregnant and not sure what she needed to do. Caroline knew she would abort this child using a coat hanger before she would subject it to the horrors Jock Ledford was capable of creating. If only Jock were dead, and if she only knew who fathered this baby, then she could be truly happy. In her heart, she just knew it had to be Daniel.

The ride so far was quiet. Eleanor looked over at her pale passenger. She knew she'd miserably failed her only daughter. She'd been too big of a coward to do what was needed and now look at her poor little princess. She wouldn't fail her now. Timing was everything; they had very little time to make plans. It appeared this secret was safe for the time being. Jon and Jennings blamed Caroline's condition on her breakup, and Eleanor hoped Jock was thinking on the same lines. The silence was finally broken at around mile marker eighty-two. "Are you going to have the baby?" Eleanor asked her daughter.

"Mommy, I don't know what I'm gonna do. Part of me would like to be a mother, but only if Jock Ledford were about six feet under."

After some thought, Eleanor spoke, "That can be arranged."

Caroline smiled. This was the first time Eleanor had seen her daughter smile in weeks.

4:00 PM

Brenda Osborne was steadily improving but had been very tight-lipped since her initial outburst. Tillie realized Brenda seemed to rest more comfortably when her sister was at her side. Luella was definitely glad to be of assistance to her older sister, but she was also excited about her motel room. She had no trouble leaving before dark each evening so she could order room service and view as much cable television as she desired.

Insisting Brenda be moved from ICU into a private room, Tillie felt it would be easier to keep her safe plus afforded all of them more comfort. Tillie hired a security firm from Oakridge, Tennessee, to provide guards to stay inside the room twenty-four hours a day. This allowed Trevor and her to get some rest. Brenda nodded in approval when Tillie told her about hiring these out-of-town guards. Then she finally spoke about the situation. "You've got to get me away from here. I know way too much."

"All right, it's just the three of us now. Are you ready to tell us what makes it so dangerous for you to stay here?"

Brenda didn't say a word. Her entire body was shaking. By decreasing her methadone dosage, her body was showing visible effects of the withdrawal. Apparently she wasn't going to be able to tell them anything today.

Thursday, May 1, 2008, 6:00 PM

The call from the commonwealth's attorney asking Daniel to join him at his office later that night took him by surprise. Only minutes after he ended his call, Joe Matt phoned Daniel explaining his mysterious phone call from Gene Lester too. They decided to ride to the meeting together. Joe Matt invited Daniel over to eat his momma Edna's pot roast before the eight o'clock meeting. It did Edna's heart good to watch the two grown boys tear into her tender chuck roast, but Joe Matt could tell by his mom's eyes, a lecture was brewing. Thwarting her chance to promote her "Edna-nomics" agenda to the men, he suggested they leave now and run instead of drive to Gene's office.

The testosterone and competitive nature of the men overruled their common sense as they sprinted most of the distance with each trying to best the other. Daniel was in the lead until he was distracted by the Lexus SUV in Gene's parking lot. Caroline Ledford, always the punctual one, was sitting in Gene's office. He thought she looked especially beautiful tonight. "Come on in, boys. I received something today that I thought you definitely would want to see," explained Gene.

The long-legged men shut the door and found themselves a seat. He gave each a copy of a letter then explained, "I received certified mail from an attorney in North Carolina. He forwarded me a statement from a man claiming to be Deek Lewis. The signature has been notarized as belonging to the twin brother of the recently deceased Dewey Lewis."

Daniel's heart pounded in his chest. Deek Lewis was the missing link he needed in order to tie Jock to Ruth Ann's murder. Gene read aloud the statement that explained the series of events leading up to the letter. After explaining he was an identical twin to Dewey Lewis, Deek told how his brother notified him about an opportunity to make three grand by pretending to be his twin for a night. He wrote that a man called Jock was the one who tutored him on what to say and do when he talked with a younger man named Jennings and even provided a cell phone for him to make the initial call. The letter claimed Deek also met with this same man after his meeting with Jennings Ledford concluded in order to receive his money. Deek wrote that Jock gave him his three thousand dollars in cash plus threw him a set of car keys and told him he could have the car providing he drove it out of state that night. Deek further stated he would be available to testify against the mayor providing they would be willing to guarantee his safety.

A pin dropping would have made a large commotion in the quiet room. Caroline actually felt hope bubbling up in her soul, hope for a real life without Jock.

"What kind of sick son of a bitch would try to frame his own flesh and blood?" Joe Matt questioned loudly as his counterpart consoled Caroline.

CHAPTER 50

Hospital News

Friday, May 2, 2008, 10:45 AM

Focused on electioneering, Jock decided to kill two birds with one stone by going to the hospital. He needed to check on the sheriff's wife who reportedly was admitted in the hospital for some mysterious ailment. First, he planned on campaigning at the hospital then planned to check on poor Brenda Osborne to make sure she was too sick to be talking.

"Jock flashed the young pretty girl seated under a sign that read "Patient Information" a big smile. For good measure, he took out one of his campaign cards planning to impress the young girl. She looked at it blankly as she tried to understand what she was supposed to do with the card. "Darling, I'm the Mayor of McWhorter."

The girl continued to stare at him with a confused expression.

Using his arsenal of charm, he said, "I don't think I've ever seen you around."

Her offensive Yankee accent was apparent as soon as she opened her mouth. "I'm not from McWhorter. I just moved down here to stay with my uncle for a short while. He's a new doctor here," she explained.

"Well. That explains it. I'd sure appreciate if you'd make sure your uncle votes for me."

"Why would I want to do that?" The young girl questioned.

The mayor didn't know how to react to the young girl's apparent disregard to his authority. Deciding he didn't have time to explain the pecking order in McWhorter, he blurted out that he needed the room number where he could find Brenda Osborne.

"I'm sorry. It says Mrs. Osborne is not accepting any visitors at this time."

"Oh? I'm sure she'll want to see me. It's okay. You can go ahead and tell me the room number. After all, I'm the mayor, and I have important business to discuss with her."

"Mister?" She looked down at the card to see what his last name was. "Ledford, I don't think you understand. I don't have a room number listed for Mrs. Osborne."

Jock felt the anger boiling just below the surface. "That's okay, honey, but will you be sure to let her know I was here checking on her?"

He didn't like this. This need for privacy could mean one of two things: the first could be that her family didn't want others to know about her problem, the second could mean she'd come out of her stupor long enough to spill her guts. He knew he had to act fast.

"I'll make sure she receives the message," the young girl stated before she dismissed him.

"Interlopers!" he managed to spit out as he headed up the hall and away from the information desk.

Knowing there was more than one way to skin a cat, Jock thought he could figure out Brenda's room by using the process of elimination. Starting on the first floor, he began popping in and out of each room to wish those in the hospital a speedy recovery. He recognized Rupert's room and saw his pretty wife sitting in a chair next to the lifeless man. Lizzie Jean had Rupert's hand tucked in hers and looked to be giving him a manicure. He cleared his throat as a way to announce himself.

Lizzie Jean looked up as she spoke, "Hello, Jock."

Jock questioned Lizzie Jean about Rupert's condition before he asked, "You have any idea where Brenda Osborne's room's located?"

Appearing to be concentrating, Lizzie Jean finally stated, "I think she's on the second floor." After giving Jock this information, Lizzie dropped her head and began her buffing motion once again.

Evidently, Lizzie Jean had just dismissed him too. "Don't these whores know the conversation isn't over until I say it's over!" he ranted to an empty elevator.

Grateful to hear the ding of the elevator door as it came to rest on the second floor, he walked out of the elevator and turned right. Noticing all the doors down this long hallway were open except one, he knew he first needed to check the room with the closed door. He didn't knock on the closed door, but instead pushed on it. The door opened slightly, but was stopped by a large buff man that stepped in the way of the door's further opening.

The security guard stuck his head out the opening in the door. "Can I help you?"

"I came to see my friend, Brenda Osborne."

"I'm sorry. You must have the wrong room."

Jock Ledford knew he was lying to him. A liar could always spot another one. "Listen, son, I know Brenda's in this room. I'm sure she wants to see me. Just go and tell her that it's the mayor," he said again thinking the title may make a difference. It wouldn't hurt for Ms. Little Noisy Britches to know he knew where she was located.

"As I said before, Mr. Mayor, you must have the wrong room." The big man purposely mocked Jock's title before shutting the door in his face.

Jock found himself standing outside a large thick wooden door. "This would not do. No sirree, this would not do at all. Someone's gonna pay dearly for this one."

"Gigs up, Aunt Brenda," Trevor bent his face over Brenda's bed and whispered when he felt the mayor was out of earshot. "You've got to tell us why the mayor is insisting on seeing you."

Brenda heard what Trevor was saying but didn't immediately respond.

At first, the twins were staying with Brenda out of a sense of duty, but now that she was awake and responsive, they both enjoyed being around her and Luella.

"Where do you want me to start?"

This time Tillie answered the obvious, "At the beginning?"

Brenda sighed before she started her walk down memory lane. "On one hand, William Osborne is one of the finest men I know, then on the other hand, he's one of the very worst men I've known. Problem is, I never knew which husband I was going to have. He has an evil side that's so sick and perverted you would never believe it even if I told you. He can go months being the normal Willie, but without warning his evil side will emerge." Brenda paused and took a deep breath as she repositioned her pillows.

Nothing in McWhorter surprised Tillie or Trevor anymore. Patiently, they waited for their aunt to continue.

"Willie knew my greatest desire in life was to be a mother. In one fit of rage, he took that from me." She could not and would never explain to anyone the gory details of this episode in her saga of her life.

"Aunt Brenda, why didn't you leave him?" Trevor thought the solution was easy.

"I tried it once, only to have my little brother killed in an accident. You see, I loved my family too much to risk it again. You've got to realize it wasn't always bad. Willie would go long periods of time between his evil spells. Sometimes, I could pretend I had a normal marriage. Still, I could never take the chance of having anyone too close."

"What about Luella?" Tillie asked.

"We've had Luella since my folks passed on. I'm sure you've figured out that Luella is a little challenged. She was a change of life baby. For some reason or another, Willie adored her, and she worshipped the ground Willie walked on. I could usually hide things from her fairly easily."

She took a sip from the straw on the tray in front of her. "I was cleaning out the spare bedroom when I found Willie's birth certificate. It was like a light bulb went off in my head. It all made perfect sense. I knew Mayor Clarence took a special interest in Willie, but I always thought the connection was through his friendship with Jock. After I found his birth certificate, I knew this relationship was much more than that—Clarence was Willie's father."

"What?" Tillie was floored. "You mean Willie and Jock Ledford are brothers?"

"Half-brothers." Trevor corrected. "Is the reason we have guards at the door because you know Willie and Jock are related?"

"Heavens no. It's the fact I know Willie and Jock were involved with killing a young girl."

Tillie grabbed Brenda's hand and moved as close to her as she could. "Are you sure?"

"I knew something was up when I saw Jock's Buick parked in front of the house one evening. I think it was on a Wednesday, but I can't swear to it. Jock knew about Willie's little problem and took full advantage of it. I saw the look on Willie's face when he came from Jock's car. His eyes were dark, and his mood was mean and excited. Trust me, I knew when something was up. Normally, I'm not brave and would have holed up and tried to stay out of Willie's way until the demon left him, but for some crazy reason I found myself compelled to find out what they were planning. Later, I overheard Willie say something about meeting Jock at the lake house. Since I knew where Jock's lake house was located, I decided to find out for myself what they were up to. As soon as Luella went to bed, I drove to Cromer Lake. I parked in the woods a good half mile or so from the house and walked in the dark to the cabin. I peaked in the windows and didn't see anything but that was when I heard a scream up in the woods. Stupid me followed the sound." Brenda's whole body started shaking.

Afraid to move a muscle, the twins froze. They were afraid she would go into convulsions, or worse, she would quit talking in the middle of this story.

Sighing a breath of relief when Brenda recovered, the twins waited to hear more of her story.

"I know beyond a shadow of a doubt it was Jock Ledford and my husband who killed the girl."

"Did they see you? Is that the reason they drugged you?" Trevor asked.

"Nope. I was used to being invisible. They never even suspected I'd followed. I thought I was home free and was starting to make my plan for freedom. Unfortunately, my plan went out the window. Luella, God love her heart, told Willie he shouldn't let me leave her alone anymore. I tried to lie and tell him I had to go out to get some Tylenol, but he could see right through me. I finally ended up telling him I followed him to the lake house. That was the last thing I remember until I woke up here. I don't know what he gave me, but I guess, he didn't want to have to deal with a dead wife until after the election."

"Wow!" It was Tillie's turn to shake. "We now have enough to put Jock in the electric chair."

Trevor, always the practical one, said, "Let's not get too excited just yet. I'm sure Jock will try to discredit Aunt Brenda. It will be his word against hers."

The twins were so busy fussing that it was a couple of minutes before they looked down at Brenda. Brenda's smile was ear to ear. She looked like a schoolgirl that had just stolen her first kiss. She made sure she had their full attention before she said, "Did I happen to mention Luella received a video camera for Christmas last year?"

In the parking lot of the hospital, Jock sat in his Buick waiting. He was biding his time as he tried to figure out his next move. He wasn't sure what Brenda had told anyone, but figured it must be something for her to have GI Joe and the Bobbsey Twins surrounding her.

The mayor lit a cigarette and waited and watched. He didn't hear or see anything unusual, but felt a presence. Continuing to look forward, he inconspicuously reached for his gun placed snugly in the gap next to his seat.

Slowly, he looked in the rearview mirror and just as he suspected his back seat was occupied. "Damn it!" the mayor exclaimed under his breath when he recognized the same little scraggly preacher man who lately haunted his every thought.

"Repent," the preacher man said the word void of any emotion.

"You go to hell!" Jock replied and flashed his weapon to his backseat passenger like it was a real threat to the ghostlike being.

The preacher man had no reaction to the man wielding the gun, but quoted Job 4:8–9, "Those who plow iniquity and sow trouble will reap the same. By the blast of God they perish."

Jock knew the Bible verse and could quote it just as good as the old man. Jock despised this Bible-quoting man more than anyone he'd ever disliked before, but he also feared him as he had feared no other before. He didn't have to look back into his rear view mirror to know the man was no longer there. The car felt empty again. Had Jock looked out the front window instead of concentrating on the rear view mirror, he would've seen a Volvo leaving the hospital's parking lot.

CHAPTER 51

The Hiding Place

Friday, May 2, 2008, 11:30 AM

With not a minute to waste, the twins seemed to telepathically communicate as they spoke, gestured, and nodded using their own twin language. While Tillie used her FBI blackberry to ask her boss for assistance in finding a safe rehab facility, Trevor sped to Brenda's house on Turtle Branch to find the hidden videotape. According to his aunt, she hid the videotape under a loose floorboard under her bed. Trevor wasn't sure how he felt about religion, but he found himself praying to the Jesus his granny had talked so much about. He prayed Willie hadn't already found her hiding place.

Upon arrival at the farmhouse, he made sure he wasn't followed before he opened his granny's car door. Once inside the house, he locked the door from the inside using the top deadbolt lock, then, placed the key in his pocket. He didn't want to have to worry about anyone walking in on him as he searched for the tape.

He easily found the bedroom then pushed the bed to the other side of the room using his arms to push while bracing with his legs. It moved easily enough on the hard plank floor. He pressed on the exposed dusty boards directly under the bed until he found a board that had some give. While down on his knees, he pried the board loose with his hands. He had to hand it to Brenda; the hiding place was perfect. It would be very difficult to find unless someone knew where to look. His lungs emptied of air when he realized that in the empty cavity underneath the board, lay only a wad of money. No signs of a videotape. Again, he prayed, "Please,

Lord! Please, don't do this to me." He ran his hand down through the dark opening to see what his visual inspection could have missed. Again, nothing.

Sitting in the middle of the floor with his hands nursing his head, his anger was working its way upward. For some reason, he channeled most of his anger toward his granny's Jesus. "Why, Lord, why?" he questioned while he kicked the nearest object, the overturned wooden plank. Just as he was about to throw an adult-sized tantrum, he stopped when he noticed the overturned board "What?" He raised his hands over his head like a football player who just scored. Taped on the rough underside of the plank was a small rectangular object that looked to be exactly the same size as a camcorder tape. His anger turned to praise as he whispered, "Thank you, Lord! Thank you!" Trevor tore the object free from the plank and cradled the small videotape just like it was a newborn baby.

Making sure the coast was clear before exiting the Osborne residence, he sprinted to his car knowing he had in his possession something worth much more than gold—something the mayor wouldn't hesitate to kill to obtain. According to Brenda, no one knew about the tape. Realizing this tape was her only hope to stop Willie's madness, she'd successfully kept this a secret during Willie's interrogation that morning.

Next order of business was to review the tape then duplicate it. If this tape contained only half of what Brenda said it did, then, it was what they needed to put Jock in the electric chair. At all costs, he needed to protect both Brenda and this videotape.

Saturday, May 3, 2008, 10:30 AM

The Kentucky Derby was held on the first Saturday of May, but Jock Ledford could've cared less which horse won that race. The only race he was concerned with happened in three days, and he was on the home stretch with the election excitement at its climax. Usually, he would be going door-to-door or at one of the various church cakewalks. Instead, what was he doing? "I'm on my way to the state police post to answer questions regarding that bitch, Geneva Vaughn's little whore granddaughter!" he ranted. "Couldn't this wait? Don't they know I've got babies to kiss and hands to shake?" Then it all made sense. Geneva was at the root of this. She must have orchestrated this questioning so it messed with his mind and caused him to lose votes.

In other circumstances, Jock would've insisted on his daughter accompanying him to this questioning, but instead Roy Allen Jones, her boss, would be meeting him at the police post. Jock no longer trusted his daughter. Instead of the asset to him and his election she'd always been, she now was a liability. Jock felt certain no one had any concrete evidence on him about anything. He felt a good lawyer would be able to throw anything against him out as hearsay or render it inadmissible. He knew Brenda Osborne had absolutely no credibility, and she would never be able to take the pressure of testifying against him. That is, if she lived long enough to testify.

On the other hand, Deek Lewis could cause him a little more difficulty if he were to show up. Even then, he had no material evidence—only his testimony, and what good was that? He was certain Deek was so stupid that even a bad lawyer could trip him up. He knew Mary Jane Tillery would keep pleading the fifth just as she'd been instructed to do.

By the time he pulled next to Roy Allen's vehicle, Jock was feeling pretty indestructible. As he and Roy Allen walked up the steps to go into the police post, he heard his name being called. He turned toward the voice. A camera flashed at the exact time he turned around.

Jock turned white as a sheet when he realized he'd just been photographed. "We've got to get that camera. I don't need that photo to be in the newspaper before the primary." Then it dawned on him the election would be done and over before the *Rockford Sun* would go to print again. He changed his mind and said, "Oh, forget it. Let Geneva have her fun. It would be too little and too late. Actually too little and too late should be her campaign slogan." Jock laughed at his own attempt at humor, but Roy Allen only politely smiled.

7:00 PM

Luella and Brenda were both so excited about going to Florida. Luella had visions of Mickey Mouse and seashells floating through her head. The rehabilitation center was located in Navarre and had been recommended as one of the most successful centers in the nation. Since Brenda wasn't the typical addict, Tillie felt certain she'd be just fine. Right now, convincing Brenda's body that she didn't need the drug was the hardest part; however, she was a fighter. The detoxification and the rehabilitation process would still be tough as she fought her body's craving for a chemical that her system had become dependent upon.

Tillie was glad Trevor volunteered to take Brenda to Florida. Trevor and Tillie thought riding in an ambulance for over twelve hours would be hard on even a healthy person. They decided to spend more of their inheritance on a chartered private flight.

Bone weary tired, the week's activities had rendered Tillie useless. Daniel poked fun at her by mocking her scared little girl routine from the other night. He told her she couldn't stay alone in that big house all by herself and guessed he'd just have to be there to protect her while Trevor was gone. Trevor made her promise she wouldn't tell Daniel about the tape just yet; this went against ever molecule in her body.

She had to hand it to Brenda. She'd videoed the yellow car and got a good picture of her husband's cruiser next to the car. Although the tape was too far away to see a lot of detail of the rape and murder, hearing the young girl's screams and pleads were heart wrenching. In the very capable hands of her colleagues, the tape was now being dissected frame by frame.

Daniel and Tillie ate soup and salad for supper before they snuggled on the couch while watching a movie. Wrapped in Daniel's arms, Tillie thought she never wanted him to let her go. She tried to put the video out of her mind. Somehow it felt wrong not to tell him; however, she'd given her brother her word, and she would not break it. With her time in McWhorter coming to an end, she knew she had to talk with Daniel. Deciding now was as good a time as any, she used the remote control to pause the movie.

"Hey!" Daniel said in protest.

She moved from the cocoon of love and sat up next to Daniel before saying, "We need to talk."

"Talk? We talk every day?"

"You know what I mean, smart ass. We need to talk about us. In case you haven't figured it out by now, I'm madly in love with you. I've got less than three weeks left on my leave, and I need to know what's next."

Daniel knew he wasn't good with these kinds of talks. Part of him wanted to drop to his knee and propose. He had an engagement ring ready for the right moment and the right girl. Problem was he didn't have either the timing or the girl figured out. At this very moment, he could see his life being with Tillie. Then, he would think about his reaction to Caroline and wasn't sure if he could totally give her up. Yet another looming problem he tried not to think about was the fact he hadn't received the results of the ballistic comparisons from the bullet that killed Albert Dean.

Finally able to find his voice, Daniel told her the best truth he could under the circumstances, "I'm in love with you too. I also think we'd make pretty babies. Actually, I like the idea of us walking on the beach with a little blond headed girl in between us holding both of our hands, a little dark-haired boy sitting on my shoulders, and your belly big and swollen with another one on the way. I can see that. Can you? Actually, I think we need to practice right now on our baby making skills since I want a big family." He began kissing her neck and moving his hands underneath her t-shirt.

Daniel's answer rendered her speechless by the verbal picture he'd painted for her. She could see the beach scene so vividly in her mind that she could actually smell the coconut flavored suntan oil. At this moment, she knew she would give up everything she'd worked so hard to obtain just to have what he was talking about. She never said a word and didn't think more about a video tape. Instead, she delighted in his touch. She wondered how he would feel about starting a family sooner rather than later when she realized what day of the month it was.

CHAPTER 52

The Photograph

Sunday, May 4, 2008, 7:22 AM

The phone continued to ring off the hook at the Vaughn's house since the first Lexington newspaper had been delivered in McWhorter. Her supporters couldn't dial Geneva's telephone fast enough. Plastered on the front page of the *Lexington Herald Leader* was a very unflattering photo of Jock Ledford. Evidently, the wind must've been blowing when the photo was taken because Jock's normally coiffed hair was standing up giving the appearance of two horns growing out the top of his head. The Kentucky State Police sign directly above Jock's head left the viewer with no false assumption of Jock's whereabouts. Roy Allen Jones was at Jock's side in his hand-tailored suit looking every bit the lawyer he was.

If a picture paints a thousand words, then this photo wrote an entire book. The article beneath the photo was very small but gave enough information to make many of the residents think twice about voting for the good mayor. The title of the article, "McWhorter's Mayor Questioned in the Death of Opponent's Granddaughter" led directly into the rest of the article's verbiage.

Geneva and Glenn Dale read the newspaper with mixed feelings. Relieved the truth was going to be revealed, they were also saddened. Secretly, Geneva hoped Jock Ledford wasn't behind the murder. It would be much easier to deal with her loss without knowing that her candidacy was what led to Ruthie's demise.

7:30 AM

Eleanor heard the shower running and knew Jock would want breakfast while he read the Sunday paper. Sundays were generally pretty safe days as long as Eleanor paid attention to what she was doing. Jock would spend time in the Bible and would at least try to pretend he had some Christianity in him before and after attending church.

While his oatmeal was cooking, Eleanor went outside to pick up the newspaper. Normally, Eleanor didn't even look at the newspaper. She was too preoccupied with her own survival than to worry about what was going on in the world around her. Transferring the rolled up newspaper from her right to her left hand, she happened to glance at the paper and saw a familiar face glaring at her. She then opened up the newspaper to get a better view.

She laid his newspaper in the exact spot she always laid it. Feeling especially brave this morning, she sprinkled a combination of brown sugar and flavorless laxative before adding a dollop of butter to finish her breakfast oatmeal masterpiece.

After what seemed an eternity, Jock entered the kitchen and gave a casual kiss on Eleanor's cheek trying to make amends for all the transgressions made throughout the other six days of the week. Eleanor thought it best to forewarn him. "Jock, honey, I don't know how to tell you this?"

"Tell me what?" he asked as his mood changed, and he eyed his wife suspiciously.

"Well, there's uh...uh..."

"Hell, woman, spit it out!" he yelled as he came toward her with his hand raised in the air.

Eleanor's larynx completely failed her so instead she just pointed to the table where his newspaper was waiting. His hand slowly returned to his side as his curiosity became more important than teaching his wife a lesson. In all of Eleanor's life, she had never heard the likes of the swear words that gushed from Jock's mouth when he saw his photograph front and center on the front page. He picked up the paper and tore it to shreds in his fit of rage. He realized he messed up by not getting that camera. The ringing of his cell phone interrupted Jock's rampage. He looked to see who was calling, then, laughed as he said, "I should have known the sick son of a bitch would have to call and rub my nose in it."

"Mayor Ledford," Jock said just like nothing was wrong.

The judge climbed into Jock's nightmare by saying, "Buddy, have you looked at the newspaper?"

"Why, that little article? That's nothing but hogwash. You wait 'til I get through with them. Me and Roy Allen had to go to the police post about Jennings a few weeks ago," he lied. "I'm going to go down to the radio and issue a disclaimer about this. You wait and see, the good folks of McWhorter will see right through Geneva's antics."

Jock hung up the phone with Judge Brown only to take a string of calls all regarding the same subject. By the time he hung up from the last caller, Jock was excited. He told everyone how he was going to own that newspaper and how Geneva had gone too far with this one.

Eleanor hurried to finish her breakfast dishes so she could get dressed for Sunday School. When Jock lied, somehow it became truth for him—so much that he could probably pass a polygraph. "Darn it!" Eleanor said inwardly as she threw out a perfectly good bowl of laxative-laced oatmeal.

10:30 AM

Promising his mother that he and Tillie would go to church with her this morning, Daniel and Tillie rushed to get dressed. Desperate for some guidance, he felt church may be the place for him to receive some much-needed direction about his life.

He was hesitant to make any decision one way or another until he found out the results of the ballistic tests on the Grant's guns. It was important for him to rule out Trevor or Tillie's involvement in the murder of Albert Dean. He couldn't imagine Tillie being involved with a murder; however, he wasn't so convinced about Trevor. He also thought that Julia could've been involved. Hopefully, it was some drug lords that shot the no-good drug dealer. One thing about it, he would know soon enough.

As in many small town churches, socializing made up a big part of the day's activities. A lot of the church folks were standing outside on the front lawn as the couple walked toward the entrance. They found Daniel's mother, Christina, seated in one of the pews toward the back of the building. "Where've you been? I've tried to call you all morning. Have you seen the Lexington paper?" Christina Brooks peppered Daniel with questions.

"Nope, what's in the paper?" he asked.

She took out of her Bible what looked to be a newspaper article.

Opening the fold, Daniel couldn't contain the chuckle that escaped his throat when he saw the devil himself standing on the steps of the police post. Tillie came to stand next to Daniel to see what was so funny.

"Can you believe it? Jock Ledford actually has horns in this picture," Daniel declared.

Before they could make more comments, the organ music officially announced the service was about to begin. A rush of sound filled the sanctuary as the congregation hurried to their pews. Just as soon as Daniel was comfortable in his seat, the song leader asked them to stand and turn their hymnals to page 144. After singing the first, second, and last verses of "When We All Get to Heaven," the congregation was allowed to sit down.

Someone seated toward the front hollered out for them not to forget about Geneva and the election. The pastor explained, "God's going to clean up McWhorter so it can be a city of hope for all who live here. God's using the Vaughns. He can use you too. You just have to be willing. The altar is open for anyone who wants to be used by God."

The sound of heavy feet hitting the hard wood surface made quite a commotion. Daniel watched Christina as she headed out the aisle with Tillie following close behind. Daniel chose to pray from his pew. As he prayed, he felt something foreign stir in him. The strong tingling sensation in his head and wet tears streaming down his cheeks were proof the Holy Spirit was moving in the church house and in Daniel's life.

Chapter 53

Monday Mania

Monday, May 5, 2008, 2:00 AM

The night was long and sleepless at the Ledford house. Jock was afraid to open his eyes, afraid of seeing a little man standing over top of him. Realizing that trying to sleep was useless, he went to Eleanor's room and woke her up so she could fix him a pot of coffee.

Sitting outside on the deck, he drank his coffee and smoked a cigarette. When he knew for certain he was alone, he began talking to his dead daddy and granddaddy just like they were sitting around the small patio table. He told them all his woes and even apologized for letting them down. After a few hours of arguing with the Ledford ghosts, reality hit Jock. Looking around at an empty table, he then knew he'd done lost his fool mind. Feeling the familiar pain in his chest, he knew he needed his heart medicine; he closed the door on the ghosts and went back inside.

In a more rational state, Jock Ledford showered and dressed in his standard khaki britches, light blue dress shirt, and short leather jacket. He backed his Buick out of the driveway just in time to see morning break over the hills. The first thing he heard on the radio was his own voice. Immediately, he reached for the dial and turned it up so he could hear his message.

"This is Mayor Ledford, the people's Mayor of McWhorter. I want to personally ask the good voters of McWhorter to not be deceived by my opponent's political strategy to discredit me. I'm still the same mayor that has served you and your family for over thirty years. I'm in the process of taking legal action against the newspaper that committed this horrendous crime against me. This is just another way my opponent is trying to discredit me and throw doubt your way. Are you gonna vote for someone with no experience that would stoop to such lowness, or are you gonna vote for an experienced mayor who will serve the community honestly? If re-elected, I vow to serve free of charge because I love this town so much and want to do what's right. Ask my opponent if she's willing to serve free of charge, and you'll see who has the town's best interest at heart. Vote for experience. Re-elect Mayor Ledford for the good of the community. This announcement was paid for by Jock Ledford."

Jock smiled as he drove. "Take that you old lying bitch! See if you can top that."

8:00 AM

Mornings were the hardest times for Caroline. She almost bypassed the toothbrush experience knowing it always ended up with a toilet bowl hug. Taking one last look into the ceiling-to-floor mirror, she was not pleased with what she saw. Even her smallest clothes were too big for her. She figured her new waif-like model appearance would be short-lived. She pulled a sweatshirt from the sweater cubby, wadded it up, and placed it under her shirt. "Look at me. Thirty-one years old, single, living in my parents' home, pregnant, and pathetic," she stated as she looked at herself at all angles trying to envision what she would look like in a few more months if she decided to keep the baby.

She couldn't let herself get excited about an infant until she knew for sure which of the men fathered it. A paternity test would be the only way she would know for sure. She read somewhere paternity could be tested while pregnant but didn't know how far along in her pregnancy she had to be.

The doctor felt she was at least six weeks pregnant. He drew blood and scheduled her back in four weeks for an ultrasound.

She didn't have the heart to tell her doctor or her mother that she didn't know who the father of the baby was. Thinking of her plight, she landed in a crying heap in the closet floor. As suddenly as she started her meltdown, she stopped it. Wiping her eyes with the back of her hand, Caroline number three forced herself to regain control over her emotions. She'd cried for the last time. It was time to take matters into her own hands. Reaching for her ankle holster at the top of her closet, she secured a gun under her pant leg. She then placed a small revolver inside her temporary cast on her arm. Her Ladysmith revolver stayed hidden in her purse. Her daddy would not lay another hand on her and live to tell about it.

No longer allowing herself to be a victim, Caroline merged all her personalities into one powerful persona and made her decision to keep the baby regardless of who fathered it. The only way to accomplish this move was to leave Daniel and McWhorter behind. Unfortunately, she needed more money than she had on hand to accomplish this feat. It occurred to her that Jon had told her something about having access to her daddy's precious Tuesday Club's money. "Wouldn't daddy just die if he only knew how many people knew about his secret club? It had to be the worst kept secret in McWhorter."

Feeling more alive than she ever remembered feeling, she now had a plan and knew exactly where to go to finish formulating it. Without a tear in her eyes, she explained to her brothers about her pregnancy; she conveniently left out the part about her being clueless on the father's identity. She told them she needed a lot of money and asked for their help. Their confused look told her she was going to have to go a little slower and spell it out for them in very simplistic terms.

"Jon, didn't you tell me that daddy told you how to access the Tuesday Club's offshore accounts?"

Neither of the brothers spoke for what seemed like minutes. Breaking the silence, Jon asked, "You don't think for one minute you're leaving us, do you?"

"No way! You're not leaving us behind in this hell hole," Jennings demanded.

Caroline frowned as she slowly replied, "Little brothers, I don't have a choice. Daddy will end up killing me, or I'll kill him. I've got to get away from here." She turned to head back up the stairs before saying, "I'm going with or without your help."

Grabbing her by her good arm, Jon said, "Oh, no you don't!" Physically turning her so she was facing him, he explained to her, "You know if I get into daddy's money, I'm as good as dead too, don't ya. It doesn't take much figuring to know I'm the only one who knows how to access it. If you go, then by hell, I'm going too!"

Caroline hadn't thought of this as an option, but she liked it. She knew that her brothers didn't have a chance at life as long as they lived in McWhorter. Immediately, she wrapped her arms around Jon's neck hugging him as hard as she could.

"You two don't reckon you're leaving me, now do ya? Hell, I was daddy's sacrificial lamb just the other day. After all, sounds like we've got us a baby to raise. We just have to find a place that's warm year round, and the women wear very little clothing. Okay?" Jennings asked before he joined the hug fest.

They commandeered Jock's office. Retrieving the passwords from the safe, Caroline helped her brothers access the account information from Jock's desktop computer.

"Holy shit!" Jennings exclaimed when they found over thirty-eight million dollars at their fingertips. In their wildest dreams, they had no idea the Tuesday Club had that kind of money. Initially, their plan involved only taking a couple million of their inheritance from the accounts, but now they decided the only way they could punish their daddy was through his money. They now wanted it all!

11:35 AM

If Gene Lester could put Jock Ledford behind bars, then his entire sham of a prosecuting attorney career would have meaning. He was unsure of the exact date when he lost all hope of being one of the good guys—the cowboy riding on a white horse.

Instead, he had somehow crossed over and become one of them. Jock Ledford and his cronies had drained him completely dry. Any desire to change the world through prevailing justice had been replaced by a padded wallet and complacency.

He should've known there were strings attached when Jock Ledford approached him about running for the commonwealth's attorney position. His young ambition blinded him. Looking back, he realized his title was nothing but an empty shell. Jock Ledford actually held the real title and power of the office. Jock was lawyer, judge, and jury for all things that happened in McWhorter. Sure, the mayor would throw him a few bones along the way, and on occasion, he would be allowed to do his job. By sending messages, Jock let him know which crimes needed to be punished and which ones needed to be left alone. As long as Gene didn't rock the boat, then come election time, a large sum of cash would be delivered by one of Jock's friends as appreciation for all his help. With very little effort, Gene would miraculously be re-elected.

At first he tried to resist but found his efforts to be of no use. He could prosecute all day long, but as long as Jock controlled the police department and the judges, then he'd never be successful at his solo attempts at justice.

Watching it over and over, he saw any man deciding to go against Jock be broken like a twig. Going against Jock was, at the very least, political suicide. Every elected official in the county was in the same predicament as he was. Gene had only two choices: appease Jock and keep a nice paycheck coming in or cross Jock and die.

Only after Gene decided to retire did an opportunity to make a real difference come about. He was fully prepared to pick up the reins and finally ride the white horse. The only way to clean up this town was to get rid of the root of the problem—Mayor Ledford. The opportunity to do just that landed in his lap.

Having debriefed Lowell Evans, his assistant commonwealth attorney, about the affidavit received from Deek Lewis, they both were now anxiously awaiting Ms. Tillie Grant's arrival. Her exact words over the phone were, "What if I have proof Jock Ledford and William Osborne killed Ruth Ann Vaughn?"

The meeting was scheduled to take place at eleven forty-five this morning at his office.

Gene's secretary had never missed a meal, and her pudgy cheeks were proof. She took lunch at eleven thirty each day and wouldn't vary. She claimed low blood sugar as the reason for her need for scheduled meals. She would have dramatic sinking spells if her food and gossip demands weren't met on time.

Purposely scheduling Tillie to come to his office after his secretary went to lunch, he thought Tillie would be safe from her nastiness. However, she must've gotten wind that something was up. Her curiosity was the only thing larger than her appetite.

Hearing Tillie's knocks on the door become increasingly louder, the men watched the secretary slowly make her descent to open it, even picking imaginary lint off the rug to slow her pace. When she got to the door, she barely opened it enough to get one chubby cheek through it before very curtly asking, "Can I help you?"

Tillie saw through the hateful woman's game, and she wasn't in the mood to play today. She said nicely but forcefully, "I have an appointment with Mr. Lester."

The secretary opened the door a few more inches and said, "Honey, you must be mistaken. Our office is closed from eleven thirty until twelve thirty each day for lunch. You'll just have to come back later." She pursed her lips and tilted her head at the pretty young girl as some type of triumph ritual.

Unfortunately for the secretary, Tillie really wasn't in the mood to deal with this kind of nonsense. Using her foot, she kicked the door opened not minding that the door hit the woman on its way to the door stop. She seemed to be making a habit of forcing her way in to places. If her use of force wasn't enough, Tillie placed her creds directly in the secretary's face. "I said I had an appointment with Mr. Lester. I'm on official business. Do you understand what obstruction of justice means?"

"Well, I never—" the dazed secretary said before she ran out the open door in tears.

"I think I'm in love," proclaimed Lowell Evans as he watched the most beautiful woman he'd ever laid eyes on head toward the office. He wasn't sure if it were the beauty or the way she kicked the door in that roused this emotion.

Tillie recognized the salt and peppered hair attorney from her younger days, but didn't know who the other man standing there ogling her was.

Clearing his voice, he introduced himself. "Lowell Evans, Assistant Commonwealth Attorney," he said in a lovely deep voice as he took her outstretched hand into his.

Sizing the man up, Tillie figured him to be in his mid-to-late thirties, blondish hair, and extremely good looking. It was his ice blue eyes that seemed to captivate her the most. Immediately, she began comparing him to her dark-haired, green-eyed boyfriend. She had to admit Mr. Evans stacked up nicely, but her Danny still won overall. Out of a lifetime of being single, she couldn't help but notice he wasn't wearing a ring on his left hand.

Tillie's FBI training took over as she began to explain the reason for her visit. "Chief Deputy Sizemore and I found Brenda Osborne, my aunt and the wife of the missing sheriff, in serious physical condition on April 22nd. She'd been drugged against her will and was on the verge of death. She has since recovered and has provided some valuable evidence regarding the death of Ruth Ann Vaughn." Tillie then handed over a package containing a DVD and three photos enlarged from the video.

Before the men had a chance to open the package or their mouths, Tillie warned them, "I don't know the ins and outs of McWhorter. I don't know if you are for or against the mayor, but I need to let you know that this information is not to leave this room. The original tape and several copies are located at the Louisville FBI office. Let me make myself perfectly clear. The mayor is going down with or without you. If any of this information leaks out, then I will make sure you're charged with obstruction. Understand?"

Gene and Lowell looked at each other and, then, to Tillie before Lowell Evans spoke with a professional but southern accent saying, "Ms. Grant, I understand and appreciate your concern. I assure you that although we don't publicly wear our knights in shining armor outfits, we are still the good guys. We want to be part of taking the mayor and his club down. The mayor is not supporting my candidacy in this election and is mad as hell that Gene is retiring without asking his permission."

Tillie smiled and let her guard down a little. Very little. "In my line of work, I have to be able to trust certain people. To be perfectly honest, I don't know who I can trust, or who I can't trust in this town."

Gene added, "Darling, I think you're wise to cover your bases. Shall we watch this DVD?"

The DVD played for a total of three minutes before she shut it off. It was plenty enough time for them to see and hear the girl calling for help and even calling out the murderers by name.

Relieved when she shut the recording off, Gene Lester didn't think he could bear another second of the torment. The photos in the package had been enlarged enough so they could clearly identify the mayor's face, his bloody clothing, and even the insignia on the ring he was wearing.

Gene took out his handkerchief and wiped his nose. Crying tears of grief for the little girl and tears of relief that McWhorter could actually be free, he then proclaimed, "We have him!"

Gene shared with Tillie the affidavit from Deek Lewis. It was all coming together. Working out their strategy, they had to be extremely careful not to tip their hand. A warrant for Jock's arrest would have to wait until Wednesday when the circuit judge was back in town. They realized waiting was a risk, but felt it would be even more of a risk if they tried to contact the judge while he was out of town. The judge could easily give Jock the heads up, but if they waited just a day, then, they could make sure the judge kept quiet. Showing their hand for even a second could give Jock an opportunity to run and never be found. They needed to play their cards very close to their chests, and just maybe they could also obtain evidence on other cronies of Jock's.

Tillie was concerned about letting the mad man run loose that long, but Gene assured her that the mayor would be followed every step of the day. "Don't worry. Jock will be so busy with the election he won't have time to get into trouble. His whole life revolves around his victory party."

Deciding the wait could possibly flush out more of the mayor's club members, they agreed not to call local law enforcement. Lowell mentioned he was good friends with the state police captain from the London post, and he knew him to be a man of honor.

Both men shook Tillie's hand as she departed; however, she noticed Lowell Evans held onto her hand for a long time as if he did not want to turn loose of it. Appreciative of the handsome attorney's subtle gesture, she was not interested in the least. The mention of the state police's involvement caused her mind to revert back to her obsession with Daniel Brooks. Only this time, her thoughts were more about her betrayal than about her feelings toward him. How in the world would she be able to explain she'd purposely hidden this huge turn in events from the man she hoped to marry?

2:00 PM

Having several reports to complete, Daniel initially didn't notice the activity going on around him at the police post. Working as a police officer was a lot like playing on a basketball team. Adrenaline pumped through the officers' bodies right before a major bust in the same way it does before the big game. After he received several noncommittal responses from his fellow officers, he went straight to his sergeant for answers.

Shutting the door for privacy, the sergeant explained to his direct report that he had purposely excluded him from a reconnaissance assignment involving his hometown. The sergeant began saying all the right things to unruffle his hurt ego for excluding him. Daniel began shutting his boss's empty words out until he vaguely caught the words *mayor* and *video tape*. Shocked, Daniel's eyes bulged as he listened to his boss talk about the mayor of McWhorter being involved in a murder.

When he referenced the FBI's involvement, Daniel stopped him. "Excuse me. Can you go back to what you said about the FBI?"

"Um ... I just said this damaging evidence came from an FBI agent."

"Male or female?"

The sergeant eyed Daniel suspiciously before answering him. "Female. Why?"

"Oh. No reason."

"How well do you know the mayor?" the sergeant asked.

"I guess I know him as well as he lets anyone know him."

"Well maybe, you could come in handy in surveillance tomorrow."

"I'd be glad to help, sir," Daniel said trying to hide his anger at Tillie. He'd been with Tillie all night, and she hadn't mentioned anything about new evidence in an investigation he was working.

He wanted to lash out, but kept his anger in check. How could he marry a woman who didn't trust him enough to share vital information with him? He felt like a fool.

Heading to his empty cubicle, he stopped when he noticed an envelope lying on his desk. The label on the front confirmed the contents as being his requested ballistic testing from his good friend. He carefully opened the package and reviewed the results.

2:50 PM

Caroline and her brothers worked most of the day making the necessary arrangements for their earthly rapture. They were going to be here one minute, and in a twinkling of an eye, they would disappear from McWhorter forever. The wire transfers were scheduled to take place at three p.m. tomorrow. Timing was critical. Showing their hand too early would be devastating; however, they knew Jock would empty the accounts if he were to lose the election. They didn't worry too much about a loss since according to Jock, he had the election already won. They couldn't risk being too late either. Banking on the fact Jock would be busy tomorrow, they didn't want him to discover the missing funds until after the polls closed at six tomorrow night. This gave them plenty of time to put their plan into place as well as keep the money safe.

Jennings was in charge of obtaining new passports with their new identities. It was going to cost a pretty penny for such a quick turnaround, but it was doable. Making the necessary travel arrangements, Jon had to scurry around to make sure all things functioned like clockwork. In charge of finding their new home, Caroline felt she had the best job. With the click of her mouse, she would be transported to different places all over the globe. She needed to find a safe place to raise a baby. Her brothers, on the other hand, gave her several prerequisites their new home needed to have. They all agreed they preferred a tropical place that predominately was English speaking. Of course, Jennings didn't care what language was spoken; he just wanted to make sure plenty of pretty women were at his disposal.

Lost in her hunt for a new life, Caroline was behind her desk at her law office with her laptop opened in front of her. Hopefully, the siblings were covering their tracks at every point and making sure to leave several dead-end goose chases when Jock tried to find them. They were not going to make it easy for him. If he did locate them, then, they were prepared to do whatever needed to be done.

The thought of shooting her daddy was fresh in her mind when she heard a sound. She looked up only to see Jock Ledford just feet from her. Instinctively, she reached for her purse with one hand and shut the laptop with the injured one. Jock lifted his hands over his head and started waving a pretend flag.

Wary of his motive, she had her revolver in her hand before asking, "What do you want?"

"Easy girl. I came to apologize. I know I've not always been the best daddy to you, but this distance between us is killing me." Jock's every word was pure sugar.

"Let's see, you beat me to a pulp and you...uh...uh..." She couldn't verbalize what happened next. Somehow by speaking it out loud, it made it real. Managing to shake the attack from her mind, she changed courses midsentence and mocked him by saying, "Then, I'm supposed to forgive you and pretend you're the best daddy ever. Well, maybe when I was younger, you could play these mind games with me, but as far as I'm concerned, you are not my daddy. You are nothing to—"

Interrupting her tirade, he said, "Okay, okay, I get it." He decided to appease her and let her have her say knowing her hours on this earth were limited. Letting the pain in his chest guide his next move, he placed one of his hands next to his hurting heart before falling into one of the wingback chairs directly facing her desk.

Caroline resisted her urge to clap for his Oscar winning performance, but instead crossed her arms with her Ladysmith clutched tightly in her right hand. "Go ahead. Spit it out. I know you wouldn't be here if you didn't need something from me."

He gave his best stab at showing the look of indignation. "I told you, I just wanted to make amends with you. I've lost a bunch of my good friends to the grave in the last few weeks. Now I feel I'm losing my family too, and this damn primary has got me torn all to pieces."

"Do you really think I care one iota about the election?"

Jock didn't answer her; instead, he stared at the ground for several minutes before he went straight to the point by asking, "I need you to work the election tomorrow. How much will it cost me to buy my charming, vote-getting daughter for one day?"

Caroline couldn't help but laugh. "I should've known. It's always been about that election with you. That's all that's ever mattered." Using her best lawyer voice, she made her demands known. "Ten thousand in cash would be a nice payment for a few hours of my time." When he didn't blink at her price, she decided to add more insult to injury. "Then, I think fifty thousand would be a nice down payment on a new home. The ten thousand is for working the election. The fifty thousand buys my silence." Actually, she thought he was coming out way ahead on this deal; a total of sixty thousand dollars for a lifetime of her misery.

Jock didn't balk or try to wrangle her price down. Instead, he said, "Consider it done." As he walked toward the door, he turned around and added, "I'll give you the money, but surely you're smart enough to know that no one would believe you anyway. It would be your word against mine, darling."

CHAPTER 54

Before the Storm

Tuesday, May 6, 2008, 3:32 AM

Today, the primary election could change the direction of McWhorter—or it could seal its fate just as it had over the past seventy-plus years. The election, however, had very little to do with Tillie's sleepless night. She knew Daniel would be upset over her betrayal but had no idea he would refuse to talk to her at all. When he finally answered his phone, the only words he said were, "How could you even think about spending your life with a man you don't trust?"

Even if he'd given her a chance to respond, she had no idea what she would've said. Each explanation she thought up seemed lame. Part of her wanted to blame her twin, but she knew she could've talked Trevor into including Daniel if she really wanted to. Bottom line was she couldn't afford more mistakes. Trusting a corrupt uncle was bad enough.

She could replay it over and over in her mind and make every excuse in the world, but the truth of the matter was he was right—she really didn't trust him. She trusted him with some things, but when lives were in the balance, she had to trust her instincts. All her police training was based on instinct, and secrecy was part of her everyday life. The fact remained that she didn't know Daniel Brooks enough to trust him when it came right down to it. Daniel Brooks shared just enough of his life with her to give her a glimpse into it, but not the full panoramic view that was needed for this level of trust.

4:30 AM

The Ledford house was very quiet. Jock was making plans in case the clerk's scheme was not foolproof. Number one on his list would be taking care of the county court clerk if he even thought of double-crossing him. Number two on his mental checklist was taking care of the golden boy himself, Daniel Brooks. He had such great plans for Daniel—that is, until Daniel made him and his daughter the laughing stocks of the town. He had to prance that little blond whore all around town making sure everyone knew where he was shaking his tallywacker. Come to think of it, he could pinpoint his downward spiral to the day Daniel Brooks came back to town. "Yep, I'm gonna make sure the golden boy knows it's entirely his fault Caroline is going to have to die tonight."

He knew number three on his list would have to wait a little bit. He could do that. After all, he was a patient man. Admittedly, Geneva taught him a thing or two over the past few weeks; however, respecting her ability didn't mean he didn't despise her. More than just despise, he deep down loathed her.

Enjoying this mental exercise of revenge, Jock made plans to dispose of his enemies one by one, starting with the ones who had betrayed him the most. This mental stimulation was actually physically stimulating him as well. Knowing exactly what to do to remedy this little problem, he picked up the phone and dialed his secretary, not minding it was very early in the morning.

"Yeah, Sissy. This is Mayor Ledford. I have some dictating I need you to do this morning. I'll run by your house. Okay. Be there in about twenty minutes."

7:30 AM

The 2008 presidential election had taken a backseat to the heated local races in Rockford County. Instead of talking about Hillary and Obama, those in Rockford County were talking about Ledford and Vaughn. Regardless of the heated elections,

Eleanor knew the pretty May weather would also contribute to a big turnout.

Responsible for decorating for Jock's victory celebration, she tried to be creative and use different themes each year. This year she decided to decorate the backroom at Hazels using patriotic red, white, and blue streamers and balloons. She stood in the doorway of the room trying to judge the reaction factor of those attending tonight. Satisfied the room would meet Jock's standards, she knew after the alcohol started flowing no one would care much about the decorations anyway.

After leaving Hazel's, her next stop would be the elementary school to help serve up the pancake breakfasts for a community fundraiser. After breakfast was served, she then had to work on the election officer's lunches. Today was one of her busiest days each year. Thankfully, one thing she didn't have to worry about was standing in line to vote. She'd already voted last week by submitting an absentee ballot to Rufus Jones, the county court clerk.

She was glad Caroline had changed her mind and would be helping today. Her daughter had always been such a big help to her. She thought it was odd her boys were also helping at the breakfast this morning instead of spending this sacred time with their daddy.

Round two would start promptly at six o'clock when the precincts closed. The precinct results would start rolling in shortly after closing. Election tabulations had come a long way in Kentucky with everything being computer driven. The fact that Kentucky rated near the nation's bottom regarding education, but was at the top of the heap regarding election tabulations, showed what the state valued. It explained just how serious small town Kentuckians were about their politics. She remembered when officials were still counting paper votes into the wee hours of the morning. Now, all Rockford County precincts should have their election results verified by eight, the celebration commence by nine, the whiskey flowing by ten, and then Eleanor could be safely tucked in her bed by eleven. Of course, this was how it happened when Jock and his candidates were victorious. She wouldn't even allow herself to think about what would happen if Jock didn't win.

11:00 AM

Knowing they needed to be fresh for the evening's verdict, Geneva and Glenn Dale purposely slept in this morning. The election was all in the Lord's capable hands now, and she knew she was a winner regardless of the outcome. She felt all along that the Lord's strategy was for her to become the mayor; however, she didn't remember him giving his personal guarantee.

Geneva liked being a housewife and had been just fine with her life before the Lord decided to take her out of her comfort zone. Holding a public office or the small salary that came with the mayor's position had never been her motivating force. Personally, she didn't care if she won or not—she just didn't want Jock Ledford to win. Regardless of the outcome, she knew life as she'd previously known would never be the same. Her life could never fit back into her old life, and it wasn't because of her weight loss either.

The couple's first stop of the day would be at their church. They rode from their house to the church only breaking the comfortable silence when they saw a dozen or more cars parked in the church's parking lot. Entering the sanctuary, they saw it was lit by candlelight with soft praise music playing over the loud speaker. Geneva latched on to Glenn Dale when she saw the altar lined with people on their knees.

Her heart was so full as she realized so many of the prayers being said were on her behalf. Through this election, her faith had grown by leaps and bounds, her church family had united, and many of her supporters learned the art of spiritual warfare. Looking back, she knew this drastic transformation didn't come about until after Ruthie died. She had to hold the Lord's promise of Romans 8:28 fast in her heart "that all things work together for good for those who are called according to his purposes." It was hard to lose her granddaughter, but to know her death furthered the kingdom at least made it tolerable.

Glenn Dale squeezed Geneva's hand before he turned toward her and reminded her what Esther 4:14 said, "Remember that like Queen Esther of the Bible, you have come to this position… for such a time as this."

CHAPTER 55

V is for Vote

Tuesday, May 6, 2008, 5:18 PM

Jock seemed undeterred by the rules governing elections. If he recognized there were undercover officers located throughout the courthouse, he didn't let it stop him from violating several state election laws. Not only was Jock seen numerous times in the voting areas, he actually assisted some voters when they cast their ballots. The close proximity of Jock's office to the courthouse proved handy on election day for him as well. His buddies congregated at his office campaign headquarters throughout the day, and Daniel witnessed a steady stream of inebriated men coming from Jock's office to vote. Another election no-no.

Daniel felt the best way to keep an eye on the mayor today was to stay close to Joe Matt and Rufus Jones in their second story makeshift office. His duty was not to apprehend Jock or gather evidence of his election transgressions, but rather to observe him for signs of flight or danger. He still hadn't spoken to Tillie today and didn't think it was a good idea to speak with her just yet. Focused on the task at hand, he was able to keep his mind occupied so he wouldn't think about her and her betrayal. Daniel had to resist the urge to confide in Joe Matt about the planned take down of the mayor. It wasn't because he didn't trust his best friend. On the contrary, Daniel knew he could trust Joe Matt with any secret. Joe Matt wasn't his patsy by any means, but all his life he'd been able to persuade, influence, or even downright manipulate Joe Matt into doing things. Come to think of it, Daniel realized he'd been able to influence a lot of people over the years without them actually realizing he was doing it. Call it one of his gifts to society. Daniel was certain Joe Matt only leaked information to Jock that they both agreed was necessary to accomplish their overall mission of taking down the Tuesday Club.

Part of him wanted Jock to know about his appointment with a jail cell, hoping it would make him careless. However, this knowledge could backfire, and instead of making the mayor careless, it could make him deadly.

The courthouse voting had been backed up all day and now the voters only had forty-two minutes left to cast their vote. Daniel watched the various voters enter and exit. At one point, Joe Matt and Rufus had their heads together whispering. Daniel acted as if he didn't notice their secrecy or the fact they acted skittish about something. Reminding him of an expression his dad used to say, he thought Rufus and Joe Matt acted as nervous as long-tailed cats in a room full of rocking chairs. He had a pretty good idea of the reason behind their anxiety.

5:10 PM

It was a little past five and Caroline and her brothers found a few minutes to touch base with one another before putting their plans in motion. Jon explained he had the cash ready. Caroline was pleased to see the transfers had been made into the new offshore account she'd set up. The Wednesday Club, as they'd taken to calling themselves, officially had over thirty-eight million dollars at their disposal. As long as Jock was winning in the polls, she didn't think he would have a reason to check the offshore accounts until much later that night.

Jennings explained the passports would be ready to pick-up in Atlanta at eight o'clock in the morning. They each had a bag packed with only bare necessities. Caroline had packed a suitcase for her mommy. Eleanor hadn't been told about their plans of escape. They felt it was best this way. They were prepared to drug and kidnap her if necessary. Either way, she was going with them.

Traveling to Atlanta in two separate vehicles, Jon felt it made the most sense for Eleanor to ride with him and for Caroline to ride with his younger brother. Upon arrival in Atlanta, they would all travel in a van to a small airport in Venice, Florida. Chartering a flight in Venice, they would journey by air to Key West, and they would test their sea legs from the Keys.

She had to hand it to her little brothers; their plans looked to be foolproof. "Oh no!" she said to herself in a panic. "Hadn't daddy always said there was no such thing as having a foolproof plan because there were just too many damn fools in the world?"

CHAPTER 56

War Dawg of Kentucky

Tuesday, May 6, 2008, 6:45 PM

The cool of the gun felt good against Jock's hot hands. Normally, he was able to figure a way out of most of his predicaments; however, no amount of figuring tonight would make everything all right. Drastic measure had to be taken. His only decisions tonight involved which act of revenge to take and in what order. The polls had been closed for forty-five minutes, and he already knew that Rufus Jones had managed to royally screw him out of the election with his foolproof idea. Geneva Vaughn won the election in a fair race—no computer guru or hocus pocus involved.

He'd enlisted someone at each precinct to call him with the results as soon as they had a tally. He knew the outcome of the election even before the officials knew it. Jock Ledford had let his daddy down. Not only was Jock Ledford officially beat, he was also financially ruined. He had a pretty good idea who was behind stealing his money. The thieves would have to pay the piper too, even if it involved every one of his own damn spawns. That money rightfully belonged to him, and he needed it to get as far away from this Godforsaken town as he could. However, he wondered if he could ever run far enough to get away from the Ledford ghosts.

Interestingly enough, Jock didn't feel the normal tug in his chest that had become the norm as of late; instead, he felt alive. He lusted for revenge. "Daniel Brooks holds the key to all this madness," he thought as he grounded the pills found in his desk drawer to a very fine powder—fine enough to pass for salt.

He couldn't think about Daniel without thinking of Tinker. Jock felt admiration, gratitude, and even a little fear when thinking about Tinker Brooks. As much as he would have liked to have forgotten, he could never forget that summer day in 1957 when Tinker saved his life. Jock let himself go back there in his mind one last time before he completely shut the door on that memory.

Even when he was young, Willie Osborne had always been a mean ole cuss. He was a head taller than the rest of the boys in his class and lorded it over everyone. On this particular day, Willie thought it would be funny to throw Jock out of the little rowboat and make him swim to shore. Cromer Lake wouldn't be considered a big lake by any means, but plenty big enough to a twelve-year-old. Jock remembered hearing Tinker pleading with Willie to go back and get him. Willie just laughed. Just when Jock was ready to let the lake take him, Tinker dove in and rescued him.

"Well, you little pussies made it after all," Willie taunted.

That was all it took for Tinker to explode. Willie didn't stand a chance as Tinker fought like a heavy-weight prize fighter. Although Jock never officially thanked Tinker, he tried to throw him some bones from time to time. However, Jock couldn't throw him anything when Tinker was drafted. Thankfully, Jock's number never came up, but Tinker and Willie weren't so lucky. Tinker returned from Vietnam possessing so-called "special" skills. Jock found out about Tinker's skills firsthand on a Tuesday morning while driving from his secret club meeting. Feeling the knife on his throat and his head pinned by the hair against the headrest of the car, he barely managed to push the car's brake pedal. He listened to Tinker talk to him in a slow whisper. "You leave my boy alone. You mess with him again, and I'll kill you. You'll never see it coming."

Having no other choice, Jock agreed. He smelled death on the blade of Tinker's Marine issued bayonet that was ready to slice into his juggler. As soon as Jock gave him his word, Tinker slipped silently out the backseat door and into the darkness of the morning.

Even Willie wouldn't mess with Tinker after Vietnam, not because of the ass whooping from his youth, but because of the wartime tales that were told about the War Dawg from Kentucky. Jock was both glad and sad when Tinker Brooks died.

Sniffing in the air, he recognized the familiar scent of Jeb's fried chicken. Best he remembered everybody loved Jeb's fried chicken, especially Daniel Brooks.

CHAPTER 57

Let the Games Begin

Tuesday, May 6, 2008 6:50 PM

Caroline was nervous, afraid some important detail had been overlooked. Watching out the window earlier, Caroline saw her daddy slip into his office shortly after the polls closed. She knew in a matter of minutes that he would emerge from his lair knowing he was missing thirty-eight million dollars and would automatically suspect Jon's involvement.

Fearful of underestimating their daddy, the siblings had to work extra hard to make sure all bases were covered. Jock always had an uncanny way of knowing things he shouldn't. Maybe he really did have a direct connection to hell.

Caroline had been intermittently taking turns at looking first at her watch, then, at the large clock hanging in Hazel's front dining room. Hazel's Diner was strategically positioned so she could sit and look out windows to see the activity on three different streets.

"Mayday, mayday, the bird's flown his coop," she whispered excitedly to her youngest brother when she called him on his cell phone. Jennings was in the courthouse verifying votes on his daddy's behalf. Caroline's call would be Jennings' cue to phone Jock with the ruse of a possibly kidnapped brother. What better way to point the finger of suspicion away from them, than to plant in Jock's mind the possibility Jon had been forced to give the passwords to the safe?

It was still light enough for Caroline to see when her daddy retrieved his telephone to take Jennings's call. Caroline's performance was up next. Even as a child, Caroline had no time to play the typical teenage drama queen role; nevertheless, in order to survive, acting skills and lying were part of her repertoire. "No, Ms. Reva, I got that bruise from falling down the stairs," she remembered telling an observant teacher. She could pull this off. She had no choice.

If Jock was knowledgeable of the missing Tuesday Club money, he didn't let on to anyone at the diner. Instead, he was all smiles when he said to Jeb, "Umm ... umm ... that fried chicken called to me from nearly a thousand yards away."

"Here, eat up now so we can celebrate later," Jeb said as he handed him a chicken leg.

Giving herself a few minutes to tame her nerves, Caroline allowed her daddy to visit with Jeb before she made her grand entrance into the kitchen.

"Well, hello, Ms. Caroline," Jock called out to her when she was in earshot.

Intent on giving him his money's worth. "Hello, Daddy. Aren't you looking all dapper?"

"Darling, why don't you go over to the courthouse and fetch your mommy?"

She smiled at him and even batted her eyes a little as she said, "Sure thing, Daddy."

Jock admired his wife as she and her frail daughter walked in the diner together. He heard Jeb's low whistle of appreciation that was meant for his wife of thirty-two years. Ordinarily, Caroline would've been the stand out, but tonight Caroline paled in comparison to her mother. Eleanor was wearing a taupe colored two-piece skirt and jacket set. Adorned with gold jewelry, she looked like leftover tinsel from one of those fancy department store's Christmas trees.

By the look in Jock's eyes, Eleanor could tell he was pleased, but what came out of his mouth contradicted his eyes, "How much did that set me back?"

"Plenty," she smiled as she answered.

Jeb made up for the mayor's lack of flattery. "You sure look purty, Ms. Eleanor. The men will all want to come to your victory party just to get to look at you."

"You're always so sweet to me, Jeb." She then looked to her husband and asked, "Caroline said you needed me?"

"Yeah, I needed to ask if you've seen Jon-Jon?"

The women looked at each other before Eleanor said, "I haven't seen him since about two when he finished his lunch delivery route."

"That was the last time I saw him too," Caroline answered.

"Jennings called me worried because Jon wasn't answering his phone," explained Jock while trying to read the expressions of the women.

"If he doesn't turn up in a little bit, we probably need to send someone to look for him," Eleanor said nonchalantly before asking her husband if he'd seen his victory room.

"Nope, I haven't seen it yet. Come show me."

Right on cue, Jeb shut the lid on one of the supper boxes, "Ms. Caroline, best I remember your Daniel sure likes my fried chicken. Why don't you take him this here supper box?"

Caroline's face lit up. "Who doesn't like your chicken? I'm sure he'd love it," she said as she took the box from Jeb's hands.

Clearly in his element, Rufus Jones was handing the election results to the radio announcer as soon as he received them. Rufus had his workers typing in the results as they were read. The middle table had a microphone in the center, and this was where Crawdad Craig, the voice of McWhorter's only radio station, was positioned.

Swimming through the foggy haze of smoke, Caroline located Daniel. He followed Caroline out the door to an isolated stairwell. It was there she handed him a styrofoam box containing fried chicken, potato salad, beans, and corn on the cob. Daniel hadn't realized he was hungry until he eyed the food much as a wolf would look at his prey before devouring it.

Content on watching Daniel eat the chicken, Caroline didn't speak. He broke the silence by saying, "I believe Jeb's changed his chicken recipe a little. Tastes a little different, but still good. Maybe better."

"I'm pregnant."

Unable to initially react, he only stared at her until he asked, "You're what?"

"At least four weeks pregnant, maybe longer. I won't know for sure until my next appointment."

Daniel knew he wanted to be a dad someday, but this was not how he envisioned the experience.

Caroline could not bring herself to tell him the child might not be his. In her mind, she willed the baby to be Daniel's and refused to think otherwise.

"Are you going to have it? What will your daddy say?" Daniel managed to ask as he began mentally calculating where he was a month ago.

"Yes. I've made my decision, and as far as I'm concerned, my daddy will never know. I just thought you should know because I'm leaving tonight. Tillie won. You and Tillie can now live happily ever after. I just thought you should know about the baby." Before giving him time to respond to her words or her plan, she turned and ran out the door.

In what seemed like slow motion, he placed his box down on the floor. He tried to follow her, but his body wasn't responding. He managed to use the banister to pull his body to an upright position. Instead of heading out the door to follow her, he detoured into the rest room.

8:30 PM

Wiping her eyes, Caroline walked in on the celebration and noticed the serious looks of those in the room. She thought to herself, "Oh, my goodness! Daddy's losing this election." Normally, she would've been happy about him losing, but today, it posed a serious problem. Jock losing the election was one thing not covered in their plan—it was the unthinkable.

Some well-meaning supporter hollered out, "Don't get down, boss. We've got five precincts left. We can still win this thing."

Jock didn't say a word. He wasn't a fool. He knew these same men and women who supported him tonight would run straight to Geneva at daybreak. The election was over for him, and he had to change his focus. He had to get his money back, and he had some lessons to teach along the way.

Drinking the last of his Jack Daniels from his tumbler, he decided it was time to make his move. He walked over to his wife and whispered in her ear, "Get your purse and follow me, dear."

Caroline was in the kitchen helping Jeb with the clean-up when she felt her daddy's gun barrel jam up against her back ribs. "Come with me, and I might let your mommy live," he whispered so only she would hear. Caroline looked around for where she laid her purse.

"This what you looking for?" he said as he raised up her purse with his left hand.

Eleanor and Caroline walked down the basement steps together with Jock following one step behind them. Mentally calculating the best way to take Jock down, Caroline decided it was too risky to show her hand now.

Clueless, Eleanor nervously asked, "What's going on? Something wrong with Jon?"

No one answered. Both Jock and Caroline were silent.

The fresh air outside was rejuvenating, but the darkness was disturbing. Caroline never remembered it being this dark on Broad Street before. Looking up, she then understood why it was so dark at this precise spot. "Oh, shit!" she said when she realized the streetlights were conveniently not working. She knew this was bad. It meant her daddy was already a step ahead. The lights had to have been disabled earlier in the week. Walking the distance to the car in complete darkness, Jock pushed Caroline toward the driver's side before he opened the door.

The car's inside light shone enough for Caroline to realize the car she was to be driving was Daniel's cruiser. "Daniel? What did you do to him? Why did you do this?" Caroline screamed when seeing her lover crumpled in the back seat of his car.

"What did I do to him? I didn't do nothing. Huh…wonder who gave him that chicken?" he asked before shutting the car door.

Screaming loudly so he could hear her through the metal and glass of the vehicle, she demanded him to tell her. "What was on that chicken?"

"Don't you worry that pretty little head of yours. It won't kill him less he ate more than two pieces," Jock said while he shoved Eleanor in the center of the seat.

Jock laughed as he watched his daughter count in her head the number of pieces she witnessed Daniel eating. The whiskey in him was making him meaner than usual.

"I don't need to tell you that if you try any funny business that I'll shoot your beautiful mommy right through the head. Be a shame to bloody up such a pretty suit." His right hand held the gun at her temple while he slipped his left arm around her neck. Eleanor didn't respond because she had escaped to the safe place in her mind.

Jock ordered her to drive down Main before he instructed her to make three more turns before he ordered her to stop. He then instructed her to shut the lights off and to back the cruiser into an unused driveway concealed by a large unkempt hedge. It was evident Jock had plans to waylay somebody coming this route. They waited in silence, not because they had nothing to say but because it was hard to talk through a gag.

9:00 PM

The basement of the Believers Baptist Church was alive with music and excitement. The announcer would proclaim Geneva the winner of a precinct, and the church band would play while the supporters sang, "Oh, victory in Jesus, my Savior forever, he sought me and bought me with his redeeming blood." They would sing the hymn until someone close to the radio speaker would signal that more results were being read. When the radio announcer declared Jock Ledford the winner of another precinct, the band played and the room was filled with the chorus, "Gonna have a little talk with Jesus. I'm gonna tell him all about my problems. He will hear my faintest cry, and he will answer by and by."

When all fifteen precincts were read and Geneva Vaughn was officially proclaimed the winner; then, the group celebrated more than fans at any NASCAR race. Everyone was crying, laughing, hugging, and praising the Lord. Relieved, Geneva started quietly praising her Jesus. This day didn't make up for all the heartache she'd endured during this election, but it did help to dull her pain as she waited for the Lord to give her the strategic plan she was to follow. McWhorter would become a lighthouse and a place of hope instead of the den of iniquity and place of evil it had been during the Ledford regime.

9:15 PM

Holding his only link to his family in his hand, Jon nearly jumped out of his seat when the phone began to ring. He knew something was wrong. It wasn't time for Jennings to call yet.

"They're gone! I can't find daddy, mommy, or Caroline." Jennings's voice was so loud that Jon had to hold the receiver a couple of inches from his ear.

"I told you to watch them like hawks. How did you let 'em get by you?"

"Damn it! I thought I was watching them. I don't understand how they got past me. Their cars are still parked in the same places, and no one remembers seeing them leave the victory party. By the way, it wasn't much of a victory party. We have a new mayor."

"New mayor? Damn it! This ain't good. Daddy will be even more pissed off and dangerous than he already was. I'm coming to help. Daddy knows we have the money, and he wants to play a cat and mouse game with us. It'll take both of us to fight him. You do realize we're gonna have to kill him?"

"Okay by me."

10:42 PM

The residents of McWhorter didn't know how to react. They didn't know whether to be happy or fear the changes that were soon to take place. "Sometimes the devil you know is better than the devil you don't," thought many of the citizens.

Joe Matt Sizemore, Rufus Jones, and Jack Brown were the last ones to leave the courthouse. Judge Brown had always tried to be Jock Ledford's wing man, but tonight he was now trying to butter up to the county court clerk.

"I reckon that Rufus here ought to take Jock's place at the helm of the Tuesday Club. Anybody that had the gonads to pull off that kind of stunt would have my vote any day of the week," said Jack with one arm wrapped around Rufus's neck and the other holding a fifth of liquor.

Joe Matt took a swig from the bottle. "Are you serious? You really don't think Jock Ledford will take this lying down, do you? Did you fools forget that Jock controls the money? Boys, without Jock there's no Tuesday Club. Both of you men are damned idiots."

Joe Matt headed toward the door, and Jack called after him, "Joe Matt, now don't you play innocent in this. Rufus here couldn't have pulled it off without you?"

Joe Matt's eyes were blazing with anger as he turned around and said, "Let's get this straight. The only reason I agreed to help Rufus was as a means to an end. I think this town has had more than enough of the Tuesday Club," he said with the true avenger coming out in him.

CHAPTER 58

The Killing Spree

Tuesday, May 6, 2008, 11:32 PM

The lights of the upcoming car cut the darkness and could be seen from Jock's vantage point for over a mile as it headed toward his trap. Neatly tucked behind the overgrown shrubs, the gray cruiser was well concealed. Since the hiding place was directly across from a stop sign, all vehicles were supposed to stop at this exact location. This gave Jock time to perfect his aim.

Caroline realized her daddy had this act of revenge planned for some time. "Don't stop, please keep going," she willed the driver of the upcoming vehicle. "Please, speed up!" Instead, the vehicle's brakes began to slow the vehicle down yards before the stop sign.

Rufus Jones, the county court clerk, never saw what exploded his head like a melon.

After the deed was done, Jock calmly opened the back door of the cruiser and threw the empty rifle onto the backseat on top of the unconscious passenger. If Jock would have looked closer, he would have realized Daniel moved slightly to keep the butt of the rifle from hitting him in the head. Starting with Caroline, Jock removed the gags and handcuffs before telling his white-faced daughter, "Start the engine!"

Eleanor came out of her shock long enough to stammer, "You…you…killed Rufus!"

Removing his gloves, he informed her, "No, dear, you are mistaken. Daniel Brooks just went on a killing spree using his own arsenal of weaponry." He turned to his daughter and said,

"Now, you little whore, you're going to take me home and get me my money."

———✐✐✐———

Daniel knew he was in the backseat of a vehicle, but he didn't recollect how he got there. His head was pounding. He could vaguely hear the voices in the front seat, but they were muffled partly by the glass partition and partly by his own cloudy mind.

He forced himself to stay awake and focus. "Caroline? Was that Caroline's voice, or no, was it Tillie's?"

———✐✐✐———

Caroline pulled the cruiser into the open garage just as her daddy had instructed, then she shut the vehicle off and started to remove the key.

"No! Leave it running," Jock stated as he closed the garage door.

She had to take action—kill Jock or beg for mercy. At this time, she chose to beg. "Please, daddy, I'll give you anything, do anything! Just leave Daniel out of this!"

Knowing he needed her cooperation for now, he relented. "Okay, leave it off, but you better do exactly as I tell you, you little, no-good-for-nothing whore." He pushed Daniel's duty weapon into her back as she walked from the garage into the laundry room. "Eleanor, honey, you're being awfully quiet. At least Caroline has gotten a little backbone. Maybe if I married a woman that had some gumption, then, maybe my kids wouldn't be such weak ass, little traitors!" Jock's voice rose with each word until it blended with a loud popping sound. Jock's blow to Eleanor's cheek caused her to fall to the floor.

Eleanor managed to stand and stagger forward. Jock followed the women through the kitchen and down the hallway until they came to his office. After they entered the room, Jock pushed his daughter toward the computer. His mouth was only inches from her face when he said, "Get me my money!" He purposely spit each syllable.

Wiping her face, Caroline knew she couldn't give him the money. She was prepared to die first. Buying some time, she played along with him until she could find the right time to make her move. Sitting in the large leather swivel desk chair. She very calmly asked, "What's your password?"

He slapped her hard across the face, "You little whore! Don't you dare play like you don't know my password! You were the one who talked your brother into giving it to you! I wasn't born yesterday."

She refused to let him hurt her. Instead, she yelled back at him. "I don't know your damn password! If you want your money, then, you better tell me what it is!"

"Damn it to hell, girl, get out of that seat!" Jock continued to mumble under his breath as he commandeered his large chair, retrieved his reading glasses, and logged into the computer. His head bobbed up and down as he pushed each key. While Jock was focused on entering his password, Caroline knew now was the time to make her move. She quietly reached for the gun strapped to her ankle. She pressed the barrel of her revolver directly into her daddy's temple. Eleanor gasped loudly.

Jock slowed his hunt and peck typing. "If you were going to kill me, girl, you would have done it a long time ago." He then swiveled his chair into Caroline hard enough to knock her off balance and easily disarmed her. Jock was now standing with Caroline's own weapon pressed directly in the center of the back of her head.

"Let her go!" Eleanor's strong voice sounded foreign.

Jock couldn't believe his ears. He didn't even turn around to look at his wife when he said, "Eleanor, dear, now's not the time to grow some gumption."

"Actually, I think it's long overdue." Her voice was smooth and controlled, and to make her final point, she made sure he could hear the click of the gun's hammer as she readied it for use.

While having one gun aimed at his daughter's head and another gun aimed at his head, Jock's body decided to fail him. With his empty hand, he reached for his chest; he could feel the pounding of his heart even in his ears. His grip on Caroline loosened; she managed to pull her third gun from her sling. Standing by her mommy, she also took aim. Both women had their guns sighted and ready to fire.

Turning to face the women, it was then when his vision began to fail. Instead of two heads, he saw three blurry heads in front of him. He managed to retrieve the pill bottle from his pocket, but the lid wasn't cooperating with him. He reached the bottle toward the blurry heads, hoping for their sympathy. It was at that precise time when he was able to recognize the owner of the extra head—the little preacher man stood slightly behind his wife and daughter.

"Daddy, you've got to be kidding. You really don't expect us to fall for this chest pain act," Caroline mocked him.

Short of breath, in agonizing pain, and lying in the middle of the floor, he managed to open his eyes wide enough for his last view of this earth to be of the yellowed dentures of the little man who had been haunting him. His face was only a couple of feet from him, and he heard him command as clear as a bell, "Repent!"

Jock shook his head and directed the gun at the man, but once again the trigger on the gun wouldn't fire. He felt his life fading away and thought once about repenting, but as the visions of his life sped before his eyes, he knew he couldn't repent. He wasn't sorry for anything. His only regret was not getting to take revenge on those who betrayed him and for letting that bitch, Geneva, beat him.

The women watched as Jock's chest failed to rise. Caroline used her watch to see how long he could hold his breath. After ten minutes passed, with her gun in front of her, Caroline slowly ventured closer to him.

Jock's eyes and mouth were wide-opened. His body lay perfectly still. He really did deserve an Oscar for this performance.

Caroline kicked him hard in the side. Nothing. Still keeping her gun aimed at his head, she placed two fingers on his neck. When she didn't get a pulse there, she tried for one at his wrist. "Mommy, I think daddy really is dead."

Eleanor began to scream like a madwoman. "Damn you!" she said before using her high heels as a weapon. Her blow landed in his crotch as she repeatedly cursed him while she kicked him again and again. Still not satisfied, she unloaded her gun into her husband's lifeless body.

"Mommy, if you didn't want to give him mouth-to-mouth, why didn't you just say so?'

Wednesday, May 7, 2008, 1:00 AM

The scene Jennings, Jon, and Joe Matt saw when entering the Ledford household was unexpected. Daniel was standing over one side of the kitchen sink puking his guts out from the ipecac syrup that Caroline had forced down him. The men stood in silence trying to determine if everything was okay or not, when they heard the familiar tapping of heels coming down the hallway.

"Hello, boys, could I offer you some sweet tea?" Eleanor said as if wearing blood splattered clothing was common place for her.

"Mommy, what the hell? Are you okay? Jon asked when he noticed her swollen eye and cheek. "Where's daddy?"

Caroline answered, "Sorry, guys but daddy decided to have a heart attack on us. Mommy got a little upset because she didn't get to use her gun. All's well except we have a little baggage to take care of before we leave McWhorter." She suddenly remembered and said, "Oh yeah, I also forgot to tell you that daddy just shot Rufus Jones using Daniel's gun."

Scratching his head, Joe Matt asked, "That all? You mean Jock really is dead? I've got to see it to believe it," he said as he and the others walked down the hallway to see for themselves.

No one said anything for a few minutes as they waited to see if Jock's chest would rise or if really was immortal. Jennings was the one ready to celebrate. "We can all stare at daddy or we can all head to the Caribbean."

"What're we going to do with daddy's body?" Caroline asked.

Joe Matt offered a solution. "I know exactly what to do with our esteemed mayor's body—something that will make right an injustice done many years ago."

Caroline faced Daniel. "You know you can come with us? Thirty-eight million dollars can buy us a lot of happiness and healing."

Groggily, he replied, "Why don't you stay now that your daddy's gone?"

"I wish it were that simple. The way I see it, we can't stay unless we want to live with the Ledford ghosts for the rest of our lives. Even though our daddy died of natural causes, there will be a whole lot of questions as to why he has about five bullet holes in him. It really will be easier for all of us if we leave. Then everyone will think Jock and his entire family left the community after he lost his mind after losing the election. I want to have a better life for my baby—a life without McWhorter and the Tuesday Club."

"Baby?" Joe Matt looked to Daniel for answers.

The light bulb went off in Daniel's eyes, "That's right. That's the last thing I remember before waking up in the backseat of the cruiser. I'm going to be a daddy!"

2:00 AM

Sixty-nine years, seven months, and three days after the original Tuesday Club members made the early morning trek to cover their crime, a total of six men and women ventured into the same remote section of McWhorter, Kentucky, to put a proper end to the Tuesday Club. All six were lost in their own thoughts—thoughts of a future, worries of a past, and plans to merge the two together so their tomorrows could be filled with happiness instead of regret.

The seventy-year-old unmarked grave was still there. The gravediggers slung dirt as fast as they could. They knew that once the dirt covered the body of Mayor Ledford, then the reign of the Tuesday Club was officially over; the remaining members and their descendents were free to live a life of their own choosing.

Jock Ledford would rest eternally side-by-side with the same slain mayor his grand pappy murdered all those years ago. No one prayed or said anything over the grave once they finished. They left in silence.

As the getaway car sped down the road heading away from the burial place, Eleanor Ledford could have sworn she saw someone standing on the side of the road. She turned to get a better look at the old man, but he was gone. Her mind must have been playing tricks on her.

5:00 AM

The avenger and the accomplice waited until the daily newspaper was delivered before they deposited their own special package. Even though the judge had been sloshed last night, he was a creature of habit, and the duo knew he would soon walk the distance to the mailbox to retrieve his daily newspaper. After their package was delivered, they left the man's fate in the hands of God and silently slipped away.

6:32 AM

The county judge executive couldn't remember how he made it home last night. "Was it a dream? Did Jock Ledford really lose? Did Rufus Jones commit the ultimate betrayal?" he asked himself. He felt it was almost too good to be true.

Slowly, he crawled out of his bed and rambled to the bathroom, his head pounding with each step. Turning on his coffee maker, he then headed out the door wearing his robe and house shoes. "Only one way to find out for sure that it wasn't a dream," he said thinking about the newspaper waiting for him in his mailbox.

Shaking his head as he crossed the wet lawn, he exclaimed, "I be damned! McWhorter without a Ledford as the mayor. Ain't that a caution?" He wondered if his buddy, Rufus, had lived through the night. He had to hand it to him. What he did took real balls. Of course, that is if he lived long enough to reap any rewards for his actions. Jock had made it perfectly clear what would be the ramification for crossing him. He thought he'd better call Jock this morning and check on his mood. After all, he still needed his Tuesday Club money. He couldn't afford to be on Jock's bad side.

He opened the small round tube to retrieve his newspaper. Reaching his hand in the dark tube, he pulled it out quickly when he felt something move against his hand. Not thinking rationally, he bent his large frame down so he could get a better look in the box thinking a squirrel or some small animal had crawled in it. As soon as his head was close enough to the opening, the timber rattler struck him on his face multiple times before he even realized what hit him. Still in a drunken haze, it took him several seconds before his brain signaled for him to react. By then, it was too late. The snake's poison was already beginning to work on his allergy-ridden system. The snake's body dropped from the mailbox and began zigzagging its way to the cover of the woods.

CHAPTER 59

Resolve and Recount

Wednesday, May 7, 2008, 8:00 AM

The lawyer acting as the official spokesperson called a special club meeting after hearing that the clerk and judge were both found dead this morning. It was presumed that the mayor had a hand in both of the deaths before he went on the run. The lawyer, chief deputy, and the protégé were the last of the surviving club members.

The lawyer called the meeting to order. "Looks like it's just the three of us left."

"We may not miss 'em, but we can definitely learn from their mistakes," the protégé said as he stood and walked the floor of the office. "Many of the members believed the Tuesday Club was a precious gift. I'm gonna tell you, it was a curse, a curse my father didn't intend to pass down to me. Remember that we may have helped the Lord out a little, but in the end, it was his decision on who died." He looked at the lawyer before saying, "And on the ones he spared."

The chief deputy interrupted, "I guess you could say there's a little avenger in all of us, with the Almighty being the true vindicator of justice. I make a final motion to dissolve the Tuesday Club. Will anyone second that motion?"

The lawyer raised his hand. "I second it."

The chief deputy then said, "All in agreement, say 'aye.'"

"Aye," said all three men in unison.

With full authority, the chief deputy proclaimed, "From this day forward, the Tuesday Club ceases to exist. As God is our witness, if at any time anyone tries to resurrect it, then we all pledge to put back on our avenger hats and stop it at all costs."

Raising their brandy glasses, they clicked them in agreement and said. "Here, here!"

8:22 AM

Tillie had plans to get up early and go to Gene Lester's office to await news of Jock Ledford's pending arrest, but every attempt to get ready resulted in the same outcome. She couldn't remember ever feeling this fatigued and sick.

If the cordless phone hadn't been located directly next to her in the bed, then she would have never been able to answer it in time. "Hello," she whispered, afraid that a loud noise would erupt the silent volcano in her stomach.

"Tillie! Why didn't you call me and tell me about what all happened in McWhorter last night?" Trevor rushed right into the conversation without any pleasantries.

Tillie sat up in her bed, "What happened? I have no clue."

"For starters, Geneva Vaughn won the election. Then Mayor Ledford lost his mind and went on some kind of killing spree. He drugged Daniel and stole his cruiser."

She held her breath thinking that Daniel had been killed.

"Jock then waylaid the county clerk and killed him using Daniel's gun. They think Jock may have had something to do with Judge Brown's death too, but they're not certain. They found him dead in his lawn this morning. Conveniently, Jock's house is burning as we speak, and no one's sure if any bodies burned with it. No one's seen Jock or any of his family since the election last night."

"What about Daniel?"

"I guess Daniel's okay. Joe Matt evidently found him gagged and bound in his cruiser in some remote location."

She sighed in relief. "Oh my gosh! I can't believe I slept through this. How's Geneva?" Tillie asked.

"They have armed guards watching her every step in case Jock tries to get to her."

"Who told you all this?"

"I called the editor from the *Rockford Sun* this morning to find out the election results, and she talked my leg off."

"When you coming home? Brenda settled in? "

"Brenda and Luella are doing fine. My flight leaves this evening."

"Hurry home, please. I need you."

CHAPTER 60

The Letter

Friday, May 9, 2008, 10:30 AM

The knock on the Grant's door was unexpected. Roy Allen Jones knocked again on the kitchen door. Louder this time. Trevor opened the door and asked the lawyer to come inside. Roy Allen politely declined the invitation. Instead, he handed Trevor a package and asked him to make sure his sister received it.

Trevor eyed it suspiciously trying to figure out if it was large enough to contain a poisonous snake. After the results of the judge's death were made public, he didn't want to take any chances. Roy Allen explained that it was a package from Daniel Brooks.

Trevor was eager to see what Daniel had sent his heartbroken sister. He hadn't told Tillie; however, he'd heard that Daniel had turned in his badge, guns, and car after the state police wouldn't honor his request for a personal leave to search for the missing Ledfords.

Tillie opened it slowly and cautiously, savoring anything that had to do with Daniel. His cell phone had been disconnected, and she had no other way of reaching him. She even called his mom and found out that Christina was as clueless about his whereabouts as she was. A letter fell to the floor when she opened the lid off the box. She picked it up and read slowly.

My Tillie,

I'm so sorry I've not been able to talk to you personally. The last few days have been very hard ones. I've had to do some heavy soul searching. Enclosed you will find a ballistic report showing that the gun in your granny's car was the same gun that killed Albert Dean Smith. I don't need to tell you what that means—it means that you, Trevor, and your redheaded friend are now suspects. What better motive than revenge of your dad's murder? If I stay here then I would have to investigate. I can't do that to you.

This may not make a lick of sense to you, but I think that report was the sign I've been looking for. This knowledge would drive a wedge between anything we hoped to have in the way of a relationship. This report has disappeared from the investigation file, and no one else will ever be the wiser of it since my friend ran the report on an unofficial request from me. Take my advice and throw the gun in the lake!

I want you to know that I love you. I'm not sure if I really ever told you in so many words or not. You are everything I ever hoped to find in a woman and then some, but sometimes love just isn't enough.

I hope you can one day find it in your heart to forgive me for so many things. I've not exactly been the most honest person with you as you will see when you read the contents of this file.

I'm going to find Caroline. I feel that I have to find her, not only because I owe it to her, but also because she's pregnant with my child. I guess you could say this was the final sign that sealed my fate. I know that it's hard for you to understand how I can be with her, but still be in love with you. It's very complicated, and if you only knew half of the hell Jock put her through; then, you would understand that she needs me. You, on the other hand, are strong. You're a survivor. You will succeed with or without me. I wish I could make more sense out of my decision, but I know it's the right one. It's the only one that I can live with. I will never forget you!

Also enclosed you will find more information on the Tuesday Club. Please don't hate me when you find out my involvement.

I will love you forever,
Your Danny

Tillie dropped the letter to the ground and fell into Trevor's arms. Neither mentioned anything about the ballistic report. Instead, Tillie tore the report into tiny pieces. Some things were better left unsaid.

"It'll be okay. We'll raise this baby. It will be just fine. You wait and see. Shhh ... it'll be okay," he cooed to her trying to calm her, but all the while he was counting the times he had been with Caroline and wondering if Daniel was marrying the right pregnant woman.

CHAPTER 61

McWhorter without the Tuesday Club

Headlines from the *Rockford Sun*:

Five Hundred Jobs coming to McWhorter

McWhorter celebrated the groundbreaking of its first big business. A five hundred seat call center had been lured by Mayor Geneva Vaughn and the others on the newly formed Industrial Authority Committee.

Former Bank President Dies

Rupert Jones died in the night of natural causes. Services will be held at First Baptist Church on June 6, 2008. Family requests that donations be made to the McWhorter Medical Center in lieu of flowers.

New Owner of the Rockford Sun

Trevor Grant, the grandson of Doctor and Mrs. Roscoe Grant used his inheritance to purchase the *Rockford Sun*. He plans to make a few gradual changes but is committed to keeping the local flavor that makes the paper a hometown must.

McWhorter's New Year's Baby receives Six-Month Supply of Diapers

Sheriff Tillie Grant gave birth to McWhorter's first New Year's baby. Daniel Edward Brooks weighed in at 5 lb 7 oz on January 1, 2009.

Edna Mattingly Sizemore Wins Sweepstakes

Edna Mattingly Sizemore can't even remember entering the Butcher Block Cooking Sweepstakes contest but was pleasantly surprised when she was presented with a large check. Edna wishes to keep the amount she won confidential.

Lizzie Jean Jones Making a Difference

Lizzie Jean Jones is requesting donations for a health care clinic she has opened in Tanzania. She and partner Dr. Nikolus Workman are opening a free clinic in this developing country in East Africa. They are seeking financial support as well as medical volunteers.

Epilogue

March 26, 2009

The couple strolled hand in hand down the beach just as the sun appeared to be slipping into the water. A lot had changed for the couple over the past ten months; they'd lost their home, left loved ones behind, and lost their identities. The change that made all the sacrifices worthwhile was pressed tightly in her baby sling against her mommy's chest. Ellie Christina's eyes were as brown as her mommy's, but unlike her mommy, her hair already had a tendency to have a mind of its own. The baby's blond curly wisps were in stark contrast to her mother's dark, thick, course hair. Back at the cottage, a whimper from this baby resulted in a fight, as her uncles, godfather, and grandmommy rushed to her side as this baby breathed new healing life into this family.

The man had another baby on his mind. This baby was his spitting image even though he'd only seen his son in photographs. He couldn't think about his son or the mother of his son without feeling regret and sadness wrap itself around his heart. Did he make the right decision? Actually, he knew the answer. He knew the decision had been made for him long before his son was conceived. The decision was made when he and his best friend made a promise at the side of a hospital bed that would allow other McWhorter sons to live a life of their own choosing and never have to worry about the stigma of being the protégé.

April 9, 2009

The office had the same old furniture that had been used in the sheriff's office for many years, but Tillie had made the office her own. Her new extended family, consisting of Brenda Osborne,

Julia Hopper, and Christina Brooks, had helped her to transform the office into an office-slash-nursery. In the corner of the room was a small baby bed with brightly colored blankets. Among Brenda, Julia, and Christina, she never lacked for babysitters. Also, between Trevor and Lowell, she never had to worry about male role models either. Even her mother, who had moved back to Kentucky, seemed more alive when she would hold baby Dan.

Tillie originally had declined her Aunt Brenda's request for her to assume the position as High Sheriff of Rockford County. She agreed to help out until they could hold another election to replace the sheriff, county judge, and county clerk. She truly hoped Joe Matt would come to his senses and come back to McWhorter and take the helm. Last she'd heard, he'd gone crazy over some foreign girl during his and Daniel's pursuit to find the Ledfords.

She missed her Danny. She didn't understand everything about the events leading up to his departure and had quit trying to understand it. She knew he would always hold a piece of her heart captive and hoped to think he felt the same way, but she had moved on for her baby's sake.

The loud ring of her desk phone jolted her back to reality. "Sheriff Grant speaking."

It was one of her deputies, "You're never going to believe it," he exclaimed.

"Believe what?"

"We think we've found Woody Ledford. Some hikers came across a vehicle and the skeletal remains at the bottom of a cliff. It's Woody Ledford's car."

Tillie was excited yet nervous by the news. "I'll be right there," she stated. It was only after she drove the curvy graveled road and parked her cruiser on the side of the road before she realized her mistake. She forgot to ask the whereabouts of the vehicle and body.

April 12, 2009

The forest leading to the once unmarked grave of the slain mayor seemed to be quieter and at peace. No longer was the blood calling out to be avenged and no longer was the grave unmarked. Mysteriously, a small grave marker appeared that read as follows:

> Here lies the bones of Jeremiah Paul Mattingly, born September 23, 1903.
>
> He was murdered by Jon R. Ledford on Tuesday, October 4, 1938.
>
> He now lies in peace.
>
> His murder was avenged by his own flesh and blood.
>
> Isaiah 1:24